BARFORD ABBEY

broadview editions
series editor: Martin R. Boyne

BARFORD ABBEY

Susannah Minifie Gunning

edited by Margaret Doody
and
Kurt Edward Milberger

broadview editions

BROADVIEW PRESS – www.broadviewpress.com
Peterborough, Ontario, Canada

Founded in 1985, Broadview Press remains a wholly independent publishing house. Broadview's focus is on academic publishing; our titles are accessible to university and college students as well as scholars and general readers. With 800 titles in print, Broadview has become a leading international publisher in the humanities, with world-wide distribution. Broadview is committed to environmentally responsible publishing and fair business practices.

© 2021 Margaret Doody and Kurt Edward Milberger

Library and Archives Canada Cataloguing in Publication

Title: Barford Abbey / Susannah Minifie Gunning ; edited by Margaret Doody and Kurt Edward Milberger.
Names: Gunning, Mrs. (Susannah), 1740?-1800, author. | Doody, Margaret Anne, editor. | Milberger, Kurt Edward, editor.
Series: Broadview editions.
Description: Series statement: Broadview editions | Originally published: London: T. Cadell; and J. Payne, 1768. | Includes bibliographical references.
Identifiers: Canadiana (print) 20200255509 | Canadiana (ebook) 20200288628 | ISBN 9781554814466 (softcover) | ISBN 9781770487871 (PDF) | ISBN 9781460407387 (EPUB)
Classification: LCC PR4729.G9 B37 2020 | DDC 823/.6—dc23

Broadview Editions
The Broadview Editions series is an effort to represent the ever-evolving canon of texts in the disciplines of literary studies, history, philosophy, and political theory. A distinguishing feature of the series is the inclusion of primary source documents contemporaneous with the work.

Advisory editor for this volume: Colleen Humbert

Broadview Press handles its own distribution in North America:
PO Box 1243, Peterborough, Ontario K9J 7H5, Canada
555 Riverwalk Parkway, Tonawanda, NY 14150, USA
Tel: (705) 743-8990; Fax: (705) 743-8353
email: customerservice@broadviewpress.com

For all territories outside of North America, distribution is handled by Eurospan Group.

Broadview Press acknowledges the financial support of the Government of Canada for our publishing activities.

Canada

Typesetting and assembly: True to Type Inc., Claremont, Canada
Cover Design: Lisa Brawn

PRINTED IN CANADA

Contents

Acknowledgements

Thanks to Jessica Kane for her assistance in preparing the text of this edition. Her diligent attention and clever reading illuminated the content and form of the novel, and her work much improved the veracity of this edition. The hard-working staff of Notre Dame Copy Center 301 deserve kudos for arranging, binding, and distributing much of this material in the form of classpacks. The staff of the Morgan Library provided brilliant last-minute primary source references with incredible ease. We owe many thanks to the students of Professor Doody's "Thinking with Abbeys" seminars at the University of Notre Dame, who provided much insight into these materials and their organization. Finally, hearty thanks to the editorial team at Broadview for bringing this volume to publication, especially Marjorie Mather, Martin Boyne, Colleen Humbert, and Tara Trueman.

Introduction

The First Appearance of an "Abbey Novel"

Barford Abbey is a compact novel in two volumes originally produced in 1768 by a young woman aged some 28 or 29 years on the eve of her marriage. The novelist, Susannah Minifie (1739/40–1800), had already had some success in the production of fiction, both by herself and in collaboration with her sister Margaret (fl. 1763–91).[1] At the end of the century, after a scandal rocked her marriage to John Gunning, Susannah became one of the leading writers for the Minerva Press, an extremely popular publishing house and lending library known for sensational bestselling fiction. The career of Susannah Minifie Gunning vividly illustrates the degree to which any amount of celebrity may endanger the standing and peace of mind of a woman who is seen as daring to encroach on the rightful privileges of aristocratic and wealthy men. In *Barford Abbey* itself, the heroine is subjected to unwanted sexual attentions that characterize this context, and Gunning's position as a novelist was later used against her in deliberate physical caricature and verbal mockery (Appendix F). That she was a novelist made her obviously a liar. We cannot understand the era in which *Barford Abbey* was written, nor the life of its author, if we do not understand the dangers that threatened any woman who entered the public sphere, for any woman acting, singing, or writing novels in the eighteenth century was out of her rightful place.

Before the scandal, *Barford Abbey* enjoyed some success. A Dublin edition followed the first London edition in 1768, and a second edition was published in 1771. The novel was also translated into French under the title *L'Abbaye ou le chateau de Barford* in 1769. It deserves to be better known today. For one thing, there is a very strong probability that it was among the many novels read by the young Jane Austen (1775–1817). In

---

1 Margaret's birth and death dates remain obscure. The dates given here indicate the years in which she was certainly active and publishing. Janice Thaddeus, "MINIFIE, Margaret," *A Dictionary of British and American Women Writers,* edited by Janet Todd (Rowman and Littlefield, 1987), p. 219, provides the first date; we provide the second in our account of the Gunninghiad affair (Appendix F).

Barford Abbey, we have, after all, a heroine named Fanny who visits and becomes effectually adopted by a family in a great house, where she learns to ride. We find an aristocratic lover named Darcey, who holds back. The good Mrs. Jenkings provides information and affection, even if she comes from a lower class—a little like Mrs. Jennings in *Sense and Sensibility*, though she is happily not widowed. We glimpse a termagant Lucy and an overbearing wife sprung from the commercial class determined to remodel her husband's estate and turn the grounds into a fashionable showplace—strongly resembling Austen's Fanny Dashwood.

However, Minifie's book provides more value than its influence on Austen. *Barford Abbey* is among the first of a new genre, which we might christen the "Abbey novel"—or simply the "Abbey fiction." It is the great-grandmother of *Downton Abbey*. Although the novel does not mention the Dissolution of the Abbeys in the sixteenth century directly (see Appendix B), it uses the abbey as a site for a story of broken relationships, a story of heredity and change, and fear of change. Susannah Minifie uses her Abbey as setting and symbol. Even within the "Gothic" tradition, Castle and Abbey remain very different. A castle is always defensive, holding some people in and keeping others out. Horace Walpole's Otranto and Ann Radcliffe's Udolpho are both defensive, violent, and over-masculine. Castles are military installations. In English history, they are associated with Norman invasion and rule. But abbeys are peaceable installations. They are intended to be hospitable and supportive of community. They relate to essential and to basic activities (farming, education, and health care) that support human existence.

An abbey is receptive, its very existence implying the arrival of strangers and the mixing of different sorts of persons. The abbeys in England had functioned for hundreds of years as centers of production and growth. Monks had cleared the land, fostered agriculture, and participated in the exchange of knowledge. An abbey functioned variously as school, asylum, hospital, and adoptive home. Religious centers attracted donations and benefactions; some monastic foundations became wealthy. However, the end arrived suddenly and sharply.

The Reformation, for both opponents and supporters in England, created a rift between past and present. The abrupt change that came to England only a few years after Martin Luther's challenge to the Church in 1517 introduced many disruptions in belief, practice, and sensibility.[1] Active iconoclasm was both cheered and lamented. Symbols and places like abbeys, once revered, became suspect. Numerous relationships were altered, including the relation of the living to the dead. With his "Act for the Dissolution of the Lesser Monasteries," King Henry VIII (r. 1509–47), with the clever assistance of Thomas Cromwell (1485–1540), took over the Church lands, the buildings, and the wealth of the monasteries and convents in England (Appendix B1). The process took only a few short years (1536–40). The Dissolution of the Abbeys caused practical disruption not least in the lives of the poor, whose social services were abruptly removed. Over 800 monasteries, convents, priories, and abbeys were dissolved. The endeavor to fight back in the so-called "Pilgrimage of Grace" (1536–37) was an unsuccessful protest, an uprising in the eastern counties rather than a civil war. What was seen as a rebellion was firmly put down, leaving the king in control. A few aristocratic leaders were executed as examples. These included Thomas Darcy, 1st Baron Darcy (c. 1467–1537), whose lands were seized and whose head was struck off on Tower Hill on 30 June 1537. Both Minifie and Austen appear to have attached importance to this surname. Lord Darcy was presumably the source of the central young male character in Minifie's novel. With great diffidence, young Darcy tries to stand up against the present controller of Barford Abbey.

The takeover by Henry VIII of the monasteries and all that they possessed gained the king new wealth and resources for a new model of internationally aggressive and imperial monarchy. This grand privatization left great buildings in ruins or effected their conversion into the proud possessions of aristocratic or newly rich takers and purchasers. The Dissolution entailed for the common people the loss of the social safety net and the disappearance of resources. It is the greatest single act of privatization in British history and foreshadows the colonial takeover to come. The king was able to sell off (or occasionally give away) abbeys to friends and supporters (Appendices B2 and B3). In Austen's *Northanger Abbey* (1817; see Appendix D3), we are told that the Tilneys' abbey had been formerly "a highly endowed convent" which had "fallen into the hands of

---

1   See Duffy, especially chapters 11 and 12, for a historical account of the Reformation in England.

an ancestor of the Tilneys on its dissolution."[1] Austen pointedly elides the exact circumstances of the "fall" of the abbey into the Tilneys' grasping hands. The Dissolution ensured current and future wealth for the king and created an influential class of people, interested parties, who would tend to remain loyal and could be counted upon to uphold the righteousness of the seizure.

Ostensibly, Minifie uses Barford Abbey as a sign of privilege. She places her abbey in Hampshire—a happy choice. That fertile and wealthy county (Austen's birthplace) had once been home to a number of rich abbeys. Highclere Castle, the real if improbable building used for the imaginary "Downton," is in Hampshire—although the fictional Downton is somewhat implausibly situated in Yorkshire, near Ripon. Barford Abbey radiates signs of wealth and rank. Its owners dine on venison from their own park, and they stroll through ornamented grounds. Barford is a dominant spot on the social landscape of the region. When Fanny, the orphan traveler, first sees it, she is naively struck by it as an Eden.

As we get further into the life of Barford Abbey, we find that it is contaminated within by possessiveness and anger, by issues of inheritance and disinheritance. The heir of this abbey is missing. The novel recycles one of the recurrent problems central to English fiction of the eighteenth and nineteenth centuries: Who is the heir? Unspoken secrets and distressing obligations cloud the truth. Young Darcey is cruelly pinned to a deathbed promise to his father, in effect a vow always to obey Sir James Powis, his guardian. Sir James, the owner of Barford, has inadvertently dismissed his own son, causing the son's stubborn exile. Furthermore, Sir James has become a very sincere believer in avarice and is overwhelming with wrong advice the timid young man who has been—until very recently—his ward. Yet Sir James is nothing like a villain—he is not at all a Montoni, the antagonist of Radcliffe's *The Mysteries of Udolpho* (1794), even though in his own fashion he is obstinate and selfish. Abbey fictions allow characters to lose and then regain their way.

At the same time, Barford Abbey displays some of the more truly benign aspects of the abbey. Like many abbeys in English fiction, it is hospitable to the disabled. In *Barford Abbey*, the chaplain Mr. Watson is blind, yet he is not only accepted but has an important role in the family. Throughout the novel, amusing

---

1 Jane Austen, *Northanger Abbey*, edited by Barbara M. Benedict and Deirdre Le Faye (Cambridge UP, 2006), 2.2.145.

scenes and vignettes point to differences in behavior and values, alerting us to differences between the old and the new. Despite some failures on the part of the new, it is not good to be manacled to the old, or subjugated to the dead. The abbey's role as a kind of hospital or sanctuary indicates that it might be better thought of as a place of renewal or rebirth rather than as a bastion of tradition or a sign of past aristocratic success. Assertions of lineage call into question the authority of primogeniture. Behind the facade of gentility and order there are disruptions, mysteries, even scandals—and a good many lies.

During the French Revolution, which began in 1789, the Revolutionary government dismantled and emptied religious houses in France—creating unease among the upper-class English. They may have detested the new Revolution but couldn't help knowing that their English Protestant ancestors had themselves acted like horrifying revolutionaries in their attack on England's religious foundations. Wealthy landowners had profited from a sacrilegious overturn. The abbey setting becomes increasingly called into use from the late 1780s to the early years of the new century. An abbey poses questions as to where our society was and is going— and what it truly values.

The abbey as trope is more than its appearance in any individual work of fiction in prose or poetry. Its influence extends over a multitude of imaginary places and personalities and poetical effects, including the Grasmere Abbey of Charlotte Smith's *Ethelinde* (Appendix D1), the Tintern Abbey about which William Gilpin (1724–1804) writes in his *Observations on the River Wye* (1770) and which William Wordsworth (1770–1850) describes in "Lines Composed a Few Miles above Tintern Abbey" (1798), and the abandoned or subjugated abbeys of Regina Maria Roche's *Children of the Abbey* (Appendix D2). Austen's sharply imagined Northanger Abbey (Appendix D3) contrasts with Sir Walter Scott's Melrose Abbey in *Lay of the Last Minstrel* (Appendix C3), the abbey that, as ruin, must be seen by moonlight. An abbey displays social hopes or fears regarding loss and restoration, continuity and alteration. Reference to an abbey always marks change as a subject. Minifie is in advance of the movement to which she importantly contributes.

Barford Abbey is a novel of the 1760s, the period introduced and almost covered by Laurence Sterne's *Tristram Shandy* (1759–67). The mid-century had produced ambitious and solid works, including Henry Fielding's *Tom Jones* and Samuel Richardson's *Clarissa* (see Appendix A3) in the 1740s. The 1750s were announced almost simultaneously by Fielding's *Amelia* (1751), Eliza Haywood's *Betsy Thoughtless* (1751), and Tobias Smollett's *Peregrine Pickle* (1751), closely followed by Richardson's *Sir Charles Grandison* (1753–54). The year 1760 was marked by the advent of a new young king, George III (r. 1760–1820). The decade developed as a self-conscious era of historical awareness, choice, and taste. Literary works moved away from the solidity of the mid-century and were more inclined to go in for half-shades, quarter-tones, and swiftly suggested complexities. This decade preferred slimmer novels, with less absolute statement and more suggestion.

This is the period of Frances Sheridan's *Memoirs of Miss Sidney Bidulph* (1761) and its *Continuation* (1767), as well as her Oriental tale *Nourjahad* (1767). *Le Neveu de Rameau* was written by Denis Diderot (1713–84) during this period, though not published. Oliver Goldsmith's comic pastoral *The Vicar of Wakefield* (1766) closely preceded Minifie's novel. These works of fiction were customarily slim—like Sterne's *Sentimental Journey* (1767) and individual volumes of his *Tristram Shandy*. Even Smollett (1721–71), one of the solids of the 1750s, produced in 1760 the Quixotic *Launcelot Greaves*, a slim novel with a hero more intent on idealism than practicality; such a figure is bound to be thought "mad." The new novels were teasing and experimental, displaying an interest in inadequacy and the problematic. This age had not allowed itself to arrive at an ideological program. Outward conquest of the world, imperial success, was less celebrated. Fantasy of various kinds, the forms and traditions of the "Oriental tale" and fairy-tale, mingled with "realism." New fictions participated in an interrogation of older generations and their values. Central questions may be raised but tend to be left unresolved, as in *Tristram Shandy*, where momentary feelings are more important than solid answers. This period is heralded by Samuel Johnson's *Rasselas* (1759) with its "Conclusion in which nothing is concluded."

Barford Abbey is told through letters written by several characters, thus employing a number of narrators. Fanny's might be the most important voice, but she is certainly not the only narrator. Epistolary narratives with multiple narrators leave matters open, prolonging the discussion into the life outside the novel. The epistolary narration ensures that our knowledge is always partial and bound to be framed by a particular and temporary point of view. The postal service in England experienced enormous growth throughout the eighteenth century, which tied the

Inspired the young Austen

country together (Appendices A1 and A5) and encouraged people to consider how to use the medium of letters to keep in contact, advance their personal agendas, and fit into larger institutions such as the artistic community or the state (Appendix A4). Early experiments with fictions in letters used the form to provide a public glimpse into private lives, often exploiting uneven social relationships for humor or drama (Appendix A2). The epistolary novel had been brought into high development by Samuel Richardson (1689–1761), whose three major novels (*Pamela*, 1741–42; *Clarissa*, 1747–48; and *Sir Charles Grandison*, 1753–54) are all told in letters. Richardson develops the technique that he termed "writing to the moment"; his characters write under the pressure of immediate stress or stimulus, recording momentary impressions too recent to have faded (Appendix A3). Thus their writing retains a feel of spontaneity and action that brings life, excitement, and uncertainty to the narrative.

This technique would be employed by Frances Burney (1752–1840) in her highly successful *Evelina, or the History of a Young Lady's Entrance into the World* (1778)—but Minifie was ten years in advance of Burney. Minifie's novel is plotted with an interior design, not as a sequence of episodes like Burney's first novel. *Barford Abbey* presents several narrators and their varying points of view, but the gaps between the personalities result in invisible spaces where what we do not know resides. The suppression of information is not incidental; it should count as an action—if at first an entirely invisible action—of the main plot.

An epistolary narrative often attempts less deliberate authority or settlement than either dominant-voice/first-person narration or reliance on authorial third person. Susannah Minifie has obviously studied Richardson's *Sir Charles Grandison*. The introduction of Miss Delves near the end creates a cheerful and slightly mocking voice of an outsider, a shrewd observer who is yet an interested party. Her character owes a good deal to Richardson's witty Charlotte Grandison; Miss Delves, crucially, does not attend Fanny's wedding—she is still an outsider. Miss Delves, suspecting any tendency in herself to harbor illusions, maintains high spirits even if these are mixed with desire and some resentment. Her story is just beginning as we leave Fanny.

Fanny's own central voice makes this orphan a less romantic figure than we may expect. She is complicated and amusing, often capable of shrewd observation. Yet she is lonely and in need of nurture and community, and the Jenkingses (who are plotters) offer her both by bringing her within the ambit of the Abbey.

Fanny is in mourning when we first meet her, but she "comes out" at the dinner party where she wears the white lutestring and the red garnets. This heroine refuses to be highly sentimental—as we see in the amusing scene where she goes to Lady Mary Sutton's Brandon Lodge and is reunited with her friend's old pets. Her kindness to animals will not allow her not to put them on a diet. Lady Mary, on the other hand, seems more idealistic, more sentimental, and in some ways more "lost" than Fanny.

Barford Abbey may seem to offer the consolations of melodrama and the comforts of marriage, but the balance of the novel reminds us that parts of life can sometimes be left out and that life's losses cannot genuinely be recovered. Something has gone missing in the Abbey; there is an empty space, an unmentionable absence. A generation is missing. The grandparents are there, but where is the generation of Father and Mother? Lady Mary Sutton is the only representative of that generation, but she did not herself generate a successor. Barren Lady Mary remains abroad among mineral waters until almost the very end. Sir James has usurped the position of Darcey's dead father. The blind chaplain is balanced by the rugged country squire Mr. Watson, who still thinks a "tye-wig" fashionable and wears a best coat purchased some twenty or more years before. Both of these quirky if appealing characters are old and incapable of taking the position of the people in their forties who are constant in their absence.

There is an unconscious discomfort in keeping company with grandparents and grandchildren but no one of middle age—a discomfort never openly announced but felt through the narrative. The discontinuity suggests that England has not managed to find a middle way—that the eighteenth century jumps from the old to the young (as indeed the national demographic shift makes literally true). Continuity is harder to come by. Arrangements and opinions are provisional rather than certain.

Abbeys Real and Imagined: *Barford Abbey*, the Novel

Barford Abbey is an achievement. Within a very small compass the novel achieves innovations in narrative manner and style. The main story works in somewhat the same manner as a mystery story; both characters and readers are misled by concealments and evasions. The story begins with the death of an apparently unimportant personage. We gather that she has been Fanny's caretaker and that the girl has hitherto lived with this woman and must grieve at her loss. But Fanny still has a friend in the evidently middle-aged Lady Mary, now abroad at a German spa for her health. With a youthful and appropriate desire to explore something different, to look forward and not back, Fanny accepts an unexpected invitation to visit the home of Mr. Jenkings, the steward of Barford Abbey, and his wife. Neither Fanny nor the reader can understand why Lady Mary does not approve of this visit.

Throughout the novel, the characters are in relationships that they themselves do not understand. Those possessing knowledge on certain points (like Lady Mary, or Mr. and Mrs. Jenkings) have their own reasons for their reluctance to impart information. Hidden emotional and social causes bring about unanticipated and even undesired effects. Central narrating characters are incapable of filling in the gaps in the narrative. At its center, the story exhibits the ill-effects brought on by the desire for control of others. Within the main narrative, as we follow it, this insistence on control—as well as techniques for accruing it—can be constantly observed, particularly in scenes between Sir James Powis and his former ward, Lord Darcey, who has only recently come of age. Beyond that immediate pressure lies the ultimate sinister contract, the death-bed promise extracted from Darcey by his father. Such a promise gains the status of a vow; it cannot be rescinded or renegotiated. Under pressure, Darcey agreed to his father's demand that the youth treat Sir James as his father. He promises to attend to Sir James's advice, but this promise has hardened into an expectation on behalf of Sir James, a law of perfect obedience whereby Sir James must have ultimate control over Darcey's marriage choice—and any other important actions.

Barford Abbey is both setting and atmosphere, a sign of power, the symbol of an originating act of will. We are uncomfortably asked, even if never directly, whether the transformation of abbeys into mansions with wealth-producing lands inevitably entails some secularization of religious law. Are moral laws merely the rules of a class? The discomfort of such questions is quietly present in the promise to his dying father extracted from young Darcey. Other novelists after Minifie will pick up the significance of the abbeys and their history. Charlotte Smith begins *Ethelinde* (1789) with a succinct and pointed account of a place:

> On the borders of the small but beautiful lake called Grasmere Water, in the county of Cumberland, is Grasmere Abbey, an old seat belonging to the family of Newenden. The abbey, founded by Ranulph Earl of Chester, for forty Cister-

cian monks, was among those dissolved by Henry the Eighth; by whom it was given, with its extensive royalties, to the family of Brandon, from whence it descended by a female to Sir Edward Newenden, its present possessor. (Appendix D1, p. 267)

The abbey is not Sir Edward's main residence, and it has by now become largely an expense. In order to sustain his wealth, Sir Edward, like *Downton Abbey*'s Robert Crawley, Earl of Grantham, has married new money. As Robert married American money, Sir Edward has taken to himself the daughter of the rich Mr. Maltravers, who has made a hefty fortune in Indian trade and commerce. Sir Edward has married for wealth—the choice that Sir James Powis of Barford Abbey incessantly urges upon his hapless ward. Sir Edward gained the money, but the bride he brought into his family has no respect for its values. Lady Newenden disdains the abbey, which she sees as a cold old building in distant and damp Cumberland. For Lady Newenden, the abbey's social symbolism of power is quite dead. Wealth, she knows, comes from exploitation of India, and expanding commerce—not from forgotten medieval religious edifices in the depths of the country: "after ... jolting in extreme heat, I come into this cold, damp, desolate place, which really is fit only for the nuns and friars that you told me, I think, used to inhabit it" (p. 280).

In Smith's novel, the abbey undergoes a second dissolution; its social meaning, its former worldly glamour and power, are now becoming invisible. *Barford Abbey* is among the first literary works to pick up an inherited privatized abbey as site and symbol of stress and change. Fanny's original enthusiastic rapture on first beholding the Abbey in its grounds proves to be ironic:

How enchanting the park! how clear the river that winds through it!——What taste,—what elegance, in the plantations!——How charmingly are Nature's beauties rang'd by art!—The trees,—the shrubs,—the flowers,—hold up their heads, as if proud of the spot they grow on!——Then the noble old structure,—the magnificent mansion of this ancient family, how does it fire the beholder with veneration and delight! The very walls seem'd to speak; at least there was something that inform'd *me*, native dignity, and virtues hereditary, dwelt within them. (pp. 41–42)

Fanny's delighted tribute arises out of her ignorance. The opening credits of many episodes of TV's *Downton Abbey* customarily make the viewer re-enact an approach to the abbey like this one, eliciting our awe at its magnificence, even while that social and aesthetic respect becomes intercut by familiarity with the trials and stresses of various inhabitants, as well as their secrets. *Barford Abbey* requires the readers to recognize the imperfections of the ideal and to share in the characters' experience, a process of change and redemption. A theme of rebirth and resurrection runs through the whole; it is not without cost that the heir is recovered. In receiving the relatively low-born Miss Delves, merely a banker's daughter, Barford will lose the exclusiveness that had nearly excluded Fanny.

Minifie's novel is light and playful, with unexpected moments of observation regarding the country life of hunting, shooting, and horse keeping that George Bernard Shaw (1856–1950) caricatured as "Horseback Hall."[1] Mr. Morgan, the old-fashioned country squire, is worth observing, whether he is teaching Fanny to ride or stuffing himself with leftovers. As Fanny develops social and self-consciousness, she sees the comic in both herself and the actions and pretenses of others, as, for instance, within the harmless and inane routines at the dinner party, with its group production of tired topics: "It was some time before the conversation became general.—First, and ever to have precedence,—the weather;—next, roads;—then houses,—plantations,—fashions,—dress,—equipage;—and last of all, politics in a thread-bare coat" (p. 99). This is not quite the "Shakespeare and musical-glasses" of Goldsmith's *The Vicar of Wakefield*, but a related study of inanity in fashion. Minifie is moving in the direction of Jane Austen with her innovative use of broken sequences, as in Mrs. Elton's monologue at the strawberry party in *Emma* (1815).

Fanny's social consciousness is not untinged with humor. Trying to be cool and stand-offish with Darcey when she justifiably believes that he has now "declared off," Fanny turns away from him in order to read, picking up a book on the windowsill. Darcey calls her bluff:

> *The Complete Pocket-Farrier; or, A Cure for all Disorders in Horses*, read his Lordship aloud, looking over my shoulder; for such was the title of the book.

---

1   George Bernard Shaw, "Heartbreak House and Horseback Hall," preface to *Heartbreak House* (1919).

What have you here, my love?

My love, indeed! Mighty free, mighty free, was it
not, my Lady? I could not avoid laughing at the
drollery of this accident, or I should have given him the
look he deserved. (p. 121)

The Complete Pocket-Farrier is a delightful title, so exactly suited
to its place and time. A "farrier," originally so-called because he
made horseshoes of iron (fer), later attended to the needs and ail-
ments of horses. Gentlemen needed do-it-yourself guides to far-
riery. Such a work, so truly suited to Horseback Hall, is not likely
to be the chosen reading matter of a young lady.

Barford Abbey offers many pieces of brilliant and innovative
writing. The quietly dramatic dinner-party scene at the end of
Volume I marks a new development within the eighteenth-
century English novel as a form. There Minifie brings off a
triumph of narrative within a little compass. Her first evening out
of mourning, Fanny wears a white gown and red garnets. Lord
Darcey dresses up for her. The jealous Miss Winter and her fatu-
ously attentive suitor tax Fanny's attention, while the thoroughly
mature visitors Lord Allan and his wife celebrate their wedding
anniversary and make pleasant if inane conversation about
venison. Then, by dint of the sort of good-natured joke that
somebody of forty-odd years such as Lord Allan may make to a
young man of twenty-one, the cat is set among the pigeons. Sir
James's suspicions flare as he fears loss of authority, and both
Darcey and Fanny are sent spinning. Miss Winter is pleased to
hear the declaration that there is no love-interest between the
two, no intention of marriage. As she exclaims to Fanny, Lord
Darcey has certainly "declared off." Fanny's and Darcey's very
different reactions to Darcey's own awkward response have now
put them at odds.

This skillfully managed scene represents Minifie's contribution to the new fiction of this period. A number of characters are
present, participating in desultory and instant conversation, not
planned address. One-on-one conversation comes most easily to
beginning dramatists and young novelists. Jane Austen was not
able to accomplish a multiple-speaker dinner-party scene like this
one until the sixth chapter of Mansfield Park (1814). Minifie's
chapter has no distinguished or worthy public theme—her
scene's dramatic effects revolve around an accidental contre-

temps, plunging both the obtuse and acutely self-conscious members of the party into a chaos of hurt, uncertainty, and unintended meanings. Beautifully brought off, the scene seems effortless. Yet no English novelist had produced anything quite like it before.

Critics in our day tend to dismiss Gunning's contributions to literature. *Barford Abbey* garnered one of the better compliments paid Gunning when a reviewer in *The Critical Review* remarked, "We cannot help making an exception of this novel from the common run of such publications. Few or none of the incidents are, indeed, new; but they are well wrought up" (Appendix E1, p. 309). Like many eighteenth-century reviews, *The Critical Review* reproduced large swaths of the novel and revealed the entirety of the plot, assuming that many readers' experience of the book was likely to be limited to the review. Reviews like this one turned sour near the end of her career, especially when it came to *Virginius and Virginia*, about which one reviewer remarked, "We would advise Mrs. Gunning to rest her literary fame on the basis of that credit, whatever it be, which she has acquired as a novellist [*sic*]. Her poetical abilities, if we may judge by this production, will never entitle her to any exalted seat among the favourites of the Muses" (Appendix E3).

Her daughter, Elizabeth, also became a novelist, publishing *The Packet* (1794) and a number of other works, including a translation of Bernard le Bovier de Fontenelle's 1686 *Plurality of Worlds* (1808). Elizabeth married James Plunkett of County Roscommon in Ireland, but marriage did not stop her from writing and publishing as it had her mother. John Gunning died in 1797. He appears to have been reconciled in the end to his wife and daughter, leaving them £8,000. To his wife he also left his estate in Ireland.[1] Susannah died on 28 August 1800 and was buried in the north cloister of Westminster Abbey. Who arranged that prestigious last resting place is a matter for speculation. It is not in Poets' Corner, where England's literary celebrities are buried, but any burial site in Westminster Abbey is important enough. Somebody must have paid for it or had considerable influence.

---

1 As reported in the *Gentleman's Magazine* (1797).

Susannah Minifie Gunning: A Brief Chronology

1065	Dedication of Westminster Abbey
1535	Henry VIII's Act for the Dissolution of the Lesser Monasteries wrests control of abbeys from the Church and places their lands and resources at the king's disposal. Many abbeys fall into disuse and ruin; others become the stately homes of aristocrats.
1694	Founding of the Bank of England
1739/40	Susannah Minifie born in Somerset. Her father is the Reverend Doctor James Minifie.
1740	Samuel Richardson's enormously popular epistolary novel *Pamela; or, Virtue Rewarded* published. It tells the story of a servant who marries her master.
1747–48	Samuel Richardson: *Clarissa*
1753–54	Samuel Richardson: *Sir Charles Grandison*
1763	Susannah and her sister, Margaret, publish their first novel, *The Histories of Lady Frances S——, and Lady Caroline S——.*
1764	Susannah publishes *Family Pictures*. Horace Walpole publishes *The Castle of Otranto*, reputedly the first gothic horror story.
1766	Susannah and Margaret publish their novel *The Picture*.
1768	*Barford Abbey*. Susannah marries Captain John Gunning (8 August).
1769	Daughter Elizabeth born. French translation of *Barford Abbey* published. *The Cottage. The Hermit,* with Margaret.
1771	Second edition of *Barford Abbey*
1775	American War of Independence begins. Captain John Gunning fights on the English side at the Battle of Bunker Hill.
1780	*The Count of Poland*
1783	*Coombe Wood*
1789	Beginning of the French Revolution. Charlotte Smith: *Ethelinde*.
1791	*Letter to Argyll*
1792	*Anecdotes of the Delborough Family*; *Virginius and Virginia*. John Gunning: *Apology*.

A Note on the Text

Barford Abbey appeared in four eighteenth-century editions, including one translation into French (*L'abbaye ou le chateau de Barford*, 1769). The first version of the novel, published in London by Thomas Cadell (1768), was reprinted in Dublin later that year by J. Exshaw, H. Saunders, and W. Collis. A second edition issued from Robinson and Roberts in London (1771), suggesting that the work experienced some popularity. No reliable contemporary edition of the novel exists, although many facsimile editions have made the text available. This edition is based on the 1768 edition of the text. We have consulted the 1771 edition in a few instances to resolve questions raised by the first edition. Every effort has been made to preserve the orthography, punctuation, and presentation of the first edition, especially the idiosyncratic use of the "double dash" (——) and "triple dash" (———), which extend across the page much farther than our customary em-dash (—) and clearly served a special purpose in Gunning's or the printer's presentation of the novel. In some instances, we have preserved errors in the first edition text unremarked to save something of the sometimes quick and untidy practices with which eighteenth-century novels like *Barford Abbey* were printed. We have also attempted to maintain the epistolary look and spacing of the first edition, which lend verisimilitude and readability to the text.

BARFORD ABBEY,

A NOVEL:
IN A
SERIES of LETTERS.
IN TWO VOLUMES.

BARFORD ABBEY,

END OF THE FIRST VOLUME.

FINIS.

FINIS.

BARFORD ABBEY,

A NOVEL:
IN A
SERIES of LETTERS.
IN TWO VOLUMES.

VOL. I.

LONDON:

Printed for T. CADELL, (Successor to Mr. MILLAR) in the
Strand; and J. PAYNE, in Paternoster-Row.

MDCCLXVIII.

BARFORD ABBEY.

LETTER I.

Lady MARY SUTTON, at the German Spaw,[1] to Miss
WARLEY, in England.

HOW distressing, how heart-rending, is my dear Fanny's
mournful detail!—It lies before me; I weep over it!—I weep
not for the departed saint: no; it is for you, myself, for all who have
experienced her god-like virtues!—Was she not an honour to her
sex? Did she not merit rewards too great for this world to bestow?—
Could the world repay her innocence, her piety, her resignation?
Wipe away, my best love, the mark of sorrow from your cheek.
Perhaps she may be permitted to look down: if so, will she smile on
those that grieve at her entering into the fullness of joy?
—Here a sudden death cannot be called dreadful. A life like hers
wanted not the admonitions of a sick-bed;—her bosom accounts
always clear, always ready for inspection, day by day were they held
up to the throne of mercy.—Apply those beautiful lines in the Spectator to her; lines you have so often admir'd.—How silent thy
passage; how private thy journey; how glorious thy end![2] Many have

---

1 Lady Mary has traveled for her health. The original "Spa" or "Spaw"
(which gives us our term "spa") is in Belgium, southeast of Liège. It possesses natural mineral water and was a resort for invalids wishing to take
the waters. Casinos started up here in the eighteenth century. If Lady
Mary were to go to a watering-place in Germany, it might be in Baden-
Baden or any one of a number of towns with "Bad" ("bath") in the name.
The curative powers of mineral waters for both drinking and bathing were
highly thought of in the eighteenth century.

2 See *Spectator* no. 133 (2 August 1711). The *Spectator* essays were frequently reprinted throughout the eighteenth century and could be found
in almost every private library. This paper by Richard Steele describes
watching at the deathbed of a friend. The first sentence is "There is a sort
of Delight, which is alternately mixed with Terror and Sorrow, in the contemplation of Death."

Contemplation of dying was a strong subject in the eighteenth century,
found both in devotional literature and in fiction. Here the reader does
not know the character who has just died; it is part of the design of the
novel that the reader should be alert in deducing the relations of various
characters to each other (which they themselves do not   (*continued*)

I known more famous, some more knowing, not one so innocent.—
Hope is a noble support to the drooping head of sorrow.—Though
a deceiver, court her, I counsel you;—she leads to happiness;—we
shall bless her deceptions:—baffling our enjoyments here, she
teaches us to look up where every thing is permanent, even bliss
most exquisite.

Mr. Whitmore you never knew, otherwise would have wonder'd how his amiable wife loiter'd so long behind.—Often she
has wish'd to be reunited to him, but ever avoided the subject in
your presence.

Keep not from me her rich bequest:—*rich* indeed,—her most
valuable treasure.—That I could fold you to my arms!—But hear
me at a distance;—hear me call you my beloved daughter,
—and suppose what my transports will be when I embrace an
only child:—yes, you are mine, till I deliver you up to a superior
affection.

Lay aside, I conjure you, your fears of crossing the sea.——
Mr. and Mrs. Smith intend spending part of this winter at Montpelier: trust yourself with them; I shall be there to receive you at
the Hôtel de Spence.

The season for the Spaw is almost at an end. My physicians
forbid my return to England till next autumn, else I would fly to
comfort,—to console my dearest Fanny.—We shall be happy
together in France:—I can love you the same in all places.

My banker has orders to remit you three hundred pounds;—
but your power is unlimited; it is impossible to say, my dear, how
much I am in your debt.—I have wrote my housekeeper to get
every thing ready for your reception:—consider her, and all my
other servants, as your own.—I shall be much disappointed if
you do not move to the Lodge immediately.——You shall not,—
must not,—continue in a house where every thing in and about
it reminds you of so great a loss.——Miss West, Miss Gardner,
Miss Conway, will, at my request, accompany you thither.—The

---

always know). We gather that young Fanny has lost the woman who was a
guardian or mother figure, and that Lady Mary, a protective friend who
seems somewhat elderly, is absent from England.

Menagerie,[1]—plantations,[2] and other places of amusement, will naturally draw them out;—you will follow mechanically, and by that means be kept from indulging melancholy.——Go an-airing every day, unless you intend I shall find my horses unfit for service:—why have you let them live so long idle?

I revere honest Jenkings;—he is faithful,—he will assist you with his advice on all occasions.——Can there be a better resource to fly to, than a heart governed by principles of honour and humanity?

Write, my dear, to Mrs. Smith, and let me know if the time is fixed for their coming over.—Say you will comply with the request my heart is so much set on;—say you will be one of the party.

My health and spirits are better:—the latter I support for your sake;—who else do I live for?—Endeavour to do the same, not only for me, but *others*, that one day will be as dear to you as you are to

Your truly affectionate,

M. SUTTON.

★ ★ ★

LETTER II.

Miss WARLEY to Lady MARY SUTTON.

Barford Abbey.

BARFORD ABBEY! *Yes*, my dearest Lady,—I date from Barford Abbey: a house I little thought ever to have seen, when I have listened hours to a description of it from Mr. Jenkings.—What are houses,—what palaces, in competition with *that*

---

1 A collection of animals, often exotic, meant for exhibition, menageries were popular among wealthy aristocrats beginning in the seventeenth century.

2 Here referring to newly planted areas of estates, especially plantings of young trees, and not the sugar plantations of the West Indies.

honour, *that* satisfaction, I received by your Ladyship's last letter!—The honour all must acknowledge;—the satisfaction is not on the surface,—*it centers in the heart.*—I feel too much to express any thing.——One moment an orphan; next the adopted child of Lady Mary Sutton.—What are titles, except ennobled by virtue! *That* only makes a coronet[1] fit graceful on the head;—*that* only is the true ornament of greatness.

Pardon my disobedience.—Can there be a stronger command than your request?—But, my Lady, I must have died,—my life *must* have been the sacrifice, had I gone to the Lodge.—The windows opposite, the windows of that little mansion where I spent nineteen happy years with my angelic benefactress;—could it be borne?—Your Ladyship's absence too;—what an aggravation!—The young ladies you kindly propose for my companions, though very amiable, could not have shut my eyes, or deaden'd my other senses.

Now let me account for being at Barford Abbey.——Was Mr. Jenkings my father, I think I could not love him more; yet when he press'd me to return with him to Hampshire,[2] I was doubtful whether to consent, till your Ladyship's approbation of him was confirmed in so particular a manner.——His son an only one;—the fine fortune he must possess;—these were objections not only of *mine*, but, I believe, of my dear, dear——Oh! my Lady, I cannot yet write her name.—Often has she check'd Mr. Jenkings, when he has solicited to take me home with him:—her very looks spoke she had something to fear from such a visit.—She loved me;—the dear angel loved me with maternal affection, but her partiality never took place of noble, generous sentiments.——Young people, she has frequently said, are, by a strict intimacy, endeared to each other. This, I doubt not, was her motive for keeping me at a distance.—She well knew my poor expectations

---

1 The word "coronet," literally "little crown," refers to the miniature crown worn by nobles below the rank of the monarch. An actual coronet is worn only on the most formal state occasions, but the term figuratively refers to the nobility

2 Lady Mary Sutton's country house is in Oxfordshire. Hampshire is a large and wealthy southern county, with rich lands and an extensive seacoast, including the ports of Portsmouth and Southampton. There are several towns named "Barford" in England. "Powis" and "Morgan" are Welsh names, interesting for people so long settled in southern England.

were ill suited to his large ones.—I know what was her opinion, and will steadily adhere to it.

Edmund, to do him common justice, is a desirable youth:—such a one as I can admire his good qualities, without another wish than to imitate them.——Monday, the tenth, I took my leave of Hillford Down, and, after a melancholy journey, arrived Tuesday evening at Mr. Jenkings's.—Nothing did I enjoy on the road;—in spight of my endeavours, tears stream'd from my eyes incessantly;—even the fine prospects that courted attention, pass'd unnotic'd.——My good conductor strove to draw me off from gloomy subjects; but in vain, till we came within a few miles of his house; then of a sudden I felt a serenity, which, for some time, has been a stranger to my breast;—a serenity I cannot account for.

Mrs. Jenkings!—never shall I forget her humanity. She flew to the chaise[1] the instant it stopp'd, receiv'd me with open arms, and conducted me to the parlour, pouring out ten thousand welcomes, intermingled with fond embraces.——She is, I perceive, one of those worthy creatures, who make it a point to consider their husbands friends as their own; in my opinion, the highest mark of conjugal happiness.

Plac'd in a great chair next the fire, every one was busied in something or other for my refreshment.—One soul,—one voice,—one manner, to be seen in the father,—mother,—son:—they look not on each other but with a smile of secret satisfaction. *To me* their hearts speak the same expressive language;—their house,—their dress,—their words, plainly elegant.——Envy never stops at such a dwelling; nothing there is fit for her service:—no pomp,—no grandeur,—no ostentation.——I slept sweetly the whole night;—sweetly!—not one disagreeable idea intruded on my slumbers.

Coming down in the morning, I found breakfast on the table, linen white as snow, a large fire,—every thing that speaks cleanliness, content, and plenty.——The first thing in a house which attracts my notice is the fire;—I conclude from that, if the hearts of the inhabitants are warm or cold.——Our conversation was interesting;—it might have lasted, for aught I know, till dinner,

---

1 Chaise pulled by a team of horses.

had it not been interrupted by the entrance of Sir James and Lady Powis.——I knew Mr. Jenkings was their steward, but never expected they came to his house with such easy freedom.——We arose as they entered:—I was surprised to see Mr. and Mrs. Jenkings appear confused;—in my opinion, their visitors accosted them more like *equals* than *dependants*.

Your Ladyship cannot imagine how greatly I was prepossessed in their favour even before they spoke.——In their manner was something that struck me excessively;—few—very few—can express the nameless beauties of grace,—never to be seen but in a carriage[1] sweetly humble.

Lady Powis seated herself opposite to me.—We called, said she, addressing Mr. Jenkings, to inquire what was become of you, fearing your Oxfordshire friends had stolen you from us;—but you have made up for your long absence, if this is the young lady, bowing to me, your wife told us was to return with you.——A politeness so unexpected,—so deliver'd,—visibly affected me:—I sat silent, listening for the reply Mr. Jenkings would make.

Pardon me, my Lady! pardon me, Miss Warley! said the good man,—I am a stranger to punctilio;[2]—I see my error:—I should have acquainted your Ladyship before with the name of this dear young Lady; I should have said she is an honour to her friends.——Need I tell Miss Warley, Sir James and Lady Powis are present:—I hope the deportment of their *servant* has confirmed it;—I hope it has.

Sir James kindly took his hand, and, turning to me, said, Don't believe him, Madam, he is not our servant;—he has been our *friend* forty years; we flatter ourselves he deems not *that* servitude.

Not your *servant*!—not your *dependant*!—not your *servant*, Sir James!——and was running on when her Ladyship interrupted him.

---

1 Mode of behaving, one's deportment and attitude.

2 From the Italian *puntiglio* or the Spanish *puntillo*, attention to a small point of order or honor in conduct.

Don't make me angry, Jenkings;—don't pain me;—hear the favour I have to ask, and be my advocate:—it is with Miss Warley I want you to be my advocate.——Then addressing herself to me, Will you, Madam, give me the pleasure of your company often at the Abbey?—I mean, will you come there as if it was your home?—Mr. and Mrs. Jenkings have comforts, I have not,—at least that I can enjoy.——Here she sigh'd deeply;—so deep, that I declare it pierced through my heart;—I felt as if turn'd into stone;—what I suppose I was a true emblem of.—— The silent friends that trickled down my cheeks brought me back from that inanimate state,—and I found myself in the embraces of Lady Powis, tenderly affectionate, as when in the arms of Mrs Whitmore.——Judge not, Madam, said I, from my present stupidity, that I am so wanting in my head or heart, to be insensible of this undeserv'd goodness.—With Mr. and Mrs. Jenkings's permission, I am devoted to your Ladyship's service.——*Our* approbation! Miss Warley, return'd the former;—yes, that you have:—her Ladyship cannot conceive how happy she has made us.—Sir James seconded his Lady with a warmth perfectly condescending:—no excuse would be taken; I must spend the next day at the Abbey; their coach was to attend me.

Our amiable guests did not move till summoned by the dinner-bell, which is plainly to be heard there.——I thought I should have shed tears to see them going.——I long'd to walk part of the way, but was afraid to propose it, lest I should appear presumptuous.—Her Ladyship perceiv'd my inclinations,— look'd delighted,—and requested my company; on which Mr Jenkings offer'd his service to escort me back.

How was I surpris'd at ascending the hill!——My feet seem'd leading me to the first garden,—the sweet abode of innocence!— Ten thousand beauties broke on my sight;—ten thousand pleasures, before unknown, danced through my heart.—Behold me on the summit;—behold me full of surprise,—full of admiration!— How enchanting the park! how clear the river that winds through it!——What taste,—what elegance, in the plantations!——How charmingly are Nature's beauties rang'd by art!—The trees,—the shrubs,—the flowers,—hold up their heads, as if proud of the spot they grow on!——Then the noble old structure,—the magnificent mansion of this ancient family, how does it fire the beholder with veneration and delight! The very walls seem'd to speak; at least there was something that inform'd *me*, native dignity, and virtues hereditary, dwelt within them.

The sight of a chaise and four,[1] standing at the entrance, hurried me from the charming pair of this paradise, after many good days ecchoed to me, and thanks respectful return'd them by the same messenger.

Mr. Jenkings, in our return, entertain'd me with an account of the family for a century past.——A few foibles excepted in the character of Sir James, I find he possesses all the good qualities of his ancestors.—Nothing could be more pleasing than the encomiums bestow'd on Lady Powis;—but she is not exempt from trouble:—the *good* and the *bad* the *great* and the *little*, at some time or other, feel Misfortune's touch. Happy such a rod hangs over us! Were we to glide on smoothly, our affections would be fixed here, and here only.

I could love Lady Powis with a warmth not to be express'd; —but—forgive me, my dear lady—I pine to know why *your* intimacy was interrupted.—Of *Lady Mary*'s steadiness and integrity I am convinc'd;—of *Lady Powis* I have had only a transitory view.—Heaven forbid she should be like such people as from my heart I despise, whose regards are agueish![2] Appearances promise the reverse;—but what is appearance? For the generality a mere cheat, a gaudy curtain.

Pardon me, dear Lady Powis—I am distress'd,—I am perplex'd; but I do not think ill of you;—indeed I cannot,—unless I find——*No*, I cannot find it neither;—something tells me *Lady Mary*, my dear honour'd Lady Mary, will acquit you.

We were receiv'd by Mrs. Jenkings, at our return, with a chearful countenance, and conducted to the dining-parlour, where, during our comfortable meal, nothing was talk'd of but Sir James

---

1 Small open carriage typically used for shorter journeys, the fact that this carriage is pulled by not one or two but four horses may signify a certain, almost absurd, grandeur. Compare *Pride and Prejudice*, where Austen describes both Mr. Bingley and Lady Catherine de Bourgh riding in "a chaise and four" (chs. 1 and 56).

2 I.e., whose opinions of others are feverish, inconstant.

and Lady Powis:—the kind notice taken of your Fanny mentioned with transport.

Thus honour'd,—thus belov'd,—dare I repine?—Why look on past enjoyments with such a wistful eye!——Mrs. Whitmore, my dear maternal Mrs. Whitmore, cannot be recall'd!——Strange perverseness!—why let that which would give me pleasure fleet away!—why pursue that which I cannot overtake!—No gratitude to heaven!—Gratitude to you, my dearest Lady, shall conquer this perverseness;—even now my heart overflows like a swoln river.

Good night, good night, dear Madam; I am going to repose on the very bed where, for many years, rested the most deserving of men!——The housekeeper has been relating many of his virtues;—so many, that I long to see him, *though only in a dream.*

Was it not before Mr. Powis went abroad, that your ladyship visited at the Abbey?—Yet, if so, I think I should have heard you mention him.—Merit like his could never pass unnotic'd in a breast so similar——Here I drop my pen, lest I grow impertinent.——Once again, good night,—my more than parent:—tomorrow, at an early hour, I will begin the recital to your Ladyship of this day's transactions——I go to implore every blessing on your head, the only return that can be offer'd by

F. WARLEY.

LETTER III.

Miss WARLEY to Lady MARY SUTTON, in continuation.

Barford Abbey.

I Think I have told your Ladyship, I was to be honour'd with the coach to convey me to the Abbey.——About half an hour after one it arriv'd, when a card was deliver'd me from Lady Powis, to desire my friends would not be uneasy, if I did not return early in the evening, as she hop'd for an agreeable party at whist,[1] Lord Darcey being at the Abbey.

---

1 Card game for four players, whist is a trick-taking game, the ancestor of bridge and the similar game, hearts. Edmond Hoyle (1672–1769) published a guide explaining how to play whist effectively.

Mrs. Jenkings informed me, his Lordship was a ward of Sir James's just of age;[1]—his estate genteel, not large;—his education liberal,—his person fine,—his temper remarkably good.— Sir James, said she, is for ever preaching lessons to him, that he must marry *prudently*;—which is, that he must never marry without an immense fortune.——Ah! Miss Warley, this same love of money has serv'd to make poor Lady Powis very unhappy.—Sir James's greatest fault is covetousness;—but who is without fault?—Lord Darcey was a lovely youth, continued she, when he went abroad; I long to see if he is alter'd by travelling.—Edmund and his Lordship were school-fellows:—how my son will be overjoy'd to hear he is at the Abbey!——I detain you, Miss Warley, or could talk for ever of Lord Darcey! Do go, my dear, the family will expect you.——Promise, said I, taking her hand,—*promise* you will not sit up late on my account.—She answer'd nothing, but pressing me to her bosom, seem'd to tell me her heart was full of affection.

The old coachman, as we drove up the lawn, eyed me attentively, saying to the footman, *It will be so, John, you may depend upon it.*——John answer'd only by a shrug.——What either meant, I shall not pretend to divine.——As I came near the house, I met Mr Jenkings almost out of breath, and, pulling the string, he came to the coach-side. I was hurrying home, my dear young Lady, said he, to—to—to——Now faith I'm afraid you'll be angry.

Angry with you, Sir!—angry with you, Mr Jenkings!—is it possible!

Then, to be plain, Madam, I was hurrying home, to request you would wear no cap.—Never shall I forget how pretty you look'd, when I saw you without one!—Of all things, I would *this day* wish you might look your best.

To satisfy him I had taken some little pains in honour to the family, I let back the hood of my cloke.—He examin'd the manner in which my hair was dress'd, and smiled his approbation;—which *smile*, though only seen in the eyes, was more expressive than a contraction of all the other features.—— Wishing me a happy day, he bid the coachman drive on.

---

1 Lord Darcey has just passed his 21st birthday.

Coming within sight of the Abbey, my heart beat as if break-ing from confinement.—I was oblig'd to call it to a severe trial,—to ask, Why this insurrection,—whence these tumults?——My monitor reply'd, Beware of self-sufficiency,—beware of its mortifying consequences.——

How seasonable this warning against the worst of foes!—a foe which I too much fear was stealing on me imperceptibly,—else why did I not before feel those sensations?—Could I receive greater honour than has been conferr'd on me by the noblest mind on earth!—by *Lady Mary*?—Could I behold greater splen-dor than Lady Mary is possess'd of!——What affection in another can I ever hope for like *Lady Mary*'s!——Thus was I arguing with myself, when the coach-door open'd, and a servant conducted me to the drawing-room,—where I was receiv'd by Sir James and Lady Powis with an air of polite tenderness;—a kind of unreserve, that not only supports the timid mind, but dignifies every word,—every action,—and gives to education and address their highest polish.

Lord Darcey was sitting in the window, a book in his hand;—he came forward as Sir James introduc'd me, who said, *Now*, my Lord, the company of *this* young Lady will make your Lordship's time pass more agreeably, than it could have done in the conver-sation of two old people.——My spirits were flutter'd; I really don't recollect his reply; only that it shew'd him master of the great art, to make every one pleas'd with themselves.

Shall I tell you, my dear Lady, what are my thoughts of *this* Lord Darcey?——To confess then, though his person is amaz-ingly elegant, his manners are still more engaging.—This I look upon to be the natural consequence of a mind illumin'd with uncommon understanding, sweetness, and refinement.

A short time before dinner the chaplain made his appear-ance,—a venerable old man, with hair white as snow:—what renders his figure to be completely venerated, is the loss of sight.[1]—Her Ladyship rising from her seat, led me towards him: Mr Watson, said she, I am going to introduce a lady whose brightest charms will soon be visible to you.——The best man in

Loyalty is his sight

---

1   Mr. Watson affords an interesting instance of the Abbey as an asylum for the disabled. A blind character is most unusual.

the world! whisper'd she, putting my hand in his;—which hand I could not avoid putting to my lips.—*Thank* you, Miss Warley, said her Ladyship, *we all* revere this gentleman.——Mr. Watson was affected, some drops stole from their dark prisons, and he bless'd me as if I had been his daughter:—my pleasure was exquisite,—it seem'd as if I had receiv'd the benediction of an angel.

Our subjects turn'd more on the celestial than the terrestrial, till dinner was serv'd up,—when I found that good *knight* which has been so long banish'd to the side-board, replac'd in his original station.[1]

Poor royalty

How different *this table* from many others! where genteel sprightly conversations are shut out; *where* such as cannot feast their senses on the genius of a *cook*, must rise unsatisfied.

A similitude of manners between your *Ladyship* and *Lady Powis*, particularly in doing the honours of the table, struck me so much, that I once or twice call'd her *Lady Mary.*—Pray, Miss Warley, ask'd she, who is this Lady Mary?

What could occasion her confusion!—what could occasion the confusion of Sir James!—Never did I see any thing equal it, when I said it was Lady Mary Sutton!—The significant looks that were interchang'd, spoke some mystery;—a mystery it would be presumption in me to dive after. Her Ladyship made no reply,—Sir James was eager to vary the subject,—and the conversation became general.

Though autumn is far advanc'd, every thing here wears the face of spring.—The afternoon being remarkably fine Lady Powis, Lord Darcey, and myself, strolled out amongst the sweets.—We walk'd a considerable time; his Lordship was all gaiety, talk'd with raptures of the improvements; declar'd every

---

[1] The "good knight" is a sirloin of beef, "Sir Loin" (an old joke). Sir James and his wife appreciate "the roast beef of old England" and, as in former times, make it a central attraction of the table. The roast is not banished, as in more fashionable companies, to the sideboard, to be sliced and served by servants. Later, Mr. Morgan helps himself with the help of Sir James's servants to an unofficial meal of "cold sirloin and pickled oysters"—digging into the leftovers (see p. 50).

thing he had seen abroad fell short of this delightful spot; and *now*, my dear Lady Powis, added he, with an air of gallantry, I can see *nothing* wanting.

Nothing wanting! return'd her Ladyship, sighing:——Ah! my Lord, *you* are not a parent!—you feel nothing of a parent's woe!— *you* do not hourly regret the absence of a beloved and only son! Don't look serious, my dear Lord, seeing him somewhat abash'd, you have hitherto tenderly loved me.—Perhaps I had a mind to augment your affection, by bringing to your recollection I was not happy.——His Lordship made no reply, but, taking her hand, lifted it respectfully to his lips.

Mr. Jenkings is this moment coming up the lawn, I see him from window;—excuse me, my dear Lady, whilst I step to ask him how he does.

I have been accounting to Mr. Jenkings for not coming home last night. Good man! every mark of favour I receive, enlightens *his countenance*.—The reasons I have given him, I shall now proceed to give your Ladyship.

I said we were walking;—I have said the conversation was interesting;—but I have not said it was interrupted by Sir James and Mr. Watson, who join'd us just as Lord Darcey had quitted the hand of Lady Powis.——A visit was propos'd to the Dairy-house, which is about a mile from the Abbey.——In our way thither, I was full of curiosity, full of inquiries about the neighbourhood, and whose seats *such* and *such* were, that enrich'd adjacent hills?—The neighbourhood, reply'd her Ladyship, is in general polite and hospitable.—*Yes*, said *Sir James*, and more smart young men, *Miss Warley*, than are to be met with in *every* county.——Yonder, continued he, live Mr. and Mrs. Finch,[1]— very rich,—very prudent, and very worthy;—they have one son, a discreet lad, who seems to promise he will inherit their good qualities.

That which you see so surrounded with woods, is Sir Thomas Slater's, a *batchelor* of fifty-five; and, let me tell you, fair Lady, the

---

1 The name of this briefly appearing character may have been suggested by the married surname of a famous and aristocratic female poet: Anne Finch, Countess of Winchilsea (1661–1720).

pursuit of *every* girl in the neighbourhood;—his estate a clear nine thousand a-year, and——Hold, hold, interrupted Lord Darcey, in compassion to *us* young fellows, say no more of this *redoubtable* batchelor.

Well then, continued Sir James, since my Lord *will* have it so,—let me draw your eye, Miss Warley, from Sir Thomas Slater's, and fix it on Lord Allen's: Observe the situation!—Nothing can be more beautiful, the mind of its owner excepted.

That house on the left is Mr Winter's.——Chance!—*strange chance!*—has just put him in possession of an immense fortune, with which he is going to purchase a *coronet* for his daughter.[1] ——The fellow does not know what to do with his *money*, and has at last found an *ape* of quality, that will take *it* off his hands.

In this manner was Sir James characterising his neighbours, when a sudden and violent storm descended.——Half a mile from the *Dairy-house*, the rain fell in such torrents, that we were wet through, before a friendly oak offer'd us its shelter.——Never shall I forget my own or Lord Darcey's figure: he stripp'd himself of his coat, and would have thrown it over Lady Powis. Her Ladyship absolutely refusing it, her cloak being thick, mine the reverse, he forc'd it upon me. Sir James assisting to put my arms into the sleeves.——Nor was I yet enough of the amazon:[2]—they even compell'd me to exchange my hat for his, lapping it, about my ears.—— What a strange *metamorphose!*——I cannot think of it without laughing!——To complete the scene, no exchange could be made, till we reach'd the Abbey.——In this droll situation, we waited for the coach; and getting in, streaming from head to toe, it more resembled a bathing machine,[3] than any other vehicle.

---

1 Mr. Winter intends to offer such a grand dowry that a nobleman will be tempted to marry her.
2 In Greek myth, Amazons were a society of female warriors. The term came to denote masculine women. Fanny jokes about her gender change as she is wearing Lord Darcey's coat and hat, while he wears her hat.
3 A little wagon specially designed to assist in sea-bathing, especially for women. The would-be bather, still dressed, got into the machine from the land or beach; the conveyance was then drawn into the sea and the bather, having changed clothing under cover, could emerge and take a modest plunge. The Powises' coach here resembles a bathing machine as a thoroughly damp conveyance.

A gentleman, who, after a chace of ten hours, had taken shelter under the roof of Sir James, was, at our return, stamping up and down the vestibule, disappointed both in his sport and dinner, shew'd an aspect cloudy as the heavens.——My mortification was scarce supportable, when I heard him roar out, in a voice like thunder, *What the devil have we here?*——I sprang to the top of the stairs in a moment,—there stopp'd to fetch breath; and again the same person, who had so genteelly accosted me, said to Lord Darcey,—*Great* improvements, upon my soul!—*You* are return'd a mighty pretty *Miss.*——What, is *this* the newest dress at Turin?——I heard no more; her Ladyship's woman came and shew'd me to an apartment,—bringing from her Lady's wardrobe a chints négligée, and a suit of flower'd muslin; in which I was soon equipp'd.

Lady Powis sent to desire I would come to her dressing-room; and, embracing me as I entered, said, with an air of charming freedom, If you are not hurt, my dear, by our little excursion, I shall be quite in spirits this evening.

I am only hurt by your Ladyship's goodness. Indeed, return'd she, I have not a close heart, but no one ever found so quick a passage to it as yourself.——Oh! Lady Mary, *this* is surely a *heart* like yours!——A *heart* like Mrs. Whitmore's!——Was you not surpris'd, *my dear,* continued her Ladyship, to be so accosted by the gentleman below?—Take no notice of what is said by Mr. Morgan.—that is his name;—he means well, and never goes into any person's house, but where his oddities are indulg'd.——I am particularly civil to him; he was an old school-fellow of Sir James's, one whose purse was always open to him. ——Sir James, Miss Warley, was rather addicted to extravagance in the beginning of his life;—*that,* in some respects, is revers'd latterly.——I have been a sufferer,—yet is he a tender generous husband. One day you shall know more.—I *had* a son, Miss Warley——Here Sir James interrupted her.——I come to tell you, said he, that Lord Darcey and myself are impatient for our tea.

O fie! Sir James, return'd Lady Powis, talk of impatience before an unmarried Lady!—If you go on at this rate, you will frighten her from any connection with your sex.——Not at all,—not at all, said Sir James; you take us for better for worse.[1]——See there, Miss Warley smiles.—I warrant she does not think my *impatience* unseasonable.—I was going to reply, but effectually stopped by her Ladyship, who said, taking my hand, Come, my dear, let us go down.——I am fond of finding excuses for Sir James; we will suppose it was not he who was impatient:—we will suppose the *impatience* to be Lord Darcey's.

Whilst regaling ourselves at the tea table, Mr. Morgan was in the dining-parlour, brightening up his features by the assistance of the cook and butler.—We were congratulating each other on the difference of our present and late situation, declaring there was nothing to regret, when Mr Morgan enter'd.—Regret! cry'd he,—what do you regret?—Not, I hope, that I have made a good dinner on a cold sirloin and pickled oysters?——Indeed I do, said Lady Powis:—Had I thought you so poor a caterer, I should have taken the office on myself.——Faith then, reply'd he, you might have eat it yourself—Forty years, my good Lady, I have made this house my home, and did I ever suffer you to direct *what*, or *when*, I should eat?——

Sir James laugh'd aloud; so did her Ladyship:—I was inclin'd to do the same,—but afraid what next he would say;—However, this caution did not screen me from particular notice.

What the duce have I here![2] said he, taking one of my hands,—a snow-ball by the colour, and feeling? and down he dropp'd it by the side of Lord Darcey's, which rested on the table.

I was never more confounded.

You are not angry, my pretty Lady, continued he:—we shall know one another better;—but if you displease me,—I shall thunder.——I keep all in subjection, except the *muleish kind*, making a low bow to Sir James. Saying this, he went in pursuit of Mr. Watson.——They soon re-enter'd together; a card-table was produc'd; and we sat down at it, whilst they solac'd themselves by a good fire.

---

1 From the vows made in the Marriage Service (Solemnization of Matrimony) in the Anglican *Book of Common Prayer*.
2 A mild curse: what the devil have we here.

My attention was frequently taken from the cards, to observe how it was possible such opposites as Mr. Watson and Mr. Morgan cou'd be entertain'd by one another's conversation.——Never saw I any two seemingly more happy!—The chearfulness of the former augmented;—the voice of the latter at least three notes lower.——This has been since explain'd to me by Lady Powis.——Mr. Morgan, she says, notwithstanding his rough appearance, is of a nature so compassionate, that, to people defective in person or fortune, he is the gentlest creature breathing.

Our party broke up at nine.——I sat half an hour after supper, then propos'd returning to Mr. Jenkings's.——Lady Powis would not hear me on this subject—I must stay that night at the Abbey:—venturing out in such weather would hazard my health.—So said Sir James; so said Lord Darcey.——As for Mr. Morgan, he swore, Was he the former, his horses should not stir out for fifty pieces,[1] unless, said he, Sir James chooses to be a fellow-sufferer with Lord Allen, who I have led such a chace this day, that he was forced to leave poor Snip on the forest.[2]
——Saying which, he threw himself back in the chair, and fell into a sound sleep.—About eleven I retir'd to my chamber;—a message first being sent to Mr. Jenkings.—Instead of going immediately to bed, I sat down and indulg'd myself with the satisfaction of writing to my beloved Lady Mary.——This morning I got up early to finish my packet;[3] and though I have spent half an hour with Mr. Jenkings, shall close it before her Ladyship is stirring.

Your commands, my dear Lady, are executed.——I have wrote Mrs. Smith; and as soon as I receive her answer, shall, with a

---

1 50 pieces of gold, or 50 guineas (£52.10s).
2 Morgan and Lord Allen have been fox hunting. Hunters on horses employed dogs to help them run down their game. Morgan boasts that Lord Allen was less successful than he and that he lost one of his fox-hounds in the woods.
3 Fanny bundles her many letters to Lady Mary into larger packets, which would have been delivered to the German Spaw by small boats, schooners, or sloops, called "packet boats." The king maintained around twenty packet boats designed to carry mail and freight between England, Europe, and other locales. Packet boats sailed daily and made small accommodations for travelers on short journeys.

joyful heart, with impatient fondness, prepare to throw at your
Ladyship's feet,

Your much honour'd,

and affectionate,

F. WARLEY.

LETTER IV.

Lord DARCEY
to the Honourable GEORGE MOLESWORTH.[1]

Barford Abbey.

P Repare your ten pieces, George![2]—Upon my honour, I was
at Barford Abbey a quarter before three, notwithstanding a
detention on the road by Lord Michell and Fletcher, driving on
Jehu for Bath, in his Lordship's phaeton and six.——You have
seen them before this,—and, I suppose, know their errand.——
The girl is an egregious fool, that is certain.—I warrant there are
a hundred bets depending.——I ask'd what he intended doing
with her if he succeeded?——*Do* with her! said his Lordship; why,
she is not more than eighteen; let her go to school: faith, Fletcher,
that's my advice.——*Let her go* to the devil after I am once sure
of her, return'd the lover; and, whipping up the horses; drove
away like lightning.

Be serious—Answer me one serious question,——Is it not
possible,—*very* possible, to have a regard, a *friendship*, for an
amiable girl, without endangering her peace or my own?—If I am
further involv'd than *friendship*,—the blame is not mine; it will lie
at the door of Sir James and Lady Powis.——Talk no more of
Lady Elizabeth's smile, or Miss Grevel's hair—Stuff!—meer stuff!

---

1 George is a member of the nobility. The term "the Honourable" ("the
 Hon.") is used for the younger son of an earl and the son of a baron, and
 also the daughter of an earl or baron. This honorific is used on calling
 cards or legal signatures, and in description or formal reference by other
 people, but is not used in speaking to the person.
2 That is, George has wagered ten guineas in a bet that Darcey here claims
 to have won.

nor keep me up after a late evening, to hear your nonsense of Miss Compton's fine neck and shoulders, or Fanny Middleton's eyes.——Come here next week, I will insure you a sight of all those graces in one form. Come, I say, you will be welcome to Sir James and his Lady as myself.——Miss Warley will smile on you.——What other inducement can you want?——Don't be too vain of Miss Warley's smiles; *for know*, she cannot look without them.

Who is Miss Warley?—What is Miss Warley?—you ask.——To your first question I can only answer, A visitor at Jenkings's.——To the second,—She is what has been so much sought after in every age, perfect harmony of mind and person.—Such a hand, George——

Already have I been here eight days:—was I to measure time, I should call them hours.——My affairs with Sir James will take up longer in settling than I apprehended.——Come therefore this week or the next, I charge you.—Come as you hope to see Miss Warley. What do you think Sir James said to me the other day?—Was Miss Warley a girl of fortune, I should think her born for you, Darcey.——As that is not the case,—take care of your heart, my Lord.—She will never attempt to draw you into scrapes:—your little favourite robin, that us'd to peck from your hand, has not less guile.

No! he will never consent;—I must only think of *friendship*.

Lady Powis doats on this paragon of beauty: scarce within their walls,—when she was mention'd with such a just profusion of praises, as fill'd me with impatience.——Lady Powis is a heavenly woman.——You do not laugh;—many would, for supposing any of that sex *heavenly* after fifty.—The coach is this moment going for Miss Warley;—it waits only for me;—I am often her conductor.—Was *you* first minister of state,—I the humble suitor whose bread depended on your favour,—not one line more, even to express my wants.

Twelve o'clock, at night.
Our fair visitor just gone;—just gone home with Edmund.——What an officious fool, to take him in the carriage, and prevent myself from a pleasure I envy him for.——I am not in

spirits;—I can write no more;—perhaps the next post:—but I will promise nothing.

I am, &c. &c.

DARCEY.

LETTER V.

The Honourable GEORGE MOLESWORTH
to LORD DARCEY.

L oLj C Ae

Bath.

COnfound your friendships!—*Friendship* indeed!—What! up head and ears in love, and not know it.——So it is necessary for every woman you think capable of friendship, to have fine eyes, fine hair, a bewitching smile, and a neck delicately turn'd.[1]——Have not I the highest opinion of my cousin Dolly's[2] sincerity?—Do I not think her very capable of *friendship*?—Yet, poor soul, her eyes are planted so deep, it requires good ones to discover she has any.——Such a hand, George!——Such a hand, Darcey!—Why, Lady Dorothy too has hands; I am often enough squeez'd by them:—though hard as a horse's hoof, and the colour of tanned leather, I hold her capable of *friendship*.——Neck she has none,—smile she has none! yet need I the determination of another, to tell me whether my regard for her proceeds from love or *friendship*?——Awake,—Awake, Darcey,—Awake:—Have you any value for your own peace?—have you any for that of Miss Warley's? If so, leave Barford Abbey.——Should you persist in loving her, for love her I know you do?—Should the quiet of such an amiable woman as you describe be at stake? To deal plainly, I will come down and propose the thing myself.—No sword,—no pistol. I mean not for *myself*, but one whose happiness is dear to me as my *own*.

Suppose your estate is but two thousand a-year, are you so fond of shew and equipage, to barter real felicity for baubles?——I am angry,—so angry, that it would not grieve me to see you leading

---

1 The word "neck" could be used as a euphemism for a lady's bosom.
2 Ungenteel nickname for the unfashionable "Dorothy."

to the altar an old hobbling dowager without a tooth.
——Be more yourself,

And I am yours,

MOLESWORTH.

★ ★ ★

LETTER VI.

Lord DARCEY to the
Honourable GEORGE MOLESWORTH.

Barford Abbey,

ANgry!—You are really angry!——Well, I too am angry with
myself.—I do love Miss Warley;—but why this to you?—
Your penetration has already discover'd it.——Yet, O Molesworth! such insurmountable obstacles:—no declaration can be
made,—at least whilst I continue in this neighbourhood.

Sir James would rave at my imprudence.—Lady Powis, whatever are her sentiments, must give them up to his opinion.—
Inevitably I lose the affection of persons I have sacredly—promised to obey,—sacredly.—Was not my promise given to a dying
father?[1]—Miss Warley has no tye; yet, by the duty she observes to
Sir James and Lady Powis, you would think her bound by the
strongest cords of nature.

Scarce a moment from her:—at Jenkings's every morning;—
on foot if good weather,—else in the coach for the convenience
of bringing her with me.—I am under no constraint:—Sir James
and her Ladyship seem not the least suspicious: this I much
wonder at, in the former particularly.

In my tête-à-têtes with Miss Warley, what think you are our subjects?——Chiefly divinity, history, and geography.—Of these
studies she knows more than half the great men who have wrote
for ages past.—On a taste for the two latter I once prided

---

1 Traditionally entailing a sacred obligation. A promise made to the dying
   cannot be renegotiated or rescinded.

myself.—An eager pursuit for the former springs up in my mind, whilst conversing with her, like a plant long hid in the earth, and called out by the appearance of a summer's sun.—This sun must shine at Faulcon Park;[1]—without it all will be dreary:—*yet* how can I draw it thither?—*Edmund*—but why should I fear *Edmund*?

Will you, or will you not, meet your old friend Finch here next Wednesday?—Be determined in your answer.—I have suspence enough on my hands to be excused from any on your account.— Sir James thinks it unkind you have not called on him since I left England;—hasten therefore to make up matters with the baronet.—Need I say the pleasure I shall have in shaking you by the hand?

DARCEY.

★ ★ ★

LETTER VII.

The Hon. GEORGE MOLESWORTH to Lord DARCEY.

Bath.

WEDNESDAY next you shall see me,—positively you shall.—Bridgman will be of the party.

I propose an immensity of satisfaction from this visit.—— Forbid it, heaven! Miss Warley's opposite should again give me a meeting at the Abbey.—After the conversation I am made to expect, how should I be mortified to have my ears eternally dinn'd with catgut work,—painting gauze,—weaving fringes,— and finding out enigmas?[2]—Setting a fine face, Miss Winter is out-done by Fletcher's Nancy.—A-propos, I yesterday saw that very wise girl step into a chaise and wheel off for Scotland, begging and praying we would make the best of it to her

---

1 Faulcon (or "Falcon") Park, Lord Darcey's estate, which brings in his £2,000 a year.
2 Molesworth mocks genteel female pastimes, such as playing stringed musical instruments, painting light materials, making fringes for clothes or furniture, and puzzling over riddles. The strings of harps, violins, violas, and guitars, etc., were made of "catgut." The word is derived from "cattle gut," denoting the processed intestines of sheep and cattle, by-products of animals killed for food or leather.

mamma.—Not the least hand had I in this affair; but, willing to help out people in distress, at the entreaties of Lord Michell, I waited on the old Lady at her lodging.

I found her in a furious plight,—raving at her servants,— packing up her cloaths, and reflecting on her relations who had persuaded her to come to Bath.—When I entered she was kneeling by a huge travelling trunk, stuffing in a green purse at one corner, which I supposed to be full of gold.

Where is Nancy?—rising from the ground, and accosting me with looks of fury;——Where is Nancy, Mr. Molesworth?

Really, *Madam*, that is a question I cannot positively answer; —but, to be sincere, I believe she is on the road to Scotland.[1]

Believe!—So you would have me think you are not one of Fletcher's clan.—But, *tell him* from me, running to the trunk after her purse, and shaking it just at my ear,—tell him, he shall never be a penny the better for this.

I took my hat, and looked towards the door, as if going.

Stop, Mr. Molesworth, (her voice somewhat lowered) why in so great a hurry?—I once thought you my friend. Pray inform me if Nancy was forced away;—or, if she went willingly.

You have no right, Madam, after the treatment I have received, to expect an answer; but justice bids me declare her going off seemed a matter of choice.

---

1 Nancy has eloped to Gretna Green, in Scotland, with Mr. Fletcher (a name sometimes spelled "Flecher" in the first edition of the text but changed to "Fletcher" throughout). Scotland kept to the older laws regarding marriage: a couple had only to stand up before witnesses and declare themselves married. In England, "An Act for the Better Prevention of Clandestine Marriage," passed by Parliament in 1753, required not only that a wedding take place in church but that the banns would have to be called for three weeks during the main Sunday service. In this way, parents or guardians could legally prevent the marriage of anyone below 21 years of age. One of the chief motives for this "Marriage Act" was to prevent heiresses or young ladies of good family from being run away with by fortune hunters.

Poor child!——You was certainly trapann'd[1] (and she put a handkerchief to her eyes).

I solemnly protest, Madam, I have seen your daughter but twice since she came to Bath.—Last night, when coming from the Rooms,[2] I saw her step into a chaise, followed by Mr. Fletcher.—They beckoned me towards them, whispered the expedition they were going upon, and requested me to break the matter to you, and intercede for their pardon.—My visit has not answered its salutary purpose—I perceive it *has not.* So saying I turned from her,—knowing, by old acquaintance, how I was to play my cards, she being one of those kind of spirits which are never quell'd but by opposition.

After fetching me from the door, she promised to hear calmly what I had to say;—and, tho' no orator, I succeeded so well as to gain an assurance, she would see them at their return from Scotland.

I left the old Lady in tolerable good humour, and was smiling to myself, recollecting the bout I had passed, when, who should come towards me but Lord Michell,—his countenance full-fraught with curiosity.

Well, George!—dear George!—what success in your embassy? —I long to know the fate of honest Fletcher.—Is he to loll in a coach and six?——or, is the coroner's inquest to bring in their verdict Lunacy?[3]

---

1 Tricked into running off. If it could be proven that Fletcher had forced or tricked Nancy, the marriage could be nullified.
2 The Bath Assembly Rooms, upper or lower, were suited to dancing, with a master of ceremonies to perform introductions.
3 The coroner (not in those days a medical man) would convene a jury to inquire into the cause of any unexplained or violent death. The jury could bring in a verdict of *felo de se* (suicide), attributing the ultimate cause to insanity. If Fletcher's attempt to gain Nancy's money through elopement (permitting the luxury of a coach and six horses) were to be unsuccessful—and Nancy's mother at first threatens to create legal bars to access to the money—Fletcher would be committing social and financial suicide.

A sweet alternative!—*As* your Lordship's assiduity has shewn the former is the highest pinnacle to which you would wish to lift a friend, I believe your most sanguine hopes are here answered.

Is it *so!*—Well, if ever Fletcher offers up a prayer, it ought to be for you, Molesworth.

Vastly good, my Lord.—What, before he prays for himself?—*This* shews your Lordship's *very* high notions of gratitude.

We have high notions of every thing.—Bucks and bloods, as we are call'd,[1]—you may go to the devil before you will find a set of honester fellows.

To the Devil, my Lord!——That's true, I believe.

He was going to reply when the three choice spirits came up, and hurried him, away to the Tuns.[2]

A word to *you*, Darcey.—Surely you are never serious in the ridiculous design.—Not offer yourself to Miss Warley, whilst she continues in that neighbourhood?—the very spot on which you ought to secure her,—unless you think all the young fellows who visit at the Abbey are blind, except yourself.—*Why*, you are jealous *already;*—*jealous* of *Edmund.*—Perhaps *even I* may become one of your tormentors.—If I like her I shall as certainly tell her *so, as* that my name is

MOLESWORTH.

[Here two Letters are omitted, one from Lady MARY to Miss WARLEY,—and one from Miss WARLEY to Lady MARY.]

---

1 Terms used of high-born young men about town, given to gambling, drinking, and other sensual pleasures.
2 His three friends, young men like himself, rushed Lord Michell away to a tavern.

LETTER VIII.

Miss WARLEY to Lady MARY SUTTON.

From Mr. *Jenkings's.*

A H! my dear Lady, how kind,—how inexpressibly kind, to promise I shall one day know what has put an end to the intimacy between the two Ladies I *so* much revere.

To find your Ladyship has still a high opinion of Lady Powis, has filled me with pleasure.—Fear of the reverse often threw a damp on my heart, whilst receiving the most tender caresses.— You bid me love her!—You say I cannot love her too well!—*This* is a command my heart springs forward to obey.

Unhappy family!——What a loss does it sustain by the absence of Mr. Powis?—*No*, I can never forgive the Lady who has occasioned this source of sorrow.—Why is her name concealed?—But what would it benefit me to come at a knowledge of it?

Pity Sir James should rather see such a son *great* than happy.— Six thousand a year, *yet* covet a fortune twice as large![1]—Love of riches makes strange wreck in the human heart.

Why did Mr. Powis leave his native country?—The refusal of a Lady with whom he only sought an union in obedience to his father, could not *greatly* affect him.—Was not such an overture *without* affection,—*without* inclination,—a blot in his fair character?—Certainly it was.—Your Ladyship seems to think Sir James only to blame.—I dare not have presumed to offer my opinion, had you not often told me, it betray'd a meanness to hide our real sentiments, when call'd upon to declare them.

Lady Powis yesterday obliged me with a sight of several letters from her son.—*I* am not mistress of a stile like *his*, or your Ladyship would have been spar'd numberless tedious moments.—

---

1 We here learn the income of Sir James, which is three times that of Lord Darcey.

Such extraordinary deckings[1] are seldom to be met with in common minds.

I told Lady Powis, last evening, that I should devote this day to my pen;—so I shall not be sent for;—a favour I am sure to have conferr'd if I am not at the Abbey soon after breakfast.— Lord Darcey is frequently my escort.—I am pleased to see that young nobleman regard Edmund as if of equal rank with himself.

Heavens! his Lordship is here!—full-dressed, and just alighted from the coach,—to fetch me, I fear.—I shall know in a moment; Mrs. Jenkings is coming up.

Even so.—It vexes me to be thus taken off from my agreeable task;—yet I cannot excuse myself,—her Ladyship is importunate.—She sends me word I *must* come;—that I *must* return with Lord Darcey.—Mrs. Finch is accidentally dropp'd in with her son.—I knew the latter was expected to meet two gentlemen from Bath,—one of them an intimate friend of Lord Darcey.—Mrs. Finch is an amiable woman;—it is to her Lady Powis wants to introduce me.

Your Servant, my Lord.—A very genteel way to hasten me down—impatient, I suppose, to see his friend from Bath.—*Well*, Jenny, tell his Lordship it will be needless to have the horses taken out.—I shall be ready in a quarter of an hour.—Adieu, my dear Lady.

Eleven o'clock at night.

Every thing has conspired to make this day more than commonly agreeable.—It requires the pen of a Littelton[2] to paint the different graces which shone in conversation.—As no such pen is

---

1 Extraordinary flourishes or ornaments. Whereas Thomas O. Beebee claims that this passage indicates Fanny's acknowledgment of her own inferior handwriting, her observations on "stile" more probably relate to fluency and exactness of expression, rather than mere flourishes of penmanship. See Beebee, *Epistolary Fiction* 44.

2 Edward Littleton (1695–1733), academic, clergyman, and poet.

at hand, will your Ladyship receive from *mine* a short description of the company at the Abbey?

Mrs. Finch is about seven and forty;—her person plain,—her mind lovely,—her bosom fraught with happiness.—She dispenses it promiscuously.—Every smile,—every accent,—conveys it to all around her.—A countenance engagingly open.—Her purse too, I am told, when occasions offer, open as her heart.—How largely is she repaid for her balsamic gifts,[1]—by seeing those virtues early planted in the mind of her son, spring up and shoot in a climate where a blight is almost contagious!

Mr. Finch is the most sedate young man I have ever seen;—but his sedateness is temper'd with a *sweetness* inexpressible;—a certain mildness in the features;—*a mildness* which, in the countenance of that great commander I saw at Brandon Lodge, appears like *mercy* sent out from the heart to discover the dwelling of *true courage.*—There is certainly a strong likeness between the Marquis and Lord Darcey;—*so strong*, that when I first beheld his Lordship I was quite struck with surprize.

Mr. Molesworth and Mr. Bridgman, the two gentlemen from Bath, are very opposite to each other in person and manner; yet both in a different degree seem to be worthy members of society.

Mr. Molesworth, a most entertaining companion,—vastly chearful,—smart at repartee; and, from the character Lord Darcey has given me of him, very sincere.

Mr. Bridgman has a good deal the air of a foreigner; attained, I suppose, by his residence some years at the court of ——, in a public character.—Very fit he appears for such an employ. —Sensible,—remarkably polite,—speaks all languages with the same fluency as his own; but then a veil of disagreeable reserve throws a dark shade over those perfections.—*Perhaps* I am wrong to spy out faults so early;—*perhaps* to-morrow my opinion may be different.—First prepossessions[2]—Ah! What would I have

---

1 Soft and soothing, like the juice of a balsam plant.
2 Compare Austen's "First Impressions"—the original title of *Pride and Prejudice* (1813).

said of *first prepossessions?*—Is it not to them I owe a thousand blessings?—*I*, who have nothing to recommend me but being unfortunate.

Something lies at my heart.—Yet I think I could not sleep in quiet, was I to drop a hint in disfavour of Mr. Jenkings;—it may not be in his *disfavour* neither:—However, my dear Lady, you shall be the judge, after I have repos'd a few hours.

Seven o'clock in the morning.

Why should I blame Mr. Jenkings?—Is not Edmund his only son?—his only child?—Is he less my friend for suspecting?—Yes, my Lady, I perceive he does *suspect.*—He is uneasy.—He supposes his son encouraging an improper affection.—I see it in his very looks:—he must think me an artful creature.—This it is that distresses me.—I wish I could hit on a method to set his heart at rest.—If I barely hint a design of leaving the neighbourhood, which I have done once or twice, he bursts into tears, and I am oblig'd to sooth him like a child.

How account for this behaviour?—Why does he look on me with the eye of fatherly affection,—yet think me capable of a meanness I *despise?*

I believe it impossible for a human being to have *more* good nature, or *more* good qualities, than Edmund; yet had he the riches of a Mogul,[1] I could never think of a connection with him.—*He*, worthy young man, has never given his father cause for *suspicion.*——I am convinced he has not.——Naturally of an obliging disposition, he is ever on the watch for opportunities to gratify his amiable inclinations:——not one such selfish motive as love to push him on.

A summons to breakfast.—Lord Darcey, it seems, is below; —I suppose, slid away from his friends to call on Edmund.——Mr. and Mrs. Jenkings are *all* smiles, *all* good humour, to their son,—— I hope it is only I who have been *suspicious.*——Lord Darcey is still with Edmund.—They are at this moment under my window,—— counselling perhaps, about a commission he wants his father to

---

1 From "Moghul," ruler of the Moghul Empire, general slang for a very wealthy man, particularly one who has made money in India.

purchase for him in the Guards.[1]—I should be glad to see this matter accommodated;—yet, I could wish, in *so* tender a point, his Lordship may not be *too* forward in advising.—Mr. and Mrs. Jenkings have such an opinion of him,—they pay such deference to what he says,—his advice *must* have weight;—and they *may* be unhappy by giving up their inclinations.

The praises of Lord Darcey are forever sounding in my ears. ——To what a height would the partiality of Mrs. Jenkings lift me? —She would *have me think*,—I cannot tell your Ladyship what she would have me think.—My hopes dare not take *such* a flight. —No!—I can perceive what their fall *must* be;—I can perceive *it*, without getting on the top of the precipice to look down.

I shall order every thing for my departure, according to your Ladyship's directions, holding myself in readiness to attend Mr. and Mrs. Smith, at the time proposed.

Oxfordshire I must revisit,—for a few days only;—having some little matters to regulate.

The silks I have purchas'd for your Ladyship are slight, as you directed, except a white and gold, which is the richest and most beautiful I could procure.[2]

How imperceptibly time slides on?—The clock strikes eleven,—in spight of the desire I have of communicating many things more.—An engagement to be with Lady Powis at twelve hastens me to conclude myself

> Your Ladyship's
>
> Most honour'd and affectionate,
>
> F. WARLEY.

---

1 At this time, one could purchase a commission as an officer in the cavalry or infantry of the English army. Edmund's request would require considerable expenditure on his father's part, and the commission would take him to London or abroad.

2 Fanny plans to bring dress materials to Lady Mary, whom she expects to see shortly after her journey to the Continent. It seems odd to take materials into France, famous for silk fabrics. Also odd is the decision to bring white and gold, youthful colors associated with weddings, to the middle-aged Lady Mary, who would not have worn white in this period.

LETTER IX.

The Honourable GEORGE MOLESWORTH to
LORD DARCEY.

Bath.

WHAT a sacrifice do you offer up to that old dog Plutus![1] —I have lost *all* patience,—all patience, I say.—*Such* a woman!—*such* an angelic woman!—But what has,—what will avail my arguments?—Her peace is gone,—if you persevere in a behaviour so *particular*,—absolutely gone.

Bridgman this morning told me, that unless I assured him you had *pretensions* to Miss Warley, he was determined to offer her his hand;—*that* nothing prevented him from doing it whilst at the Abbey, but your mysterious conduct, which he was at a loss how to construe.—Not to offend *you*, the *Lady* or *family* she is with, he apply'd, he said, to *me*, as a friend of each party, to set him right.

Surely, Bridgman, returned I, you wish to keep yourself in the dark; or how the duce have you been six days with people whose countenances speak so much sensibility, and not make the discovery you seek after?

Though her behaviour to us; continued I, was politeness itself, was there nothing more than *politeness* in her address to Lord Darcey?—Her smiles *too*, in which Diana and the Graces[2] revel, saw you not *them*, how they played from one to another, like sunbeams on the water, until they fixed on him?—Is the nation in debt?[3]—So much is Darcey in love;—and you may as well pay off one, as rival the other with success.

Observe, my friend, in what manner I have answered for you.——Keep her, therefore, no longer in suspense.—Delays of this sort are not only dangerous, but cruel.—Why delight to torture what we most admire?—From a boy you despised such

---

1 The Greek god of wealth: hence "plutocracy," the rule of the rich.
2 Diana, Roman goddess of chastity; the Graces, Greek goddesses Aglaia, Thalia, and Euphrosyne, emblems of charm, beauty, and creativity.
3 Yes. England was severely in debt in the 1760s after fighting the Seven Years' War (1756–63).

actions.—Often have I known Dick Jones, when at Westminster,[1] threshed by your hand for picking poor little birds alive.—*His* was an early point;—but for *Darcey*, accoutred with the breast-plate of honour, even before he could read the word that signifies its intrinsic value,—*for him* to be falling off,—falling off at a time *too*, when Virtue herself appears in person to support him!

Can you say, you mean not to injure her?—Is a woman only to be injured, but by an attempt on her virtue?—Is it *no* crime, *no* fault, to cheat a young innocent lovely girl out of her affections, and give her nothing in return but regret and disappointment?

Reflect, what a task is mine, thus to lay disagreeable truths plainly before you.—To hear it pronounced, that Lord and Lady Darcey are the happiest couple on earth, is the hope that has pushed me on to this unpleasing office.

Bridgman is just set out for town.—I am charg'd with a profusion of respects, thanks, &c. &c. &c. which, if you have the least oeconomy, will serve for him, and

Your very humble servant,

MOLESWORTH.

LETTER X.

Lord DARCEY to
the Honourable GEORGE MOLESWORTH.

Barford Abbey.

BRIDGMAN!—Could Bridgman dare aspire to Miss Warley!—He offer her his hand!—*he* be connected with a woman whose disposition is diametrically opposite to his own!—*No*,—that would not have done, though I had never seen her.—Let him seek for one who has a heart shut up by a thousand locks.

After his *own* conjectures,——after what *you* have told him,——should he *but* attempt to take her from me, by all that is sacred, he shall repent it dearly.

---

1 Once the school of Westminster Abbey, Westminster School is an expensive upper-class school for boys that offers a classical education.

Molesworth! *you* are my friend,—I take your admonitions well;——but, surely, you should not press thus hardly on my soul, knowing its uneasy situation.—My state is even more perplexing than when we parted:—I did not then know she was going to France.—*Yes*, she is absolutely going to *France.*—Why leave her friends here?—Why not wait the arrival of Lady Mary Sutton in England?

I have used every dissuasive argument *but one.*——That shall be my last.——If *that* fails I go——I positively go with her.——It is your opinion that she loves me.—Would it were mine!—*Not* the least partiality can I discover.——Why then be precipitate?—— Every moment she is gaining ground in the affections of Sir James and Lady Powis.—*Time* may work wonders in the mind of the former.—Without his consent never can I give my hand;—the commands of a dying father forbid me.——*Such* a father!—O George! you did not know him;—*so* revered,—*so* honour'd,—*so* belov'd! not more in public than in private life.

My friend, behold your son!—*Darcey*, behold your father!—*As* you reverence and obey Sir James, *as* you consult him on all occasions, *as* you are guided by his advice, receive my blessing.— These were his parting words, hugg'd into me in his last cold embrace.—No, George, the promise I made can never be forfeited.—I sealed it on his lifeless hand, before I was borne from him.

Now, are you convinc'd no mean views with-hold me?—You despise not more than I do the knave and coxcomb; for no other, to satiate their own vanity, would sport away the quiet of a fellow-creature.——Well may you call it cruel.—*Such* cruelties fall little short of those practised by *Nero* and *Caligula.*[1]

Did it depend on myself only, I would tell Miss Warley I love, *every time* I behold her enchanting face; *every time* I hear the voice of wisdom springing from the seat of innocence.

No shadow of gaining over Sir James!—*Efforts* has not been wanting:—I mean *efforts* to declare my inclination.——I have fol-

---

1 Famously cruel and wildly erratic Roman emperors Caligula (Gaius Caesar Germanicus, 12–41 CE) and Nero (Claudius Caesar Augustus Germanicus, 37–68 CE).

low'd him like a ghost for days past, thinking at every step how I should bless *this* or *that* spot on which he consented to my happiness.—Pleasing phantoms!——How have they fled at sight of his determin'd countenance!——Methought I could trace *in it* the same obduracy which nature vainly pleaded to remove.—In *other* matters my heart is resolute;—*here* an errant coward.—No! I cannot break it to him whilst in Hampshire.—When I get to town, a letter *shall* speak for me.—Sometimes I am tempted to trust the secret to Lady Powis.—She is compassionate;—she would even risk her own peace to preserve mine.—Again the thoughts of involving her in fresh perplexities determines me against it.

Had my father been acquainted with that part of Sir James's character which concerned his son, I am convinc'd he would have made some restrictions in regard to the explicit obedience he enjoined.—But all was hushed whilst Mr. Powis continued on his travels; nor, until he settled abroad, did any one suspect there had been a family disagreement:—*even* at this *time* the whole affair is not generally known.—The name of the lady to whom he was obliged to make proposals, is in particular carefully concealed.— I, who from ten years old have been bred up with them, am an entire stranger to it.—*Perhaps* no part of the affair would ever have transpired, had not Sir James made some discoveries, in the first agitation of his passion, before a large company, when he received an account of Mr. Powis's being appointed to the government of ———. No secret can be safe in a breast where every passage is not well guarded against an enemy which, like lightning, throws up all before it.

Let me not forget to tell you, amongst a multiplicity of concerns crowding on my mind, that I have positively deny'd Edmund to intercede with his father regarding the commission.—A bare surmise that he is my rival, has silenced me.—Was I ungenerous enough to indulge myself in getting rid of him, an opportunity now offers;—but I am *as* averse to such proceedings as *he* ought to be who is the friend of Molesworth, and writes the name of

DARCEY.

LETTER XI.

The Honourable GEORGE MOLESWORTH
to Lord DARCEY.

Bath.

BELIEVE me, my dear Lord, I never suspected you capable of designs you justly hold in abhorrence.—If I expressed myself warmly, it was owing to your keeping from me the knowledge of those particulars which have varied every circumstance.—I saw my friend a poor restless being, irresolute, full of perplexities.—I felt for him.—I rejoice now to find from whence this *irresolution*, those *perplexities* arose.——She is,—she must,—by heaven! she shall be yours:—A reward fit only for *such* great—*such* noble resolutions.

You talk of a *last* argument—Forbear *that* argument.—You *must* not use it before you have laid your intentions open to Sir James.——*Neither* follow her to France.——What, as you are situated, would *that* avail?—Prevent her going, *if* you can.—*Such* a woman, under the protection of Lady Mary Sutton, *must* have many advantageous proposals.

I understand *nothing* of features,—I know *nothing* of physiognomy, if you have any uneasiness from Bridgman.—It was not marks of a violent passion he betrayed;—rather, I think, an ambition of having his taste approved by the world;—but we shall know more of the matter when I meet him in town.

Stupidity!—Not see her partiality!—not see that she loves you!—She will some time hence own it as frankly with her lips, as her eyes have told you a thousand times, did you understand their language.—The duce a word could *I* get from them.—Very uncivil, I think, not to *speak* when they *were* spoke to.—They will be ready enough, I suppose, with their *thanks* and *applauses*, when I present her hand to be united with her heart. That office shall be *mine:*—*Something* tells me, there is to be an alteration in *your* affairs, sudden as unexpected.

I go to the rooms this evening for the last time.—To-morrow I set out for Slone Hall,[1] in my way to London.——Here I shall

---

1 Elsewhere, Stone Hall.

spend two or three days happily with my good-natured cousin Lady Dorothy.—Perhaps we may take an airing together as far as your territories.—I shall now look on Faulcon-Park with double pleasure.—Neither that or the agreeable neighbourhood round it will be ever bridled over by a haughty dame.—(Miss Warley, forbid it.)—Some such we see in *high as well as low life.*—Haughtiness is the reverse of true greatness; therefore it staggers me to behold it in the former.

A servant with a white favour![1]——What can this mean?—

Upon my word, Mr. Fletcher, you return with your fair bride sooner than I expected.—*A card too.*—Things must be finely accommodated with the old Lady.——Your Lordship being at too great a distance to partake of the feast, pray regale on what calls me to it.

"Mrs. Moor and Mr. and Mrs. Fletcher's compliments to Mr. Molesworth.—My son and daughter are just return'd from Scotland, and hope for the pleasure of Mr. Molesworth's company with eight or ten other friends, to congratulate them this evening on their arrival.—Both the Ladies and Mr. Fletcher will be much disappointed, if you do not accept our invitation."

True as I live, *neither added or diminished* a tittle,—and wrote by the hand of Fletcher's Desdemona.[2]—Does not a man richly deserve thirty thousand pounds with a wife like *this?*—Not for *twice* that sum would I see such nonsense come from her I was to spend my life with.

Pity Nature and Fortune has such frequent bickerings! When one smiles the other frowns.—I wish the gipsies would make up matters, and send us down their favours wrapp'd up together.

---

1 A white rosette or some such token accompanying a note of invitation and signifying the celebration of a wedding.

2 In William Shakespeare's *Othello* (c. 1603), Desdemona elopes with the eponymous hero of the play. Molesworth mocks the romantic folly of Nancy's elopement and the quick change on the part of Nancy's mother, now willing to celebrate the marriage. Fletcher, in defiance of the Marriage Act, has greatly enriched himself through this elopement, obtaining a dowry of £30,000.

Considering the friendship you have honour'd Edmund with, I have no idea he can presume to think of Miss Warley, *seeing* what he must *see*.

I shall expect to find a letter on my arrival in St. James's Street.[1]—Omit not those respects which are due at Barford Abbey.

Yours,

MOLESWORTH.

LETTER XII.

Lord DARCEY to the Honourable GEORGE MOLESWORTH.

Barford Abbey.

I Should be in a fine plight, truly, to let her go to France without me!—Why, I am almost besides myself at the thoughts of an eight days separation.—Was ever any thing so forgetful!—To bring no other cloaths here but mourning!—Did she always intend to encircle the sun with a sable cloud?—Or, why not dispatch a servant?—A journey into Oxfordshire is absolutely necessary.——Some *other* business, I suppose; but I am not enough in her confidence to know of what nature.—Poh! love!—Impossible, and refuse me so small a boon as to attend her!—requested too in a manner that spoke my whole soul.—Yes; I had near broke through all my resolutions.——This I did say, If Miss Warley refuses her dear hand, pressing it to my lips, in the same peremptory manner,—what will become of him who without it is lost to the whole world?——The reply ventur'd no further than her cheek;—there sat enthron'd in robes of crimson.——I scarce dar'd to look up:—her eyes darted forth a ray so powerful, that I not only quitted her hand, but suffered her to leave the room without my saying another word.——This happened at Jenkings's last evening; in the morning she was to set out with the old gentleman for Oxfordshire.—I did not attempt seeing her again 'till that time, fearing my presence might be unpleasing, after the confusion I had occasion'd.

---

1 The first edition reads "St. James's Sreet."

Sick of my bed I got up at five; and taking a gun, directed my course to the only spot on earth capable of affording me delight.——The outer gate barr'd:—no appearance of any living creature, except poor Cæsar.—He, hearing my voice, crept from his wooden-house, and, instead of barking, saluted me in a whining tone:—stretching himself, he jumped towards the gate, licking my hand that lay between the bars.—I said many kind things to this faithful beast, in hopes my voice would awaken some of the family.——The scheme succeeded.—A bell was sounded from one of the apartments; that opposite to which I stood.—A servant opening the window-shutters, I was tempted to keep my stand.——A white beaver[1] with a green feather, and a riding-dress of the same colour, plainly told me this was the room where rested all my treasure, and caused in my mind such conflicts as can no more be described by *me* than felt by *another*.—Unwilling to encrease my tortures I reeled to an old tree, which lay on a bank near;—there sat down to recover my trembling.——The next thing which alarmed me was an empty chaise, driving full speed down the hill.—I knew on *what* occasion, yet could not forbear asking the post-boy.——He answered, To carry some company from yonder house.——My situation was really deplorable, ——when I beheld my dear lovely girl walking in a pensive mood, attir'd in that very dress which I espied through the window.—Heavy was the load I dragged from head to heel; yet, like a Mercury,[2] I flew to meet her.—She saw me,—— started,——and cry'd, Bless me! my Lord! what brings you hither at this early hour?—The real truth was springing to my lips, when, recollecting her happiness might be the sacrifice, I said, examining the lock of my gun,—I am waiting, Miss Warley, for that lazy fellow Edmund:—he promised to shew me an eye[3] of pheasants——If you are not a very keen sportsman, returned she, what says your Lordship to a cup of chocolate?— —It will not detain you long;—Mrs. Jenkings has some ready prepared for the travellers.

She pronounced *travellers* with uncommon glee;—at least I thought so,—and, nettled at her indifference, could not help

---

1 Beaver hat.
2 Roman messenger of the gods.
3 A rare collective noun, now meaning flock.

replying, *You* are *very* happy, madam;—*you* part with your friends *very* unreluctantly, I perceive.

If any thing ever appeared in my favour, it was now.—Her confusion was visible;——even Edmund observed it, who just then strolled towards us, and said, looking at both attentively, What is the matter with Miss Warley?

With me, Edmund? she retorted,—nothing ails me.—I suppose you think I am enough of the fine lady to complain the whole day, because I have got up an hour before my usual time.

His tongue was *now* silent;—his eyes *full* of enquiries.—He fixed them on us alternately,—wanting to discover the situation of our hearts.—Why so curious, Edmund?—Things cannot go on long at this rate.—*Your* heart must undergo a strict scrutiny before I shall know what terms we are upon.

No words can paint my gratitude for worthy Jenkings.—He went to the Abbey, on foot, before breakfast was ended, to give me an opportunity of supplying his place in the chaise.—At parting he actually took one of my hands, joined it with Miss Warley's, and I could perceive petitions ascending from the seat of purity.——I know to what they tended.—I *felt*, I *saw* them. ——The chaise drove off. I could have blessed him.——May my blessings overtake him!—May they light where virtue sits enshrin'd by locks of silver.

Yes, if his son was to wound me in the tenderest part, for the sake of *such* a father, I think,——I know not what to think.— Living in such suspense is next to madness.

She treats him with the freedom of a sister.——She calls him Edmund,——leans on his arm, and suffers him to take her hand.—The least favour conferred on me is with an air *so* reserved, *so* distant, as if she would say, I have not for you the least sentiment of tenderness.

Lady Powis sends to desire I will walk with her.—A sweet companion am I for a person in low spirits!—That her's are not high is evident.——She has shed many tears this morning at parting with Miss Warley.

Instead of eight days mortification we might have suffer'd twenty, had not her Ladyship insisted on an absolute promise of returning at that time.—Farewel till then.

Yours,

DARCEY.

★ ★ ★

LETTER XIII.

Miss WARLEY to Lady MARY SUTTON.

From the Crown, at ——.

HERE am I, ever-honour'd lady, forty miles on the road to that beloved spot, where, for nineteen years, my tranquility was uninterrupted.——Will a serene sky always hang over me?—It will be presumption to suppose it,—when thousands, perhaps, endowed with virtues the most god-like, have nothing on which they can look *back* but dark clouds,—nothing to which they can look *forward* but gathering storms.—Am I a bark only fit to sail in fair weather?—Shall I not prepare to meet the waves of disappointment?

How does my heart beat,—how throb,—to give up follies which dare not hide themselves where a passage is made *by* generosity, *by* affection unbounded.—Yes, my dear Lady, this is the only moment I do not regret being absent from you;—for could my tongue relate what my pen trembles to discover?—No!

Behold *me* at your Ladyship's feet!—behold *me* a supplicant suing for my returning peace!——*You* only, can restore it.—Command that I give up my preference for Lord Darcey, and the intruder is banished from my heart:——*then* shall I no more labour to deceive myself:—*then* shall I no more blindly exchange certain peace for doubtful happiness,—a *quiet* for a *restless* mind.—Humility has not fled me;—my heart has not fallen a sacrifice to title, pomp, or splendor.—Yet, has it not foolishly, unasked, given itself up?——Ah! my Lady, not entirely unask'd neither; or, why, from the first moment, have I seen him shew *such* tender, *such* respectful assiduities?—why *so* ardently solicit to attend me into Oxfordshire?—why ask, if I refused my hand in the same peremptory manner, what would become of the man who without it was lost to the whole world?—But am I not too vain?—Why should this man be Lord Darcey?—Rather one rising to his imagination, who he might possibly suppose was entrapped by my girlish years.—A few, a very *few* weeks, and I am gone from him forever.—If your Ladyship's goodness can pardon the confession I have made, no errors will I again commit of the kind which now lies blushing before you.

Next to your Ladyship Mr. Jenkings is the best friend I have on earth.—He *never* has suspected, or *now* quite forgets his suspicions.——Not all my entreaties could prevent him from taking this long journey with me.—His age, his connections, his business, every thing is made subservient to my convenience—Whilst I write he is below, and has just sent up to know if I will permit a gentleman of his acquaintance, whom he has met accidentally at this inn, to dine with us.—Why does he use this ceremony?— I can have no objection to any friend of *his*.—Dinner is served up.—I shall write again at our last stage[1] this evening.

Senny

From the Mitre at ——.[2]

Past twelve at night!—An hour I used to think the most silent of any:—but *here* so much the reverse, one reasonably may suppose the inhabitants, or guests, have mistaken midnight for mid-day.

I will ring and enquire, why all this noise?

A strange bustle!—Something like fighting!——Very near, I protest.——Hark! bless me, I shall be frightened to death!—The chambermaid not come! Would I could find my way to Mr. Jenk-

---

1 Stopping point used to rest, water, and refresh worn-out horses, and to collect additional freight, mail, or passengers. On longer journeys, stages would include overnight stays at inns.

2 An inn would be called "The Mitre" only in a city that was the residence of a bishop and the site of a cathedral. Here, the reference is probably to the still-extant Mitre Inn in Oxford.

ings's room!—Womens voices, as I live!——Begging!—praying!—Ah! ah! now they cry, Take the swords away!—Take the swords away!—Heaven defend us! to be sure we shall be all killed.

One o'clock.

Not kill'd, but terrified out of my senses.—Well, if ever I stop at this inn again——

You remember, Madam, I was thrown into a sad fright by the hurry and confusion without.—I dropped my pen, and pulled the bell with greater violence.—No one came;—the noise increas'd.—Several people ran up and down by the door of my apartment.——I flew and double lock'd it.—But, good God! what were my terrors, when a voice cried out, She cannot be brought to life!—Is there no assistance at hand?—no surgeon near?—I rushed from my chamber, in the first emotions of surprize and compassion, to mix in a confused croud, *unknowing* and *unknown.*—I ventur'd no further than the passage. Judge my astonishment, to perceive there, and in a large room which open'd into it, fifty or sixty well dressed people of both sexes:—*Women*, some crying, some laughing:——*Men* swearing, stamping, and calling upon others to come down and end the dispute below.—I thought of nothing *now*, but how to retreat unobserv'd:—when a gentleman, in regimentals,[1] ran so furiously up the stairs full against me, that I should have been instantly at the bottom, had not his extended arm prevented my flight.

I did not stay to receive his apologies, but hastened to my chamber, and have not yet recovered my trembling.—Why did I leave it?—Why was I so inconsiderate?

Another alarm!—Some one knocks at the door!—Will there be no end to my frights?

If one's spirits are on the flutter, how every little circumstance increases our consternation!—When I heard the tapping at my door, instead of enquiring who was there, I got up and stood against it.

---

1 In army uniform, with insignia of his regiment.

Don't be afraid, *Mame*,[1] said a voice without; it is only the chambermaid come with some drops and water.[2]—With drops and water! replied I, letting her in—who sent you hither?

Captain Risby, *Mame*, one of the officers:—he told me you was frighten'd.

I am oblig'd to the gentleman;—but set down the drops, I do not want any.—Pray tell me what has occasioned this uproar in your house?

To be sure, *Mame*, here has been a terrifying noise this night.—It don't use to be so;—but our *Town*'s Gentlemen have such a dislike to *Officers*, I suppose there will be no peace while they are in town.—I never saw the Ladies dress'd so fine in my life; and had the Colonel happen'd to ask one of the *Alderman*'s daughters to dance, all would have gone on well.

You have an assembly then in the house?

O yes, *Mame*, the assembly is always kept here.—And, as I was saying, the Colonel should have danced with one of our Alderman's daughters:—instead of that, he engag'd a daughter of Esquire Light, and introduced the Major and a *handsome Captain* to her two sisters.—Now, to be sure, this was enough to enrage the best Trade's-People in the place, who can give their *young Ladies* three times as much as Mr. Light can his daughters.[3]

I saw she was determin'd to finish her harangue, so did not attempt to interrupt her.

_____

1 Ma'am, a pseudo-genteel pronunciation.
2 Composing drops taken in a small glass of water, probably a mild form of laudanum or opium.
3 An assembly is a regular meeting for a dance party, often the major entertainment of a country town. Minifie's novel emphasizes the vulgarity of the provincial group. A group of middle-class persons holds this assembly with its vulgar uproar over social position. The officers supply much-needed male partners, but delight in their presence is soon punctured by the officers' social views. The Colonel prefers Esquire Light, a landowner, to the town tradesman, and his daughters above even the Alderman's daughter. The shopkeepers are richer, with bigger dowries for their girls, and these families are—in their town's eyes—of higher status. Hence a fight breaks out.

One of us chambermaids, *Mame*, continued she, always assist the waiters;—it was my turn this evening; so, as I was stirring the fire in the card-room, I could hear the Ladies whisper their partners, if they let strangers stand above them, they might dance with whom they could get for the future.—They were busy about the matter when the Colonel enter'd with Miss Light, who though she is *very* handsome, *very* sensible, and all that, it did not become her to wear a silver silk;—for what, as *our Ladies* said, is family without fortune?——But I am running on with a story of an hour long.—So *Mame*, as soon as the Colonel and his partner went into the dancing-room,—*one* cry'd, Defend me from French'd hair, if people's heads are to look like towers;[1]—*another*, her gown sleeves were too large;—a *third*, the robeings too high;—a *fourth*, her ruff too deep:—in short, *Mame*, her very shoe-buckles shared the same fate.

This recital put me out of all patience:—I could not endure to see held up a picture, which, though out of the hands of a dauber, presented a true likeness of human nature in her most deprav'd state.—Enough, Mrs Betty, said I, now pray warm my bed; it is late, and I am fatigued.

O! to be sure, *Mame*; but will you not first hear what was the occasion of the noise?—The country-dances, continued she, not waiting my reply, began; and *our Town's Gentlemen* ran to the top of the room, leaving the *Officers* to dance at the bottom.[2]—This put them in *so* violent a passion, that the Colonel swore, if *our* Gentlemen persisted in their ill manners, not a soul should dance.—So, *Mame*, upon this *our* Gentlemen let some of the Officers stand above them;—and there was no dispute till after ten.—What they quarrelled about then I don't know;—but, when I came into the room, they were all going to fight;—and fight they certainly would, if they could have got *our* Gentlemen down stairs.——Not one of them would stir, which made the others so mad, that they would have pulled them down, had not the Ladies

---

1 Hair piled high on top of the head with the help of pads and supplementary hair in the fashionable French style, which was to reach ridiculous heights in the 1770s but that Minifie notices here.

2 The term "country-dance" comes from the French *contredanse*. The dancers in pairs formed two lines of couples, the couples of highest status leading off. That the townspeople place themselves at the top of the line offends the Colonel and the officers, who threaten not to dance.

interfered.—Then it was, Mame, I suppose, you heard the cries and shrieks; for every one that had *husbands, brothers,* or *admirers* there, took hold of them; begging and praying they would not fight.——Poor Miss Peggy Turner will have a fine rub; for she always deny'd to her *Mamma,* that there was any thing in the affair between her and Mr. Grant the Attorney. Now she has discovered all, by fainting away when he broke from her to go to the other end of the room.

I hope there has been no blood shed?

None, I'll assure you, *Mame,* in this house; what happens out of it is no business of mine. Now, *Mame,* would you please to go to bed? By all means, Mrs. Betty.——So away went my communicative companion. Being much tired, I shall lay down an hour or two, then reassume my pen.

Four o'clock in the morning.

Not able to close my eyes, I am got up to have the pleasure of introducing to your Ladyship the Gentleman who I mention'd was to dine with us at the other inn. Judge my surprize, when I found him to be the worthy Dean of H—— going into Oxfordshire to visit his former flock;—I knew him before Mr. Jenkings pronounced his name, by the strong likeness of his picture.

I even fancied the beautiful pair stood before me, whose hands he is represented joining.[1] It is much to be regretted so fine a piece should be hid from the world.——Why should not *this* be proportion? The *other* portraits which your Ladyship has drawn, are even allowed by Reynolds[2] to be masterly.——Let me therefore entreat, next time he comes to the Lodge, my favourite may *at least* have a chance of being called from banishment.

---

1 Fanny has seen Lady Mary's painting of her parents' marriage but does not know that is what the scene is. The Dean performed the marriage ceremony for her father and mother. The Dean has a private talk with Mr. Jenkings and is caught up on the current situation at this point. This painting by Lady Mary of the secret wedding (a painting that appears later in the narrative) is one she does not show, although her other paintings are displayed.

2 Portrait painter and founder of the Royal Society of Arts, Sir Joshua Reynolds (1723–92).

The Dean was almost discouraged from proceeding on his journey, by hearing of your Ladyship's absence, and the death of Mrs. Whitmore.—He was no stranger to what concern'd me, tho' I could be scarce an inhabitant of Hillford-Down at the time *he* left it.——I suppose his information was from Mr. Jenkings; I could see them from the window deep in discourse, walking in the Bowling-Green, from the moment the Dean got out of his chaise till dinner.

The latter expressed infinite satisfaction when I joined them; looking with such stedfast tenderness, as if he would trace on my countenance the features of some dear friend.—His sincere regard for Mr. and Mrs. Whitmore, and the gratitude he owes your Ladyship, must make him behold me with a favourable eye, knowing how greatly I have been distinguish'd by the two latter.

He had a stool put into his chaise; assuring us we could fit three conveniently.—We came from the last inn together, and are to travel so the remainder of the journey.

After your Ladyship's strict commands, that I look on Brandon-Lodge[1] as my home, I shall make it such the few days I stay in Oxfordshire;—and have presumed on your indulgence, to request Mr. Jenkings will do the same.—The Dean's visit is to Mr. Gardener, which will be happy for me, as that Gentleman's house is so near the Lodge.—I hope to see the tops of the chimneys this evening.—

My heart would jump at the sight, if I expected your Ladyship to meet me with open arms.—Extatic thought!—unfit to precede those disappointments which must follow thick on one another. Can there be greater!—to pass the very house, once inhabited by—O my Lady!—Heaven! how will your and her image bring before me past happy scenes!

If this is the Dean's voice, he is got up early. The horses putting to, and scarce five o'clock! Here comes a messenger, to say they are ready. So rest my pen, till I again take it up at Brandon-Lodge.

---

1 Lady Mary's home is merely a "lodge," originally simply the gatekeeper's lodge at the entrance to a landowner's fine estate, not itself a mansion.

I never saw such general joy as appeared through the village at sight of the Dean.—The first person who espy'd him ran with such speed into every house, that by the time we reached Mr. Gardener's gate, the chaise was surrounded by a hundred people.—Mr. and Mrs. Gardener stepping out, were saluted by the Dean. What, our old friend! cried they.——What, our old friend!—Good God!—and Miss Warley too!—This is a joyful surprize, indeed! and would have taken me out by force, if I had not persisted in going to the Lodge.—Your Ladyship is enough acquainted with these good people, to know they would part with any thing rather than their friends.—I have not yet seen Miss Gardener: she was gone on a walk with Miss West and Miss Conway.

The Dean showered a thousand marks of regard on all around him;——the meanest not escaping his notice.—In this tumult of pleasure I did not pass unregarded.——Your Ladyship and Mrs. Whitmore still live in their hearts; the pure air of Hillford-Down will not mix with the cold blast of ingratitude.

May the soft pillow I am going to repose on, shut not out from my mind the load of obligations which rest on it!—The remembrance is balm to my soul, either in my sleeping or waking hours.

Nine o'clock.

Scarce out of my bed half an hour!—How have I over-slept myself! Mrs. Bennet has prevailed on Mr. Jenkings to have some breakfast.—Good, considerate woman!—indeed, all your Ladyship's domestics are good and considerate.—No wonder, when you treat them so very different from *some people* of high rank.[1] Let those who complain of fraud, guilt, negligence, or want of respect from their dependants, look in here;—where they will see honesty, virtue, and reverence attend the execution of every command.——Flowers must be planted before they can take root.—Few, very few endeavour to improve an uncultivated soil, notwithstanding how great the advantage is to the improver.

I last night receiv'd pleasure inexpressible, by sending for the servants to acquaint them of your Ladyship's returning health;

---

1 The novel often discusses the treatment of servants.

and feasted on the satisfaction they expressed.—In a moment all the live creatures were brought.—I am satisfied, my Lady, if any of them die in your absence, it must be of fat.——My old acquaintances Bell and Flora[1] could hardly waddle in to pay their compliments; the parrot, which used to squall the moment she saw me, is now quite dumb; shewing no mark of her favour, but holding down her head to be scratched;—the turtle-doves are in the same case.—I have taken the liberty to desire the whole crew might be put to short allowance.

John said, he believed it was natural for every thing to grow fat here; and was much afraid, when I saw the coach-horses, I should pronounce the same hard sentence against them, desiring orders to attend me with the carriage this morning.—I told him my stay would be so short, I should have no time for an airing.

The gardener has just sent me a blooming nosegay; I suppose, to put me in mind of visiting his care, which I intend, after I have acquainted your Ladyship with an incident that till this moment had escaped my memory.——The Dean, Mr. Jenkings, and myself, were drinking a cup of chocolate before we sat out from the inn where I had been so much hurried, when captain Risby sent in his name, desiring we would admit him for a moment. His request being assented to, he entered very respectfully, said he came to apologize for the rudeness he was guilty of the last night.—The Dean and Mr. Jenkings presently guessed his meaning; I had been just relating the whole affair, which I was pleased to find did not disturb their rest.—I assured Captain Risby, far from deeming his behaviour rude, I was obliged to him for his solicitude in sending a servant to my chamber. He said he had not been in bed, determining to watch our setting out, in hopes his pardon would be sealed:—that to think of the accident he might have occasioned, gave him great pain.

Pardon me, Madam, addressing himself to me; and you, Sir, to Mr. Jenkings; if I ask one plain question: Have *you*, or at least has not *that Lady*, relations out of England? I have a friend abroad—I have heard him say his father is still living;—but then he has no sister;—or a certain likeness I discover would convince me.

---

1 Dogs.

Undoubtedly he took me for Mr. Jenkings's daughter:—what he meant further I cannot divine.

Mr. Jenkings reply'd, You are mistaken, Sir, if you think me the father of this Lady.—The chaise driving up that moment to the door, he shook him by the hand, and led me towards it; the Captain assisting me in getting in.

I wish I could have satisfied my curiosity.——I wish I had known to whom he likened me.—Perhaps his eyes misinformed him—perhaps he might have taken a cheerful glass after the last night's encounter:—yet he resembled not a votary of Bacchus;[1] ——his complexion clear;—hair nicely comb'd;—coat without a spot;—linen extremely fine and clean.—But enough of him.— [Here comes the Dean, walking up the avenue escorting a party of my old acquaintances.]

Adieu! dearest honour'd Lady, till my return to Hampshire.

F. WARLEY.

★ ★ ★

LETTER XIV.

The Honourable GEORGE MOLESWORTH
to LORD DARCEY.

London.

*W*AS every any thing so forgetful, to bring no other clothes here but mourning?

Really, my Lord, this favours a good deal of the matrimonial stile. Was you, commenced Benedict, I should think you had received lessons from the famous L——, who takes such pains with his pupils, that those whose attendance is frequent, can, in, the space of three months after the knot is tied, bring their wives to hear patiently the words—*forgetful,—ridiculous,—absurd,* —*pish—poh,*—and a thousand more of the same significant meaning.—I hear you, my Lord:—*it is true,* I am in jest; and know you would scorn to say even a peevish thing to a wife.

---

1 Roman god of wine.

Why fret yourself to a skeleton about an absence of eight days?—How could you suppose she would let you go into Oxfordshire?—Proper decorums must be observed by that sex.—Are not those despicable who neglect them?—What would you have said, had she taken Edmund with her?—Don't storm:—on reflection you will find you had no greater right to expect that indulgence.

I have this morning had a letter from Dick Risby, that unfortunate, but worthy cousin of mine, just returned from the West-Indies to take on him the command of a company in Lord ——'s regiment. What a Father his!—to abandon *such* a son.—Leave him to the wide world at sixteen,—without a shilling, only to gratify the pride and avarice of his serpent daughter,—who had art sufficient to get this noble youth disinherited for her waddling brat, whose head was form'd large enough to contain his mother's mischief and his own.—In vain we attempted to set aside the will:——my brother would not leave England whilst there remained the least hopes for poor Risby.

I always dreaded Dick's going abroad, well knowing what a designing perfidious slut his sister was, from her very infancy.—Her parents drew down a curse by their blind indulgence:—even her nurse was charg'd not to contradict her; she was to have every thing for which she shewed the least inclination.

Lord Eggom and myself being near of an age with our cousins, were sometimes sent to play with them in their nursery;[1] and, though boys of tolerable spirit, that vixen girl has so worried us by her tyrannic and impatient temper, that we have often petitioned, at our return home, to be put to bed supperless.——If sweet-meats were to be divided, she would cry to have the whole; the same in regard to cards,—shells,—money, or whatever else was sent for our entertainment.—When she has pinched us black and blue,—a complaint to her mother has

---

1 Children were an important topic in the eighteenth century. Here, Molesworth's remembrance of the past behavior of Dick's sister argues that children's play displays their true tempers. Some theorists of childhood like Jean-Jacques Rousseau in his *Emile, or On Education* (1762), suggest that spoiling by adults can lead to cruelty as well as greed in the child. Hence, Lucy should not have been excused for her bad behavior simply because she was the youngest.

been made by Dick, who could not bear to see us so used, though he was obliged to take such treatment himself; the only redress we should receive was—Poh! she is but a baby.—I thought you had all known better than to take notice of what *such* a *child* as Lucy does——Once, when this was said before her, she flew at me, and cry'd, I will pinch again, if I please;—papa and mamma says I shall,—and so does nurse; and I don't mind what any body else says.—I waited only for my revenge, till the two former withdrew; when sending the latter for a glass of water, I gave *Miss* such a glorious tacking,[1] as I believe she has never tasted the like before or since.——In the midst of the fray, I heard nurse running up, which made me hasten what I owed on *my own* account, to remind her of the *favours* she had conferred on Lord Eggom and her brother.——If such a termagant in her infant state,—judge what she must be at a time of life when her passions are in full vigour, and govern without controul!——I have just shewn the method of rearing this diabolical plant, that you may not wonder at its productions.—I shall see justice overtake her, notwithstanding the long strides she is making to escape.

Dick will be in town with us most part of the winter:—I have wrote him to that purpose, and mention'd your name. He will rejoice to see you:——I have often heard him regret your acquaintance was of so short standing.—Bridgman set out for York the day before I arrived; his servants inform me he is not expected back this three weeks.

I like our lodgings vastly; but more so as the master and mistress of the family are excessively clean and obliging; two things so material to my repose, that I absolutely could not dispense patiently with either.—This it was which made me solicitous about taking a house; I am now so happily situated, I wish not to have one in town whilst I remain a batchelor. Heaven knows how long that will be!—Your nonpareil has given me a dislike to all my former slight prepossessions.

Lady Elizabeth Curtis!—I did once indeed think a little seriously of her:—but *such* a meer girl!—Perhaps the time she has spent in France, Germany, and the Lord knows where, may have changed her from a little bewitching, smiling, artless creature—

---

1 Tackling.

to a *vain, designing, haughty,*—I could call a coquet by a thousand names;—but Lady Elizabeth *can*-not, *must* not be a coquet.—Cupid, though, shall never tye a bandage over my eyes.—The charms that must fix me are not to be borrow'd;—I shall look for them in her affection to her relations;—in a condescending[1] behaviour to inferiors;—above all, when she offers up her first duties.—If she shines here, I shall not follow her to the card-table, or play-house:—every thing must be right in a heart where duty, affection, and humility, has the precedence.

The misfortune of our sex is this: when taken with a fine face, we enquire no further than, Is she *polite?*—Is she *witty?* Does she *dance* well?—sing well?—in short, is she fit to appear in the *Beau Monde;*[2] whilst good sense and virtues which constitute real happiness, are left out of the question.

How does beauty,—politeness—wit,—a fine voice,—a graceful movement, charm!—But how often are we deceiv'd by them.—An instance of which I have lately seen in our old friend Sir Harry. No man on earth can pity that poor soul more than I do; yet I have laughed hours to think of his mistake. *So mild—so gentle*—said he, George, a week before his marriage, I should have said *execution,*—it is impossible to put her out of humour.—If I am not the happiest man breathing, it must be my own fault.

What was my astonishment when I call'd on him in my way to town, and found this mild *gentle mate* of his, aided by a houseful of her relations, had not only deprived him of all right and authority in the *Castle*, but almost of his very speech!

I dropt in about one, told the Baronet I came five miles out of my way for the pleasure of saluting his bride, and to drink a bottle of claret[3] with him.—He was extremely glad to see me; and ventured to say so, *before* I was introduced to the *Ladies*:—but I saw by his sneaking look, no such liberty must be taken in *their* pres-

---

1 Kind and courteous to those of lower social status; one cannot condescend to one's social equals.
2 French: beautiful world. An expression that denotes the world of the wealthy, successful, and elegant.
3 Fine red wine.

ence.—My reception was gracious enough, considering all communication is cut off between him and his former acquaintance.

Scarce was I seated, before the old Dowager asked me, if her daughter had not made *great* alterations in the little time she had been at the Castle.

Alterations, Madam! I reply'd;—upon my honour, they are so visible, no person can avoid being struck with them.—How could your father and mother, Sir Harry, bear to live in such an wood?[1] looking and speaking disdainfully.——He smiled obsequious—hemm'd—trembled, and was silent.—I hope, continued she, not to see a tree remaining near this house before the next summer.——We want much, Mr. Molesworth, turning to me with quite a different look and voice, to have the pleasure-ground laid out:—but really her Ladyship has had so much to set in order *within doors*, that it has taken off her attention a good deal from what is necessary to be done *without*.—However, Sir, you shall see our design; so, my dear, speaking to her daughter, let Sir Harry fetch the plan.

It is in my closet, returned her Ladyship, and I don't chuse to send *him* there;—but I'll ring for Sally.

I had like that moment to have vow'd a life of celibacy——I saw him redden;—how could he avoid it, if one spark of manhood remain'd?

The indignation I felt threw such a mist before my eyes, that when the plan was laid on the table, I could scarce distinguish temples from clumps of shrubs, or Chinese seats from green slopes.——Yet this *reptile* of a husband could look over my shoulder, hear the opinion of every one present, without *daring* to give his own.

I was more out of patience at dinner.—Bless me, says her Ladyship, how *aukward* you are when I *bid* you cut up any thing!—the mother and daughter echoing, *Never* was there *such a*

---

1 Sir Harry's domineering new wife exhibits her lack of taste in desiring to cut down trees and introduce fashionable lawns, shrubs, and garden ornaments. People who want to destroy trees feature as heartless vulgarians in a number of novels in the later eighteenth century.

carver as *Sir Harry!*—Well, I vow, cry'd the latter, it is a strange thing you will not remember, so often as I have *told you*, to lay the meat handsome in the dish.

Good God! thought I, can this man live out half his days? ——And, faith, if I had not drank five bumpers of Madeira,[1] I could not have stood the sight of his fearful countenance.

He perceived I was distress'd, and whisper'd me as I mounted my horse,—You see how it is, Molesworth; breeding women[2] *must* not be contradicted.—

I do, I do see how it is, return'd I; and could not for my soul forbear saying, I shall rejoice to hear of a *delivery.*

This is the day when the important affairs of the m——y are to be settled;[3] the papers will inform you; but can a man in love have any relish for politics?—Pray, divest yourself of that plague, when you attend the house.[4]—I should drop to hear you say you espouse *this* or *that* cause, for the love of *Miss Warley*, instead of your *country.*

Next Friday!—Well, I long to see you after a dreadful, dreadful absence of *eight days.*—There is something confounded ridiculous in all this stuff; nor can I scarce credit that a man should pine, fret, and make himself unhappy, because he is loosed from the apron-strings of his Phillida[5] for a few days.— I see you shrug;—but my fate is not dependent on your prognostications.——Was it so, I know where I should be,—down amongst the *dead* men; down amongst the *dead* men.—[6]

---

1 Rich, sweet wine from Madeira. Five bumpers would be five giant glasses full.
2 Pregnant women.
3 Ministry, i.e., the Prime Minister and his Cabinet.
4 Darcey is of age and entitled to sit in the House of Lords, the Upper House of Parliament. Molesworth suggests that the new Lord should get rid of love when he settles in as a legislator.
5 Poetic name for a rustic beloved.
6 Refrain of a drinking song. The phrase "the dead men" refers jocularly to the empty bottles strewn on the floor.

However, I would consent to be rank'd in the nᵤ
Cupid's slain, could I be hit by just such a dart as pierc'd

Vulcan[1] certainly has none ready made that will do, unless ᵢ
sharpens the points of those which have already recoiled.

But hold; I must descend from the clouds, to regale myself on
a fine turtle[2] at the Duke of R——d's. What an *epicure!* Talk of
feasting my palate, when my eyes are to meet delicacies of a far
more inviting nature!—There *was* a time I should have been
envy'd *such* a repast:—*that* time is fled;—*you* are no longer a
monopolizer of beauty;—can sing but of *one*,—talk but of *one*,—
dream but of *one*,—and, what is still more extraordinary, love but
one.—

Give *me* a heart at large;—such confin'd notions are not for

MOLESWORTH.

★ ★ ★

LETTER XV.

Lord DARCEY to the Honourable GEORGE
MOLESWORTH.

Barford Abbey.

I ENVY not the greatest monarch on earth!——She is
return'd with my peace;—my joy;—my very soul.——Had
you seen her restorative smiles! they spoke more than my pen can
describe!—She bestow'd them on me, even before she ran to the
arms of Sir James and Lady Powis.—Sweet condescension!——
Her hand held out to meet mine, which, trembling, stopt half
way.——What checks,—what restraint, did I inflict on myself!—
Yes, that would have been the decisive moment, had I not perceiv'd the eyes of Argus[3] planted *before, behind,* on *every side* of Sir

---

1 Roman god of fire, volcanoes, and metalworking.
2 The English associated eating turtles with wealth and luxury because they
   were imported from the West Indies. The fad so severely diminished turtle
   populations that we eat fewer turtles today rather because they are less
   accessible 'than because of distaste for them.
3 In Greek myth, a giant with a hundred eyes.

James.—God! how he star'd.—I suppose my looks made some discovery.—Once more I must take thee up, uneasy dress of hypocrisy;—though it will be as hard to girt on, as the tight waist-coat on a lunatic.[1]

Never has a day appear'd to me so long as *this*.—*Full* of expectation, *full* of impatience!—All stuff again.——No matter; it is not the groans of a sick man, that can convey his pain to another:—to feel greatly, you must have been afflicted with the same malady.

I suppose you would laugh to hear how often I have open'd and shut the door;—how often look'd out at the window,—or the multiplicity of times examined my watch since ten this morning!——Needless would it likewise be to recount the impatient steps I have taken by the road-side, attentive to the false winds, which would frequently cheat me into a belief, that my heart's treasure was approaching.——Hark! I should say, that must be wheels;—stop and pause;—walk forwards;—stop again, till every sound have died upon my ear.

Harrass'd by expectation, I saunter'd a back way to Jenkings's;—enquired of Mrs. Jenkings, what time she thought her husband might be home; and taking Edmund with me to my former walk, determined to sound *his* inclinations.—I waved[2] mentioning Miss Warley's name till we had gone near a quarter of a mile from the house; still expecting he would begin the subject, which at this juncture I suppose particularly engaged his attention; but perceiving he led to things quite opposite, I drew him out in the following manner:

So you really think, Edmund, your father will not be out after it is dark?

I have not known, my Lord, that he has for many years; rather than venture, I believe, he would stop the night at Oxford. Very composedly he said this, for I watched his looks narrowly.——

---

1 Invented in the eighteenth century, straitjackets were thought a more humane restraint for the mentally ill.
2 Waived.

Edmund, confess, confess *frankly*, said I; has not *this* day been the longest you ever knew?

The longest I ever knew! Faith your Lordship was never more out: far from thinking so, I am startled to find how fast the hours have flown; and want the addition of at least three, to answer letters which my father's business requires.

Business, *Edmund!* and does *business* really engross so much of your attention, when you know who is expected in the evening? Ah! *Edmund*, you are a sly fellow: never tell me, you want to lengthen out the tedious hours of *absence.*

Tedious hours of absence! Ho! ho! my Lord, I see now what you are at; your Lordship can never suppose me *such* a fool as to——

Fool!——My supposition, *Edmund*, pronounces you a man of sense; but you mistake my meaning.

I do not mistake, my Lord; surely it must be the height of folly to lift my thoughts to Miss Warley. Suppose my father can give me a few thousands,—are these sufficient to purchase beauty, good sense, with every accomplishment?——No, no, my Lord, I am not such a vain fellow;—Miss Warley was never born for *Edmund Jenkings*—She told me *so*, the first moment I beheld her.

Told you so? what then, you have made pretensions to her, and she told you *so?*

Yes, my Lord, she told, me *so.*—That is, her *eyes*, her whole graceful *form*, spoke it.—Was I a man of family,—a man of title, with a proper knowledge of the world,—I would not deliberate a moment.

How comes it then, Edmund, that you are so assiduous to oblige her?——You would not run and fly for every young lady.—

True, my Lord, it is not every one would repay me with smiles of condescension. Suffer me to assure your Lordship, when I can oblige Miss Warley, my ambition is gratified.—Never, *never* shall a more presumptuous wish intrude to make me less worthy of the honour I receive from your Lordship's notice.——

This he spoke with energy;—such energy,—as if he had come at the book of my heart, and was reading its contents. I knew his regard for my dear amiable girl, and the danger of betraying my secret, or should have treated him with unbounded confidence:——I therefore only applauded his sentiments;—told him a man who could think thus nobly,——honour'd me in his friendship;—that mine to him should be unalterable; call'd him brother; and by the joyful perturbations of my soul, I fear I gave him some idea of what I strove to hide.

The curtain of night was dropping by slow degrees, when a distant sound of wheels interrupted our conversation.—We stood listening a moment, as it approach'd nearer. Edmund cry'd out,—They are come; I hear Cæsar's voice; and, taking a hearty leave, ran home to receive them.—I directed my course towards the Abbey, in hopes the chaise had proceeded thither, and found I had steer'd right, seeing it stand at the entrance.

Mr. Jenkings did not get out; Lady Powis refused to part with Miss Warley this night. Whilst I write, I hope she is enjoying a sweet refreshing sleep. O! Molesworth! could I flatter myself she dreams of me!——

To-morrow Lord and Lady Allen, Mr. and Mrs. Winter, dine here; consequently Miss Winter, and her *fond* admirer, Lord Baily.—How often have I laugh'd to see that cooing, billing, pair?[1] It is come home, you'll say, with a vengeance.—Not so neither.—I never intend making such a very fool of myself as Lord Baily.—Pray, Madam, don't sit against that door;—and pray, Madam, don't sit against this window.—I hear you have encreased your cold;——you speak hoarse:—indeed, Madam, you speak hoarse, though you won't confess it.——In this strain has the monkey ran on for two hours.——No body must help him at table but Miss Winter.—He is always sure to eat whatever is next her.—She, equally complaisant, sends her plate to him;—

---

1 Lord Darcey satirically refers to Lord Baily and Miss Winter as a pair of doves (or, as we might say, "lovebirds"). Birds are said to "bill" when they touch one another's beaks, as if kissing.

desires he will have a bit of the same.—Excessively high, my Lord;—you never eat any thing so well done.——The appearance of fruit is generally the occasion of great altercation:—What! venture on peaches again, Miss Winter?——Indeed, my Lord, I shall only eat this small one;—that was not half ripe which made me sick yesterday.——No more nuts; I absolutely lay an embargo[1] on nuts,—No more, nonsense: I absolutely lay an embargo on nonsense, says Molesworth to

DARCEY.

★ ★ ★

LETTER XVI.

Miss WARLEY to Lady MARY SUTTON.

Barford Abbey.

ONCE more, my dear Lady, I dispatch a packet from this place,—after bidding adieu to the agreeable Dean,—— Brandon Lodge,——and my friends in that neighbourhood.

How long I shall continue here, God only knows.—If my wishes could avail, the time would be short, very short, indeed.— I am quite out of patience with Mr. and Mrs. Smith; some delay every time I hear from them.—First, we were to embark the middle of this month;—then the latter end;—now it is put off till the beginning of the next:—perhaps, when I hear next, it will be, they do not go at all.—Such weak resolutions are never to be depended on;—a straw, like a magnet, will draw them from side to side.

I think I am as much an inhabitant of this house as of Mr. Jenkings's:—I lay here last night after my journey, and shall dine here this day; but as a great deal of company is expected, must go to my *other* home to dress.——To-morrow your Ladyship shall command me.

---

1 A legal prohibition against an imported product. There is a sexual connotation to improper social concern over someone's eating or not eating in this period.

From Mr. Jenkings's.

Rejoice with me, my dear Lady.——You *will* rejoice, I know, you *will*, to find my eyes are open to my folly.——How could I be so vain, so presumptuous!—Yes, it must be vanity, it must be presumption to the highest,—gloss it over as I will,—to harbour thoughts which before this your Ladyship is acquainted with.—Did you not blush for me?—did you not in contempt throw aside my letter?—Undoubtedly you did.—Go, you said.—I am sure, dear Madam, you *must* let me not again behold the weakness of that poor silly girl.—But this is my hope, you are not apt to judge unfavourably, *even* in circumstances that will scarce admit of palliation.——Tell me, my dear Lady, I am pardoned; tell me so, and I shall never be again unhappy.—How charming, to have *peace* and *tranquility* restor'd, when I fear'd they were for *ever* banish'd my breast!—I welcomed the friends;——my heart bounded at their return;—I smiled on them;—soothed them;—and promised never more to drive them out.

Thank you, Lord Allen;——again, I thank you:—can I ever be too grateful?——You have been instrumental to my repose.

The company that dined at the Abbey yesterday were Lord and Lady Allen, Lord Baily, Mr. Mrs. and Miss Winter.—This was the first day I changed my mourning;——a white lutestring, with the fine suit of rough garnets[1] your Ladyship gave me, was my dress on the occasion.—But let me proceed to the incident for which I stand indebted for the secret tranquility, the innate repose I now possess in a *superlative* degree.—

When I went to Mr. Jenkings's to dress for dinner, Lord Darcey attended me, as usual:—the coach was to fetch us.—I thought I never saw his Lordship in such high good humour; what I mean is, I never saw him in such spirits.—To speak the truth, his temper always appears unruffled;——sometimes a little gloomy; but I suppose he is not exempted from the common ills of life.—He entertained me on the way with a description of the company expected, interlarding[2] his conversation with observa-

---

1 Fanny's first venture out of mourning, a dress of white glossy silk (from Italian *lustrino*) with a "suit," or set of necklace, bracelet, and earrings of simple and inexpensive dark red garnets.

2 To alternate or mix, a cooking term that literally means to add a layer of fat, especially bacon, between other ingredients.

tions tending to raise my vanity. Notwithstanding his seeming sincerity, I was proof against such insinuations.——If he had stopp'd *there*,—well, if he had stop'd *there*;—what then?—Why then, perhaps, I should not have betray'd the weakness of my heart.——But I hope my confusion pass'd unobserv'd;——I hope it was not seen before I could draw my handkerchief from my pocket: if it should, heavens! the very thought has dyed me scarlet.

I am running on as though your Ladyship had been present in Mr. Jenkings's parlour,—in the coach,—and at table, whither I must conduct you, my dear Lady, if your patience will bear a minute recital.——First, then, to our conference in the parlour, after I was dress'd.

My coming down interrupted a *tête-à-tête* between his Lordship and Edmund. The latter withdrew soon after I entered;—it look'd some-how as if designed;—*it vexed me*;—mean it how he would, *it much* disconcerted me:—I *hate*, I *despise* the least appearance of design.—In vain did I attempt to bring him back; he only answer'd he would be with us instantly.

I was no sooner seated, than his Lordship placed himself by me; and fetching a deep sigh, said, I wish it was in my power to oblige Miss Warley as much as it is in hers to oblige me.——

My Lord, I cannot conceive how I have it in my power to oblige you. He took my hand,—Yes, Madam, to make *me* happy,—for ever happy,—to make *Sir James* and *Lady Powis happy*, you have only to determine not to quit your native country.

Stop! my Lord, if you mean my going to *Montpellier*, I am determin'd.——And are you *really* determin'd, Miss Warley?—his face overspread with a dreadful paleness.

I am, my Lord.

But what are you determin'd? Are you determined to distress your friends?

I wish not to distress my friends: nothing would give me so much pain; but I *must* go;—indeed I *must*.

He rose up;—walk'd about the room,—came back to his seat again, looking quite frantic.——Good God! why should that sex practise so many arts? He pray'd,—intreated,—left no argument untried.

I cannot picture his countenance, when I declared myself resolved.——He caught both my hands, fixed his eyes stedfastly upon me.

Then you are inflexible, Madam?—Nothing can move you to pity the most wretched of his sex.—Know you the person living that could prevail?—If you do,—say so;—I will bring him instantly on his knees.

There is not in the world, my Lord, one who could prevent me from paying my *duty*, my *affection*, my *obedience*, to *Lady Mary Sutton*: if due to a parent, how much more from me to Lady Mary;—a poor orphan, who have experienced from her the most maternal fondness?

The word *orphan* struck him; he reeled from me and flung himself into a chair opposite, leaning his head on a table which stood near.

I declare he distress'd me greatly;—I know not what my thoughts were at that moment;—I rose to quit the room; he started up.

Don't leave me, Miss Warley;—don't leave me. I *will* keep you no longer in the dark: I *must* not suffer in your opinion,—be the consequence——

Here we were interrupted by Edmund.—I was sorry he just then entered;—I would have given the world to know what his Lordship was about to say.

When we were in the coach, instead of explaining himself, he assumed rather a chearful air; and asked, if my time was fix'd for going to France?

Not absolutely fix'd, my Lord; a month or two hence, perhaps. This I said, that he might not know exactly the time when I shall set out.

A month or *two!* O! that will be just the thing, just as I could wish it.——

What does your Lordship mean?

Only that I intend spending part of the winter in Paris; and if I should not be deemed an *intruder*, perhaps the same yacht may carry us over.

I was never more at a loss for a reply.

Going to France, my Lord! in a hesitating voice.—I never heard,—I never dreamt,—your Lordship had such an intention.

Well, you do not forbid it, Miss Warley? I shall certainty be of your party:

I *forbid it*, my Lord! *I forbid it!* What right have *I* to controul your Lordship's actions? Besides, we should travel so short a way together, it would be very immaterial.

Give me Leave, Madam, in this respect to be the judge; perhaps every one is not bless'd with that *happy* indifference.— What may be very *immaterial* to *one*,—may be matter of the *highest* importance to *another*.

He pronounced the word *immaterial*, with some marks of displeasure. I was greatly embarrass'd: I thought our conversation would soon become too interesting.

I knew not what to do.—I attempted to give it a different turn; yet it engrossed all my attention.—At length I succeeded by introducing my comical adventure at the inn, in our way to Oxfordshire: but the officer's name had escaped my memory, though I since recollect it to be Risby.

This subject engaged us till we came within sight of the drawing-room windows.—There are the visitors, as I live! said I. Your Lordship not being dress'd, will, I suppose, order the coach to the other door.——To be plain, I was glad of any excuse that would prevent my getting out before them.—Not *I*, indeed, Miss Warley, reply'd he:—Dress is never of consequence enough to draw me two steps out of my way.—If the spectators yonder will fix their eyes on an old coat rather than a fine young Lady, *why* they have it for their pains.

By this time the door was open'd; and Sir James appearing, led me, with his usual politeness, to the company. I was placed by her Ladyship next Miss Winter, whose person I cannot say prejudiced me in her favour, being entirely dispossessed of that winning grace which attracts strangers at a first glance.

After measuring me with her eye from head to toe, she sent my dimensions in a kind of half smile across the room to Lord Baily; then vouchsafed to ask, how long I had been in this part of the world? which question was followed by fifty others, that shewed she laboured under the violent thirst of curiosity; a thirst never to be conquered; for, like dropsical people, the more they drink in, the more it rages.[1]

My answers were such as I always return to the inquisitive.—Yes, Madam;—No, Madam;—very well;—very good;—not certain;—quite undetermin'd.—Finding herself unsuccessful with *me*, she apply'd to *Lady Powis*; but alas! poor maiden, she could drain nothing from that fountain; the streams would not flow;—they were driven back, by endeavouring to force them into a wrong channel.

These were not certainly her first defeats, by the clever way of hiding her chagrin:—it is gone whilst she adjusts the flower in her bosom,—or opens and shuts her fan twice.—How can *she* be mortified by trifles,—when the *Lord* of *her heart*,—the sweet, simpering, fair-faced, Lord Baily keeps his eyes incessantly fixed on her, like centinels on guard?—They cannot speak, *indeed they cannot*, or I should expect them to call out every half hour, "All is well."

I admire Lord and Lady Allen; I say, I admire them: their manners are full of easy freedom, pleasing vivacity.—I cannot admire all the world; I wish I could.—Mr. and Mrs. Winter happen not to suit my taste;—they are a kind of people who look down on every one of middle fortune;—seem to despise ances-

---

1 Dropsy is the eighteenth-century term for the medical condition edema, from the Greek for "swelling," which causes fluid to accumulate beneath the skin and in other parts of the body.

try,—yet are always fond of mixing with the great.——Their rise was too sudden;—they jump'd into life all at once.—Such quick transitions require great equality of mind;——the blaze of splendor was too much for their *weak* eyes;—the *stare* of surprise is still visible.

It was some time before the conversation became general.— First, and ever to have precedence,—the weather;—next, roads;—then houses,—plantations,—fashions,—dress,—equipage;—and last of all, politics in a thread-bare coat.

About ten minutes before dinner, Lord Darcey joined us, dress'd most magnificently in a suit of olive velvet, embroider'd with gold;—his hair without powder,[1] which became him infinitely.—He certainly appear'd to great advantage:—how could it be otherwise, when in company with that tawdry, gilded piece of clay?——And to sit by him, of all things!—One would really think it had been designed:—*some* exulted, *some* look'd mortified at the contrast.——Poor Miss Winter's seat began to grow very uneasy;—she tried every corner, yet could not vary the light in which she saw the *two opposites*.——Why did she frown on *me*?—why cast such contemptuous glances every time I turn'd my eye towards her?—Did *I* recommend the daubed coxcomb;—or represent that her future joys depended on title?—No! it was vanity, the love of grandeur,——that could make her give up fine sense, fine accomplishments, a princely address, and all the noble requisites:—yes, my Lady, such a one, Lord Darcey tells me, she has refused.—Refused, for what? For folly, a total ignorance in the polite arts, and a meaness of manners not to be express'd: yet, I dare say, she thinks, the sweet sounds of *my Lady*, and *your Ladyship* is *cheaply* purchased by such a sacrifice.

When we moved to go into the dining-parlour, Miss Winter bow'd for me to follow Lady Allen and her mother; which after I had declined, Lady Powis took me by the hand, and said, smiling, No, Madam, Miss Warley is one of us.[2]—If *so*, my

---

1 Orris root powder used to color the hair or a wig white.
2 Access to the dining room was conducted as a procession in order of rank. Lady Powis spares Miss Winter from having to follow Miss Warley, but she favors Miss Warley by indicating that she is one of the family, thus giving her a superior position. She will leave the room last.

Lady—and she swam out of the room with an air I shall never forget.

Lord Darcey took his place at table, next Lord Allen;—I sat opposite, with Miss Winter on my right, and Lord Baily on my left.—Sorry I was, to step between the Lovers; but ceremony required it; so I hope they do not hate me on that account.—Lord Allen has a good deal of archness in his countenance, though not of the ill-natur'd kind.——I don't know how, but every time he look'd across the table I trembled; it seem'd a foreboding of what was to follow.

He admired the venison;—said it was the best he had ever tasted from Sir James's park;—but declared he would challenge him next Monday, if all present would favour him with their company.——Lady Allen seconded the request so warmly, that it was immediately assented to.—

What think you, said his Lordship, it is to the *young* folks that I address myself, of seeing before you a couple who that day has been married twenty years, and never frown'd on one another?

Think! said Lord Darcey, it is very possible.

Possible it certainly is, reply'd Lady Powis; but very few instances, I believe—

What say you, Miss Warley? ask'd his Lordship: you find Lord Darcey supposes it very possible.—Good God! I thought I should have sunk: it was not so much the question, as the manner he express'd it in. I felt as if my face was stuck full of needles: however, I stifled my confusion, and reply'd, I was quite of Lady Powis's opinion.

Well, what say you, Miss Winter?

How I rejoiced! I declare I could hardly contain my joy, when he address'd himself to her.

What say I, my Lord? Return'd she; why, *truly*, I think it must be your own faults, if you are not treated *civilly*.—The Devil! cry'd he.

O fie! O fie! my Lord, squeaked my left hand neighbour.—
And why O fie! retorted his Lordship: Is *civility* all we have to
expect?

We can *claim* nothing else, said the squeaker.—If the dear
creatures condescend to *esteem* us, we ought to consider it a particular indulgence.

And so, Miss Warley, cry'd Lord Allen, we are only to be
esteemed now-a-days. I thank God my good woman has imbibed
none of those modern notions. Her actions have convinced the
world of that long ago.

Poh! my Lord, said Lady Allen, we are old-fashion'd people:—
you must not talk thus before Gentlemen and Ladies bred in the
present age.

Come, come, let me hear Lord Darcey speak to this point,
continued his Lordship. He is soon to be *one of us:*—we shall
shortly, I am told, salute him *Benedick.*

On this Sir James threw down his knife and fork with emotion,
crying, This is news, indeed! This is what I never heard before!
Upon my word, your Lordship has been very secret! looking full
at Lord Darcey. But you are of *age,* my Lord, so I have no *right* to
be consulted; however, I should be glad to know, who it is that
runs away with your heart. This was spoke half in jest, half in
earnest.

In a moment my neck and face were all over crimson.——I felt
the colour rise;—it was not to be suppress'd.—I drew my handkerchief from my pocket;—held it to my face;—hemm'd;—call'd
for wine and water;—which, when brought, I could scarcely
swallow; spoke in a low voice to Miss Winter;—said she had a
poor stomach, or something like it.

Lord Darcey too was confus'd.——Why did I look up to
him?—He was pale, instead of red.—I saw his lips move, but
could not hear what he said for more than a minute; occasion'd by an uncommon noise which just then rush'd through
my head:——at length sounds grew distinct, and I heard this
sentence——*every* word is inscribed where it can *never* be
erazed——

Upon my honour, Lord Allen, I have never made proposals to any woman; and *further*, it is a matter of doubt, whether I ever shall.

By this time I had lost all my colour;—charming cool—and calm,—no perturbation remaining.

Nothing disagreeable now hung on my mind, except a certain thoughtfulness, occasion'd by the recollection of my folly.—

Miss Winter's eyes sparkled, if it is possible for grey ones to sparkle, at the declaration Lord Darcey had just made; and, of a sudden, growing very fond of *me*, laid her hand on mine, speaking as it were aside,—Well, I was never *more* surprized! I as *much* believed him engaged to a *certain* young Lady,—squeezing my thumb,—as I think I am living.——Nay, I would not have credited the contrary, had I not heard him declare off[1] with my *own* ears.—I see how it is; Sir James must chuse a wife for him.—

To all which I only answered, Lord Darcey, Madam, is certainly the best judge of his actions:—I make no doubt but Sir James will approve his Lordship's choice.

After what I have related, common subjects ensued:—the cloth being removed,[2] I withdrew to the Library, intending to sit with Mr. Watson half an hour, who was confined by a cold. He holds out his hand to take mine the moment he hears my footstep.—I look on him as an angel: his purity, his mildness, his resignation speak him one.—

Lord Darcey entered as I was about to join the company; however, I staid some minutes, that my quitting the room might not seem on *his* account.

I am glad you are come, my Lord, said Mr. Watson; sitting with such a poor infirm man has made Miss Warley thoughtful.—— Upon my word, Sir, returned I, it was only the fear of increasing your head-ach that made me silent.—I never was in higher

---

1 A man who has "declared off" has clearly stated that he has ceased pursuit, or is just not that into you.
2 Table cloth removed after dining.

spirits.—I could sing and dance this very moment. Well then, dear Miss Warley, cried his Lordship, let me fetch your *guitarre.*

With all my heart, my Lord; I am *quite* in tune.——Taking leave of Mr. Watson, I return'd to the company.—His Lordship soon followed. Again repeating his request, in which every person join'd, I sung and play'd several compositions.

Miss Winter was next call'd upon and the guitarre presented to her by Lord Darcey.——A long time she absolutely refused it; declaring she had not learnt any new music this year.—What does that signify, Miss Winter? said her mother; you know you have a sweet voice.

Bless me! Madam! how can you say so?—To be sure, I should sing to great advantage *now.*

Well, Nancy, you'll oblige *Papa?*—says the old Gentleman; I know you'll oblige *Papa,*—stalking over to her on the tops of his toes.

Here the contest ended; *Miss* taking the guitarre, condescended to oblige her *Papa.*

She really sings and plays well:——if her manner had been less affected, we should have been more entertain'd.—The company staid supper, after which Lord Darcey came with me home.—I made *no* objection:——of all things, I would make *none*—after what pass'd at table. Fortunate event! how I rejoice in my recovered tranquillity!

The thoughts, the pleasing thoughts of freedom have kept me from sleep; I could not think of repose amidst my charming reflections. Happy, happy change!

It is past two o'clock!—At all times and all seasons,

I am, my dear Lady,

Yours invariably,

F. WARLEY.

★ ★ ★

LETTER XVII.

Miss WARLEY to the same.

From Mr. Jenkings's.

SENT for before breakfast!—Nobody in the coach!——Well, I am glad of that, however.—Something very extraordinary must have happen'd.—I hope Lady Powis is not ill.—No other message but to desire I would come immediately.—I go, my dear Lady; soon as I return will acquaint you what has occasion'd me this *early* summons.

Eight o'clock at Night.

No ill news! quite the reverse:—I am escaped from the house of festivity to make your Ladyship a partaker.

My spirits are in a flutter.—I know not where to begin.—I have run every step of the way, till I am quite out of breath.—— Mr. Powis is coming home,—absolutely coming home to settle;—married *too*, but I cannot tell all at once.—Letters with an account of it have been this morning receiv'd. He does not say who his wife is, only one of the best women in the world.

She will be received with affection;—I know she will.—Lady Powis declares, they shall be folded together in her arms.

It was too much for Sir James, he quite roared again when he held out to me the letter.—I don't believe he has eat a morsel this day.—I never before saw a man so affected with joy.—Thank God! I left him pure and calm.

The servants were like mad creatures, particularly those who lived in the family before Mr. Powis left England.—He seems, in short, to be considered as one risen from the dead.——

I was in such haste on receiving Lady Powis's message, that I ran down to the coach, my hat and cloak in my hand.——Mr. and Mrs. Jenkings were talking to the coachman.—I soon perceived by them something pleasing had happen'd.—They caught me in their arms, and I thought would have smother'd me in their embraces; crying out, Mr. Powis is coming home, my dear;—Mr. Powis is coming home:——for God's sake, Madam, make haste up to the Hall.

In getting into the coach, I stepp'd on my apron, and fell against the opposite door.—My right arm was greatly bruis'd, which I did not perceive till I drew on my glove.

The moment I alighted, I ran to the breakfast-parlour; but finding no one there, went directly to her Ladyship's dressing-room.——She open'd the door, when she heard me coming. I flew to her.—I threw my arms about her neck, and all I could say in my hurry was, Joy, Joy, Joy!

I am all joy, my love, she return'd—I am made up of nothing else. I quitted her to run to Sir James, who was sitting in a great chair with a letter held out. I believe I kiss'd him twenty times before I took it;—there could be no harm in that surely.—Such endearments I should have shewn my father, on the like tender occasion. He wept, as I have said, till he quite roared again.—I laid his head on my shoulder, and it was some time before I would mention his son's name.

Lord Darcey held one of Sir James's hands: he was in the room when I enter'd; but I declare I never saw him till he spoke. He is safe *now*,—after what happened yesterday,—safe from any impu-tation on *my* account.—

Very kind and very civil, upon my word! O! your Ladyship never heard such a fuss as he made about the scratch on my arm.——I affect to look pleased when he speaks to me, that he might not take it into his head I am mortified.

He must be the happiest creature in the world; I honour him for the grateful affection he shews Sir James and Lady Powis.

Breakfast stood on the table: not a soul had broke their fast.—Her Ladyship was here, there, and every where.—I was sadly afraid they would be all sick; at length I prevailed on them to drink a cup of chocolate.—

Mr. Watson, good man! notwithstanding his indisposition, got up at eleven.—I met him coming from his apartment, and had the pleasure of leading him to the happy family.—

His congratulations were delivered with such serene joy,—such warmth of affection,—as if he had cull'd the heart-felt satisfaction of both *parents*.

The word *happy* echoed from every mouth; each sentence began and ended with it.—What the heart feels is seldom to be disguised.—Grief will speak,—if not by the tongue, it will out;—it hangs on the features, sallows the skin, withers the sinews, and is a galling weight that pulls towards the ground.—Why should a thought of grief intrude at this time?—Is not my dear Lady Mary's health returning?——Is not felicity restor'd to this family?——Now will my regret at parting be lessened;—now shall I leave every individual with minds perfectly at ease.

Mr. Powis is expected in less than a month, intending to embark in the next ship after the Packet.—How I long to see him!——But it is very unlikely I should; I shall certainly have taken my leave of this place before he arrives.—By your Ladyship's permission, I hope to look in upon them, at our return to England.

What genteel freedoms men give themselves after *declaring off*, as Miss Winter calls it?—I had never so many fine things said to me before;—I can't tell how many;—quite a superabundance;—and before Sir James *too!*—But no notice is taken; he has cleared himself of all suspicion.—He may go to town as soon as he will.——His business is done;—yes, he did it yesterday.

I wish I may not laugh out in the midst of his fine speeches.
——

I wish your Ladyship could see this cool attention I give him.—But I have nettled him to the truth this afternoon:—his pride was alarm'd;—it could certainly proceed from *no other* cause, after he has *declared off*.

I was sitting at the tea-table, a trouble I always take from Lady Powis, who with Sir James was walking just without the windows, when Lord Darcey open'd the door, and said, advancing towards me with affected airs of admiration,—How proud should I be to see my house and table so graced!—Then leaning over the back of my chair, Well, my angel! how is the bad arm? Come, let me see, attempting to draw off my glove.

Oh! quite well, my Lord; withdrawing my hand carelessly.

For heaven's sake, take more care of yourself, Miss Warley; this might have been a sad affair.

Depend on that, my Lord, for my own sake.

For your *own sake!* Not in consideration of any other person?

Yes; of *Lady Mary Sutton, Sir James* and *Lady Powis, good Mr. Jenkings* and *his wife,* who I know would be concerned was I to suffer much from any accident.

Then there is no *other* person you would wish to preserve your life for?

Not that I know at present, my Lord.

Not that you know at *present!* so you think you may one day or *other?*

I pretend not, my Lord, to answer for what *may* happen; I have never seen the *person* yet. I was going to say something further, I have really forgot what, when he turn'd from me, and walked up and down the room with a seeming discomposure.

If you are sincere in what you have said, *Miss Warley; if* you are *really* sincere, I do pronounce——Here he burst open the door, and flew out the instant Sir James and Lady Powis entered.

When the tea was made, a footman was sent to Lord Darcey; but he was no where to be found.

This is very strange, said her Ladyship; Lord Darcey never used to be out of the way at tea-time. I declare I am quite uneasy; perhaps he may be ill.

Oh! cry'd Sir James, don't hurry yourself; I warrant he is got into one of his old reveries, and forgets the time.

I was quite easy. I knew his abrupt departure was nothing but an air:——an air of consequence, I suppose.——However, I was willing to be convinced, so did not move till I saw the Gentleman sauntering up the lawn. As no one perceived him but myself, I slid out to the housekeeper, and told her, if her Lady enquir'd for me, I was gone home to write Letters by to-morrow's post.

You have enough of it now, I believe, my dear Lady; two long letters by the same packet:—but you are the repository of my joy, my grief, the very inmost secrets of my soul.——You, my dear Lady, have the whole heart of

F. WARLEY.

★ ★ ★

LETTER XVIII.

Lord DARCEY to the Honourable GEORGE MOLESWORTH.

Barford Abbey.

RUIN'D and undone, as I hope for mercy!—undone too by my own egregious folly!——She is quite lost,—quite out of my power.—I wish Lord Allen had been in the bottom of the sea;—he can never make me amends;—no, if he was to die to-morrow and leave me his whole fortune.—

I told you he was to dine here yesterday.——I cannot be circumstantial.—He did dine here;——to my utter sorrow he did.

Oh what a charming morning I spent!—Tho' my angel persisted in going to France, yet it was in a manner that made me love her, if possible, ten thousand times more than ever.—Good God! had you seen how she look'd!—But no matter now;—I must forget her angelical sweetness.——Forget did I say?——No, by heaven and earth——she lives in every corner of my heart.—I wish I had told her my whole soul.—I was going to tell her, if I had not been interrupted.—It is too late now.—She would not hear me: I see by her manners she would not hear me. She has learnt to look with indifference:—even smiles with indifference.—Why does she not frown? That would be joy to what her smiles afford.—I hate such smiles; they are darts dipp'd in poison.—

Lord Allen said he heard I was going to be marry'd:—*What was that to him?*—Sir James look'd displeased. To quiet *his* fears I assured *him*—God! I know not what I assured him——something very foreign from my heart.

She blushed when Sir James asked, to whom?—With what raptures did I behold her blushes!—But she shrunk at my answer.——I saw the colour leave her cheek, like a rose-bud fading beneath the hoary frost.

I *will* know my fate.—I will be with you in a few days,—if Sir James should consent.—*What if he should consent?*—She is steeled against my vows—my protestations;——my words affect her not;—the most tender assiduities are disregarded:—she seems to attend to what I say, yet regards it not.

Where are those looks of preference fled,—those expressive looks?—I saw them not till now:—it is their loss,—it is their sad reverse that tells me what they were. She turns not her head to follow my foot-steps at parting;—or when I return, does not proclaim it by advancing pleasure tip-toe to the windows of her soul.—No anxiety for my health! No, she cares not what becomes of me.—I complain'd of my head, said I was in great pain;—heaven knows how true! My complaints were disregarded.—I attended her home. She sung all the way; or if she talked, it was of music:—not a word of *my poor head*;—no charges to draw the glasses up going back.[1]

There was a time, Molesworth—there was a time, if my finger had but ached, it was, My Lord, you look ill. Does not Lady Powis persuade you to have advice? You are really too careless of your health.

Shall she be *another's?*—Yes; when I shrink at sight of what lies yonder,—my sword, George;—that shall prevent her ever being *another's.*

---

1 Raise the coach windows so that the driver cannot hear what is said. Keeping the windows down signals there will be no private conversation.

Tell me you believe she will be mine:—it may help to calm my disturbed mind.—Be sure you do not hint she will be *another's*.

Have I told you, Mr. Powis is coming home?—I cannot recollect whether I have or not;—neither can I pain myself to look back.

All the world has something to comfort them, but your poor friend.—Every thing wears the face of joy, till I turn my eyes inwards:—*there it is* I behold the opposite;—*there it is* where Grief has fix'd her abode.—Does the fiend ever sleep? Will she be composed by ushering in the happy prospects of others?—Yes, I will feel joy.—Joy did I say? Joy I cannot feel.—Satisfaction then?—Satisfaction likewise is forbid to enter.—What then will possess my mind, on recollecting peace is restor'd, where gratitude calls for such large returns?—I'll pray for them;—I'll pray for a continuance of their felicity.—I'll pray, if they have future ills in store, they may light on the head of Darcey.——Yes, he can bear more yet:—let the load be ever so heavy, he will stoop to take up the burthen of his friends;——such friends as Sir James and Lady Powis have been to

DARCEY.

LETTER XIX.

The Honourable GEORGE MOLESWORTH
to LORD DARCEY.

London.

WELL, give me the first salute of your fair bride;—*and for your bride* I'll ensure Miss Warley.——Why there is not a symptom but is in your favour.—She is nettled; can't you perceive it?—Once a studied disregard takes place, we are safe:—nothing will hurt you now, my Lord.——

You have been stuttering falsehoods.—From what I can gather, you have been hushing the Baronet at the expence of your own and Miss Warley's quiet.—If you have, never mind it; things may not be the worse.—Come away, I advise you; set out immediately.—See how she looks at parting.—But don't distress her;—

I charge you not to distress her.——Should you play back her own cards, I will not answer for the pride of the sex.——

Sir James's consent once gained, and she rejects your proposals, lay all your letters to me on the subject before her.—I have them by me.—These cannot fail of clearing every doubt; she will be convinced then how sincerely you have loved her.—

You surprise me concerning Mr. Powis:—I thought he was settled in his government for life;—or rather, for the life of his father.—However, I am convinced his coming over will be no bad thing for you;—he has suffered too much from avarice, not to assist another so hardly beset.—

Was not his settling abroad an odd affair!—If he determined to remain single till he had an opportunity of pleasing himself, why did he leave England?—The mortification could not be great to have his overtures refused, where they were made with such indifference.——

As he has lived so many years a batchelor, I suppose there will be now an end to that great family.—

What a leveller is avarice! How does it pull down by attempting to raise? How miserable, as Seneca says, in the desire?—how miserable in attaining our ends?—The same great man alledges, that as long as we are solicitous for the increase of wealth, we lose the true use of it; and spend our time in putting out, calling in, and passing our accounts, without any substantial benefit, either to the world, or to ourselves.——[1]

If you had ever any uneasiness on Bridgman's account, it must be now at an end.—Married, and has brought his bride to town.—What a false fellow!—From undoubted authority, I am assured the writings have been drawn six months:——so that every thing must be concluded between him and his wife, at the very time he talked to me of Miss Warley.—I wash my hands from any further acquaintance with concealed minds:—there must be something very bad in a heart which has a dark cloud drawn

---

1 From Roman Stoic philosopher Seneca's *De Beata Vita* [On the Happy Life] (c. 58 CE), Book XII.

before it.—Virtue and innocence need no curtain:—they were sent to us naked;—it is their loss, or never possessing them,—that makes caution necessary, to hide from the world their destined place of abode.—Without entering a house, and being conversant with its inhabitants, how is it possible to say, if they are worthy or unworthy:——so if you knock, and are not admitted, you still remain doubtful.—But I am grown wise from experience;—and shall judge, for the future, where a heart is closely shut up, there is nothing in it worth enquiring after.

I go on Thursday to meet Risby, and conduct him to town. It would give us great joy, at our return, to shake you by the hand. ——What can avail your staying longer in the midst of doubts, perplexities, racks, tortures, and I know-not-what. Have you any more terms to express the deadly disorder?——If you have keep them to yourself; I want not the confounded list compleat:—no, no, not I; faith.——

I go this evening to see the new play, which is at present a general subject of conversation.——Now, was I a vain fellow—a boaster— would I mention four or six of the prettiest women about town, and swear I was to escort them.——Being a lover of truth, I confess I shall steal alone into an upper box, to fix my attention on the performance of the piece.——Perhaps, after all is over, I may step to the box of some sprightly, chatty girl, such as lady ****,—hear all the scandal of the town, ask her opinion of the play, hand her to her chair, and so home, to spend a snug evening with Sir Edward Ganges, who has promised to meet me here at ten.

Yours,

MOLESWORTH.

* * *

LETTER XX.

Lady MARY SUTTON to Miss WARLEY.

German Spaw.

NO, my dear, *Lord Darcey* is not the man he appears.—— What signifies a specious outside, if within there's a narrow heart?——Such must be his, to let a virtuous love sit imprisoned in secret corners, when it delights to dwell in open day.

Perhaps, if he knew my intentions, all concealments would be thrown aside, and he glory to declare what at present he meanly darkly hints.——By my consent, you should never give your hand to one who can hold the treasures of the mind in such low estimation.

When you mention'd your happy situation, the friendly treatment of Sir James and Lady Powis, I was inclined to think for *many* reasons, it would be wrong to take you from them;——now I am convinced, the pain *that* must occasion, or the danger in crossing the sea, is not to be compared to what you might suffer in your *peace* by remaining where you are.——When people of Lord Darcey's rank weigh long a matter of this nature, it is seldom the scale turns of the right side;—therefore, let not *Hope*, my dear child, flatter you out of your affections.

Do not think you rest in security:—tender insinuations from a man such as you describe Lord Darcey, may hurt your quiet.

I speak not from experience;—Nature, by cloathing me in her plainest garb, has put all these hopes and fears far from me.

I have been ask'd, it is true, often, for my fortune;——at least, I look upon asking for my heart to be the same thing.—Sure, I could never be such a fool to part with the latter, when I well knew it was requested only to be put in possession of the former!

You think Jenkings suspects his son has a *too* tender regard for you;—*you* think he is uneasy on that account.——Perhaps he is uneasy;—but time will convince you his suspicions, his uneasiness, proceed not from the *cause you imagine.*——He is a good man; you cannot think too well of him.

I hope this letter will find you safe return'd to Hampshire. I am preparing to leave the Spaw with all possible expedition: I should quit it with reluctance, but for the prospect of visiting it again next summer, with my dear Fanny.

At Montpelier[1] the winter will slide on imperceptibly: many agreeable families will there join us from the Spaw, whose good-humour and chearful dispositions, together with plentiful draughts of the Pouhon Spring, have almost made me forget the last ten years I have dragg'd on in painful sickness.

The family in which I have found most satisfaction, is Lord Hampstead's:—every way calculated to make themselves and others happy;——such harmony is observed through the whole, that the mechanism of the individuals seem to be kept in order by one common wheel.——I rejoice that I shall have an opportunity of introducing you to them.—We have fixed to set out the same day for Montpelier.

Lady Elizabeth, the eldest daughter, has obligingly offer'd to travel in my coach, saying, she thought it would be dull for me to go alone.

It is impossible to say which of the two sisters, was it left to my choice, would be my companion, as both are superlatively pleasing.——They possess, to a degree, what I so much admire in our sex;—a peculiar softness in the voice and manner; yet not quite so sprightly, perhaps, as may be thought necessary for some misses started up in this age; but sufficient, I think, for those who keep within certain bounds.—It requires an uncommon share of understanding, join'd with a great share of wit, to make a very lively disposition agreeable. I allow, if these two ingredients are happily blended, none can chuse but admire, as well as be entertain'd with, such natural fine talents:——on the contrary, where one sees a pert bold girl apeing such rare gifts, it is not only the most painful, but most absurd sight on earth.

Lady Elizabeth, and her amiable sister Sophia strive to hide every perfection they possess;——yet these I have just mention'd, with all others, will on proper occasions, make their appearance through a croud of blushes.——This timidity proceeds partly from nature,—partly from the education they have received under the best of mothers, whose tenderness for them would not suffer her to assign that momentous task to any but herself;

---

1 Montpellier, a popular resort for invalids. Lady Mary plans to leave "Spaw" and travel to Montpellier in the south of France, where she expects Fanny to join her.

fearing, as she has often told me, they would have had a thousand faults overlook'd by another, which her eye was ever on the watch to discover. She well knew the most trivial might be to them of the worst consequence:—when they were call'd to an account for what was pass'd, or warn'd how to avoid the like for the future, her manner was so determin'd and persuasive, as if she was examining her own conscience, to rectify every spot and blemish in it.

Though Lady Hampstead's fondness for her daughters must cause her to admire their good qualities, like a fine piece of perspective, whose beauties grow upon the eye,——yet she has the art not only to conceal her admiration, but, by the ascendency her tenderness has gain'd, she keeps even from themselves a knowledge of those perfections.—To this is owing the humility which has fortified their minds from the frequent attacks flattery makes against the unstable bulwarks of title and beauty.

Matchless as these sisters appear, they are to be equalled in their own, as well as the other sex.—I hope you will allow it in *one*, when you see Lord Hallum: he is their brother as much by *virtue* as *birth*.—I could find in my heart to say a thousand things of this fine youth;——but that I think such subjects flow easier from a handsome young woman than a plain old one.—Yet don't be surpriz'd;——unaccountable things happen every day;—if I *should* lend a favourable ear to this Adonis![1]—Something whispers me I shall receive his proposals.—An excuse, on these occasions, is never wanting; mine will be a good one:—that, at my death, you may be left to the protection of this worthy Lord.—— But, first, I must be assured you approve of him in that light;— being so firmly attach'd to my dear Fanny, to your happiness, my Love, that the wish of contributing to it is the warmest of your ever affectionate

M. SUTTON.

★ ★ ★

---

1 In Greek mythology, the beautiful mortal lover of the goddess Aphrodite.

LETTER XXI.

Lord DARCEY to the Hon. GEORGE MOLESWORTH.

Barford Alley.

FIVE days more, and I am with you.——Saturday morning!—Oh that I may support the hour of trial with fortitude!—I tremble at the thought;—my blood freezes in my veins, when I behold the object I am to part from.—

I try in vain to keep out of her sight:—if I attempt to leave the room where she is, my resolutions are baffled before I reach the door.——Why do I endeavour to inflict so hard a penance! —Because I foolishly suppose it would wean me.—Wean me *from what?*—From virtue.—No, Molesworth, it is not *absence*; ——it is not time itself can deaden the exalted image;—it neither sickens or dies, it blooms to immortality.

Was I only to be parted from beauty, *that* I might meet again in every town and village.——I want you to force me from the house.—Suppose I get up early, and slip away without taking leave.——But that will not do;—Sir James is ceremonious;— Lady Powis may deem it disrespect;—above all, Miss Warley, *that dear, dear Miss Warley,*——if *she* should think me wanting in regard, all then must be at an end.

Ha! Sir James yonder on the terrace, and alone! Let me examine his countenance:—I see no clouds;—this is the time, if ever!—Miss Warley not yet come up from Jenkings's!—If successful, with what transports shall I run to fetch her!—*Yes, I will* venture;—*I will* have one trial, as I hope for mercy.——

*

As I hope for mercy, I see, were my last words.—I do indeed hope for it, but never from Sir James.

Still perplexed;—still miserable!—

I told you Miss Warley was not come from Jenkings's; but how I started, when I saw her going to Lady Powis's dressing-room!

I was hurried about her in a dream, last night.—I thought I had lost her:—I hinted it when we met;—that moment I fancied she eyed me with regard;—she spoke *too* in a manner very different from what she has done some days past.—Then I'll swear it,—for it was not illusion, George,—her whole face had something of a sweet melancholy spread over it;—a kind of resignation in her look;—a melting softness that droop'd on her cheek:—I felt what it expressed;——it fir'd my whole frame;—it sent me to Sir James with redoubled eagerness.

I found him thoughtful and complaisant: we took several turns, before I could introduce my intended subject; when, talking of my setting out, I said, Now I have an opportunity, Sir James, perhaps I may not have another before I go, I should be glad of your sentiments in regard to my settling in life.—

How do you mean, my Lord; as to the choice of a wife?——

Why, I think, Sir, there's no other way of settling to one's satisfaction.

To be sure, it is very necessary your Lordship should consider on those matters,—especially as you are the last of a noble family:—when, you do fix, I hope it will be *prudently.*

Prudently, Sir James! you may depend on it I will never settle my affections *imprudently.*

Well, but, my Lord, what are your notions of *prudence?*

Why, Sir, to make choice of a person who is virtuous, sensible, well descended.——*Well descended Jenkings has assured me she is.*

You say nothing, my Lord, of what is *most* essential to happiness;—nothing of the *main point.*

Good-nature, I suppose you mean:—I would not marry an ill-natur'd woman, Sir James, for the world.

And is good-nature, with those you have mention'd, the only requisites?

I think they are the chief, Sir.

You and I differ much, my Lord.—Your father left his estate encumbered;[1] it is not yet clear; you are of age, my Lord: pray, spare yourself the trouble of consulting me, if you do not think of *fortune.*

Duty to the memory of my rever'd father, the affection and gratitude I owe you, Sir James, calls for my obedience:—without *your* sanction, Sir, never shall my hand be given.

He seem'd pleas'd: I saw tears starting to his eyes; but still he was resolv'd to distress me.

Look about you, my child; look about you, Darcey;—there's Lady Jane Marshly, Miss Beaden, or——and was going on.

Pardon me, Sir James, for interrupting you; but really, I cannot take any Lady on recommendation: I am very difficult, perhaps *perverse* in this point; my first attachment must be merely accidental.[2]

Ah! these are the notions that ruin half the young fellows of this age.——*Accidental likings—First love,*—and the devil knows what, runs away with half the old family estates.—Why, the least thing men ought to expect, even if they marry for *love*, is sixpence for a *shilling.*[3]—Once for all, my Lord, I must tell you, your interest is to be consulted before your inclinations.

Don't be ruffled, Sir James; *don't* let us talk warmly of a matter which perhaps is at a great distance.

I wish it may be at a *great distance*, my Lord.—*If what I conjecture is true*——Here he paus'd, and look'd so sternly, that I expected all would out.

---

1 In debt.

2 "My first love-connection must simply happen, come of its own accord," rather than being planned and contrived. Darcey is trying to resist the tradition of arranged marriage, a custom which has already affected Sir James's son. Sir James contemptuously connects "Accidental likings—First love,—and the devil knows what" as follies dangerous to the estate.

3 Twelve pence make one shilling; the match is a financial loser.

What do you *conjecture*, Sir?—Yes, I ask'd him what.—

Your Lordship must excuse my answering that question. *I hope*
I am wrong;—*I hope* such a thing never enter'd your thoughts:—
if it has—and he mutter'd something I could not understand;
only I heard distinctly the words *unlucky,——imprudent,——
unforeseen.——*I knew enough of their meaning to silence me.—
Shaking him by the hand, I said, Well, Sir James, if you please, we
will drop this subject for the present.—On which the conversation ended.

What a deal of patience and philosophy am I master of, to be
here at my pen, whilst two old men are sucking in the honey
which I should lay up for a winter's store?—Like Time, nothing
can stand before her:—she mows down all ages.—Even Morgan,
that man who us'd to look on a fine woman with more indifference than a horse or dog,—is now new-moulded;—not one oath
in the space where I have known twenty escape him:—instead of
following his dogs the whole morning, he is eternally with the
ladies.

If he rides out with my angel, for he's determin'd, he says, to
make her a complete horsewoman, I must not presume to give
the least direction, or *even* touch the bridle.

I honour him for the tender regard he shews her:—yes, I go
further; *he* and *Mr. Watson* may *love* her;—they do *love* her, and
glory in declaring it.——I *love* them in return;—but they are the
only two, of all the race of batchelors within my knowledge, that
should make *such* a declaration with impunity.

Let me see: I shall be in London Saturday evening;—Sunday,
no post;—Monday, *then* I determine to write to Sir James;—
Wednesday, I may have an answer;—*Thursday,*—who knows but
Thursday!—nothing is impossible; who knows but *Thursday* I
may return to all my hopes?——How much I resemble a shut-
tlecock![1] how am I thrown from side to side by hope and fear;
now up, now down; no sooner mounted by one hand than
lower'd by another!

---

1 The object hit back and forth in badminton.

This moment a gleam of comfort steals sweetly through my heart;—but it is gone even before I could bid it welcome.—Why so fast!—to what spot is it fled?—Can there be a wretch more in need, who calls louder for its charitable ray than

DARCEY.

LETTER XXII.

Miss WARLEY to Lady MARY SUTTON.

From Mr. Jenkings's.

NOW, my dear Lady, the time is absolutely fix'd for our embarkation; the 22d, without fail.—Mr. Smith intends coming himself, to accompany me to London.—How very good and obliging this!—I shall say nothing of it to Lady Powis, till Lord Darcey is gone, which will be Saturday:—*he* may go to France, if he pleases, but not with *me.*——

When I received Mrs. Smith's letter, he was mighty curious to know who it was from:—I found him examining the seal,[1] as it lay on the table in Mr. Jenkings's parlour.—Here is a letter for you, Miss Warley, a good deal confus'd.——So I see, my Lord: I suppose from Lady Mary Sutton.

I fancy not;—it does not appear to be directed in the same hand with that my servant brought you last from the post-office.—I broke the seal; it was easy to perceive the contents gave me pleasure.

There is something, Miss Warley, which gives you particular satisfaction.

You are right, my Lord, I never was better pleas'd.

Then it is from Lady Mary?

No, not from Lady Mary.

---

1   Wax pressed to close a letter, usually carrying the emblem of the sender. Seals were supposed to protect the privacy of letters, which could not be opened without breaking the wax.

From Mrs. Smith, *then?*—Do I guess *now?*—You say nothing; oh, there it is.—I could not forbear smiling.

Pray tell me, only *tell me,* and he caught one of my hands, if this letter does not fix the *very* day of your setting out for France?

I thought him possest with the spirit of divination.——What could I do, in this case?—Falshoods I despise;—evasions are low, *very* low, indeed:—yet I knew he ought not to be trusted with the contents, even at the expence of my veracity.—I recollected myself, and looked grave.

My Lord, you must excuse me; this affair concerns only myself; even Lady Powis will not be acquainted with it yet.

I have done, if Lady Powis is not to be acquainted with it.—I have no right;—I say *right.*—Don't look so, Miss Warley—*I believe I did stare a little*—Time will unfold,—will cast a different light on things from that in which you now see them.

I was confus'd;—I put up my letter, went to the window, took a book from thence, and open'd it, without knowing what I did.

The Complete Pocket-Farrier; or, A Cure for all Disorders in Horses, read his Lordship aloud, looking over my shoulder; for such was the title of the book.[1]

What have you here, my love?

My love, indeed! Mighty free, mighty free, was it not, my Lady? I could not avoid laughing at the drollery of this accident, or I should have given him the look he deserved.——I thank God I am come to a state of *indifference;* and my time here is so short, I would willingly appear as little reserv'd as possible, that he might not think I have chang'd my sentiments since his *declaring off:* though I must own I have; but my pride will not suffer me to betray it to him.

---

1 The book Fanny picks up is a do-it-yourself book for the care of horses, highly typical of the kind of reading matter to be found in what Bernard Shaw (1856–1950) calls "Horseback Hall," the home of country gentry.

If he has distress'd me,—if he has led my heart a little astray,—I am recovered now:—I have found out my mistake.—Should I suffer my eye to drop a tear, on looking back, for the future it will be more watchful;—it will guard, it will protect the poor wanderer.

He is very busy settling his affairs with Sir James:——three hours were they together with Mr. Jenkings in the library;—his books all pack'd up and sent away, to be sure he does not intend returning *here* again soon.

I suppose he will settle;—he talks of new furnishing his house;—has consulted Lady Powis upon it.—If he did not intend marrying, if he had no Lady in his eye——

But what is all this to me? Can he or his house be of any consequence to my repose?—I enjoy the thoughts of going to France without him:—I suppose he will think me very sly, but no matter.—

That good-natur'd creature Edmund would match me to a prince, was it in his power.—He told me, yesterday, that he'd give the whole world, if I was not to go to France.—Why so, Edmund?—I shall see you again, said I, at my return to England.

Ay, but what will *somebody* do, in the mean time?

Who is *somebody?*

Can't you guess, Miss Warley?

I do guess, Edmund. But you was never more mistaken; the person you mean is not to be distress'd by *my* absence.

He is, upon my honour;—I know *he is.*—Lord Darcey loves you to distraction.

Poh! Edmund; don't take such things into your head: I know *you* wish me well; but don't be so sanguine!—Lord Darcey stoop to think of *me!*

Stoop to think of *you*, Miss Warley!——I am out of all patience: stoop to think of *you!*—I shall never forget *that.*——

Greatly as I honour his Lordship, if he conceals his sentiments, if he trifles in an affair of such importance,——was he the first duke in the kingdom, I hold him below the regard even of such a one as *I* am.——Pardon my curiosity, madam, I mean no ill; but surely he has made proposals to you.

Well, then, I will tell you, Edmund;—I'll tell you frankly, he never *has* made proposals:—and further, I can answer for him, he never *will*.—His belief was stagger'd;—he stood still, his eyes fixed on the ground.

Are you *really* in earnest, Miss Warley?

Really, Edmund.

Then, for heaven's sake, go to France.—But how can you tell, madam, he never intends to make proposals?

On which I related what passed at table, the day Lord Allen dined at the Abbey.—Nothing could equal his astonishment; yet would he fain have persuaded me that I did not understand him;—call'd it misapprehension, and I know not what.

He *will* offer you his hand, Miss Warley; he certainly *will*.—— I've known him from a school-boy;—I'm acquainted with every turn of his mind;—I know his very looks;—I have observ'd them when they have been directed to you:—he will, I repeat,—he will offer you his hand.

No! Edmund:—but if he *did*, his overtures should be disregarded.

Say not so, Miss Warley; for God's sake, say not so again;—— it kills me to think you *hate* Lord Darcey.

I speak to you, Edmund, as a friend, as a brother:—never let what has pass'd escape your lips.

If I do, madam, what must I deserve?—To be shut out from your confidence is a punishment only fit for such a breach of trust.—But, for heaven's sake, do not *hate* Lord Darcey.

Mr. Jenkings appeared at this juncture, and look'd displeas'd.—How strangely are we given to mistakes!—I betray'd the same confusion, as if I had been really carrying on a clandestine affair with his son.—In a very angry tone he said, I thought, Edmund, you was to assist me, knowing how much I had on my hands, before Lord Darcey sets out;——but I find business is not *your* pursuit:—I believe I must consent to your going into the army, after all.—On which he button'd up his coat, and went towards the Abbey, leaving me quite thunderstruck. Poor Edmund was as much chagrined as myself.—A moment after I saw Mr. Jenkings returning with a countenance very different,— and taking me apart from his son, said, I cannot forgive myself, my dear young Lady;—can you forgive me for the rudeness I have just committed?——I am an old man, Miss Warley;—I have many things to perplex me;—I should *not*,—I know I should not, have spoke so sharply to Edmund, when you had honour'd him with your company.

I made him easy by my answer; and since I have not seen a cloud on his brow.—I shall never think more, with concern, of Mr. Jenkings's suspicions.—Your Ladyship's last letter,—oh! how sweetly tender! tells me *he* has *motives* to which *I* am a stranger.

We spent a charming day, last Monday, at Lord Allen's. Most of the neighbouring families were met there, to commemorate the happy festival.—Mr. Morgan made one of the party, and return'd with us to the Abbey, where he proposes waiting the arrival of his godson, Mr. Powis.——If I have any penetration, most of his fortune will center *there*,——For my part, I am not a little proud of stealing into his good graces:—I don't know for what, but Lady Powis tells me, I am one of his first favourites; he has presented me a pretty little grey horse, beautifully caparison'd; and hopes, he says, to make me a good horsewoman.

As I have promis'd to be at the Abbey early, I shall close this letter; and, if I have an opportunity, will write another by the same packet.—Believe me ever, my dearest Lady, your most grateful and affectionate

F. WARLEY.

END OF THE FIRST VOLUME.

BARFORD ABBEY,

A NOVEL:

IN A

SERIES of LETTERS.

IN TWO VOLUMES.

VOL. II.

LONDON:

Printed for T. CADELL, (Successor to Mr. MILLAR) in the
Strand; and J. PAYNE, in Paternoster-Row.

MDCCLXVIII.

LETTER XXIII.

Miss WARLEY to Lady MARY SUTTON.

From Mr. Jenkings's.

O H what a designing man is Lord Darcey!——He loves me not, yet fain would persuade me that he does.——When I went yesterday morning to the Abbey, I met him in my way to Lady Powis's dressing-room.——Starting as if he had seen an apparition, and with a look which express'd great importance, he said, taking my hand, Oh! Miss Warley, I have had the most dreadful night!—but I hope *you* have rested well.

I have rested very well, my Lord; what has disturb'd your Lordship's rest?

What, had it been *real* as it was *visionary,* would have drove me to madness.—I dreamt, Miss Warley,——I dreamt every thing I was possess'd of was torn from me;—but now—*and here stopt.*

Well, my Lord, and did not the pleasure of being undeceiv'd overpay all the pain which you had been deceiv'd into?

No, my angel!——Why does he call me his angel?

Why, no: I have such a sinking, such a load on my mind, to reflect it is possible,—only possible it might happen, that, upon my word, it has been almost too much for me.

Ah! my Lord, you are certainly wrong to anticipate evils; they come fast enough, one need not run to meet them:——besides, if your Lordship had been in reality that very unfortunate creature, you dreamt you were, for no rank or degree is proof against the caprice of Fortune,—was nothing to be preserv'd entire?—— Fortune can require only what she gave: fortitude, peace, and resignation, are not her gifts.

Oh! Miss Warley, you mistake: it was not riches I fancied myself dispossess'd of;—it was, oh my God!——what my peace, my *very* soul is center'd in!——and his eyes turn'd round with so wild a stare, that really I began to suspect his head.[1]

I trembled so I could scarce reach the dressing-room, though just at the door.—The moment I turn'd from him, he flew like lightning over the stairs; and soon after, I saw him walking with Sir James on the terrace. By their gestures I could discover their conversation was not a common one.

Mr. Morgan comes this instant in sight;—a servant after him, leading my little horse.—I am sorry to break off, but I must attend him;—he is so good, I know your Ladyship would be displeas'd, was I to prolong my letter at the expence of his favour.— Yours, my much honour'd,—my much lov'd Lady,——with all gratitude, with all affection,

F. WARLEY.

LETTER XXIV.

Miss WARLEY to the same.

From Mr. Jenkings's.

NOW, my dearest Lady, am I again perplex'd, doubting, and embarrass'd:—yet Lord Darcey is gone,—gone this very morning,—about an hour since.

Well, I did not think it would evermore be in his power to distress me;——but I have been distress'd,—greatly distress'd!—I begin to think Lord Darcey sincere,—that he has always been sincere.—He talks of next *Thursday*, as a day to unravel great mysteries:—but I shall be far enough by that time; sail'd, perhaps.—Likely, he said, I might know before Thursday.—I wish any body could tell me:—I fancy Sir James and Lady Powis are in the secret.

Mr. Jenkings is gone with his Lordship to Mr. Stapleton's,— about ten miles this side London, on business of importance:— to-morrow he returns; then I shall acquaint him with my leaving this place.——Your Ladyship knows the motive why I have hith-

---

1 To think him mentally deranged, mad.

erto kept the day of my setting out a secret from every person,—even from Sir James and Lady Powis.

Yesterday, the day preceding the departure of Lord Darcey, I went up to the Abbey, determin'd to exert my spirits and appear chearful, cost what it would to a poor disappointed heavy heart.—Yes, it was disappointed:—but till then I never rightly understood its situation;—or perhaps would not understand it;—else I have not examin'd it so closely as I ought, of late.—Not an unusual thing neither: we often stop to enquire, what fine seat *that?*—whose magnificent equipage *this?*—long to see and converse with persons so surrounded with splendor;—but if one happen to pass a poor dark cottage, and see the owner leaning on a crutch at the door, we are apt to go by, without making any enquiry, or betraying a wish to be acquainted with its misery.——

This was my situation, when I directed my steps to the Abbey.—I saw not Lord Darcey in an hour after I came into the house;——when he join'd us, he was dress'd for the day, and in one hand his own hat, in the other mine, with my cloak, which he had pick'd up in the Vestibule:—he was dreadfully pale;—complain'd of a pain in his head, which he is very subject to;—said he wanted a walk;—and ask'd, if I would give him the honour of my company.—I had not the heart to refuse, when I saw how ill he look'd;—though for some days past, I have avoided being alone with him as much as possible.

We met Lady Powis returning from a visit to her poultry-yard.[1]—Where are my two runabouts going *now?* she said.——Only for a little walk, madam, reply'd Lord Darcey.

You are a sauce-box, said she, shaking him by the hand;—but don't go, my Lord, *too far* with Miss Warley, nodding and smiling on him at the same time.—She gave me a sweet affectionate kiss, as I pass'd her; and cried out, You are a couple of pretty strollers, are you not!—But away together; only I charge you, my Lord, calling after him, remember you are not to go *too far* with my dear girl.

---

1 Ladies of the manor, in the tradition of their forebears, often busied them-selves with keeping poultry, either simple domestic fowl for the table or more exotic new breeds.

We directed our steps towards the walk that leads to the Hermitage,[1] neither of us seeming in harmony of spirits.—His Lordship still complaining of his head, I propos'd going back before we had gone ten paces from the house.

Would Miss Warley then prevent me, said he, from the last satisfaction I might ever enjoy?—You don't know, madam, how long——it is impossible to say how long——if ever I should be so happy again——I look forward to Wednesday with impatience;—if that should be propitious,—*Thursday* will unravel *mysteries*; it will clear up *doubts*;—it will perhaps bring on an event which you, my dearest life, may in time reflect on with pleasure;—you, my dearest life!——pardon the liberty,—by heaven! I am sincere!

I was going to withdraw my hand from his: I can be less reserv'd when he is less free.

Don't take your hand from me;——I will call you Miss Warley;——I see my freedom is depleasing;——but don't take your hand away; for I was still endeavouring to get it away from him.

Yes, my angel, I will call you *Miss Warley*.

Talk not at this rate, my Lord: it is a kind of conversation I do not, nor wish to understand.

I see, madam, I am to be unhappy;—I know you have great reason to condemn me:—my whole behaviour, since I first saw you, has been one riddle.

Pray, my Lord, forbear this subject.

---

1 A picturesque structure that suggests a hermit's retreat. From the early eighteenth century it became increasingly fashionable to decorate the grounds of estates with such structures. A "hermit" is customarily seen as a pious person or repentant sinner engaged in solitary religious devotion in the wilderness. One landowner is supposed to have hired a man to act the part of the hermit on his grounds, but he found the job too lonely. The reference to the "hermitage" chimes in with the subtle—and partly secularized—religious themes of this abbey novel, including penance, patience, and rebirth.

No! if I never see you more, Miss Warley,——this is my wish that you think the worst of me that appearances admit;—think I have basely wish'd to distress you.

Distress me, my Lord?

Think so, I beseech you, if I never return.—What would the misfortune be of falling low, even to the most abject, in your opinion, compared with endangering the happiness of her whole peace is my ardent pursuit?—If I fail, I only can tell the cause:— you shall never be acquainted with it;—for should you regard me even with pity,—cool pity,—it would be taking the dagger from my own breast, and planting it in yours.

Ah! my Lady, could I help understanding him?——could I help being moved?—I was moved;—my eyes I believe betrayed it.

If I return, continued he, it is you only can pronounce me happy.—If you see me not again, think I am tost on the waves of adverse fortune:—but oh think I again intreat *you*,—think me guilty. Perhaps I may outlive—no, that will never do;—you will be happy long before that hour;——it would be selfish to hope the contrary. I *wish* Mr. Powis was come home;—I *wish*—All my *wishes* tend to one great end.—Good God, what a situation am I in!—That the Dead could hear my petitions!——that he could absolve me!—What signifies, whether one sue to remains crumbled in the dust, or to the ear which can refuse to hear the voice of reason?

I thought I should have sunk to see the agony he was work'd up to.—I believe I look'd very pale;—I felt the blood thrill through my veins, and of a sudden stagnate:—a dreadful sickness follow'd;—I desir'd to sit;——he look'd on every side, quite terrified;——cry'd, Where will you sit, my dearest life?——what shall I do?—For heaven's sake speak;—speak but one word;—speak to tell me, I have not been your murderer.

I attempted to open my mouth, but in vain; I pointed to the ground, making an effort to sit down:—he caught me in his arms, and bore me to a bench not far off;——there left me, to fetch some water at a brook near, but came back before he had gone ten steps.——I held out my hand to his hat, which lay on the ground, then look'd to the water.—Thank God!—thank God! he said, and went full speed, to dip up some:—he knelt down, trembling, before me;—his teeth chatter'd in his head whilst he offer'd the water.

I found myself beginning to recover the moment it came to my lips.—He fix'd his eyes on me, as if he never meant to take them off, holding both my hands between his, the tears running down his face, without the contraction of one feature.—If sorrow could be express'd in stone, he then appear'd the very statue which was to represent it.

I attempted to speak.

Don't speak yet, he cried;——don't make yourself ill again: thank heaven, you are better!—This is some sudden chill; why have you ventur'd out without clogs?[1]

How delicate,—how seasonable, this hint! Without it could I have met his eye, after the weakness I had betrayed?—We had now no more interesting subjects; I believe he thought I had *enough* of them.

It was near two when we reach'd the Abbey. Sir James and Mr. Morgan were just return'd from a ride;——Lady Powis met us on the Green, where she said she had been walking some time, in expectation of her strollers,—She examin'd my countenance very attentively, and then ask'd Lord Darcey, if he had remember'd her injunctions?

What reason, my Lady, have you to suspect the contrary? he returned—Well, well, said she, I shall find you out some day or other;—but her Ladyship seem'd quite satisfied, when I assured her I had been no farther than the Beech-walk.[2]

Cards were propos'd soon after dinner: the same party as usual.——Mr. Morgan is never ask'd to make one;—he says he would as soon see the devil as a card-table.—We kept close at it 'till supper.—I could not help observing his Lordship blunder'd a little;—playing a diamond for a spade,—and a heart for a

---

1 Without thick-soled shoes, or more likely "without pattens."
2 "Beach-walk" in the original. A path winding among beech trees.

club,——I took my leave at eleven, and he attended me home.

Mr. and Mrs. Jenkings were gone to bed,—Edmund was reading in the parlour; he insisted on our having a negus[1] which going out to order, was follow'd by Lord Darcey:—I heard them whisper in the passage, but could distinguish the words, *if she is ill, remember, if she is ill*—and then Edmund answer'd, You may depend on it, my Lord,—as I have a soul to be saved:—does your Lordship suppose I would be so negligent?

I guess'd at this charge;——it was to write, if I should be ill, as I have since found by Edmund,—who return'd capering into the room, rubbing his hands, and smiling with such significance as if he would have said, Every thing is as it should be.

When his Lordship had wish'd us a good night, he said to me,—*To-morrow*, Miss Warley!——but I will say nothing of *to-morrow*;——I shall see you in the morning. His eyes glisten'd, and he left the room hastily.—Whilst Edmund attended him out, I went to my chamber that I might avoid a subject of which I saw his honest heart was full.

On my table lay the Roman History;[2] I could not help giving a peep where I had left off, being a very interesting part:—from one thing I was led to another, 'till the clock struck three; which alarm made me quit my book.

Whilst undressing, I had leisure to recollect the incidents of the pass'd day: sometimes pleasure, sometimes pain, would arise, from this examination;—yet the latter was most predominant.

When I consider'd Lord Darcey's tender regard for my future, as well as present peace,—how could I reflect on him without gratitude?—When I consider'd his perplexities, I thought thus:—they arise from some entanglement, in which his heart is not engag'd.—Had he confided in me, I should not have weaken'd his

---

1 Warm drink made of wine, brandy, lemon, and nutmeg.
2 Likely one of the volumes from Nathaniel Hooke's four-volume *Roman History, from the Building of Rome to the Ruin of the Commonwealth* (1738–71).

resolutions;——I would no more wish him to be guilty of a breach of honour, than surrender myself to infamy.——I would have endeavour'd to persuade him *she* is amiable, virtuous, and engaging.—If I had been successful, I would have *frown'd* when he *smil'd;*—I would have been *gay* when he seem'd *oppress'd;*—— I would have been *reserv'd, peevish, supercilious;*—in short, I would have counterfeited the very reverse of what was likely to draw him from a former attachment.

To live without him must be my fate; since that is almost inevitable, I would have strove to have secur'd his happiness, whilst mine had remain'd to chance.—These reflections kept me awake 'till six, when I fell into a profound sleep, which lasted 'till ten; at which time I was awaken'd by Mrs. Jenkings to tell me Lord Darcey was below; with an apology, that she had made breakfast, as her husband was preparing, in great haste, to attend his Lordship.

This was a hint he was not to stay long; so I put on my cloaths with expedition; and going down, took with me my whole stock of resolution; but I carried it no farther than the bottom of the stairs;——there it flew from me;—never have I seen it since:——that it rested not in the breast of Lord Darcey, was visible;——rather it seem'd as if his and mine had taken a flight together.

I stood with the lock of the door in my hand more than a minute, in hopes my inward flutterings would abate.——His Lordship heard my footstep, and flew to open it;—I gave him my hand, without knowing what I did;—joy sparkled in his eyes and he prest it to his breast with a fervour that cover'd me with confusion.

He saw what he had done;—he dropp'd it respectfully, and inquiring tenderly for my health, ask'd if I would honour him with my commands before he set out for Town?—What a fool was I!—Lord bless me!—can I ever forget my folly? What do you think, my Lady! I did not speak;—no! I could not answer;——I was *silent;*—I was *silent,* when I would have given the world for one word.——When I did speak, it was not to Lord Darcey, but, still all fool, turn'd and said to Mr. Jenkings, who was looking over a parchment, How do you find yourself, Sir? Will not the journey you are going to take on horseback be too fatiguing? No, no, my good Lady; it is an exercise I have all my life been us'd to: to-morrow you will see me return the better for it.

Mrs. Jenkings here enter'd, follow'd by a servant with the breakfast, which was plac'd before me, every one else having breakfasted.—She desir'd I would give myself the trouble of making tea, having some little matters to do without.—This task would have been a harder penance than a fast of three days;—but I must have submitted, had not my good genius Edmund appear'd at this moment; and placing himself by me, desir'd to have the honour of making my breakfast.

I carried the cup with difficulty to my mouth. My embarrassment was perceiv'd by his Lordship; he rose from his seat, and walk'd up and down.—How did his manly form struggle to conceal the disorder of his mind!——Every movement, every look, every word, discover'd Honour in her most graceful, most ornamental garb: *when* could it appear to such advantage, surrounded with a cloud of difficulties, yet shining out and towering above them all?

He laid his cold hand on mine;—with precipitation left the room;—and was in a moment again at my elbow.—Leaning over the back of my chair, he whisper'd, For heaven's sake, miss Warley, be the instrument of my fortitude; whilst I see you I cannot—there stopt and turn'd from me.—I saw he wish'd me to go first,—as much in compassion to myself as him. When his back was turn'd, I should have slid out of the room;—but Mr. Jenkings starting up, and looking at his watch, exclaim'd, *Odso*,[1] my Lord! it is past eleven; we shall be in the dark. This call'd him from his reverie; and he sprang to the door, just as I had reached it.—Sweet, generous creature! said he, stopping me; and you will go *then?*—Farewell, my Lord, replied I.——My dear, good friend, to Mr. Jenkings, take care of your health.——God bless you both!——My voice faulter'd.

Excellent Miss Warley! a thousand thanks for your kind condescension, said the good old man.——Yet one moment, oh

---

1 A declaration of surprise: a contraction of "God so" (as we might say "My God!").

God! yet one moment, said his Lordship; and he caught both my hands.

Come, my Lord, return'd Mr. Jenkings; and never did I see him look so grave, something of disappointment in his countenance;——come, my Lord, the day is wasting apace. Excuse this liberty:—your Lordship has been *long* determin'd,—have *long* known of leaving this country.—My dearest young Lady, you will be expected at the Abbey.—I shall, indeed, replied I;—so God bless you, Sir!—God bless you, my Lord! and, withdrawing my hands, hasten'd immediately to my chamber.

I heard their voices in the court-yard:—if I had look'd out at the window, it might not have been unnatural;—I own my inclinations led to it.—Inclination should never take place of prudence;—by following one, we are often plung'd into difficulties;—by the other we are sure to be conducted safely:——instead, then, of indulging my curiosity, to see how he look'd—how he spoke at taking leave of this dwelling;—whether his eyes were directed to the windows, or the road;—if he rid[1] slow or fast;—how often he turn'd to gaze, before he was out of sight:—instead of this, I went to Mrs. Jenkings's apartment, and remain'd there 'till I heard they were gone, then return'd to my own; since which I have wrote down to this period. Perhaps I should have ran on farther, if a summons from Lady Powis did not call me off. I hope now to appear before her with tolerable composure.——I am to go in the coach alone.—Well, it will seem strange!—I shall think of my *late* companion;—but time reconciles every thing.——*This* was my hope, when I lost my best friend, the lov'd instructress of my infant years.—*Time*, all healing *Time*! to *that* I fear I must look forward, as a lenitive against many evils.

Two days!—only two days!——and then, adieu, my dear friends at the Abbey;——adieu, my good Mr. and Mrs. Jenkings!—and you *too*, my friendly-hearted Edmund, adieu!

Welcome,——doubly welcome, every moment which brings me nearer to that when I shall kiss the hands of my honour'd Lady;—when I shall be able to tell you, in person, ten thousand things too much for my pen;—when you will kindly say, Tell me

---

1 Rode.

all, my Fanny, tell me every secret of your heart.—Happy
sounds!——pleasing sounds! these will be to your grateful and
affectionate]

F. WARLEY.

LETTER XXV.

Miss WARLEY to the same.

From Mr. Jenkings's.

NOW, my dear Lady, am I ready for my departure:——Sir
James and Lady Powis reconciled to my leaving them;——
yet how can I call it reconciled, when I tear myself from their
arms as they weep over me?——Heavens! how tenderly they love
me!—Their distress, when I told them the day was absolutely
fix'd; when I told them the necessity of my going, *their* distress
nothing could equal but my *own.*——I thought my heart would
have sunk within me!—Surely, my Lady, my affection for them is
not a common affection;—it is *such* as I bear your dear self;—it is
such as I felt for my revered Mrs. Whitmore.—I cannot dwell on
this subject—indeed I cannot.

I almost wish I had not kept the day so long a secret.—But
suppose I had not,—would their concern have been lessen'd?—

I would give the world, if Mr. Jenkings was come home:—his
wife is like a frantic woman; and declares, if I persist in going, I
shall break the heart of her and her husband.—Why do they love
me so well?—It cannot be from any deserts of mine:——I have
done no more than common gratitude demands;—the affection I
shew them is only the result of their own kindness.—Benevolent
hearts never place any thing to their own account:
——they look on returns as presents, not as just debts:—so,
whether giving or receiving, the glory must be their's.]

I fancy Mr. Smith will not be here 'till to-morrow, his Lady
having wrote me, he intended spending the evening with an
acquaintance of his about six miles from the Abbey.

How I dread the hour of parting!—Poor Mr. Watson!—I fear
I shall never see *him* more.—Mr. Morgan *too*! but he is likely to
live many years.—There is something in this strange man exces-

sively engaging⌐——If people have roughness, better to appear in the voice, in the air and dress, than in the heart: a want of softness *there*, I never can dispense with.—What is a graceful form, what are numberless accomplishments, without humanity? I love, I revere, the honest, plain, well-meaning Mr. Morgan.⌉

Hark! I hear the trampling of horses.—Mr. Jenkings is certainly return'd.—I hasten down to be the first who shall inform him of my departure.

How am I mortified to see Aaron return without his master!—Whilst Mrs. Jenkings was busied in enquiries after the health of her good man, I was all impatience for the contents of a letter she held in her hand, unopen'd: having broke the seal, and run her eye hastily over it, she gave it me.——I think my recollection will serve to send it verbatim to your Ladyship.

Mr. JENKINGS to Mrs. JENKINGS.

"My Dear,

I dispatch Aaron to acquaint you it is impossible for me to be home till Wednesday. Mr. Stapleton is gone to London: I am obliged to attend Lord Darcey thither. I love his Lordship *more* and *more*.—He has convinc'd me *our* conjectures were not without foundation.——Heaven grant it may end to *our* wishes!——There are, he thinks, difficulties to be overcome. Let him think it:—his happiness will be more exquisite when he is undeceiv'd.——Distribute my dutiful respects to Sir James, Lady Powis, and Miss Warley; next to yourself and our dear Edmund, they are nearest the heart of your truly affectionate husband

JENKINGS."

I will make no comments on this letter; it cannot concern *me*.—What can I do about seeing Mr. Jenkings before I go?——

Lord bless me! a chaise and four just stopp'd; Mr. Smith in it.——Heavens! how my heart throbs!—I did not expect him 'till to-morrow: I must run to receive him.—How shall I go up to the Abbey!—how support the last embrace of Sir James and Lady Powis!

Ten at Night, just come from the Abbey.
Torn in pieces!—my poor heart torn in pieces!—I shall never see them more;—never again be strain'd to their parental bosoms.——Forgive me, my dearest Lady, I do not grieve that I am coming to *you*; I grieve only that I go from *them*.—Oh God! why must my soul be divided?

Another struggle too with poor Mrs. Jenkings!—She has been on her knees:—yes, thus lowly has she condescended to turn me from my purpose, and suffer Mr. Smith to go back without me.——I blush to think what pain, what trouble I occasion.—She talks of some *important event* at hand. She says if I go, it will end in the destruction of us all.—What can she mean by an *important event?*—Perhaps Lord Darcey—but no matter; nothing, my dear Lady, shall with-hold me from you.— The good woman is now more calm. I have assured her it is uncertain how long we may be in London: it is only that has calm'd her.—She says, she is *certain* I shall return;—she is *certain*, when Mr. Powis and his Lady arrives, *I must* return. ——Next Thursday they are expected:—already are they arrived at Falmouth:[1]—but, notwithstanding what I have told Mrs. Jenkings, to soften her pains at parting, I shall by Thursday be on my voyage;—for Mr. Smith tells me the Packet will sail immediately.—Perhaps I may be the messenger of my own letters:——but I am determin'd to write on 'till I see you;—that when I look them over, my memory may receive some assistance.——Good night, my dearest Lady; Mrs. Jenkings and Mr. Smith expects me.

F. WARLEY.

LETTER XXVI.

Lord DARCEY to Sir JAMES POWIS.

London.

EVEN whilst I write, I see before me the image of my expiring father;—I hear the words that issued from his death-like lips;——my soul feels the weight of his injunctions;—*again* in my imagination I seal the sacred promise on his livid hand;——and

---

1 Port in Cornwall. From 1688, Falmouth was a Royal Mail Packet Station.

my heart bows before Sir James with all that duty which is indispensable from a child to a parent.

Happiness is within my reach, yet without *your* sanction I *will* not, *dare* not, bid it welcome;—I *will* not hold out my hand to receive *it.*——Yes, Sir, I love Miss Warley; I can no longer disguise my sentiments.—On the terrace I should not have disguis'd them, if your warmth had not made me tremble for the consequence.—You remember my arguments *then*; suffer me now to reurge *them.*

I allow it would be convenient to have my fortune augmented by alliance; but then it is not *absolutely* necessary I should make the purchase with my felicity.—A thousand chances may put me in possession of riches;—one event only can put me in possession of content.——Without *it,* what is a fine equipage?—what a splendid retinue?—what a table spread with variety of dishes?

Judge for me, Sir James; *you* who *know,* who *love* Miss Warley, judge for me.——Is it possible for a man of my turn to see her, to talk with her, to know her thousand *virtues,* and not wish to be united to them?——It is to your candour I appeal.—*Say* I *am* to be happy, *say* it only in one line, I come immediately to the Abbey, full of reverence, of esteem, of gratitude.

Think, dear Sir James, of Lady Powis;—think of the satisfaction you hourly enjoy with that charming woman; then will you complete the felicity of

DARCEY.

★★★

LETTER XXVII.

Sir JAMES POWIS to Lord DARCEY.

Barford Abbey.

I Am not much surpris'd at the contents of your Lordship's letter; it is *what* Lady Powis and I have long conjectur'd; yet I must tell, you, my Lord, notwithstanding Miss Warley's great merit, I should have been much better pleas'd to have found myself mistaken.

I claim no right to controul your inclinations: the strict observance you pay your father's last request, tempts me to give my
opinion very opposite to what I should otherwise have done.—
Duty like yours ought to be rewarded.—If you will content yourself with an incumber'd estate rather than a clear one, why—
why—why—faith you shall not have my approbation 'till you
come to the Abbey. Should you see the little bewitching Gipsy
before I talk with you, who knows but you may be wise enough
to make a larger jointure than you can afford?[1]

I am glad your Lordship push'd the matter no farther on the
terrace: I did not then know how well I lov'd our dear girl.—My
wife is *so* pleas'd,—*so* happy,—*so* overjoy'd,—at what she calls
your noble disinterested regard for her Fanny, that one would
think she had quite forgot the value of *money*.——I expect my son
to-morrow.—Let me have the happiness of embracing you at the
same time;—you are both my children, &c. &c.:

J. POWIS.

LETTER XXVIII.

Lord DARCEY to the Honourable GEORGE MOLESWORTH.

Barford Abbey.

FULL of joy! full of surprize! I dispatch a line by Robert.
——Fly, Molesworth, to Mr. Smith's, in *Bloomsbury-Square*:
——tell my dearest, dear Miss Warley, but tell her of it by degrees,
that Mr. Powis is her *father!*—Yes! her *father*, George;—and the
most desirable woman on earth, her mother!—Don't tell her of it

---

1 Sir James is thinking ahead to the marriage articles or prenuptial agreement.
While her husband lived, a wife had a right to bare maintenance and also to
a certain annual sum for "pin money," an allowance for clothes, gifts, and
personal service. As a widow she would have a right to an annual income, so
a settled sum, or lands yielding such a sum in annual rents—the widow's
"jointure"—had to be set aside for this purpose. But a shrewd bridegroom
and his lawyer could make sure that her "jointure" did not take a large bite
out of the estate. Sir James fears that Darcey would be tempted to make too
large a settlement on the penniless Fanny, whom Sir James characterizes
here with some disapproval as a "bewitching Gipsy." Such practices among
the upper and propertied classes are in opposition to the spirit of the Marriage Service itself, in which the groom promises to "endow" his wife "with
all [his] worldly goods."

neither; you will kill her with surprise.—Confounded luck! that I did not know she was in London.

I shall be with you in less than two hours, after Robert:——I send him on, with orders to ride every horse to death, lest she should be set out for Dover.

Jenkings is now on the road, but he travels too slow for my wishes.—If she is gone, prepare swift horses for me to follow:—I am kept by force to refresh myself.—What refreshment can I want!——Fly, I say, to Miss Powis, now no longer Miss Warley.—Leave her not, I charge you;—stir not from her;—by our friendship, Molesworth, stir not from her 'till you see

DARCEY.

LETTER XXIX.

The Honourable GEORGE MOLESWORTH
to RICHARD RISBY, Esq;

Dover.

OH Dick! the most dreadful affair has happen'd!——Lord Darcey is distracted and dying; I am little better.—Good God! what shall I do?—what can I do?——He lies on the floor in the next room, with half his hair torn off.—Unhappy man! fatigue had near kill'd him, before the melancholy account reach'd his ears.—Miss Warley, I mean Miss Powis, is gone to the bottom.——She sunk in the yacht that sailed yesterday from Dover for Calais.—Every soul is lost.—The fatal accident was confirm'd by a boat which came in not ten minutes before we arriv'd.—There was no keeping it from Lord Darcey.—The woman of the Inn we are at has a son lost in the same vessel: she was in fits[1] when we alighted.—Some of the wreck is drove on shore.——What can equal this scene!—Oh, Miss Powis! most amiable of women, I tremble for your relations!——But Darcey, poor Darcey, what do I feel for you!—He speaks:—he calls for me:——I go to him.

★

Oh, Risby! my heart is breaking; for once let it be said a man's heart can break.—Whilst he rav'd, whilst his sorrows were loud,

---

1 Fainting fits.

there was some chance; but now all is over. He is absolutely dying;—death is in every feature.——His convulsions how dreadful!—how dreadful the pale horror of his countenance!——But then so calm,—so compos'd!—I repeat, there can, be no chance.—

Where is Molesworth? I heard him say as I enter'd his apartment: come to me, my friend,—*holding out his hand*—come to me, my friend.—Don't weep;—don't let me leave you in tears. ——If you wish me well, rejoice:—think how I should have dragg'd out a miserable number of days, after——oh, George! after—Here he stopp'd.—The surgeon desir'd he would suffer us to lift him on the bed.—No, he said, in a faultering accent, if I move I shall die before I have made known to my friend my last request.—Upon which the physician and surgeon retir'd to a distant part of the room, to give him an opportunity of speaking with greater freedom.

He caught hold of my hand with the grasp of anguish, saying, Go, go, I entreat you, by that steady regard which has subsisted between us,—go to the unhappy family:—if they can be comforted; ay, if they *can*, you must undertake the task.—*I* will die without you.—Tell them I send the thanks, the duty, of a dying man;—that they must consider me as their own. A few, a *very* few hours! and I shall be their own;——I shall be united to their angel daughter.—Dear soul, he cried, is it for this,—for this, I tore myself from you!——But stop, I will not repine; the reward of my sufferings is at hand.

Now, you may lift me on the bed;—now, my friend, pointing to the door,—*now*, my dear Molesworth, if you wish I should die in——*there fainted.*——He lay without signs of life so long, that I thought, all was over.——

I cannot comply with his last request;—it is his last I am convinc'd;—he will never speak more, Risby!—he will never *more* pronounce the name of Molesworth.

Be yours the task he assign'd me.—Go instantly to the friends you revere;—go to Mr. and Mrs. Powis, the poor unfortunate parents.—Abroad they were to you as tender relations;—in England, your first returns of gratitude will be mournful.—You have seen Miss Powis:—it could be no other than that lovely creature whom you met so accidentally at ——: the likeness she bore to her father startled you. She was then going with Mr. Jenkings into Oxfordshire:—you admired her;—but had you known her mind, how would you have felt for Darcey!

Be cautious, tender, and circumspect, in your sad undertaking.——Go first to the old steward's, about a mile from the Abbey; if he is not return'd, break it to his wife and son.—They will advise, they will assist you, in the dreadful affair;—I hope the poor old gentleman has not proceeded farther than London.— Write the moment you have seen the family; write every melancholy particular: my mind is only fit for such gloomy recitals.— Farewell! I go to my dying friend.

Yours,

MOLESWORTH.

***

LETTER XXX.

Captain RISBY to the Honourable GEORGE
MOLESWORTH.

Barford Abbey.

WHAT is the sight of thousands slain in the field of battle, compar'd with the scene I am just escap'd from!—How can I be circumstantial!—where am I to begin!——whose distress shall I paint first!—can there be precedence in sorrow!

What a weight will human nature support before it sinks!— The distress'd inhabitants of this house are still alive; it is proclaim'd from every room by dreadful groans.—You sent me on a raven's message:——like that ill-boding bird I flew from house to house, afraid to croak my direful tidings.

By your directions I went to the steward's;—at the gate stood my dear friends, Mr. and Mrs. Powis, arm in arm.——I thought I should have sunk;—I thought I should have died instantly.—I was turning my horse to go back, and leave my black errand to be executed by another.

They were instantly at my side;——a hand was seiz'd by each,—and the words Risby!——captain Risby!—ecchoed in my ears.——What with their joyous welcomes,—and transported countenances, I felt as if a flash of lightning had just darted on my head.—Mrs. Powis first perceiv'd the alteration; and ask'd if I was well;——if any thing had happen'd to give me concern?

Certainly there has, said Mr. Powis, or *you* are not the same man you *was*, Risby.——It is true, Sir, return'd I;——it is true, I am not *so* happy as when I last saw *you*;—my mind is disagreeably situated;—could I receive joy, it would be in knowing this amiable woman to be Mrs. Powis.

You both surprise and affect us, replied he.

Indeed you do, join'd in his Lady; but we will try to remove your uneasiness:—pray let us conduct you to the Abbey; you are come to the best house in the world to heal grievances.——Ah, Risby! said my friend, all there is happiness.—Dick, I have the sweetest daughter: but Lord Darcey, I suppose, has told you every thing; we desir'd he would; and that we might see you immediately.—Can *you* tell us if his Lordship is gone on to Dover?

He is, returned I.——I did not wait his coming down, wanting to discover to you the reason of my perplexities.

What excuse after saying this, could I make, for going into the steward's?——For my soul, I could not think of any.—Fortunately it enter'd my head to say, that I had been wrong directed;—that a foolish boy had told me this was the strait road to the Abbey.

Mr. and Mrs. Powis importun'd me to let the servant lead my horse, that I might walk home with them.——*This* would never do.——I could not longer trust myself in *their* company, 'till I had reconnoitred the family;—'till I had examin'd who *there* was best fitted to bear the first onset of sorrow.—I brought myself off by saying, one of my legs was hurt with a tight boot.

Well then, go on, Risby, said Mr. Powis: you see the Abbey just before you; my wife and I will walk fast;——we shall be but a few minutes behind.

My faculties were quite unhing'd, at the sight of the noble structure.—I stopp'd, paus'd, then rode on; stopp'd again, irresolute whether to proceed.——Recollecting your strict injunctions, I reach'd the gate which leads to the back entrance; there I saw a well-looking gentleman and the game-keeper just got off their horses:—the former, after paying me the compliment of his hat, took a brace of hares from the keeper, and went into the house.—I ask'd of a servant who stood by, if that was Sir James Powis?

No, Sir, he replied; but Sir James is within.

Who is that gentleman? return'd I.

His name is Morgan, Sir.

Very intimate here, I suppose—is he not?

Yes, very intimate, Sir.

Then *he* is the person I have business with; pray tell him *so*.

The servant obey'd.—Mr. Morgan came to me, before I had dismounted; and accosting me very genteely, ask'd what my commands were with him?

Be so obliging, Sir, I replied, to go a small distance from the house; and I will unfold an affair which I am sorry to be the messenger of.

Nothing is amiss, Sir, I hope: you look strangely terrified; but I'll go with you this instant.——On that he led me by a little path to a walk planted thick with elms;[1] at one end of which was

---

1 Such an elm walk signals earlier landscape design. Only confident landowners could plan such an impressive avenue, as elms take a long while to reach maturity. Impressive plantings of great deciduous trees (especially oaks and elms) are a sign of wealth, status, continuity of lineal ownership, and an assured estate. The "pond just by" mentioned shortly after may be part of the old landscaped design, though unromantic ponds are found close to farmyards for the sake of drink for horses and cattle.

a bench, where we seated ourselves.—*Now*, Sir, said Mr. Morgan, you may *here* deliver what you have to say with secrecy.——I don't recollect to have had the honour of seeing *you* before;—but I wait with impatience to be inform'd the occasion of this visit.

You are a friend, I presume, of Sir James Powis?

Yes, Sir, I am: he has *few* of longer standing, and, as times go, *more* sincere, I believe.—But what of that?—do you know any harm, Sir, of me, or of my friend?

God knows I do not;—but I am acquainted, Mr. Morgan, with an unfortunate circumstance relative to Sir James.

Sir James! Zounds,[1] do speak out:—Sir James, to my knowledge, does not owe a shilling.

It is not money matters, Sir, that brought me here:——heaven grant it was!

The devil, Sir!—tell me at once, what is this damn'd affair? Upon my soul, you must tell me immediately.

Behold!—read, Sir—what a task is mine! (*putting your letter into his hands.*)

Never was grief, surprize, and disappointment so strongly painted as in him.—At first, he stood quite silent; every feature distorted:—then starting back some paces, threw his hat over the hedge;—stamp'd on his wig;—and was stripping himself naked, to fling his clothes into a pond just by, when I prevented him.

Stop, Sir, I cried: do not alarm the family before they are prepar'd.—Think of the dreadful consequences;—think of the unhappy parents!—Let us consult how to break it to them, without severing their hearts at one blow.

Zounds, Sir, don't talk to me of breaking it; I shall go mad:—you did not know her.——Oh! she was the most lovely, gentle

---

1 Exclamation derived from "God's wounds."

creature!——What an old blockhead have I been!——Why did I not give her my fortune?—*then* Darcey would have married her;—*then* she would not have gone abroad;—*then* we should have sav'd her. Oh, she was a sweet, dear soul!—What good will my curst estates do me *now*?——You shall have them, Sir;—any body shall have them—I don't care what becomes of *me*.—Do order my horse, Sir;——I say again, do order my horse. I'll never see this place more.——Oh! my dear, sweet, smiling girl, why would you go to France?

Here I interrupted him.

Think not, talk not, Sir, of leaving the family in such a melancholy situation.—Pray recollect yourself.——You *ought* not to run from your friends;——you *ought* to redouble your affection at this hour of trial.—Who *can* be call'd friends, but those who press forward, when all the satisfactions of life draw back.—You are not;—your feeling heart tells me you are not one of the many that retire with such visionary enjoyments.—Come, Sir, for the present forget the part you bear in this disaster:—consider,—pray, consider her poor parents; consider what will be their sufferings:——let it be our task to prepare them.

What you say is very right, Sir, return'd he.——I believe you are a good christian;—God direct us,—God direct us.——I wish I had a dram:[1]—faith, I shall be choak'd.—Sweet creature!—what will become of Lord Darcey!—I never wanted a dram so much before.—Your name, Sir, if you please.—I perceive we shall make matters worse by staying out so long.

I told him my name; and that I had the honour of being intimately acquainted with Mr. and Mrs. Powis.

He continued,—You will go in *with me*, Sir.—How am I to act!—I'll follow your advice——We must expect it will be a dreadful piece of work.——

Caution and tenderness, Mr. Morgan, will be absolutely necessary.

But where is my hat?—where is my wig?—have I thrown them into the pond?

---

1 A shot of hard liquor.

It is well the poor distress'd man recollected he had them not; or, bare-headed as he was, I should have gone with him to the house.——I pick'd them up, all over dirt; and, well as I could, clean'd them with my handkerchief.

Now, Sir, said I, if you will wipe your face,—for the sweat was standing on it in large drops,—I am ready to attend you.

So I must *really* go in, captain.——I don't think I can stand it;—you had better go without me.—Upon my soul, I had sooner face the mouth of a cannon—If you would blow my brains out, it would be the kindest thing you ever did in your life.

Poh! Don't talk at this rate, Sir.—Do we live only for ourselves?——

But *will* you not leave us, captain;—*will* you not run from us, when all is out?

Rather, Sir, suspect me of cowardice.——I should receive greater satisfaction from administering the smallest consolation to people in distress, than from whole nations govern'd by my nod.

Well, captain, I *will* go;—I *will* do any thing you desire me, since you are so good to say you will not leave us.

But, notwithstanding his fair promise, I never expected to get him within the doors.——He was shifting from side to side:—sometimes he would stand still,—sometimes attempt to retreat.——When we were just at the house, a servant appear'd:—of whom he enquir'd, if Mr. and Mrs. Powis were return'd; and was inform'd the latter was within;—the former gone out in pursuit of us. We likewise found the Ladies were with Sir James in the library. I sent in my name: it was in vain for me to expect any introduction from my companion.

Mrs. Powis flew to meet me at the door:—Mr. Morgan lifted up his eyes, and shook his head.—I never was so put to it:—I knew not what to say, or how to look.——Welcome, Mr. Risby, said the amiable, unfortunate, unsuspecting mother;—doubly welcome at this happy juncture.——Let me lead you to parents, introducing me to Sir James and Lady Powis, from whom I have receiv'd all my felicity.

You need not be told my reception:——it is sufficient that you know Sir James and her Ladyship.—My eyes instantly turn'd on the venerable chaplain: I thought I never discover'd so much of the angel in a human form.

Mrs. Powis ask'd me a thousand questions;—except answering *them*, I sat stupidly silent.—It was not so with Mr. Morgan: he walk'd, or rather ran up and down;—his eyes fix'd on the floor,—his lips in motion.—The Ladies spoke to him: he did not answer; and I could perceive them look on each other with surprize.

Mr. Powis enter'd:—the room seem'd to lift up:——I quite rambled when I rose to receive his salute.—Mr. Morgan was giving me the slip.—I look'd at him significantly;—then at Mr. Watson;—as much as to say, Take him out; acquaint him with the sorrowful tidings.—He understood the hint, and immediately they withdrew together.

Come, dear Risby, pluck up, said Mr. Powis:—do not you, my friend, be the only low-spirited person amongst us.——I fear Mr. Risby is not well, return'd Lady Powis.—We must not expect to see every one in high spirits, because *we* are:—*our* blessings must be consider'd as *very* singular.—You have not mention'd Fanny to your friends.

Indeed, Madam, I have, replied he.——Risby knows, I every minute expect my belov'd daughter.——But tell me, Dick;—tell me, my friend;—all present are myself;—fear not to be candid; ——what accident has thrown a cloud of sadness over your once chearful countenance?—Can I assist you?—My advice, my interest, my purse, are all your own.——Nay, dear Risby, you must not turn from me.—I did turn, I could hold it no longer.—

Pray Sir, said Mrs. Powis, do speak;—do command us; and she condescended to lay her hand on mine.—Lady Powis, Sir James too, both intreated I would suffer them to make me happy.——Dear worthy creatures, how my heart bled! how it still bleeds for them!—

I was attempting some awkward acknowledgment, when Mr. Watson enter'd, led by Mr. Morgan.—I saw he had executed the task, which made me shudder.—Never did the likeness of a being celestial shine more than in the former! He mov'd gently forward,—plac'd himself next Lady Powis;——pale,—trembling,—sinking.——Mr. Morgan retir'd to the window.——

Now,—now,—the dreadful discovery was at a crisis.——Mr. Watson sigh'd.—Lady Powis eyed him with attention; then starting up, cried, Bless me! I hear wheels: suppose, Mr. Watson, it should be Fanny!——and after looking into the lawn resum'd her chair.

Pardon me, Lady Powis, said. Mr. Watson in a low-voice; why *this* impatience?——Ah Madam! I could rather wish you to check than encourage *it*.

Hold, hold, my worthy friend, return'd Sir James; do you forget four hours since how you stood listening at a gate by the road-side, saying, you could hear, tho' not see?

We must vary our hopes and inclinations, reply'd Mr. Watson. ——Divine Providence——there stopp'd;—not another word.— He stopp'd;—he groan'd;——and was silent.—Great God! cried Mr. Powis, is my child ill?—Is my child dead? frantickly echoed Mrs. Powis—Heaven forbid! Exclaim'd Sir James and his Lady, arising.——Tell us, Mr. Watson;—tell us, Mr. Risby.

When you are compos'd,—return'd the former——Then, our child is dead,—really dead! Shriek'd the parents.—No, no, cried Lady Powis, clasping her son and daughter in her arms,——she is not dead; I am sure she is not dead.

Mr. Watson, after many efforts to speak, said in a faultering voice,—Consider we are christians:—let that bless'd name fortify our souls.

Mrs. Powis fell on her knees before him,—heart-rending sight!——her cap torn off,—her hair dishevell'd,—her eyes fix'd;—not a tear,—not a single tear to relieve the bitter anguish of her soul.

Sir James had left the room;—Lady Powis was sunk almost senseless on the sopha;——Mr. Powis kneeling by his wife, clasping her to his bosom;—Mr. Morgan in a corner roaring out his affliction;——Mr. Watson with the voice of an angel speaking consolation.——I say nothing of my own feelings.— God, how great!—how inexpressible! when Mrs. Powis, still on her knees, turn'd to me with uplifted hands,—Oh Mr. Risby! cried she,—can *you*,—can *you* speak comfort to the miserable?——Then again addressing Mr. Watson,——Dear, saint, only say she lives:—I ask no more; only say she lives.—My best love!—my life!—my Fanny! said Mr. Powis, lifting her to the sopha;—live,—live,—for my sake.——Oh!—Risby, are *you* the messenger?—his head fell on my shoulder, and he sobb'd aloud.

Lady Powis beckon'd him towards her, and, looking at Mrs. Powis with an expressive glance of tenderness,—said Compose yourself, my son;—what will become of *you*, *if*—He took the meaning of her words, and wrapping his arms about his wife, seem'd for a moment to forget his own sorrow in endeavours to sooth her.

What an exalted woman is Lady Powis!

My children, said she, taking a hand from each,—I am thankful: whom the Lord loveth he chasteneth.[1]——Let us follow his great example of patience,—of resignation.—What is a poor span?——*Ours* will be eternity.

I whisper'd Mr. Morgan, a female friend would be necessary to attend the Ladies;—one whom they lov'd,—whom they confided in, to be constantly with them in their apartments.—He knew just such a woman, he said; and went himself to fetch Mrs. Jenkings.——Lady Powis being unable longer to support herself, propos'd withdrawing.—I offered my arm, which she accepted, and led her to the dressing-room.——Mrs. Powis follow'd; almost lifeless, leaning on her husband:—there I left them together, and walk'd out for a quarter of an hour to recover my confus'd senses.

At my return to the library, I found Sir James and Mr. Watson in conversation.—The former, with a countenance of horror and distraction,——Oh Sir! said he, as I came near

---

1 Hebrews 12:6.

him,—do I see you again?—are you kind enough not to run from our distress?

Run from it, Sir James! I reply'd;—no, I will stay and be a partaker.

Oh Sir! he continued, you know not *my* distress:—death only can relieve *me*—*I* am without *hope*, without *comfort*.

And is this, Sir James, what you are arriv'd at? said the good chaplain.——Is this what you have been travelling sixty years after?——Wish for death! yet say you have neither hope or comfort.—Your good Lady, Sir, is full of both;—*she* rejoices in affliction:—*she* has long look'd above this world.

So might I, he reply'd,—had I no more to charge myself with than she has.—*You* know, Mr. Watson,——*you* know how faulty I have been.

Your errors, dear Sir James, said he, are not remember'd.—Look back on the reception you gave your son and daughter.

He made no reply; but shedding a flood of tears, went to his afflicted family.

Mr. Watson, it seems, whilst I had been out, acquainted him with the contents of your letter;—judging it the most seasonable time, as their grief could not then admit of increase.

Sir James was scarce withdrawn, when Lady Powis sent her woman to request the sight of it.—As I rose to give it into her hand, I saw Mr. Morgan pass by the door, conducting an elderly woman, whom I knew afterward to be Mrs. Jenkings. ——She had a handkerchief to her eyes, one hand lifted up;—and I heard her say, Good God! Sir, what shall I do?—how can I see the dear Ladies?—Oh Miss Powis!——the amiable Miss Powis!

Mr. Morgan join'd us immediately, with whom and Mr. Watson I spent the remainder of this melancholy evening: at twelve we retir'd.

So here I sit, like one just return'd from the funeral of his best friend;——alone, brooding over every misery I can call together.—The light of the moon, which shines with uncommon splendor, casts not one ray on my dark reflections:—nor do the objects which present themselves from the windows offer one pleasing idea;—rather an aggravation to my heart-felt anguish.——Miserable family!—miserable those who are interested in its sad disaster!——

I go to my bed, but not to my repose.

*

         Nine o'clock in the morning.
How sad, how gloomy, has been the approach of morning!—About six, for I had not clos'd my eyes,—somebody enter'd my chamber. I suppos'd it Mr. Morgan, and drew aside my curtain.—It was not Mr. Morgan;—it *was* the poor disconsolate father of Miss Powis, more agitated, if possible, than the preceding night.—He flung himself on my bed with agony not to be express'd:—

Dear Risby, said he, *do* rise:—*do* come to my apartment.—Alas! my Fanny—

What new misfortune, my friend? ask'd I, starting up.—My wife! return'd he!—she is in fits;—she has been in fits the whole night.——Oh Risby! if I should lose *her*, if I should lose my *wife!*—My parents *too*, I shall lose them!—

Words could not lessen his affliction. I was silent, making what haste I could to huddle on my clothes;—and at his repeated intreaties follow'd him to his wife.—She was sitting near the fire drowned in tears, supported by her woman. I was pleas'd to see them drop so plentifully.—She lifted up her head a little, as I enter'd.—How alter'd!—how torn to pieces with grief!——Her complexion once so lovely,—how changed in a few hours.

My husband! said she, in a faint voice, as he drew near her.—Then looking at me,—Comfort him, Mr. Risby;—don't let him sob so.—Indeed he will be ill;—indeed he will.—Then addressing him, Consider, she who us'd to be your nurse is now incapable of the task.—His agitation was so much increas'd by her words and manner, that I attempted to draw him into another apartment.—Your intentions are kind, said she, Mr. Risby;—but I *must* not lose my husband:—you see how it is, Sir, shaking her head;—try to sooth him;—talk to him *here* but do not take him from *me*.—

Then turning to Mr. Powis,—I am better, my love,—don't frighten yourself:—we must learn to be resign'd.—Set the example, and I will be resign'd, said he,—wiping away the tears as they trickled down her cheek;—if my Fanny supports herself, I shall not be quite miserable.

In this situation I left them, to close my letter.

What is become of poor Lord Darcey? For ever is he in my thoughts.——*His* death will be an aggravation to the general sorrow.—Write instantly:—I wait your account with impatience; yet dread to receive it.

Yours,

RISBY.

LETTER XXXI.

The Honourable GEORGE MOLESWORTH
to RICHARD RISBY, Esq;

Dover.

S AY not a word of it;—no, not for the world;—the body of Miss Powis is drove on shore.—If the family choose to have her brought down, it may be done some time hence.—I have order'd an undertaker to get a lead coffin,[1] and will take care to have her remains properly deposited.—It would be an act of cruelty at present to acquaint her friends with this circumstance.—I have neither leisure or spirits to tell you in what manner the body was found, and how I knew it to be miss Powis's.

---

1 The body, perhaps already in a wooden box, would be put into a lead-lined container tightly sealed, leak-proof and smell-proof, to be transported by wagon to the distant burial site.

The shore is fill'd with a multitude of people.—What sights will they gaze on to satisfy their curiosity!——a curiosity that makes human nature shrink.

I have got three matronly women to go with the undertaker, that the body may be taken up with decency.

Darcey lives;—but *how* does he live?—Without sense; almost without motion.

God protect the good old steward!—the worthy Jenkings!——He is with you before this;——he has told you everything. I could not write by him:——I thought I should never be able to touch a pen again.—He had left Dover before the body was found.—What conflicts did he escape! But as it is, I fear his grey hairs will go down with sorrow to the grave.[1]—God support us all!

MOLESWORTH.

LETTER XXXII.

Captain RISBY to the Honourable GEORGE MOLESWORTH.

Barford Abbey.

MY heart bleeds afresh.——Her body found! Good heaven!——it *must* not,—*shall* not come to the knowledge of the family.—At present they submit with a degree of resignation.—Who knows but a latent hope might remain?—Instances have been known of many saved from wrecks;—but her body is drove on shore.—Not a glimmering;—possibility is *now* out of the question.—The family are determin'd to shut themselves out from the world;——no company ever more to be admitted;—never to go any where but to the church.——Your letter was deliver'd me before them.——I was ask'd tenderly for poor Lord Darcey.——What could I answer?——Near the same; not worse, on the whole.—They flatter themselves he will recover:—I encourage all their flattering hopes.

---

1 Allusion to Genesis 44:29: And if ye take this also from me, and mischief befall him, ye shall bring down my grey hairs with sorrow to the grave.

Mrs. Jenkings has never been home since Mr. Morgan fetch'd her;——Mr. Jenkings too is constantly here;—sometimes Edmund:—except the unhappy parents, never was grief like theirs!

Mr. Jenkings has convinc'd me it was Miss Powis which I saw at ——. Strange reverse of fortune since that hour!

When the family are retir'd I spend many melancholy hours with poor Edmund;—and from him have learnt the reason why Mr. Powis conceal'd his marriage,—which is *now* no secret.—— Even Edmund never knew it till Mr. and Mrs. Powis return'd to England.—Take a short recital:—it will help to pass away a gloomy moment.

WHEN Mr. Powis left the University, he went for a few months to Ireland with the Lord-Lieutenant; and at his return intended to make the Grand Tour.——In the mean time, Sir James and Lady Powis contract an intimacy with a young Lady of quality, in the bloom of life, but not of beauty.——By what I can gather, Lady Mary Sutton is plain to a degree,— with a mind——But why speak of her mind?—let that speak for itself.

She was independent; her fortune noble;—her affections disengag'd.—Mr. Powis returns from Ireland: Lady Mary is then at the Abbey.——Sir James in a few days, without consulting his son, sues for her alliance.—Lady Mary supposes it is with the concurrence of Mr. Powis:—*his* person,—*his* character,—*his* family, were unexceptionable; and generously she declar'd her sentiments in his favour.—Sir James, elated with success, flies to his son;—and in presence of Lady Powis, tells him he has secur'd his happiness.——Mr. Powis's inclinations not coinciding,—— Sir James throws himself into a violent rage.——Covetousness and obstinacy always go hand in hand:—both had taken such fast hold of the Baronet, that he swore—and his oath was without reservation—he would never consent to his son's marrying any other woman.——Mr. Powis, finding his father determin'd,——and nothing, after his imprecation, to expect from the entreaties of his mother,—strove to forget the person of Lady Mary, and think only of her mind.——Her Ladyship, a little chagrin'd Sir James's proposals were not seconded by Mr. Powis, pretended immediate business into Oxfordshire.——The

Baronet wants not discernment: he saw through her motive; and taking his opportunity, insinuated the violence of his son's passion, and likewise the great timidity it occasion'd:—he even prevail'd on Lady Powis to propose returning with her to Brandon Lodge.

The consequence of this was, the two Ladies set out on their journey, attended by Sir James and Mr. Powis, who, in obedience to his father, was still endeavouring to conquer his indifference.——

Perhaps, *in time*, the amiable Lady Mary might have found a way to his heart,—had she not introduc'd the very evening of their arrival at the Lodge, her counter-part in every thing but person:—there Miss Whitmore outshone her whole sex.—— This fair neighbour was the belov'd friend of Lady Mary Sutton, and soon became the idol of Mr. Powis's affections, which render'd his situation still more distressing.——His mother's disinterested tenderness for Lady Mary;—her own charming qualifications;—his father's irrevocable menace, commanded him one way:—Miss Whitmore's charms led him another.

Attached as he was to this young Lady, he never appear'd to take the least notice of her more than civility demanded;——tho' she was of the highest consequence to his repose, yet the obstacles which surrounded him seem'd insurmountable.

Sir James and Lady Powis retiring one evening earlier than usual,—Lady Mary and Mr. Powis were left alone. The latter appear'd greatly embarrass'd. Her Ladyship eyed him attentively; but instead of sharing his embarrassment,—began a conversation of which Miss Whitmore was the subject.—She talk'd so long of her many excellencies, profess'd *such* sincerity, *such* tenderness, *for her*, that his emotion became visible:—his fine, eyes were full of fire;——his expressive features spoke what she, had long wish'd to discover.—You are silent, Sir, said she, with a smile of ineffable sweetness; is my lovely friend a subject that displeases you?—

How am I situated! replied he.——Generous Lady Mary, dare I repose a confidence in your noble breast?——Will you permit me that honour?—*Will* you not think ill of me, if I disclose——

No, I cannot——presumption—I *dare* not——She interrupted him:

Ah Sir!—you hold me unworthy,—you hold me incapable of friendship.—Suppose me your sister:——if you had a sister, would you conceal any thing from *her?*—Give me then a *brother;*—I can never behold *you* in any other light.

No, my Lady;——no, return'd he, I deserve not *this* honour. ——If you knew, madam,——if you knew all,—you *would,* you *must* despise me.

Despise you, Mr. Powis!——she replied;——despise you for loving Miss Whitmore!

Exalted goodness! said he,——approaching her with rapture: take my heart;——do with it as you please;——it is devoted to your generosity.

Well then, said she, I command *it,*——I command *it* instantly to be laid open before me.——*Now* let it speak;—*now* let it declare if I am not the bar to its felicity:——if—

No, my good angel, interrupted he, dropping on his knees,— and pressing her hand to his lips;—I see it is through you,—— through you only,——I am to expect felicity.

Before Lady Mary could prevail on Mr. Powis to arise, Sir James, whom they did not expect,—and who they thought was retir'd for the night, came in quest of his snuff-box;——but with a countenance full of joy retir'd precipitately, bowing to Lady Mary with the same reverence as if she had been a molten image cast of his favourite metal.[1]

In this conversation I have been circumstantial, that you might have a full view of the noble, disinterested Lady Mary Sutton: ——you may gather now, from whence sprang her unbounded affection for the incomparable, unfortunate Miss Powis.

You will not be surprised to find a speedy marriage took place between Mr. Powis and Miss Whitmore, to which none were

---

1 An image or idol made of gold.

privy but the Dean of H——, who perform'd the ceremony,—Lady Mary,—Mrs. Whitmore (the mother of Mrs. Powis),—— Mr. and Mrs. Jenkings.——Perhaps you think Lady Powis ought to have been consulted:—I thought so *too*; but am *now* convinc'd she would have been the wretchedest woman in the world, had she known her son acting diametrically opposite to the will of his father in so material a point.

To put it out of the power of every person intrusted with this momentous secret to divulge it,—and to make Mr. Powis perfectly easy,—each bound themselves at the altar where the ceremony was perform'd, never to make the least discovery 'till Mr. Powis thought fit to declare his marriage.

What an instance have I given you of *female* friendship!—Shew me such another:—our sex are a test of *their* friendships.

How many girls have I seen,—for ever together arm in arm,—whispering their own, perhaps the secrets of all their neighbours;——when in steps a young fellow of our cloth,——or any other, it signifies not the colour,—and down tumbles the tottering basis.——Instead of *my dear* and *my love*, it is *sly creature, false friend*, could any one have thought Miss Such-a-one possess'd of so much art?——then out comes intrigues, family-affairs, losses at cards,—in short, every thing that has been treasur'd up by two industrious fair ones seven years before.

Don't think me satyrical:—I am nice;[1]——*too* much so, perhaps.—The knowledge of *such* as constitute this little narrative, and *some* other minds like *theirs*, has made me rather *too* nice, as I said before:—a matter of little consequence, as I am situated.——Can I look forward to happy prospects, and see how soon the fairest felicity is out of sight?——This afflicted family, Molesworth, has taught me to forget,—that is, I ought to forget.——But no matter;—never again let me see Lady Sophia;—never lead me a second time into danger:—she is mortal, like Miss Powis.—Lord Darcey! poor Lord Darcey!

If recollection will assist me, a word or two more of Mr. and Mrs. Powis.

---

1 Particular.

Lady Sophia——the deuce is in me! you know who I mean;—
why write I the name of Lady Sophia?—upon my honour, I have
given over all thoughts of that divinity—Lady Mary I should have
said, a few months after the nuptials of her friends, wrote to Mr.
Powis, who was then at Barford Abbey, an absolute refusal, in
consequence of a preconcerned plan of operation.—Immediately
after this, she set out with Mrs. Powis for London, whose *situation* made it necessary for her to leave Hillford Down.

You will suppose, on the receipt of this letter, how matters
were at the Abbey:—Sir. James rav'd; even Lady Powis thought
her son ill us'd; but, in consideration of their former intimacy,
prevail'd on Sir James never to mention the affair, though from
this time all acquaintance ceas'd between the families.

In order to conceal the marriage, it was inevitable Mr. Powis
must carry his wife abroad;——and as he intended to travel
before the match was thought of with Lady Mary,—his father
now readily consented that he should begin his tour.—This
furnish'd him with an excuse to go immediately to town,——
where he waited 'till the angel that we all weep for, made her
appearance.

But what, you ask, was Mrs. Powis's excuse to leave
England, without being suspected?——Why, I'll tell you: by
the contrivance of Lady Mary, together with Mrs. Whitmore,
it was believ'd she had left the world;——that she died in town
of a malignant fever;—that—but I cannot be circumstantial.
——Miss Powis, after her parents went abroad, was brought
down by Lady Mary, and consign'd to the care of her grandmother, with whom she liv'd as the orphan child of some
distant relation.

Whilst Mr. and Mrs. Powis were travelling through Italy, he
apply'd to his friend the Lord-Lieutenant,—and by *that* interest
was appointed to the government of ——. It was here my
acquaintance with them commenc'd: not that I suspected Miss
Glinn to be Mrs. Powis, though I saw her every day.——*Glinn*
was a name she assum'd 'till she returned to England.—A thousand little circumstances which render'd her character unsus-
pected, I want spirits to relate.—Suffice it to say,—the death of
Mrs. Whitmore;—a daughter passing on the world for an

orphan;—and the absence of Lady Mary Sutton;——made them resolve to hazard every thing rather than leave their child unprotected.——Alas! for what are they come home?

Nothing is impossible with a Supreme Being.——Lord Darcey *may* recover.—But why this ray of hope to make the horrors of my mind more dreadful?—He is *past* hope, you say.—

RISBY.

LETTER XXXIII.

The Honourable GEORGE MOLESWORTH
to RICHARD RISBY, Esq;

Dover.

RISBY, I am lifted above myself!—I am overcome with surprise!—I am mad with joy!—Is it possible!—can it be!—But Lord Darcey's servant has swore it;—yes, he has swore, a letter directed in Miss Powis's *own* hand, lay on the counter in a banker's shop where he went to change a bill: the direction was to Lady Mary Sutton:—he has put many for the same Lady into the post-office.—I *run*, I *ride* or rather *fly* to town.

You may jump, you may sing, but command your features before the family.—Should it be a mistake of John's, we kill them twice.

If I live to see the resurrection of our hopes, John shall be with you instantly.——On second thought, I will not dispatch this, unless we have a bless'd certainty.

MOLESWORTH.

★★★

LETTER XXXIV.

The Honourable GEORGE MOLESWORTH to the same.

London.

ARE you a mile from the Abbey, Dick?——Are you out of sight,——out of hearing?——John, though you should offer to kill him, dare not deliver letter or message 'till you are at a proper distance.

Miss Powis lives!——Restore peace within the walls.—As I hope to be pardon'd for my sins, I have seen, I have spoke to her.—She lives!—Heavenly sound! it should be convey'd to them from above.—She lives! let me again repeat it.—Proclaim the joyful tidings:—but for particulars have patience 'till I return to the man, to the friend my life is bound up in.—I have seen him in every stage. Brightest has he shone, as the taper[1] came nearer to an end.—The rich cordial must be administered one drop at a time.—Observe the caution.

MOLESWORTH.

LETTER XXXV.

Captain RISBY to
the Honourable GEORGE MOLESWORTH.

Barford Abby.

WELL, Molesworth,——well—I can go no farther;——yet I *must*;—*John*, poor faithful *John*, says I *must*;—says he shall be sent back again.—But I have lost the use of my fingers:—my head bobs from side to side like a pendulum. Don't stamp, don't swear: they have a few drops of your cordial more than I intended.—It operates well.—I long to administer a larger potion.—Could you see how I am shifted—now here—now there—by the torrent of joy, that like a deluge almost drives reason before it;—I say, could you see me, you would not wonder at the few unconnected lines of
Yours,

RISBY.

---

1 A slender candle.

LETTER XXXVI.

The Honourable GEORGE MOLESWORTH to
RICHARD RISBY, Esq;

Dover.

D ARCEY bears the joyful surprise beyond imagination:
——it has brought him from death to life.—

Hear in what manner I proceeded.—You may suppose the
hurry in which I left Dover:——I took no leave of my friend;
——his humane apothecary[1] promis'd not to quit him in my
absence:—I gave orders when his Lordship enquir'd for me, that
he should be told particular business of my *own* had call'd me to
town express.——It happen'd very convenient that I left him in a
profound sleep.

Away I flew,—agitated betwixt *hope* and *fear.*—harrass'd by
fatigue;—not in a bed for three nights before;—nature was almost
wore out, when I alighted at the banker's.

I accosted one of the clerks, desiring to speak with Mr. or Mrs.
Delves:[2]—the former not at home, I was immediately conducted
to the latter, a genteel woman, about forty.——She receiv'd me
politely; but before I could acquaint her with the occasion of my
visit, the door open'd, and in stepp'd a pretty sprightly girl, who
on seeing me was going to retire.—Do you want any thing, my
love? said Mrs. Delves. Only, Madam, she replied, if you think it
proper for Miss Warley to get up.

Miss Warley! exclaim'd I.——Great God! Miss Warley!—Tell
me, Ladies, is Miss Warley *really* under your roof?—Both at once,

---

1 In the eighteenth century, when in need of medical attention, most
people, even the well-to-do, turned to the apothecary who could diagnose
and give pills and knew as much about the human body as—sometimes
even more than—a university-trained physician. Surgeons were in
demand for broken bones and wounds. Both apothecaries and surgeons
were considered low-class, as they touch ugly and dirty things and work
with their hands, whereas physicians were thought higher-class. The status
of the medical professions was to rise enormously in the nineteenth
century, erasing some of these class distinctions.

2 [Gunning's note:] The name of the banker.

for *both* seem'd equally dispos'd to diffuse happiness, answer'd to my wishes.

I threw myself back in my chair:—the surprise was more than I could support.—Shall I tell you all my weakness?—I even shed tears;—yes, Dick, I shed tears:—but they were drops of heart-felt gladness.

The Ladies look'd on each other.—Mrs. Delves said in a tone that shew'd she was not without the darling passion of her sex,

Pardon me, Sir; I think I have heard Miss Warley has *no* brother,—or I should think *your* emotion I saw him before me.— But whoever you are, this humanity is noble.—Indeed, the poor young Lady has been extremely ill.

I am not her brother, Madam, return'd I.—It is true, she has *no* brother;—but *she has* parents, *she has* friends, who lament her dead:—*their* sorrow has been *mine.*

I fear, Sir, return'd she, it will not end here.——I grieve to tell you, the Miss Warley you speak of is not with me;—I know nothing of that Lady:——my Miss Warley has no parents.

I still persisted it was the same; and, to the no small gratification of both mother and daughter, promis'd to explain the mystery.—But before I began, Miss Delves was sent to desire Miss Warley would continue in bed an hour longer, on account of some visitors that had dropp'd in accidentally.

Soon as Miss Delves return'd, I related every particular.—I cannot tell you half that pass'd;—I cannot describe their astonishment:—but let me *tell* you, Miss Powis is just recover'd from the small-pox;—that this was the second day of her sitting up: ——let me *tell* you *too* her face is as beautiful as ever.[1]——On mature deliberation, it was determin'd, for the sake of Miss

---

1 Small-pox is a dangerous, often lethal, disease, typically involving eruptions on the body and very high fever, even delirium. The author is anxious to reassure us that Fanny is not scarred or disfigured by this illness, which frequently left large, permanent pock marks on the skin of a survivor.

Powis's health, she must some time longer think her name Warley.

I din'd with my new acquaintance, on their promising to procure an interview for me with Miss Powis in the afternoon.

It was about five when I was admitted to her presence.—I found her in an elegant dressing-room, sitting on a sopha: her head a little reclin'd.——I stepp'd slow and softly: she arose as I enter'd.—I wonder not that Darcey adores her; never was a form so perfect!

My trembling knees beat one against another.——My heart,— my impatient heart flew up to my face to tell its joyful sensations.—I ventur'd to press her hand to my lips, but was incapable of pronouncing a syllable.—She was confus'd:——she certainly thought of Darcey, when she saw his friend.—I took a chair next her.—I shall not repeat our conversation 'till it became interesting, which began by her asking, if I had heard lately any accounts from Barford Abbey?——Lord Darcey, Madam, I reply'd, has receiv'd a letter from Sir James.

Lord Darcey! she repeated with great emotion.—Is Sir James and Lady Powis well, Sir?

His Lordship, reply'd I, awkwardly, did not mention particulars.——I believe,—I suppose.——your friends are well.

I fear, said she sighing, they will think me an ungrateful creature.——No person, Mr. Molesworth, had ever such obligations to their friends as I have.——This family, looking at the two Ladies, must be rank'd with my best.——Their replies were polite and affectionate.——Can you tell me, Sir, continued she, if Lord—here her face was all over crimson——heavens! I mean, if Mr. Powis and his Lady are at the Abbey?—Why did she not say Lord Darcey? I swear the name quiver'd on her lips.

I answer'd in the affirmative;——and sitting silent a moment,—she ask'd how I discover'd her to be still in England. ——I said by means of a servant:—true enough, Dick:—but then I was oblig'd to add, this servant belong'd to Mr. Delves, and that he accidentally happen'd a few hours since to mention her name whilst I was doing business in the shop.—She was fond of dwelling on the family at the Abbey;—on Mr. and Mrs. Jenkings;—and once when I mention'd my friend, when I said how happy I should make him at my return;—pleasure, the most difficult to be conceal'd of any sensation, sprang to her expressive eyes.

I suppose she will expect a visit from his Lordship.—If she is angry at being disappointed, no matter: the mistake will be soon clear'd up.

The moment I left her, I stepp'd into a chaise that waited for me at the door, and drove like lightning from stage to stage, 'till I reach'd this place;—my drivers being turn'd into Mercuries by a touch more efficacious than all the oaths that can be swore by a first-rate blood.

I did not venture into Darcey's apartment 'till he was inform'd of my return.—I heard him impatiently ask to see me, as I stood without the door. This call'd me to him;—when pulling aside the curtain he ask'd, Who is that?—Is it Molesworth?—Are you come, my friend? But what have you seen?—what have you heard?——looking earnestly in face.——*I* am past joy,—past feeling pleasure even for you, George;——yet tell me why you look not so sorrowful as yesterday.—

I ask'd what alteration it was he saw:—what it was he suspected.—When I have griev'd, my Lord, it has been for you.—— If I am now less afflicted, you must be less miserable.——He started up in the bed, and grasping both my hands in his, cry'd. Tell me, Molesworth, is there a possibility,—a bare possibility?— I ask no more;—only tell me there is a possibility.

My Lord,—my friend,—my Darcey, nothing is impossible.

By heaven! he exclaim'd, you would not flatter me;—by heaven she lives!

Ask me not farther, my Lord.——What is the blessing you most wish for?——Suppose that blessing granted.—And you, Risby, suppose the extasy,——the thankfulness that ensued.—— He that is grateful to man, can he be ungrateful to his Maker?
Yours,

MOLESWORTH.

LETTER XXXVII.

Miss POWIS to Lady POWIS.

London.

THINK me not ungrateful, my ever-honour'd Lady, that I
have been silent under the ten thousand obligations which
I receiv'd at Barford Abbey.—But indeed, my dear Lady, I have
been *very* ill.—I have had the small-pox:—I was seiz'd delirious
the evening after my arrival in Town.—My God! what a wretch
did I set out with!—Vile man!—Man did I say?—*No*; he is a disgrace to *manhood*.—How shall I tell your Ladyship all I have suffer'd?—I am weak,—*very* weak;—I find myself unequal to the
task.—

This moment I have hit on an expedient that will unravel
all;—I'll recall a letter[1] which I have just sent down to be put
into the post-office;—a letter I wrote Lady Mary Sutton immediately on my arrival here;—but was seiz'd so violently, that I
could not add the superscription, for which reason it has lain by
ever since.—I am easy on Lady Mary's account:—Mr. Delves
has acquainted her of my illness:—like wise the prospect of my
recovery.

Consider then, dear Lady Powis, the inclos'd as if it was
address'd to yourself.

I cannot do justice to the affection,—the compassion,——
the tender assiduity I have experience'd from Mr. Delves's
family:—I shall always love them; I hope too I shall always be
grateful.

God grant, my dear Lady;——God grant, dear Sir James, that
long ere this you may have embrac'd Mr. and Mrs. Powis.—My
heart is with *you*:—it delights to dwell at Barford Abbey.

---

1 [Gunning's note:] This was the same Lord Darcey's servant saw on the
counter.

In a few days I hope to do myself the honour of writing to your Ladyship again.—One line from your dear hand would be most gratefully receiv'd by your oblig'd and affectionate

F. WARLEY.

P.S. My good friends Mr. and Mrs. Jenkings shall hear from me next post.

LETTER XXXVIII.

Miss POWIS to Lady MARY SUTTON.

London.

OH my dear Lady! what a villain have I escap'd from?— Could your Ladyship believe that a man, who, to all appearance, has made a good husband to your agreeable neighbour upwards of twelve years, and preserv'd the character of a man of honour;—could you believe in the decline of life he would have fallen off? No; he cannot have fallen: such a mind as his never was exalted.——It is the virtues of his wife that has hitherto made his vices imperceptible;—that has kept them in their dark cell, afraid to venture out;——afraid to appear amidst her shining perfections.——Vile, abandon'd Smith!—— But for the sake of his injur'd, unhappy wife, I will not discover his baseness to any but yourself and Lady Powis.——Perhaps Mrs. Smith may not be unacquainted with his innate bad principles;—perhaps she conceals her knowledge of them, knowing it vain to complain of a disorder which is past the reach of medicine.——What cure is there for mischief lurking under the mask of hypocrisy?—It must be of long standing before that covering can grow over it:—like a vellum on the eye,[1] though taken off ever skillfully, it will again spread on the blemish'd sight.

How am I running on!—My spirits are flutter'd:—I begin where I should end, and end where I should begin.——Behold me, dearest Madam, just parted from my Hampshire friends,— silent and in tears, plac'd by the side of my miscreant conductor.——You know, my Lady, this specious man *can* make himself

---

1 A membrane on the eye, i.e., a cataract.

vastly entertaining: he strove to render his conversation particularly so, on our first setting out.

We had travell'd several stages without varying the subject, which was that of our intended tour, when I said I hop'd it would conquer Mrs. Smith's melancholy for the death of her brother.— How did his answer change him in a moment from the *most* agreeable to the *most* disgustful of his sex!

My wife, Miss Warley, with a leer that made him look dreadful, wants your charming sprightliness:——it is a curs'd thing to be connected with a gloomy woman.—

Gloomy, Sir! casting at him a look of disdain; do you call mildness, complacency, and evenness of temper, *gloomy?*

She is much altered, Madam;——is grown old and peevish; ——her health is bad;—she cannot live long.

Mrs. Smith can never be *peevish*, Sir;—and as to her *age*, I thought it pretty near your *own.*

No, no, Madam, you are quite mistaken; I am at least five years younger.

Five years, Sir! what are five years at *your* time of life!

Come, come, Miss Warley, laying his huge paw on my hand, and in a tone of voice that shew'd him heartily nettled,—even at *my* time of life I can admire a beautiful young Lady.—If my wife should die,—*old as I am*—men *older* than myself, with half my estate, have married some of the finest women in the kingdom.

Very likely, Sir;—but then it is to be suppos'd the characters of *such* men have been particularly amiable.——No man or woman of honour can esteem another whose principles are doubtful.

This was a pretty home-thrust; it put him more on his guard for the present: but had he behav'd like an angel, I must have hated him. He was *very* respectful, *very* ceremonious, and *very* thoughtful, 'till we arrived at the inn where we were to stop the night; and had so much art not to seem displeas'd, that I refus'd giving him my company at supper, under pretence of indisposition.——Indeed, I was far from well: a child which I had seen a few hours before fresh in the small-pox, a good deal disconcerted me.—After fixing on my room, not to appear suspicious, I went down at his request, to eat a bit of cake and drink a glass of wine, before I retired for the night.——I had scarce swallow'd it when he left me, as he said, to speak to the drivers. I wished him a good night as he went out, and took an opportunity a few moments after to go to my chamber.—When there I lock'd the door, and sat myself down to undress; but I began to be greatly alarm'd by something that mov'd under the bed.—Judge my surprize,—judge my horror,—on taking the candle and examining, to see there a man!—But how was that surprize,—that horror increased, on discovering him to be the vile Smith!——I gave a loud scream, and ran towards the door; but had not power to turn the key, before he caught me in his arms.—

Be calm, Miss Warley, cried the monster;—hear what I have to say.——Suffer me to tell you, that I love you to distraction;—that I adore you.

Adore me, vile man! said I, breaking from him:—leave me this instant—begone:—leave me, I say, instantly.——Again I scream'd.

No, by heaven! he reply'd, I will not go 'till you have heard and pardon'd me.——Here I stand *determin'd* to be heard:—*hear* me, or this moment is my last.—With that he drew out a pistol, and held it to his breast.

And *dare* you, said I, collecting all my resolution,—*dare* you rush into eternity, without one virtue to offer up with your polluted soul?—I pronounc'd these words with steadiness.—*He* trembled, he look'd like a criminal at the hour of execution.—Letting the pistol drop from his hand, the base dissembler fell on his knees before me.—Nobody hearing my cries,—nobody coming to my assistance, I was oblig'd to hear, and pretend to credit his penitential protestations. God knows how my ears might have been farther shock'd with his odious passion;—what indignities I might have suffer'd,—had I not heard some person passing by the door of my apartment:——on which I ventur'd to give another scream.—The door was instantly burst open; and whilst an elderly Gentleman advanc'd towards me, full of surprize, the detested brute slipp'd away.—This Gentleman, my good deliverer, was no other than your Ladyship's banker, who when he was acquainted with my name, insisted on taking me to Town in his own coach, where he was returning from a visit he had made at Salisbury.——I did not ask, neither do I know what became of Smith; but I suppose he will set out with his wife immediately for Dover.—Thank God! I am not of the party.—How I pity poor Miss Frances Walsh, a young Lady who, he told me, was waiting at his house in Town to go over with them.—I am but just arriv'd at Mr. Delves's house.—Mr. and Mrs. Delves think with me, that the character of the *unworthy* Smith should not be expos'd for the sake of his *worthy* wife.—The family here are all amiable.—I could say a great deal more; but my head aches dreadfully.——This I must add, I have consented, at the tender intreaties of Mr. and Mrs. Delves, to remain with them 'till a proper opportunity offers to throw myself at your Ladyship's feet.——My head grows worse:——I must lay down my pen.—This bad man has certainly frighten'd me into a fever.

[The following lines were added after Miss Powis's recovery.]

I hope, my dear Lady, before this you have Mr. Delves's letter;——if so, you know I have had the small-pox.—You know too I am out of danger.——How can I be thankful enough for so many escapes!—This is the first day I have been able to hold a pen.——I am permitted to write no more than the name of your honour'd and affectionate

F. WARLEY.

LETTER XXXIX.

Captain RISBY to the Honourable GEORGE
MOLESWORTH.

Barford Abbey.

WILL all the thanks,—all the gratitude,—the parents blessings,—their infinity of joy, be contain'd in one poor sheet?—No:—Was I to repeat half,—only half of what they send you, I might write on for ever.——One says you shall be their son;—another, their brother;—a third, that you are a man most favour'd of heaven;——but all agree, as a reward for your virtues you are impower'd to heal afflictions:——in short, they want to make me think you can make black white.——But enough for the vanity of one man.

I dread your coming to the Abbey.—We that are here already, shall only, then, appear like pismires:[1]——but let me caution my friend not to think his head will touch the clouds.

What man can bear to be twice disinherited?—Mr. Morgan's estate, which the other day I was solely to possess, is now to devolve on the Honourable George Molesworth.—*But mark me:*—As I have been disinherited for you,—*you* as certainly will be disinherited for Lord Darcey.

See what a man of consequence I am.—Does Captain Risby say *this?*—Does Captain Risby say *that?*—Does Captain Risby think well of it?

Expect, George, to behold me push'd into perferment against my will;——all great people *say* so, you know;—expect to behold me preside as governor of this castle.——Let me enjoy it then;——let me plume myself beneath the sun-beam.

If to witness the honours with which I am surrounded, is insufficient to fill your expanded heart;—if it looks out for a warmer gratification; you shall see, you shall hear, the exulting parents:—you shall see Mr. Morgan revers'd;——Mr. Watson restor'd to *more* than sight;——the steward and his family worthy every *honour* they receive from this *honourable* house.

I hear my *shadow.*—Strange, indeed! to hear *shadows;*——but more so to hear them swear.—Ha! ha! ha!—Ha! ha! ha!—I cannot speak to it for laughing.—Coming, Sir!——coming, Mr. Morgan!——Now is he cursing me in every corner of the house;—I suppose dinner is on the table.

This moment return'd from regaling myself with the happy family:—I mean Sir James and Lady Powis, with their joyful inmates.—Mr. and Mrs. Powis are set out for London.—As an addition to their felicity, Lady Powis had a letter from her grand-daughter the instant they were stepping into the chaise.

---

1 Ants.

For one hour I am at your command:——take, then, the particulars which I was incapable of giving you by John.—

I was sitting in the library-window, talking to Mr. Watson; the Ladies, Sir James, and Mr. Morgan, in the dressing-room, when I saw John riding down the great road a full gallop.——At first I thought Lord Darcey had been dead; then, again, consider'd his faithful servant would not have come post with the news:— however, I had not patience to go through the house, but lifting up a sash, jump'd out before he could reach the stable-yard.—— Without speaking, I enquired of his face what tidings; and was answer'd by a broad grin. I had nothing to fear from his message.

Well, John, said I, running up to him,—how is your Lord? how is Mr. Molesworth?—

Better, I thank God, Sir;—better, I thank God! With that he turned his horse, and was riding across the lawn.—

Zounds, John, where are you going?—where are you going?

Follow me, Sir;—follow me (setting up a brisk trot). If you kill me, I dare not deliver letter or message before we are at a distance from the Abbey.

I thought him mad, but kept on by the side of his horse 'till we came to the gate of a meadow, where he dismounted.

Now, Sir, said he, with a look that bespoke his consequence, ——have patience, whilst I tie up my horse.

Patience, John! (and I swore at him) I am out of all *patience*.

With that he condescended to deliver your letters.——I rambled with surprise at the contents, and fell against a hedge. ——John, who by this time had fasten'd his steed, came up to me just as I recover'd my legs;——and speaking close to my ear,— 'Twas *John Warren*, Sir, was the *man* who found out the Lady; 'twas *I* was the *man*, Sir.

I shook him heartily by the hand, but for my soul could not utter a syllable.—I hope you are not ill, Sir, said the poor fellow, thinking me seiz'd speechless.—

No, John;—no, reply'd I; it is only excess of pleasure.——You are a welcome messenger:——you have made your fortune.

John Warren, and please your honour, has made his dear Lord happy;—that is more *pleasurable* to him than all the riches in the world.

You are an honest, good creature, John.

Ay, Captain; but was it not very sensible to remember the young Lady's hand-writing?——Would a powder-headed monkey[1] have had the forecast?

Oh very sensible, John;—very sensible, indeed!——Now go [to] the Abbey;——ask for my servant;—say you was sent by Mr. Molesworth to enquire for the family; but do not mention you have seen me:—I shall return by a different way.

John mounted immediately, and I walk'd full speed towards the house. I found Mr. Morgan taking long strides up and down the dining-parlour, puffing, blowing, and turning his wig on every side.

Where have you been, Captain? I have sent to seek you.—— Lord Darcey's servant is without;—come to enquire how things are *here*.——I would not let them send his message up;—but I have been out myself to ask for his Lordship.

Well, Sir, and what says the servant?

Says!——Faith I hardly know what he says;—something about hopes of him:—to be plain, I should think it better if *hope* was out of the question.——If *he* and all of *us* were dead——But see John yourself; I will send him to you.

As he was just without the door, I drew him back,—and turn'd the key.—

---

1 In the navy, a powder monkey is a young boy who brings the gun powder to the gunners. "Powder-headed" introduces the hair powder often used by the better class of male servant.

Come hither, Sir;——Come hither, Mr. Morgan:—I have something of importance to communicate.

D—n ye, Captain, what's the matter now? (staring.)—I'll hear no more bad news:—upon my soul, I'll run out of it (attempting to open the door).

Hold, Sir; why this impatience?—Miss Powis *lives!*—Will you run from me now?—Miss Powis *lives!*—With that he sent forth a horrid noise;—something betwixt howling and screaming.—It reach'd the dressing-room, as well it might:—had the wind sat that way, I question if the village would not have been alarm'd.—Down ran Sir James and Mr. Powis into the library;—out jump'd Mr. Morgan.—I held up my hand for him to retreat:—he disregarding the caution, I follow'd.—Sir James was inquiring of a servant whence the noise had proceeded.

It was I, said Mr. Morgan, rubbing his sides, and expressing the agitation of joy by dumb shew;—it was I, beating one of my damn'd dogs for running up stairs.[1]

If that is all, said Mr. Powis,—let us return to my mother and wife, who are much hurried.—Away we went together, and the affair of the dog pass'd very well on the Ladies.

I sat musing for some moments how to introduce the event my heart labour'd to give up.—*Every* sigh that escap'd,—*every* sorrowful look that was interchang'd, I *now* plac'd to *my* own account, because in my power to reverse the scene.

Addressing myself to Mr. Powis, I ask'd if he knew Lord Darcey's servant was below.—He shook his head;—No, he answer'd.——Then it is all *over*, Risby, I suppose, in a low voice?—I hardly wish for his *own* sake he may recover:—for *ours*, it would be selfish.

He was not worse, I reply'd:—there was hope,——great hope he would do well.

Blessings attend him! cried Mrs. Powis,—tears starting afresh to her swoln eyes;——then you really think, Mr. Risby, he may recover?

---

1 We know this is just Mr. Morgan's excuse to cover a "horrid noise," the howling sound he himself has just emitted. But Morgan startles us with his cruelty to animals, even if in this case fictitious.

If he does, Madam, return'd! he is flatter'd into life.——Flatter'd! said Mr. Powis eagerly;—how flatter'd?

Why, continued I, he has been told some persons are sav'd from the wreck.

Up they all started, surrounding me on every side:—— there seem'd but one voice, yet each ask'd if I credited the report.

I said I did.——

Down they dropp'd on their knees, praying with uplifted hands their dear,—dear child may be of the number.—Though nothing could equal the solemnity of this scene, I could scarce command my countenance, when I saw Mr. Morgan standing in the midst of the circle, his hat held up before his face, and a cane under his arm.

As they rose from their knees,—I gave them all the consolation I thought at that moment they were capable of sustaining;—and assur'd them no vigilance would be wanting to come at particulars.——I was ask'd, if there was any letter from Mr. Molesworth?——When answer'd in the affirmative,——the next question was, if it related to what I had just disclos'd?—I equivocated in my reply, and withdrew to write the few unconnected lines sent by John.

After he was dispatch'd, I return'd immediately to the hopeing,——fearing family.—Mr. Watson was sitting amidst them:—he seem'd like a Being of purity presiding over hearts going to be rewarded for resignation to the Divine will.

He heard me as I enter'd: he rose from his seat as I came near him, and pressing one of my hands between both his, whisper'd, I have seen Mr. Morgan.——Then raising his voice, You are the messenger of joy, Mr. Risby;—complete the happiness you have begun:——all present, pointing round, are prepar'd to receive it.

Here drops my pen.——I must not attempt this scene:—a Shakespeare would have wrote it in tears.

How infinite,——how dazzling the beauty of holiness!—Affliction seems to have threaten'd this amiable family, only to
encrease their love,—their reverence,—their admiration of Divine
Omnipotence.——Blessings may appear, as a certain great man
remarks, under the shape of pain, losses, and disappointments;
——but let us have patience, and we shall see them in their own
proper figures.

If rewards even in this world attend the *virtuous*, who would be
deprav'd?—Could the loose, the abandon'd, look in on this happy
mansion, how would their sensual appetites be pall'd!—How
would they hate,—how detest the vanity,—the folly that leads to
vice!——If pleasure is their pursuit, here they might see it speaking at *mouth* and *eyes:*——*pleasures* that fleet not away;—*pleasures*
that are carried beyond the grave.

What a family is this to take a wife from!——Lord Darcey's
happiness is insur'd:—in my conscience, there will not be such
another couple in England.

Preparations are making to welcome the lovely successor of
this ancient house;—preparations to rejoice those whose satisfactions are scanty;—to clothe the naked,—to feed the hungry,[1]—to
let the stately roof echo with songs and mirth from a croud of
chearful, honest, old tenants.

I often hear Mrs. Jenkings crying out in extasy,——My
angel!——my sweet angel!——As to the old gentleman and
Edmund, they actually cannot refrain from tears, when Miss
Powis's name is mention'd.——Sir James and her Ladyship are
never easy without these good folks.——It has ever been an
observation of mine, that at an unexpected fortunate event, we
are fond of having people about us who feel on the same occasion.

Mr. Morgan is quite his own man again:——he has been
regaling himself with a fine hunt, whilst I attended Sir James and
my Lady in an airing round the park.—After dinner we were
acquainted with all his losses and crosses in the dog and horse
way.—He had not seen *Filley* rubb'd down this fortnight:—the
huntsman had lost three of his best hounds:—two spaniels were

1 See Matthew 25:34–36.

lame;—and one of his running horses glander'd.[1]——He concluded with swearing, as things turn'd out, he did not matter it *much*;—but had it happen'd three weeks since; he should have drove all his servants to the devil.——Enough of Mr. Morgan.—Adieu, Molesworth!——Forget not my congratulations to your noble, happy, friend.

RISBY.

LETTER XL.

The Honourable GEORGE MOLESWORTH to
RICHARD RISBY, Esq;

Dover.

A LL is happiness, Dick!—I see nothing else; I hear of nothing else.——It is the *last* thing I take leave of at night;——the *first* thing I meet in the morning.——*Yesterday* was full of it!—*yesterday* I dined with Mr. and Mrs. Powis and their charming daughter, at the Banker's.—To look back, it seems as if I had gone through all the vexations of my life in the last three weeks.

Darcey would not let me rest 'till I had been to congratulate them, or rather to satisfy his own impatience, being distracted to hear how Miss Powis bore the great discovery.—Her fortitude is amazing!—But Sir James has had every particular from his son; therefore I shall be too late on that subject.

The following short epistle I receiv'd from Mr. Powis, as I was setting off for Town.

Mr. POWIS to the Honourable GEORGE MOLESWORTH.

London.

"The first moment I can tear myself from the tender embraces of all my hopes;—the first moment I can leave my belov'd daughter, I come to Dover;——I come to acknowledge my gratitude to the noble-minded Molesworth;——I come to testify my affection to the generous, disinterested Lord Darcey.——We

---

1 Afflicted by glander, a contagious disease in horses.

pray for the recovery of his Lordship's health.——When that is establish'd, not one wish will be wanting to complete the felicity of

J. POWIS."

The more I know of *this* family, the more I admire them.—— I *must* be their neighbour, that's certain.—*Suppose* I petition for a little spot at one end of the park; *suppose* you throw up your commission; and we live together two snug batchelors.

Darcey vows he will go to Town next week.—If fatigue should cause him to relapse, what will become of us *then*?—But I will not think of that *now*.

We shall come down a joyful cavalcade[1] to the Abbey.——I long to see the doors thrown open to receive us.——School-boy like, I shall first count days;——next hours;——then minutes: though I am your's the same here, there, and every where.

MOLESWORTH.

LETTER XLI.

The Honourable GEORGE MOLESWORTH to the same.

London.

BUILD in the park, and live batchelors!——Pish!——A horrid scheme!—I give it up.—Over head and ears, Dick!

Last Monday arriv'd at his Lordship's house in *St. James's-Square*,[2] the Right Honourable the Earl and Countess of Hampstead,—Lord Hallum,—the Ladies Elizabeth and Sophia Curtis.

True, as I hope to be sav'd;—and as *true*, that Lady Elizabeth and Sophia *are* blooming as angels.

Three times have I sat down, *pen* in my hand, *paper* folded, yet could not tune my mind to write one word.—Over head and ears! I say.—

---

1 Procession of riders on horseback.
2 Fashionable area of London.

Past one in the morning!—All silent! Let me try if I can scribble now.

First, I must tell you the body drove on shore at Dover, which I concluded was Miss Powis's, is discover'd to be a Miss Frances Walsh, going over in the yacht which was unfortunately castaway;—the corpse much defac'd:—but what confirm'd it to be the body of Miss Powis, was a handkerchief taken from the neck mark'd F W.——Poor young Lady! her friends, perhaps, are suffering the excesses of grief which *you* and I have so lately witness'd.—But *this* is a subject I shall not dwell on.

I came to Town this evening with Darcey:——he bore the journey very poorly;—sinking, fainting, all the way.—When we got to our lodgings, and he was put into a bed, recovering a little, he press'd me to go to the Banker's.—I saw his impatience, and went immediately.

My name was no sooner sent up, than Mr. Powis flew to receive me.——Welcome, my friend! said he; you come opportunely. We have a noble family with us that has been just wishing to see Mr. Molesworth.—He had time for no more; the door open'd.—What was my surprize to be embrac'd by Lord Hampstead and Lord Hallum, by them led to the Countess and our two divinities, *whose* mild eyes,—*whose* elegant deportment, told me *Loves* and *Graces* had put a finishing stroke to the great work of *virtue* and *humility*.——Lady Mary Sutton,——yes, Lady Mary Sutton too was there: she advanc'd towards me, Miss Powis in her hand.

I have the honour, said Mr. Powis, of presenting Lady Mary Sutton (the source of all my felicity) to Mr. Molesworth.—Then addressing himself to her Ladyship, Permit me, Madam, to introduce to you the friend I love.

If ever I wish'd to shine, it was then:——I would have given the world for eloquence;—nay, common understanding.—The former I *never* possess'd:—A surprize and pleasure had flown away with the latter.—Miss Powis has that looks through one's very soul;——a sweet compassionate eye: the dignity it expresses bespeaks your confidence.—She perceived my embarrassment, and said, Come, Mr. Molesworth, let me have the satisfaction of placing you next Lady Mary. So down sat the stupid blockhead.——Her Ladyship is very chatty, and very affable: she said a thousand obliging things; but half was lost upon me, whilst I watch'd the lips of my fair Elizabeth.

Mr. Mrs. Powis, and Lady Mary, enquired affectionately after the health of Lord Darcey. When I said he was come to Town, up flew the heart's tell-tale to the face of Miss Powis.—Her father and mother ask'd, if they might have the happiness of waiting on his Lordship next morning.——I arose to assure them what joy their visit would occasion; when having settled the hour, and so forth, I slid to a chair vacant between Lady Elizabeth and Lady Sophia.—How enchanting *did* they look!—how enchanting *did* they speak!—No reserve;—all frankness;—the same innocence in their manners as at fifteen;—the vivacity of the French,—the sedateness of the English, how charmingly blended!

Risby, thou art a fortunate fellow: Lady Sophia speaks of thee with esteem.

The sweet syrens[1]—*syrens* only by attraction—held me by the ear upwards of an hour.——From them I learnt Lady Mary Sutton came to England, on receiving an account from Mr. Delves that Miss Powis had the small-pox.—Happy for us, Dick, they lov'd Lady Mary too well to stay behind her!

As I was listening to their entertaining descriptions of places abroad, we were join'd by Lord Hallum.——Molesworth, said his Lordship, I will not suffer these girls to engage you solely:—My prating sisters are grown so saucy that I am obliged to be a very tyrant.

A spirited conversation ensued, in which the cherub sisters bore away the palm.

More and more sick of my batchelor notions!—Yet I aver, that state should be my choice, rather than swallow one grain of indifference in the matrimonial pill, gilder'd over ever so nicely.——Think what *must* be my friendship for Darcey, to tear myself from this engageing circle before nine!—As I was taking my leave, Lady Mary stepp'd towards me.—To-morrow, Mr. Molesworth, said her Ladyship, I bespeak the favour of your company and

---

1 In Greek mythology, the sirens were dangerously attractive females who inhabited the shore and sang sailors to shipwreck on the rocks.

Lord Darcey's to dine with me in *Pall-Mall*:[1]——I bow'd, and answer'd both for his Lordship and myself.

We shall rejoice, continued she, to congratulate your friend on his recovery,——looking with peculiar meaning at Miss Powis.—— I think by *that* look there will be an interview between the *lovers*, though I did not say so much to Darcey.——He requires sleep: none would he have had, if he knew my surmises.——I'll to bed, and dream of Lady Elizabeth;—*so* good night, Dick.

Twelve o'clock at noon.
Mr. and Mrs. Powis this moment gone;——Lord Darcey dressing to meet them in *Pall-Mall.*—Yes, they are to be there;—and the whole groupe of beauties are to be there;—Miss Powis,—Lady Elizabeth,—Lady Sophia,—and the little sprightly hawk-eyed Delves.—Risby, *you* know nothing of *life*; you are *dead* and *buried*.

I will try to be serious.—Impossible! my head runs round and round with pleasure.—The interview was affecting to the last degree.—Between whom?—Why Darcey, Mr. and Mrs.——faith I can write no more.

MOLESWORTH.

LETTER XLII.

The Hon. GEORGE MOLESWORTH to the same.

London.

T HE day of days is over!

I am too happy to sleep:—exquisite felicity wants not the common supports of nature.——In such scenes as I have witness'd, the *soul* begins to know herself:—she gives us a peep

---

1 Lady Mary Sutton is evidently truly wealthy, even if she only rents rather than owning a town house in ultra-fashionable Pall Mall. The name came from a seventeenth-century game, the ancestor of croquet. The area became a street near the royal palaces, at the very heart of London. In the eighteenth century it was known as the former residence of Prince Frederick (1707–51) (later to be the Prince Regent's Carleton House) and was a haunt of members of the aristocracy.

into futurity:—the enjoyments of this day has been all her own.

Once more I regain the beaten path of narrative.

Suppose me then under the hands of hair-dressers, valets, &c. &c. &c. I hate those fellows about me:—but the singularity of this visit made me undergo their tortures with tolerable patience.—Now was the time when Vanity, under pretence of respect, love, and decorum, usher'd in her implements.

It was about two when we were set down at Lady Mary Sutton's.—Darcey trembled, and look'd so pale at coming out of his chair, that I desir'd a servant to shew us to a room, where we might be alone 'till Mr. Powis was inform'd of our being in the house.——He instantly came with Lady Mary.——Tender welcomes and affectionate caresses fill'd him with new life.—Her Ladyship propos'd he should first see Miss Powis in her dressing-room;—that none should be present but Mr. and Mrs. Powis, her Ladyship, and your humble servant.

Judge how agreeable this must be to his Lordship, whose extreme weakness consider'd, could not have supported this interview before so much company as were assembled in the drawing-room.

The plan settled, Lady Mary withdrew to prepare Miss Powis for our reception.—A footman soon came with a message from her Ladyship that she expected us.

I was all compassionate at this moment:—the conflicts of my feeble friend were not to be conceal'd.——We follow'd Mr. Powis;—the door open'd;—Darcey turn'd half round, and laying his cold clammy hand on mine, said, Oh Molesworth! my happiness is in view!—how can I meet it?

Inimitable creature!—Can I describe your reception of my friend?—can I describe the dignity of beauty;—the melting softness of sensibility;—the blushing emotion of surprize?—No, Risby;—impossible!

The Ladies stood to receive us; Miss Powis supported between her mother and Lady Mary;—*she* all graceful timidity;—*they* all extasy and rapture.—Do you not expect to see Darcey at the feet of his mistress?——No; at Mrs. Powis's, at Lady Mary's, he fell.

The eyes of his Adorable glisten'd.——He was rais'd, and embrac'd tenderly——by the parents,——by Lady Mary.——Mr. Powis said, presenting him to his delighted daughter, *You*, my dear, must make *our* returns of gratitude to Lord Darcey;—giving him her more than passive hand, which he press'd to his lips with fervor, saying, *This* is the hour my soul has flown up to petition ——Dearest, best of women! tell me I am welcome.

She attempted to reply;—it was only an attempt.

She does bid you welcome, return'd Mr. Powis;——her *heart* bids you welcome.

Indeed, said she, I am not ungrateful:——*indeed*, my Lord, I am not insensible to the obligations you have laid me under.

As these words escap'd her, you must certainly take in the whole countenance of Darcey.

By this time we were seated, and Lady Mary return'd to the company.

Honour'd as I am, said his Lordship, addressing Miss Powis, will you permit me, Madam, in presence of your revered parents,——in presence of the friend to whom every wish of my heart has been confess'd;——will you permit me to hope you are not offended by my application to Sir James?——May I hope for your——

Friendship, my Lord (reply'd she, interrupting him); you may command my friendship.

Friendship! (retorted he) Miss Powis, starting up:—is that *all* I am to expect?—Can I accept your *friendship?*—No, Madam, the man who would have died for you aspires to more than friendship;—he aspires to your *love*.

I am no stranger, my Lord, return'd she, to the honour you intend me;——I am no stranger to *your* worth;——but I have scruples;—scruples that seem to me insurmountable.

I never saw him so affected.

For heaven's sake, Madam, he answer'd, don't drive me to despair:——tear not open the wound which the hand of Mercy has just clos'd:—my shatter'd frame will not bear another rub from fortune.——*What scruples?*——Tell me, Miss Powis, I conjure you.

You have none, my dear child, said Mrs. Powis. You have none, Fanny, said Mr. Powis, but what his Lordship can remove.

Indeed, Sir!——indeed, Madam! replied she, I meant not to give Lord Darcey pain.——Then turning to him in a tender, soothing accent,——Your peace, my Lord, has never been lightly regarded by me.——Here he brighten'd up,—and said, taking her hand, You know not, Miss Powis, from the first moment I saw you, how ardent,—how steady has been my love.

Why *then* my Lord, resum'd she,—why endeavour to gain my affections, yet hide your preference for me from the *world*;—even from *myself?*——Think of the *day* Lord Allen dined at the Abbey;—think what pass'd in a walk preceding *that* you set out for town:——on both these,—on many others, how mysterious your conduct?——If you thought me worthy your regard, my Lord, why *such* mysteries?

For God's sake, my dear,—dear Miss Powis, said Darcey, suffer me to vindicate myself.——Pardon me, my Lord (continued the angel that harangued him) hear me patiently another moment, and I will listen to your vindication.

She went on.

From whence can I suppose, my Lord, your embarrassments proceeded, if not from *some* entanglement grown irksome?—— No; before I can promise *myself* happiness, I must be first satisfied I do not borrow that *happiness* from *another.*

Another, Madam! repeated he, throwing himself at her feet: ——May all my brighter prospects fly me;—may my youth be blighted by the loss of reason if I have ever lov'd *another*!

She was affected with the solemnity of his air: one pearly drop stray'd down her cheek;—one that escap'd the liquid body of tenderness assembled in her eyes:—she could not speak, but held out her snowy hand for him to be seated.

He obey'd; and placing himself next her, so clearly accounted for that part of his conduct she call'd mysterious, that Mr. and Mrs. Powis both at once exclaim'd, Now, my dear, complete our felicity;—now all your *scruples must* be over.

And do you, said she, my tender, my indulgent parents, rising and throwing herself into their arms;—do you say it is in *my* power to complete your felicity?—*Will* confessing a preference for Lord Darcey;—*will* declaring I wish you to prefer him to your daughter;—will *that* complete it?

My friend caught the blushing beauty from the arms of her parents, and, frantic with joy, folded her to his bosom, standing as if he wonder'd at his own happiness.

What innocence in the look of Miss Powis, when she greatly acknowledg'd her heart!—How reverse from *this* innocence, *this* greatness, is the *prudish hypocrite*, who forbids *even* her features to say she is susceptible of love! You may suppose a profusion of friendly acknowledgments fell to *my* share; but I am not vain enough to repeat them.

It is well Lady Elizabeth stands portress[1] at the door of my heart:—there is such bustling and pushing to get in;—but, notwithstanding her Ladyship's vigilance, Miss Powis has slipp'd by, and sits perch'd up in the same corner with Darcey.

If you go back to Lady Mary's dressing-room, you will find nobody *there*:—but give a peep into the dining-parlour, and you will see us just set down at dinner;—*all* smiling,—*all* happy;—an inexhaustible fountain of pleasure in every breast.

I will go down to Slone Hall;[2]—give Lady Dorothy a hint that she has it now in her power to make one man happy;—*a hint* I

---

1 Guardian of the door.
2 Here "Slope Hall" in the original.

believe she never had before.—A snug twenty thousand added to my present fortune,——the hand of Lady Elizabeth,—and then, Risby, get hold of my skirts, and you mount with me.

Next Tuesday prepare, as governor of the castle, for a warm siege.—*Such* a battery of eyes,—*such* bundles of darts,——*such* stores of smiles,——*such* a train of innocence will be laid before the walls, as never was withstood!—No; I shall see you *cap-à-pée*[1] open the gates to the besiegers.——Away goes my pen.——I write no more positively.

MOLESWORTH.

LETTER XLIII.

Miss DELVES to Mrs. DELVES.

Barford Abbey.

ARE you well, Madam? Is my dear father well? Tell me you are, and never was so happy a creature as your daughter. I tremble with pleasure,——with joy,——with delight:—but I *must*——my duty, my affection, every thing says I *must* sit down to write.—You did not see how we were marshall'd at setting out:—I wish you could have got up early enough:—never was there such joyous party!

All in Lady Mary's dining-room by seven;——the fine equipages at the door;——servants attending in rich new liveries, to the number of twenty;—Lord Darcey and his heavenly bride that is to be,—smiling on each other,—smiling on all around;——Lady Mary Sutton—yes, *she* is heavenly *too*;—I believe I was the only earthly creature amongst them;—Lord and Lady Hampstead,——the angelic Ladies Elizabeth and Sophia,—Mr. Molesworth,——the generous, friendly, open-hearted Mr. Molesworth,——Lord Hallum.——But why mention him last?—Because, Bessy,[2] I suppose he was *last* in your thoughts.—Dear Madam, how can you think so?

In Lady Mary's coach went her Ladyship, Lord Darcey, Mrs. and Miss Powis:——in Lord Hampstead's, his Lordship, Lady

---

1 From the Old French *cap à pied* (head to foot), i.e., fully armed.
2 Nickname for Elizabeth.

Hampstead, Lady Elizabeth, and Mr. Molesworth:—in Lord Darcey's, Lady Sophia, Mr. Powis, Lord Hallum, and your little *good-for-nothing*:—in Mr. Powis's, the women-servants.—We lay fifty miles short of the Abbey, and the next evening reach'd it at seven.

We reach'd Barford Abbey, I say:—but what shall I say *now?*— I cannot do justice to what I have seen of duty,——of affection,— of joy,—of hospitality.—Do, dear Madam, persuade my father to purchase a house in *this* neighbourhood.

Servants were posted at the distance of six miles to carry intelligence when we should approach.——I suppose in their way back it was proclaim'd in the village:—men, women, and children, lined the road a mile from the Abbey, throwing up their hats with loud huzzaing;—bells ringing in every adjacent parish;—bonfires on every rising ground;——in short, we were usher'd in like conquerors.——The coachmen whipp'd up their horses full speed through the park;——thump, thump, went my heart, when by a number of lights I discover'd we were just at the house.

What sensations did I feel when the carriages stopp'd!——At the entrance stood Sir James and Lady Powis,——the Chaplain,—Mr. Morgan,—Captain Risby,——you know their characters, Madam;——every servant in the house with a light:—but who could have stay'd within at this juncture?

The first coach that drove up was Lady Mary's. Out sprang Lord Darcey, Miss Powis in his hand; both in a moment lock'd in parental embraces.——Good heaven, what extasy!—I thought Mr. Watson and Mr. Morgan would have fought a duel which should first have folded Miss Powis in his arms, whilst Sir James and Lady Powis quitted her to welcome Lady Mary.——We were all receiv'd tenderly affectionate:—a reception none can have an idea of, but those who have been at Barford Abbey.

In my way to the house, I suppose I had a hundred kisses:— *God knows from whom.*—What can I say of Lord Hampstead's family?—what of Mr. Molesworth?——The general notice taken of him is sufficient.——Absolutely that charming man will be spoil'd.——Pity to set him up for an idol!——I hope he will not *always* expect to be worshipp'd.——Mr. Risby *too*——Well, I'll mention you all, one after another, as fast as possible.——Let me see, where did I leave off?——Oh! we were just out of our carriages.——And now for the pathetics:——an attempt;—a humble attempt only.

Lady Powis, Lady Mary, and their darling, had given us the slip.—What could be done?——I mean with Mr. Morgan:—he was quite outrageous.—What could be done? I repeat.—Why Sir James, to pacify him, said, we should all go and surprize them in his Lady's dressing-room.——We did go;—we did surprize them;—great God! in what an attitude!—The exalted Lady Powis at the feet of Lady Mary;——Miss Powis kneeling by her;——she endeavouring to raise them.—I said it would be an attempt at the pathetics;—it must be an attempt:—I can proceed no farther.

To be sure, Mr. Morgan is a queer-looking man, but a great favourite at the Abbey.——He took Miss Powis on his knee;—call'd her a hundred times his dear, dear daughter;—and I could not forbear laughing, when he told her he had not wore a tye-wig[1] before these twenty years. This drew me to observe his dress, which, unless you knew the man, you can have no idea how well it suited him:—a dark snuff-colour'd coat with gold buttons, which I suppose by the fashion of it, was made when he accustomed himself to *tye-wigs*;—the lace a rich orrice;[2] but then it was so immoderately short, both in the sleeves and skirts, that whilst full dress'd he appeared to want cloathing.

The *next* morning,——ay, the *next* morning, then it was I lost my freedom.—Disrob'd of his gingerbread coat, I absolutely fell a sacrifice to a plain suit of broad cloth,——or rather, to a noble, plain heart.—Now pray, dear Madam, do not cross me in my *first* love;——at least, *see* Mr. Morgan, before you command me to give him up:——and you, sweet Sir, steal to a corner of your new possession, whilst I take notice of those who are capering to my fingers ends.

---

1 A wig with a sort of pig-tail tied with a bow, standard formal wear for gentlemen in the late eighteenth century.
2 A coat or jacket of a buff or brown color, adorned with lace including thread of silver or gold.

You have seen Miss Powis, Madam, on Mr. Morgan's knee;——you have heard him say enough to fill any other girl than myself with jealousy:—nay, Madam, you may smile;—he really makes love to me.——But for a moment let me forget my lover;—let me forget his *melting* sighs,—his *tender* protestations,——his *persuasive* eloquence,—his air *so* languishing:—let me forget them *all*, I say, and lead you to the library, where by a message flew Miss Powis.—A look from her drew me after:—I suppose Lord Darcey had a touch from the same magnet.

A venerable pair with joy next to phrenzy caught her in their extended arms, as the door open'd. My *kind*, my dear, *ever* dear friends, said the lovely creature,—and is it *thus* we meet? is it *thus* I return to you?——Mr. Jenkings clasp'd her to him; but his utterance was quite choak'd:—the old Lady burst into a flood of tears, and then cried out,—How great is thy mercy, O God!—Suffer me to be grateful.——Again she flew to their arms;—again they folded her to their bosoms.——Lord Darcey too embrac'd them;—he condescendingly kiss'd their hands;—he said, next to the parents of his Fanny,—next to Lady Mary, they were most dear to him.——Miss Powis seated herself between them, and hung about the neck of Mrs. Jenkings;—whilst his Lordship, full of admiration, look'd as if his great soul labour'd for expression.——

Overcome with tender scenes, I left the library.——I acquainted Lady Mary who was there, and she went to them immediately.——Mr. Watson and Mr. Morgan for a quarter of an hour were all my own;—captain Risby, Mr. Molesworth, Lady Elizabeth and Sophia, being engag'd in a conversation at another part of the room:—you may *guess* our subject, Madam;——but I declare, whilst listening to Mr. Watson, I thought myself soaring above earthly enjoyments.——

Sir James, who had follow'd Lady Mary, soon return'd with her Ladyship, Miss Powis, Lord Darcey, and, what gave me heart-felt pleasure, the steward and his wife;—an honour they with difficulty accepted, as they were strangers to Lord Hampstead's family.——

Who says there is not in this life perfect happiness?—I say they are mistaken:—such felicity as I here see and partake of, cannot be call'd imperfect.——How comes it that the domestics of *this* family *so* much surpass those of *other* people?—how is it *one* interest governs the whole?—I want to know a thousand mysteries.——I could write,—I could think eternally,—of the first happy evening.——First happy evening do I say? And can the days that crown that eve be forgot?——Heaven forbid! at least whilst I have recollection.——My heart speaks so fast to my pen, that fain my fingers would,—but cannot keep up with it.

The next morning Lord Darcey introduc'd to us the son of Mr. Jenkings.——A finer youth I never saw!—Well might the old gentleman be *suspicious*.—Few fathers would, like *him*, have sacrificed the interest of a son, to preserve that of a friend.——To know the real rank of Miss Powis;—her ten thousand virtues;—her great expectations; yet act with so *much* caution!—with an anxiety which the most sordid miser watching his treasure, could not have exceeded! and for *what?*—Why lest involuntarily she might enrich his belov'd son with *her* affections.——Will you part with me to this extraordinary man?——Only for an hour or two.——A walk is propos'd.——Our ramble will not be farther than his house.——You say I may go. Thank you, Madam: I am gone.

*

Just return'd from the steward's, so cramm'd with sweet-meats, cake, and jellies, that I am absolutely stupified.

I must tell you who led Miss Powis.—Lord Darcey, to be sure.——No, Madam; I had the favour of his Lordship's arm:——it was Edmund.——I call him Edmund;—every body calls him Edmund;——*yes,* and at Lord Darcey's request *too.*—Never shall I forget in what a graceful manner!—But his Lordship does every thing with grace.—He mention'd something of past times, hinting he should not always have courted him to *such* honour, presenting the hand of his belov'd.

I wish I could send you her look at that moment; it was all love,—all condescension.——I say I cannot send it.——Mortifying! I cannot even borrow *it.*

Adieu, dear Madam!—Adieu, dear Sir!—Adieu, you best of parents!——It is impossible to say which is most dear to your ever dutiful and affectionate

E. DELVES.

LETTER XLIV.

Miss DELVES to the same.

Barford Abbey.

LOST my heart *again!*——Be not surpriz'd, Madam; I lose and find it ten times a day;—yet it never strays from Barford Abbey.—The last account you had from me it was button'd inside Mr. Morgan's hunting-frock:——since that, it has been God knows with whom:—sometimes wrapt in a red coat;—sometimes in a blue;—sometimes in a green:—but finding many competitors flew to black, where it now lies snug, warm, and easy.—Restless creature! I will never take it home again.

What think you, Madam, of a *Dean* for a son-in-law?

What do I think? you say.——Why the gentlemen of the church have too much sense and gravity to take my madcap off my hands.——Well, Madam, but suppose the Dean of H—— now you look pleas'd.—Oh, the Dean of *H*——! What the *Dean,* Bessy, that Lady Mary used to talk of:—the *Dean* that married Mr. and Mrs. Powis.

As sure as I live, Madam, the *very* man:—and *to-morrow,—to-morrow* at ten, he is to unite their lovely daughter with Lord Darcey.—Am I not *very* good,—*extremely* good, *indeed,* to sit down and write,—when every person below is solacing themselves on the approach of this happy festival?

I would suffer shipwreck ten times;—ten times would I be drove on uninhabited islands, for such a husband as Lord Darcey.——Miss Powis's danger was only imaginary, yet *she* must be *so* rewarded.—Well, she shall be rewarded:——she *ought* to be rewarded:——Lord Darcey shall reward her.

But is it not *very* hard upon your *poor* girl, that *all* the young smarts we brought down, and *that* which we found *here*, should have dispos'd of their hearts?—*All*;——even Lord Hallum,—*he* who used to boast so much of freedom,——now owns he has dispos'd of his.—

But to whom?——Aye: that's a question.—

They think, perhaps, the *old* stuff will do well enough for poor me!——Thanks to my genius, I can set *my* cap at any thing.[1]

Why there's something tolerable in the sound of a Dean's Lady.——Let me see if it will do.—"The *Deans*'s coach;—the *Dean*'s servants."——Something better this than a plain *Mr.* ——

Here comes Miss Powis. Now shall I be forc'd to huddle this into my pocket.——I am resolv'd she shall not see the preferment I have chalk'd out for myself.——No, no; I must be secret, or I shall have it taken from me.

This Miss Powis,——*this* very dutiful young Lady, that I used to have set up for a pattern,—*now* tells me that I *must* write no more; that you will not expect to hear from me 'till the next post.—If I *must* take Miss Powis's advice in every thing;— if I *must* be guided by *her*;—you know *who* said this, Madam;— why then there is an end of my scribbling for this night.—But remember it is not *my* fault.—No, indeed, I was sat down as sober sedate as could be.——Quite fit for a Dean's Lady?— Yes;—quite fit, indeed.—Now comes Lady Elizabeth and Lady Sophia.—Well, it is impossible, I find, to be dutiful in this house.

*

Thursday, twelve o'clock at noon.
Bless my soul! one would think I was the bride by my shaking and quaking! Miss Powis is—Lady Darcey.—Down drops my

---

1 Try to attract a man. As a banker's daughter, Miss Delves is of a lower class than her new associates, which is why she does not attend the wedding.

letter:——Yes, dear Madam, I see you drop it to run and tell my father.

I may write on *now*;—I may do what I will;—Lord and Lady Darcey are *every* thing with *every* body.

Well as I love them, I was not present at the ceremony:——I don't know why neither.—Not a soul but attended, except your poor foolish girl.——At the window I stood to see them go, and never stirr'd a step 'till they return'd.—Mr. Molesworth gave her away.——I vow I thought near as handsome as the bride-groom.——But what signifies my thinking him handsome?—I'll ask Lady Elizabeth by and bye what she thinks.—Now for a little about it, before I attire myself with implements of destruction.— The Dean is not *quite* dead yet; but if he live out this day,—I say, he is invulnerable.

Let us hear no more of yourself:—tell us of Lord and Lady Darcey.

Have patience, Madam, and I will,

Well, *their* dress?—Why *their* faces were dress'd in smiles of love:—Nature's charms should always take place of art.——You see with what order I proceed.

Lord Darcey was dress'd in white richly lac'd with gold;—— Lady Darcey in a white lutestring négligée flounc'd deep with a silver net;—no cap, a diamond sprig; her hair without powder; a diamond necklace and sleeve-knots;[1]—bracelets set round with diamonds; and let me tell you, her jewels are a present from my first Adorable;——on the knowledge of which I discarded him.—No, no, Mr. Morgan; you are not a *jewel* of yourself neither.—Lady Darcey would have wore quite a morning disha-bille,[2] if the vain old Gentleman had not requested the con-trary:—so forsooth, to humour him, we must be all put out of our way.

---

1 The lack of powder or any other headdress makes Fanny's outfit rather modern and more akin to our contemporary wedding attire than to eigh-teenth-century formal wear.

2 Dressed in a careless and informal manner.

There they are on the lawn, as I hope to live, going to invite in Cæsar.——Only an old dog, Madam, that lives betwixt this house and the steward's.

Lady Elizabeth and Mr. Molesworth, Lady Sophia and Captain Risby,—Oh, I long to be with you!——throw no more gravel to my window.——I *will* be dutiful;—in spite of your allurements, I *will*.

I left them in the library, inspecting a very charming piece,[1] just brought from Brandon Lodge, done by the hand of Lady Mary Sutton.—Upon my word, they have soon conn'd it over:—but I have not told you it is the portraits of Mr. and Mrs. Powis;——my dear Dean too joining their hands.——

God defend me! there he is, hopping out.—I wish he had kept within.—Why, Sir, I should have been down in a moment: then we might have had the most comfortable tête-à-tête.

Seriously, Madam—now I am *really* serious—can you believe, after beholding Lord and Lady Darcey, I will ever be content with a moderate share of happiness?—No; I will die first.—To see them at this instant would be an antidote for indifference.—Not any thing of foolish fondness:—no; that will never be seen in Lord and Lady Darcey.——Their happiness is not confin'd:—we are all refreshed by it:—it pours forth from their hearts like streams flowing from a pure fountain. ——I think I said I could not go to church:—no, not for the world would I have gone:——I expected Miss Powis would be crying, fainting, and I know not what.——Instead of all this .fuss, not a tear was shed.——I thought every body cried when they were married:—those that *had*, or had *not* cause.—Well, I am determin'd to appear satisfied, however, if the yoke is a little galling.

How charming look'd Miss Powis, when she smil'd on Lord Darcey!—On Lord Darcey? On every body I mean.—And for him—But I must forget his air,——his words,—his looks, if ever I intend to say love, honour, and obey.——Once I am

---

1 The painting by Lady Mary Sutton recording the wedding of Fanny's parents.

brought to say love,—honour and obey will slide off glibly enough.[1] I must go down amongst them. Believe me, Madam, I shut myself up to write against intreaties,—against the most persuasive eloquence.

This is the day when the Powis family are crown'd with felicity.—I think on it with rapture.——I will set it down on the heart of your dutiful and affectionate

E. DELVES.

LETTER XLV.

Miss DELVES to the same.

Barford Abbey.

S URELY I must smell of venison,—roast beef, and plumb-puddings.—Yes, I smell of the Old English hospitality.—*You,* Madam, have no tenants to regale so;——are safe from such troubles on my account.——Will you believe me, Madam, I had rather see their honest old faces than go to the finest opera ever exhibited.——What think you of a hundred-and-seven chearful farmers sitting at long tables spread with every thing the season can afford;—two hogsheads of wine[2] at their elbows;——the servants waiting on them with assiduous respect:——Their songs still echo in my ears.

I thought the roof would have come down, when Lord and Lady Darcey made their appearance.——Some sung one tune,—some another;—some paid extempore congratulations;—others that had not a genius, made use of ballads compos'd on the marriage of the King and Queen.—One poor old soul cried to the Butler, because he could neither sing or repeat a verse.—Seeing his distress, I went to him, and repeated a few lines applicable to

---

1 From the marriage service in the Anglican Book of Common Prayer. The woman (not the man) must promise "to love, honour and obey" her husband.

2 A barrel used for storing food, liquid, and other commodities. Although there were several attempts, including an act of Parliament, to standardize the size of a hogshead, sizes varied until the nineteenth century by product and locality. Two hogsheads of wine, however, would likely have been around 100 imperial gallons (455 liters).

the occasion, which he caught in a moment, and tun'd away with the best of them.

Lord and Lady Hampstead are so delighted with the honest rustics, that they declare every Christmas their tenants shall be regal'd at Hallum Grove.

What can one feel equal to the satisfaction which arises on looking out in the park?—Three hundred poor are there feasting under a shed erected for the purpose;—cloath'd by Sir James and Lady Powis;—*so* clean,—*so* warm,—*so* comfortable, that to see them at this moment, one would suppose they had never tasted of poverty.

Lord Darcey has order'd two hundred guineas to be given amongst them,—that to-morrow might not be less welcome to them than this day.

For my part, I have only two to provide for out of the number;——a pretty little boy and girl, that pick'd me up before I came to the shed.——The parents of those children were very good, and gave them to me on my first application.

Here comes Mrs. Jenkings.——*Well*, what pleasing thing have you to tell me, Mrs. Jenkings?

Five hundred pounds, as I live, to be given to the poor to-morrow from Lady Mary Sutton.—

What blessings will follow us on our journey! I believe I have not told you, Madam, we set out for Faulcum Park[1] on Monday.—*Not* to stay:—no, I thank God we are *not* to stay.—If Lord and Lady Darcey were to inhabit Faulcum Park, yet it would not be to *me* like Barford Abbey.——Barford Abbey is to be their home whilst Sir James and Lady Powis live.

Lord Hallum wants me to walk with him.——Not I, indeed: —I hate a *tête-à-tête* with heartless men.—On second thoughts, I will go.

---

1 Faulcon Park.

Oh Madam! out of breath with astonishment!—What think you?—I am the confidante of Lord Hallum's passion;—with permission too of the earl and countess.——Heavens! and can you guess, Madam, who it is he loves?—Adieu, my *dear*,—dear *Dean*!—Need I say more?——Will you not spare the blushes of your happy daughter,

E. DELVES?

FINIS.

Appendix A: "Writing to the Moment": The Epistolary Style

1. From Daniel Defoe, *Tour thro' the Whole Island of Great Britain* (Vol. 2; London: G. Strathan, 1725), pp. 135–37

[Daniel Defoe (1660–1731) was a notorious English writer, business-man, and reputed spy. His novel *Robinson Crusoe* (1719) is often credited with helping to define the genre. In his three-volume *Tour* (1724–27), Defoe provides a blend of fictional and nonfictional accounts derived from his extensive travels around Great Britain. In this excerpt, Defoe discusses the recent successes of the post office in connecting the diverse parts of Great Britain with each other, with the European continent, and with other parts abroad.]

The *Post Office*, a Branch of the Revenue formerly not much valued, but now, by the additional Penny upon the Letters, and by the visible Increase of Business in the Nation, is grown very considerable. This Office maintains now, Pacquet Boats to *Spain* and *Portugal*, which never was done before: So the Merchants Letters for *Cadiz* or *Lisbonne*, which were before Two and Twenty Days in going over *France* and *Spain* to *Lisbonne*, oftentimes arrive there now, in Nine or Ten Days from *Falmouth*.

Likewise, they have a Pacquet from *Marseilles* to *Port Mahone*, in the *Mediterranean*, for the constant Communication of Letters with his Majesty's Garrison and People in the Island of *Minorca*.

They have also a Pacquet from *England* to the *West-Indies*; but I am not of Opinion, that they will keep it up for much Time longer, if it be not already let fall.

This Office is kept in *Lombard Street*, in a large House, formerly Sir *Robert Viner*'s, once a rich Goldsmith; but ruined at the shutting up of the *Exchequer* [...].

The *Penny Post*, a modern Contrivance of a private Person, one Mr. *William Dockraw*, is now made a Branch of the general Revenue by the *Post Office*; and though, for a Time, it was subject to Miscarriages and Mistakes, yet now it is come also into so exquisite a Management, that nothing can be more exact, and 'tis with the utmost Safety and Dispatch, that Letters are delivered at the remotest Corners of the Town, almost as soon as they could be sent by a Messenger, and that from Four, Five, Six, to Eight Times a Day, according as the Distance of the Place makes it practicable; and you may send a Letter from *Ratcliff* or

Limehouse in the *East*, to the farthest Part of *Westminster* for a Penny, and that several Times in the same day.

Nor are you tied up to a single Piece of Paper, as in the *General Post-Office*, but any Packet under a Pound weight, goes at the same Price.

I mention this the more particularly, because it is so manifest a Testimony to the Greatness of this City, and to the great Extent of Business and Commerce in it, that this Penny Conveyance should raise so many Thousand Pounds in a Year, and employ so many poor People in the Diligence of it, as this Office employs.

We see nothing of this at *Paris*, at *Amsterdam*, at *Hamburgh*, or any other City, that ever I have seen, or heard of.

2. From Samuel Richardson, *Letters Written To and For Particular Friends, on the Most Important Occasions* (London: C. Rivington, 1741)

[Samuel Richardson (1689–1761), a successful printer and publisher, was commissioned in 1739 by two other publishers to provide a volume of exemplary letters designed to teach others how to conduct their correspondence. While designing his "letter-writer," Richardson began inventing characters and scenes, even whole narratives. He became so intrigued by the inventive task that he developed some of the letters printed here into his first epistolary novel, *Pamela* (1741).]

Preface

The following Letters are publish'd at the Solicitation of particular Friends, who are of Opinion, that they will answer several good Ends, as they may not only direct the *Forms* requisite to be observed on the most important Occasions; but, what is more to the Purpose, by the Rules and Instructions contained in them, contribute to *mend the Heart*, and *improve the Understanding*.

NATURE, PROPRIETY OF CHARACTER, PLAIN SENSE, and GENERAL USE, have been the chief Objects of the Author's Attention in the penning of these Letters; and as he every-where aimed to write to the *Judgment*, rather than to the *Imagination*, he would chuse, that they should generally be found more *useful* than *diverting:* Tho', where the Subjects require *Strokes of Humour*, and *innocent Raillery*, it will be seen, perhaps, that the Method he has taken, was the Effect of *Choice*, and not merely of *Necessity*.

The Writer is no Friend to long Prefaces; but it may be necessary, however, to say, what he has *aimed at* in this Performance; and to leave his *Merit* to the *Execution* of it, to proper Judges.

He has endeavour'd then, in general, throughout the great Variety of his Subjects, to inculcate the Principles of *Virtue* and *Benevolence*; to describe *properly*, and recommend *strongly*, the SOCIAL and RELATIVE DUTIES; and to place them in such *practical* Lights, that the Letters maybe serve for Rules to THINK and ACT by, as well as Forms to WRITE after.

Particularly, he has endeavoured to point out the Duty of a *Servant*, not a *Slave*; the Duty of a *Master*, not a *Tyrant*; that of the *Parent*, not as a Person morose and sour, and hard to be pleased; but mild, indulgent, kind, and such an one as would rather govern by *Persuasion* than *Force*.

He has endeavour'd to direct the young Man in the Choice of his *Friends* and *Companions*; to excite him to *Diligence*; to discourage *Extravagance*, *Sottishness*, and *Vice* of all Kinds.

He has aimed to set forth, in a Variety of Cases, to *both Sexes*, the Inconveniences attending *unsuitable Marriages*; to expose the Folly of a *litigious Spirit*; to console the *Unhappy*; to comfort the *Mourner*. And many of these by Arguments, tho' *easy* and *familiar*, yet *new* and *uncommon*.

With regard to the Letters of *Courtship*, the Author has aimed to point out such Methods of Address, to a young Man, as may stand the Test of the *Parents Judgment*, as well as the *Daughter's Opinion*; and, at the same time, that they should not want the proper Warmth of Expression, which Complaisance, and Passion for the beloved Object, inspire, (and is so much expected in Addresses of this Nature) they should have their Foundation laid in *common Sense*, and a *manly Sincerity*; and, in a Word, be such as a *prudent Woman* need not blush to receive, nor a *discreet Man* be ashamed to look back upon, when the *doubtful Courtship* is changed into the *matrimonial Certainty*.

With this View he has also attempted to expose the *empty Flourishes*, and *incoherent Rhapsodies*, by which *shallow Heads*, and *designing Hearts*, endeavor to exalt their Mistresses into *Goddesses*, in hopes of having it in their Power to sink them into the Characters of the *most Credulous* and *Foolish* of their Sex.

Orphans, and *Ladies of independent Fortunes*, he has particularly endeavour'd to guard against the insidious Arts of their *flattering* and *selfish* Dependents, and the *clandestine* Addresses of *Fortune-hunters*, those Beasts of Prey, as they may well be called, who spread their Snares for the *innocent* and *thoughtless* Heart.

These, among other no less material Objects, have been the Author's principal *Aim*: How well he has *succeeded*, must, as has been hinted, be left to the Judgment of the candid Reader.

XII. *Against a sudden Intimacy, or Friendship, with one of a short Acquaintance.*

Cousin Tom,

I AM just setting out for *Windsor*, and have not time to say so much as I would on the Occasion upon which I now write to you. I hear that Mr. *Douglas* and you have lately contracted such an Intimacy, that you are hardly ever asunder; and as I know his Morals are not the best, nor his Circumstances the most happy, I fear he will, if he has not already done it, let you see, that he better knows what he does in seeking *your* Acquaintance, than you do in cultivating *his*.

I am far from desiring to abridge you in any necessary or innocent Liberty, or to prescribe too much to your Choice of a Friend: Nor am I against your being complaisant to *Strangers*; for this Gentleman's Acquaintance is not yet a Month old with you; but you must not think every Man whose Conversation is agreeable, fit to be immediately treated as a Friend: Of all Sorts, hastily contracted Friendships promise the least Duration or Satisfaction; as they most commonly arise from Design on one Side, and Weakness on the other. *True Friendship* must be the Effect of long and mutual Esteem and Knowledge: It ought to have for its Cement, an Equality of Years, a Similitude of Manners, and, pretty much, a Parity in Circumstance and Degree. But, generally speaking, an Openness to a Stranger carries with it strong Marks of Indiscretion, and not seldom ends in Repentance.

For these Reasons, I would be glad you would be upon your Guard, and proceed cautiously in this new Alliance. Mr. *Douglas* has Vivacity and Humour enough to please any Man of a light Turn; but were I to give my Judgment of him, I should pronounce him fitter for the Tea-table, than the Cabinet. He is smart, but very superficial; and treats all serious Subjects with a Contempt too natural to bad Minds; and I know more young Men than one, of whose good Opinion he has taken Advantage, and has made them wiser though at their own Expence, than he found them.

The Caution I here give you, is the pure Effect of my Experience in Life, some Knowledge of your new Associate, and my Affection for you. The Use you make of it will determine, whether you merit this Concern from

Your affectionate Kinsman.

XV. *From a young Lady to her Father, acquainting him with a Proposal*
of Marriage made to her.

Honoured Sir, *Nottingham, April* 4.

I THINK it my Duty to acquaint you, that a Gentleman of this
Town, by Name *Derham*, and by Business a Linen-draper, has
made some Overtures to my Cousin *Morgan*, in the way of Courtship to me. My Cousin has brought him once or twice into my
Company, which he could not well decline doing, because he has
Dealings with him; and has a high Opinion of him, and his Circumstances. He has been set up Three Years, and has very good Business,
and lives in Credit and Fashion. He is about Twenty-seven Years old,
and a likely Man enough: He seems not to want Sense or Manners;
and is come of a good Family. He has broke his Mind to me, and
boasts how well he can maintain me: But, I assure you, Sir, I have
given him no Encouragement; and told him, that I had no Thoughts
of changing my Condition, yet awhile; and should never think of it but
in Obedience to my Parents; and I desired him to talk no more of that
Subject to me. Yet he resolves to persevere, and pretends extraordinary
Affection and Esteem. I would not, Sir, by any means, omit to
acquaint you with the *Beginnings* of an Affair, that would be want of
Duty in me to conceal from you, and shew a Guilt and Disobedience
unworthy of the kind Indulgence and Affection you have always shewn
to, Sir,

Your most dutiful Daughter.

My humble Duty to my honour'd Mother, Love to my Brother and
Sister; and Respects to all Friends. Cousin *Morgan*, and his Wife and
Sister desire their kind Respects. I cannot speak enough of their Civil-
ity to me.

XVI. *The Father's Answer, on a Supposition that he approves not of the*
young Man's Addresses.

Dear Polly, *Northampton, Apr.* 10

I HAVE received your Letter dated the 4th Instant, wherein you
acquaint me of the Proposals made to you, thro' your Cousin
Morgan's Recommendation, by one Mr. *Derham*. I hope, as you assure
me, that you have given no Encouragement to him: For I by no means
approve of him for your Husband. I have inquired of one of his Towns-
men, who knows him and his Circumstances very well; and I am
neither pleased with them, nor with his Character; and wonder my

Cousin would so inconsiderately recommend him to you. Indeed, I doubt not Mr. *Morgan*'s good Intentions; but I insist upon it, that you think nothing of the Matter, if you would oblige

Your indulgent Father.

Your Mother gives her Blessing to you, and joins me in the above Advice. Your Brother and Sister, and all Friends, send their Love and Respects to you.

XVII. *The Father's Answer, on a Supposition that he does not disapprove of the young Man's Addresses.*

My dear Daughter, *Northampt. Apr.* 10

I N Answer to yours of the 4th Instant, relating to the Addresses of Mr. *Derham,* I would have you neither wholly encourage nor discourage his Suit; for if, on Inquiry into his Character and Circumstances, I shall find that they are answerable to your Cousin's good Opinion of them, and his own Assurances, I know not but his Suit may be worthy of Attention. But, my Dear, consider, that Men are deceitful, and always put the best Side outwards; and it may possibly, on the strict Inquiry, which the Nature and Importance of the Case demands, come out far otherwise than it at present appears. Let me advise you therefore, to act in this Matter with great Prudence, and that you make not yourself too cheap; for Men are apt to slight what is too easily obtained. Your Cousin will give him Hope enough, while you don't absolutely deny him; and in the mean time, he may be told, that you are not at your own Disposal; but intirely resolved to abide by my Determination and Direction, in an Affair of this great Importance: And this will put him upon applying to me, who, you need not doubt, will in this Case, as in all others, study your Good; as becomes

Your indulgent Father.

Your Mother gives her Blessing to you, and joins with me in the above Advice. Your Brother and Sister, and all Friends, send their Love and Respects to you.

XVIII. *The young Gentleman's Letter to the Father, apprising him of his Affection for his Daughter.*

Sir, *Northampton, April* 12.

I TAKE the Liberty, tho' personally unknown to you, to declare the great Value and Affection I have for your worthy Daughter, whom I have had the Honour to see at my good Friend Mr. *Morgan*'s. I should think myself intirely unworthy of *her* Favour, and of *your* Approbation, if I could have a Thought of influencing her Resolution but in Obedience to your Pleasure; as I should, on such a Supposition, offer an Injury likewise to that Prudence in *herself*, which I flatter myself, is not the least of her amiable Perfections. If I might have the Honour of your Countenance, Sir, on this Occasion, I would open myself and Circumstances to you, in that frank and honest manner which should convince you of the Sincerity of my Affection for your Daughter, and at the same time of the Honourableness of my Intentions. In the mean time, I will in general say, That I have been set up in my Business in the Linen-drapery way, upwards of Three Years; that I have a very good Trade for the Time: That I had 1000 *l.* to begin with, which I have improved to 1500 *l.* as I am ready to make appear to your Satisfaction: That I am descended of a creditable Family; have done nothing to stain my Character; and that my trade is still further improveable, as I shall, I hope, inlarge my Bottom. This, Sir, I thought but honest and fair to acquaint you with, that you might know something of a Person, who sues to you for your Countenance, and that of your good Lady, in an Affair that I hope may prove one Day the greatest Happiness of my Life; as it *must* be, if I can be blessed with that, and your dear Daughter's Approbation. In Hope of which, and the Favour of a Line, I take the Liberty to subscribe myself, Good Sir,

Your most obedient humble Servant.

XIX. *From the Cousin to the Father and Mother, in Commendation of the young Gentleman.*

Dear Cousins, *Northampton, Apr. 12.*

I GIVE you both Thanks for so long continuing with us the Pleasure of Cousin *Polly*'s Company. She has intirely captivated a worthy Friend of mind, Mr. *Derham*, a Linen-draper of this Town. And I would have acquainted you with it myself, but that I knew and advised Cousin *Polly* to write to you about it; for I would not for the world any thing of this sort should be carried on unknown to you, at my House, especially. Mr. *Derham* has shewn me his Letter to you; and I believe every Tittle of it to be true; and really, if you and my Cousin approve it, as also Cousin *Polly*, I don't know where she can do better. I am sure I should think so, if I had a Daughter he could love.

Thus much I thought myself obliged to say; and with my kind Love to your other Self, and all my Cousins, as also my *Wife*'s, and *Sister*'s, I remain

Your affectionate Cousin.

XX. *From the Father, in Answer to the young Gentleman.*

Sir, *Nottingham, April* 16.

I HAVE received yours of the 12th, and am obliged to you for the good Opinion you express of my Daughter. But I think she is yet full young to alter her Condition, and imbark in the Cares of a Family. I cannot but say, that the Account you give of yourself, and your Application to *me*, rather than first to try to engage the Affections of my Daughter, carry a very honourable Appearance, and such as must be to the Advantage of your Character. As to your Beginning, Sir, that is not to be so much looked upon, as the *Improvement*; and I doubt not, that you can make good Proof what you assert on this Occasion. But still I must needs say, that I think, and so does her Mother, that it is too early to incumber her with the Cares of the World; and as I am sure she will do nothing in so important an Affair without our Advice, so I would not, for the world, in a Case so nearly concerning her, and her future Welfare, constrain her in the least. I intend shortly to send for her home; for she has been longer absent from us, than we intended; and then I shall consult her Inclinations; and you will excuse me to say, for she is my Daughter, and a very good Child, tho' I say it, that I shall then determine myself by what, and by what shall appear to offer most for her Good. In the mean time, Sir, I thank you for the Civility and commendable Openness of yours; and am,

Your Humble Servant.

The Father in this Letter referring pretty much to the Daughter's Choice, the young Gentleman cannot but construe it as an Encouragement to him, to prosecute his Addresses to *her*; in which he doubles his Diligence, (on the Hint, that she will soon return to *Nottingham*) in order to gain a Footing in her good Will; and she, finding her Father and Mother not averse to the Affair, ventures to give him some room to think his Addresses not indifferent to her; but still altogether on Condition of her Parents Consent and Approbation. By the Time then, that she is recalled home, (nothing disagreeable having appeared in the young Gentleman's Behaviour, and his general Character being consistent with his Pretensions) there may be supposed some Degree of Familiarity and Confidence to have pass'd between them; and she gives him Hope, that she will receive a Letter from him, tho' she will not promise an Answer; intirely referring to her Duty to her Parents, and their good Pleasure. He attends her on her Journey a good Part of the way, as far as she will permit; and when her Cousin, his Friend, informs him of her safe Arrival at *Nottingham*, he sends the following Letter.

XXI. *From the young Gentleman to his Mistress on her Arrival at her* *Father's.*

Dear Madam,   *May 25.*

I HAVE understood with great Pleasure your safe Arrival at your Father's House; of which I take the Liberty to congratulate your good Parents, as well as your dear Self. I will not, Madam, fill this Letter with the Regret I had to part with you, because I have no Reason nor Merit, at present, to expect that you should be concerned for me on this Score. Yet, Madam, I am not without Hope, from the Sincerity of my Affection for you, and the Honesty of my Intentions, to deserve in time, those Regards which I cannot at present flatter myself with. As your good Father, in his kind Letter to me, assured me, that he should consult your Inclinations, and determine by them, and by what should offer most for your Good; how happy should I be, if I could find my humble Suit not quite indifferent to your dear Self, and not rejected by Him! If what I have already opened to him as my Circumstances, be not unacceptable, I should humbly hope for Leave to pay you and him a Visit at *Nottingham*; or if this be too great a Favour, till he has made further Enquiry, that he would be pleased to give himself that Trouble, and put it in my Power, as soon as possible, to convince him of the Truth of my Allegations, upon which I desire to stand or fall in my Hopes of your Favour and his. For I think, far different from many in the World, that a Deception in an Affair of this weighty Nature, should be less forgiven than in any other. Since then, dearest Madam, I build my Hopes more on the Truth of my Affection for you, and the Honour of my Intentions, than any other Merit, or Pretensions, I hope you will condescend, if not to become an Advocate for me, which would be too great a Presumption to expect, yet to let your good Parents know, that you have no Aversion to the Person or Address of, dearest Madam,

> *Your for ever-obliged, and affectionate humble*
> *Servant,*

My best Respects attend your good father and Mother, and whole Family.

As this puts the Matter into such a Train, as may render more Writing unnecessary; the next Steps to be taken, being the Inquiry into the Truth of the young Man's Assertions, and a Confirmation of his Character; and then the Proposals on the Father's Part of what he will give with his Daughter; all which may be done best by word of Mouth, or Interposition of Friends; so we shall have no Occasion to pursue this Instance of Courtship further.

LIII. *To a young Lady, advising her not to change her Guardians, nor to encourage any clandestine Addresses.*

Dear Miss,

THE Friendship which long subsisted between your prudent Mother and me, has always made me attend to your Welfare with more than a common Concern: And I could not conceal my Surprize at hearing, that you intend to remove the Guardianship of yourself and Fortune, from the Gentlemen to whom your tender Parents committed the Direction of both. I am afraid, my Dear, your Dissatisfaction arises more from sudden Distaste, than from mature Reflection. Mr. *Jones* and Mr. *Pitt* were long the intimate Friends and Companions of your Father; for more than Thirty Years, he had experience'd their Candor and Wisdom; and it was their Fitness for the Trust, that induced him to leave you to their Care; and will you reflect upon his Judgment?

They are not less wise now, than when he made his Will; and if they happen to differ from your Judgment in any thing of Moment, what Room have you to suppose yourself better able to judge of the Consequences of what you desire, than they. I do not undervalue your good Sense, and yet I must tell you, that (the Difference of Years consider'd, and their Knowledge of the World, which yet you can know little of) it would be strange if they did not know better than you, what was proper for you; and their Honesty was never yet disputed. Upon these Considerations, who is most probably to blame, should you happen to disagree? From such Men, you will never meet more Restraints than is necessary for your Happiness and Interest; for nothing that can injure *you* in any respect, can add to *their* Advantage or Reputation. I have known several young Ladies of your Age impatient of the least Controul, and think hardly of every little Contradiction; but when, by any unadvised Step, they have released themselves, as they call it, from the Care of their try'd Friends, how often they have had Cause to repent their Rashness? How seldom do you hear those Ladies, who have subjected themselves to what some reckon the greatest Restraints while young, repent the Effects of them when grown up?

To mention the single Article about which, generally, these Differences arise, that of Marriage: What good Fruits can a Lady hope, from the insidious Progress of a clandestine Address? A man who can be worth a Lady's Acceptance, will never be ashamed or afraid to appear openly. If he deserves to succeed, or is conscious that he does what need of concealing his Designs from her Friends? Must it not be with a View to get her in his Power, and by securing a Place in her Affections, make her Weakness give Strength to *his* Presumption, and forward those Pretensions that he knew would otherwise be rejected with Scorn?

Let me tell you, my dear Miss, that you neither want Sense nor Beauty; and no young Gentleman can be ashamed of being *known* to love you. Consider this well, and despise the Man who seeks the Aid of back doors, bribed Servants, and Garden-walls to get Access to your Person. If he had not a meaner Opinion of your Understanding than he ought; he would not hope for Success from such *poor Methods*. Let him see then, how much he is mistaken, if he thinks you the giddy Girl his clandestine Conduct seems to call you. *In time* advise with your try'd Friends. Trust no Servant with Secrets you would not have known to your Equals or Guardians; and be sure ever to shun a servile Confidant, who generally makes her Market of her Mistress, and sells her to the highest Bidder.

I hope, dear Miss, you will seriously reflect upon all I have said, and excuse the well-meant Zeal of

Your sincere Friend.

Instructions to young Orphan Ladies, as well as others, how to judge of Proposals of Marriage made to them without their Guardians or Friends Consent, by their Milaners, Mantua-makers,[1] *and other Go-betweens*

A YOUNG Orphan Lady, of an independent Fortune, receivable at Age, or Day of Marriage, will hardly fail of several Attempts to engage her Affections. And the following general Rules and Instructions will be of Use to her on these Occasions:

In the first place, she ought to mistrust all those who shall seek to set her against her Guardian, or those Relations to whom her Fortune or Person is intrusted: And, next, to be apprehensive of all such as privately want to be introduced to her, and who avoid treating with her Guardian first for his Consent. For she may be assur'd, that if a young Man has Proposals to make, which he himself thinks would be

---

1 Milliners: makers of hats, particularly for women, originally in the Italian city of Milan. Mantua-makers: makers of loose gowns or robes, originally in the Italian city of Mantova. These two Italian place names became part of the English language of fashion in the early seventeenth century.

accepted by a Person of *Years* and *Experience*, he will apply in a regular way to her Friends; but if he has not, he will hope to engage the young Lady's Affections by the means of her *Milaner*, her *Mantua-maker*, or her *Servant*, and so by Bribes and Promises endeavor to make his way to her Favour, in order to take Advantage of her Youth and Inexperience: For this is the constant Method of *Fortune-hunters*, to which many a worthy young Lady of good Sense and good Fortune has owed her utter Ruin.

The following are generally the Methods taken by this Set of Designers:

These industrious Go-betweens, who hope to make a Market of a young Lady's Affections, generally by Letter, or Word of Mouth, if they have Opportunity, set forth to the young Lady:

"That there is a certain young Gentleman of *great Merit*, of a *handsome Person*, and *fine Expectations*, or *prosperous Business*, who is fallen deeply in Love with her. And very probably, the young Lady, having no bad Opinion of herself, and loving to be admired, believes it very easily.

That he has seen her at *Church*, or the *Opera*, the *Play*, the *Assembly*, &c. and is impatient to make known his Passion to her.

That he is unwilling to apply to her *Guardian* till he *knows* how his Address will be received by *herself*.

That, besides, it may very probably be the Case, that her Guardian may form Obstacles, which may not be reasonable on *her Part* to give into.

That, if he has *Daughters* of his own, he would perhaps rather see them marry'd *first*.

That he may not care to part with her *Fortune*, and the *Reputation* and *Convenience* the *Management* of it may give him.

That he may design to marry her, when he *thinks proper*, to some Person agreeable to his *own* Interest or Inclinations, without consulting *hers* as he ought.

That, therefore, it would be best, that her Guardian should know *nothing* of the Matter till she saw whether she could approve the Gentleman or not.

That even *then* she might *encourage* his Address, or *discountenance* it as she *pleased*.

That for her the *Proposer's* part, she had *no Interest* in the world, one way or the other; and no *View*, but to serve the young Lady, and to oblige a young Gentleman so well qualify'd to make her happy." And such-like plausible Assurances; ending, perhaps, "with desire to bring on an *Interview*, or, if that will not be admitted, that she will receive a Letter from him."

This kind of Introduction ought always to be suspected by a prudent young Lady. She ought with *Warmth* and *Resentment* to discourage the *officious Proposer*. She ought to acquaint her,

"That she is resolved never to give way to a Proposal of this Importance, without the *Consent* and *Approbation* of her *Guardian* or *Friends*.

That her good Father or Mother, who had *seen the World*, and had *many Years* Experience of her Guardian's *Honour* and *Qualifications* for such a Trust, knew what they did, when they put her under his Care.

That he had always shewn an *honest* and *generous* Regard for her Welfare.

That she took it very unkindly of the Proposer, to offer to inspire her with *Doubts* of his *Conduct*, when she had *none* herself, nor *Reason* for any.

That it was Time enough when he gave her *Reason*, to be apprehensive of his sinister Designs, or of his preferring his *own* Interest to *hers*.

That it was a very strange Attempt to make her mistrust a *Friend*, a *Relation*, a *Gentleman*, who was chosen for this Trust by her *dear Parents*, on *many Years Experience* of his Honour and Probity, and of whose Goodness to her, *for so long time* past, she herself had many Proofs: And this in Favour of a Person who had a *visible Interest* to induce him to this Application; whose *Person* she hardly *knew*, if *at all*; whose *Professions* she could not *judge* of; who began by such mean, such groundless, such unworthy Insinuations: Who *might*, or *might not*, be the Person he pretended; and who wanted to induce her to prefer *himself*, on *no* Acquaintance at all, to a *Gentleman* she had so many Years *known*; and whose *Honour*, good *Character*, *Reputation*, and *Conscience*, were all engaged to her as so many Pledges for his honourable Behaviour to her.

That she the *Proposer*, and the young Gentleman *too*, must have a very indifferent Opinion of her *Gratitude*, her *Prudence*, her *Discretion*, to make such an Attempt upon her.

That if he could approve himself a Man of *Years* and *Experience*, who was not to be imposed upon by *blind Passion*, in the Light he wanted to appear in to *her*, why should he not apply to *him first?*

That surely it was a very *ungenerous* as well as *suspicious* Method of Proceeding, that he could find no *other way* to give her an Opinion of *himself*, but by endeavouring to depreciate the Character of a *Gentleman*, who, by this Method plainly appeared to his *own Apprehension* to stand in the way of his Proceedings; and *that too* before he had *try'd him*; and which shewed, that he himself had not hope of succeeding, but by *Arts* of *Delusion*, *Flattery*, and a *clandestine Address*, and had nothing but her *own Inadvertence* and *Inexperience* to build upon.

That, therefore, it behoved her, had she *no other* Reason, to reject with *Resentment* and *Disdain* a Conduct so affrontive of her *Understanding*, as well as *selfish* and *ungenerous* in the Proposer.

That, therefore, she would not countenance any *Interview* with a Person *capable* of acting in such a manner, nor receive any *Letter* from him.

And lastly, that she desires never to hear of this Matter again, from her the *Proposer*, if she would have her retain for her that good Opinion, which she had hitherto had."

This prudent Reasoning and Conduct will make the Intervener quit her Design upon the young Lady, if she is not wholly abandoned of all Sense of Shame, and corrupted by high Bribes and Promises; and in this Case, the young Lady will judge how unfit such a Person is either for her *Confident* or *Acquaintance*. Nor will the Lady lose an humble Servant *worthy* of being *retain'd* or *encouraged*: For if he be the Person he *pretends*, he will directly apply to her *Guardian*, and have a high Opinion of *her* Prudence and Discretion; and if she hears no more of him, she may conclude, he could not make good his Pretensions to a Person of *Discernment*, and will have Occasion to rejoice in escaping his designing Arts with so little Trouble to herself.

If a Lady has had actually a Letter delivered her from such a Pretender, and that by means of a Person who has any Share in her Confidence, and wants a Form of a Letter to send to the Recommender to discourage the Proceeding; the following, which has been sent with good Effect, on a like Occasion may be proper.

Letter XCV.

Mrs. Pratt,

I INCLOSE the Letter you put into my Hands, and hope it will be the last I shall ever receive from you or any body else on the like Occasion. I am intirely satisfied in the Care and Kindness of my

Guardian, and shall encourage no Proposal of this sort, but what comes recommended to me by *his* Approbation. He knows the World. I do not; and that which is not fit for *him* to *know*, is not fit for *me* to *receive*; and I am sorry either you or the Writer looks upon me in so weak a Light, as to imagine I would wish to take myself out of the Hands of so *experienced* a *Friend*, to throw myself into those of a *Stranger*. Yet I would not, as this is the first Attempt of the kind from you, and that it may rather be the Effect of Inconsideration, than Design, shew it my Guardian; because he would not perhaps impute it to so favourable a Motive in you, as I am willing to do, being

Your Friend and Servant.

3. From Samuel Richardson, "Preface" to *Clarissa* (Vol. 1; London: S. Richardson, 1748), pp. iii–viii

[Undoubtedly one of the world's greatest novels, Richardson's seven-volume *Clarissa* is also the greatest epistolary novel. Whereas the heroine of *Pamela* achieves a "happy ending," *Clarissa* is a complex tragedy. The characters' own narratives provide insights into their interior selves as well as the social pressures at work upon them. In this excerpt from the novel's "Preface," Richardson develops a narrative theory that dwells upon the resources of the epistolary novel, especially its ability to capture life in what he elsewhere referred to as "writing to the moment."]

THE following History is given in a Series of Letters, written principally in a double, yet separate, Correspondence;

Between Two young Ladies of Virtue and Honour, bearing an inviolable Friendship for each other, and writing upon the most interesting Subjects: And

Between Two Gentlemen of free Lives; one of them glorying in his Talents for Stratagem and Invention, and communicating to the other in Confidence, all the secret Purposes of an intriguing Head, and resolute Heart.

But it is not amiss to premise, for the sake of such as may apprehend Hurt to the Morals of Youth from the more freely-written Letters, That the Gentlemen, tho' professed Libertines as to the Fair Sex, and making it one of their wicked Maxims, to keep no Faith with any Individuals of it who throw themselves into their Power, are not, however, either Infidels or Scoffers: Nor yet such as think themselves freed from the Observance of other moral Obligations.

On the contrary, it will be found, in the Progress of the Collection, that they very often make such Reflections upon each other, and each upon himself, and his Actions, as reasonable Beings, who disbelieve not a future State of Rewards and Punishments (and who one day propose to reform) must sometimes make:—One of them actually reforming, and antidoting the Poison which some might otherwise apprehend would be spread by the gayer Pen, and lighter Heart, of the other.

And yet that other, altho' in unbosoming himself to a *select Friend*, he discover Wickedness enough to intitle him to general Hatred preserves a Decency, as well in his Images, as in his Language, which is not always to be found in the Works of some of the most celebrated modern Writers, whose Subjects and Characters have less warranted the Liberties they have taken.

Length will naturally be expected, not only from what has been said, but from the following Considerations:

That the Letters on both Sides are written while the Hearts of the Writers must be supposed to be wholly engaged in their Subjects: The Events at the Time generally dubious:—So that they abound, not only with critical Situations; but with what may be called *instantaneous* Descriptions and Reflections; which may be brought home to the Breast of the youthful Reader:—As also, with affecting Conversations; many of them written in the Dialogue or Dramatic Way.

To which may be added, that the Collection contains not only the History of the excellent Person whose Name it bears, but includes The Lives, Characters, and Catastrophes, of several others, either principally or incidentally concerned in the Story.

But yet the Editor to whom it was referred to publish the Whole in such a Way as he should think would be most acceptable to the Public was so diffident in relation to this Article of *Length*, that he thought proper to submit the Letters to the Perusal of several judicious Friends; whose Opinion he desired of what might be best spared.

One Gentleman, in particular, of whose Knowledge, Judgment, and Experience, as well as Candor, the Editor has the highest Opinion, advised him to give a Narrative Turn to the Letters; and to publish only what concerned the principal Heroine;—striking off the collateral Incidents, and all that related to the Second Characters; tho' he allowed the Parts which would have been by this means excluded, to be both instructive and entertaining. But being extremely fond of the affecting Story, he was desirous to have every-thing parted with, which he thought retarded its Progress.

This advice was not relished by other Gentlemen. They insisted, that the Story could not be reduced to a Dramatic Unity, nor thrown into the Narrative Way, without divesting it of its Warmth; and of a great Part of its Efficacy; as very few of the Reflections and Observations, which they looked upon as the most useful Part of the Collection, would, then, find a Place.

They were of Opinion, That in all Works of This, and the Dramatic Kind, STORY, or AMUSEMENT, should be considered as little more than the *Vehicle* to the more necessary INSTRUCTION: That many of the Scenes would be render'd languid, were they to be made less busy: And that the Whole would be thereby deprived of that Variety, which is deemed the Soul of a Feast, whether *mensal* or *mental*.

They were also of Opinion, That the Parts and Characters, which must be omitted, if this Advice were followed, were some of the most natural in the whole Collection: And no less instructive; especially to *Youth*. Which might be a Consideration perhaps overlooked by a Gentleman of the Adviser's great Knowledge and Experience: For, as they observed, there is a Period in human Life, in which, youthful Activity ceasing, and Hope contenting itself to look from its own domestic Wicket upon bounded Prospects, the half-tired Mind aims at little more than *Amusement*.—And with Reason; for what, in the *instructive* Way, can appear either *new* or *needful* to one who has happily got over those dangerous Situations which call for Advice and Cautions, and who has fill'd up his Measures of Knowledge to the Top?

Others, likewise gave *their* Opinions. But no Two being of the same Mind, as to the Parts which could be omitted, it was resolved to present to the World, the Two First Volumes by way of Specimen; and to be determined with regard to the rest by the Reception those should meet with.

If that be favourable, Two others may soon follow; the whole Collection being ready for the Press: That is to say, If it be found necessary to abstract or omit some of the Letters in order to reduce the Bulk of the Whole.

Thus much in general. But it may not be amiss to add, in particular, that in the great Variety of Subjects which this Collection contains, it is one of the principal Views of the Publication,

To caution Parents against the undue Exertion of their natural Authority over their Children, in the great Article of Marriage:

And Children against preferring a Man of Pleasure to a Man of Probity, upon that dangerous, but too commonly received Notion, *That a Reformed Rake makes the best Husband.*

4. Samuel Johnson, *Rambler*, No. 152 (31 August 1751)

[One example of the many short periodicals, such as the *Tatler* (1709–11) and the *Spectator* (1711–12), that appeared in the eighteenth century, the *Rambler* published 208 articles from 1750–52. In these papers, Samuel Johnson (1709–84), poet, literary critic, and eventual author of the period's famous *Dictionary of the English Language* (1755), explores a variety of subjects ranging from religion and morality to art and politics. In this excerpt, Johnson discusses "the epistolary style."]

—————————*Tristia mœsium*
Vultum verba decent, iratum plena minarum.

Hor.[1]

"It was the wisdom," says *Seneca*, "of ancient times, to consider what is most useful as most illustrious." If this rule be observed with regard to works of genius, there is scarcely any species of composition which deserves more to be cultivated than the epistolary style, since none is of more various or frequent use, through the whole subordination of human life.

It has yet happened, however, among the numerous writers which our nation has produced, equal, perhaps always in force and genius, and of late in elegance and accuracy, to those of any other country, very few have endeavoured to distinguish themselves by the publication of letters, except such as were written in the discharge of public trusts, and during the transaction of great affairs; which, though they may afford precedents to the minister, and memorials to the historian, are of very little use as examples of the familiar style, or models of private correspondence.

If it be inquired by foreigners, how this deficiency has happened in the literature of a country, where every man indulges himself with so little danger in speaking and writing, may we not, without either bigotry or arrogance, inform them, that it must be ascribed to our contempt of trifles, and to our due sense of the dignity of the public; that we do not think it reasonable to fill the world with volumes from which nothing can be learned; nor expect that the employments of the busy, or the amusements of the gay, should give way to narratives of our private affairs, complaints of absence, expressions of fondness, or declarations of fidelity.

A slight perusal of the epistolary writings by which the wits of *France* have signalized themselves, will prove that other nations need not be discouraged from the like attempts by the consciousness of inability: for surely it is not very difficult to relate trifling occurrences,

---

1 The quotation comes from the first-century BCE Roman poet Horace's *Ars Poetica* (105–06): "Sorrowful words become the sorrowful, angry words become the angry." See *Horace: Satires, Epistles, Art of Poetry*, translated by H.R. Fairclough (Loeb Classical Library, Harvard UP, 1929).

to magnify familiar incidents, to repeat adulatory professions, to accumulate servile hyperboles, and produce all that can be found in the despicable remains of *Voiture* and *Scarron*.[1]

Yet, as much of life must be passed in affairs which become considerable only by their frequent occurrence, and much of the pleasure which our condition allows must be produced by giving elegance to trifles, it is necessary to learn how to become little without becoming mean, to maintain the necessary intercourse of civility, and fill up the vacuities of action by agreeable appearances. It had therefore been of advantage, if such of our writers as have excelled in the art of decorating insignificance, had supplied us with a few sallies of innocent gaiety, effusions of honest tenderness, or exclamations of unimportant hurry.

Precept has generally been posterior to performance. No man has taught the art of composing any work of genius, but by the example of those who performed it without any help than vigour of imagination, and rectitude of judgment. As we have few letters, we have likewise few criticisms upon the epistolary style. The observations with which *Walsh*[2] has introduced his pages of inanity, are such as give very him little claim to the rank which *Dryden* has assigned him amongst the critics. *Letters*, says he, *are intended as resemblances of conversation; and the chief excellencies of conversation, are good humour and good breeding.* This remark, equally valuable for its novelty and propriety, he dilates and enforces with an appearance of compleat acquiescence in his own discovery.

No man was ever in doubt about the moral qualities of a letter. It has been always known, that he who endeavours to please, must appear pleased; and he who would not provoke rudeness, must not practise it. The question among those who endeavor to establish rules for an epistolary performance, is only how gaiety or civility may be most properly expressed; as among the critics in history, it is not contested, whether truth ought to be preserved, but by what mode of diction it is best adorned.

As letters are written on all subjects, in all states of mind, and on all occasions, the epistolary style cannot be reduced to settled rules, or described by any single characteristic; and perhaps we may safely disentangle our minds from critical embarrassments, by determining that a letter has no peculiarity but its form, and that nothing is necessary to be refused admission into a letter which is proper in any other method

---

1 Vincent Voiture (1597–1648), society wit whose lively personal letters ("remains") were published after his death; Paul Scarron (1610–60), member and mocker of high society, wrote comic poems, plays, and a major novel (*Le roman comique*).

2 William Walsh (1662–1708), an English poet and literary critic. Here Johnson refers to Walsh's *Letters and Poems, Amorous and Gallant* (1692).

of treating the same subject. The qualities of the epistolary style most frequently required, are ease and simplicity, an even flow of unlaboured diction, and an artless arrangement of obvious sentiments. But these directions however strongly they may be inculcated by the speculatist, are no sooner applied to use, than their scantiness and imperfection become evident. Letters are written to the great and to the mean, to the learned and the ignorant, at rest and in distress, in sport and in passion. Nothing can be more improper than ease and laxity of expression, when the importance of the subject impresses solicitude, or the dignity of the person exacts reverence.

That letters should be written with strict conformity to nature, is true; because nothing but conformity to nature can make any composition beautiful or just. But it is natural to depart from familiarity of language upon occasions not familiar. Whatever elevates the sentiments, will consequently raise the expression; whatever fills us with hope or terrour, will produce some perturbation of images, and some figurative distortions of phrase. Wherever we are studious to please, we are afraid of trusting our first thoughts, and endeavour to recommend our opinion by studied ornaments, by accuracy of method, and elegance of style.

If the personages of the comic scene be allowed by *Horace* to raise their language in the transports of anger to the turgid vehemence of tragedy, the epistolary writer may without censure likewise comply with the varieties of his matter. If great events are to be related, he may, with all the solemnity of an historian, deduce them from their causes, connect them with their concomitants, and trace them to their consequences. If a disputed position is to be established, or a remote principle to be investigated, he may detail his reasonings with all the nicety of the syllogistick method. If a menace is to be averted, or a benefit implored, he may, without any violation of the edicts of criticism, call every power of rhetoric to his assistance, and try every inlet at which passion enters the heart.

Those letters that have no other end than the entertainment of the correspondent, are perhaps more properly to be regulated by critical precepts; because the matter and style are equally arbitrary, and rules are more necessary, as there is more power of choice. In letters of this kind, some conceive art graceful, and others think negligence amiable; some model them by the sonnet, and will allow them no means of delighting, but the soft lapse of calm mellifluence; others adjust them by the epigram, and expect pointed sentences and forcible periods. The one party considers exemption from faults as the height of excellence, the other looks upon neglect of excellence as the most disgusting fault; one avoids censure, the other aspires to praise; one is always in danger of insipidity, the other continually on the brink of affectation.

When the subject has no intrinsic dignity, it must necessarily owe all its attractions to artificial embellishments, and may catch at all advantages which the art of writing can bestow. He that, like *Pliny*,[1] sends his friend a portion for his daughter, will, without *Pliny*'s eloquence or address, find means of exciting gratitude, and securing acceptance; but he that has no present to make, but a garland, a ribbon, or some petty curiosity, must endeavour to recommend it by his manner of giving it.

The purpose for which letters are written when no intelligence is communicated, or business transacted, is to preserve in the minds of the absent either love or esteem. To excite love, we must impart pleasure; and to raise esteem, we must discover abilities. Pleasures will generally be given, as abilities are displayed by scenes of imagery and points of conceit, unexpected sallies and artful compliments. Trifles always require exuberance of ornament. The building which has no strength, can be valued only for the art of its decorations. The stone must be polished with care, which hopes to be valued as a diamond; and words ought surely to be laboured when they are intended to stand for things.

5. Rev. John Trusler, "The PENNY-POST," *The London Advisor and Guide* (London: Printed for the Author, 1786), pp. 84–86

[John Trusler (1735–1820) was an English priest whose life spanned much of the eighteenth century. He engaged in several literary projects, mostly of the compendium and encyclopedic variety, and he eventually established his own printing and bookselling business. *The London Advisor and Guide*, which appeared in two editions (1786 and 1790), offered helpful tips and tricks for visiting, working, and living in London. In this excerpt, Trusler discusses the expanded penny post, which allowed for the cheap and rapid exchange of letters.]

1. HAS five principal offices; viz. the chief Penny-post office in Throgmorton-street;[2] the Westminster, in Coventry-street; St. Clements, in Blackmoor-street, Clare-market; the Hermitage, in Queen-

---

1　Gaius Plinius Caecilius Secundus (Pliny the Younger, 61–c. 113 CE), a Roman author and magistrate. According to one of his letters, Pliny sent 50,000 sesterces (a small silver coin) to his friend Quintilian so that the latter could outfit his daughter with clothes and servants before her wedding.

2　First established in London in 1680, the penny post allowed delivery of letters and packages weighing up to one pound for the uniform rate of one penny within the bounds of a particular local area. By the middle of the eighteenth century, there were penny posts in many towns and cities in the United Kingdom.

street, Little Tower-hill; the Southwark, St. Saviour's Church-yard, Borough.

2. Letters to be sent out of town must be put into these offices before ten at night, to be forwarded by the first delivery the next day.

3. To prevent the frequent delays of Penny-post letters, the public are requested to be particularly careful to send them to the Penny-post receiving-houses, from whence they are collected every four hours, and delivered four times a day to all parts of London; for when they are put by mistake into the General Post-office, or the receiving-houses for general-post letters, they cannot be collected till late in the evening, and besides the delay thereby, the penny which ought to have been paid with them must of necessity be charged to the persons they are directed to.

4. Letters are much accelerated by being put in at any of the five principal offices, instead of the receiving-houses, from whence they must be collected and sent to those offices.

5. For the port of every letter or packet, passing or repassing within the cities of London or Westminster, the Borough of Southwark and their suburbs, (which letter or packet is not to exceed the weight of 4 ounces, unless coming from or passing to the General-Post) one penny upon putting in the same as also a penny upon the delivery of such as are directed to any place beyond the said cities, borough, or suburbs, within the district of the penny-post delivery.

6. The triangular stamp on all Penny-post letters shews the day they are brought to one of these principal offices; and the round stamp the hour they are given to the letter carriers.

7. This post carries parcels under four ounces to most places within ten miles of London.

8. To expedite the delivery, it is adviseable to write on the outside, the day of the week, and the hour the letter is put into the office.

9. If you sent any thing of value by the post, it is proper that the person who delivers it at the office should be able to prove the contents; but the office has given the following directions concerning this matter. Unless letters containing things of value be left open, to be so carried to one of the five principal offices above-mentioned, there to be seen and entered, the letter-carrier will no ways be made answerable for their miscarriage.

10. Those who send bank-notes by the post, are advised by the post-office to cut them in two pieces, obliquely, so as to have the words on the left, as below, in one piece, and those on the right in the other, and send them at two different times, one half at one time and one at another, as a security, in case the mail is robbed.

No. 5515.

I promise to pay to	Mr. Abraham Newland, ·
Or bearer, on demand, the	Sum of TEN Pounds
	London, May 5, 1783.
£. TEN.	For the Gov. and Comp. of
Entd. J. Fleetwood	the Bank of England,
	J. GREENWAY

In case of loss the Bank will pay the money, on producing one half of the note.

11. With respect to the Penny-post, the public are desired to be very distinct in their directions, particularly to lodgers, by mentioning their landlord's sign and name, for want of which many cannot be delivered. And as a check on the letter-carrier, those that he returns after three days enquiry will be sent to the writer gratis, if their residence can be discovered.

12. Nothing above four ounces will be conveyed by the penny-post, except passing to or from the general post-office.

13. Those who wish to find persons in London, not having their directions, may often find them out by enquiring at the post-office among the letter-carriers, at the time the letters are delivered to them.

Appendix B: The Dissolution of the Abbeys

1. **An Act for the Dissolution of the Lesser Monasteries** (1535), *The Statutes at Large:Vol. 2: From the First Year of King Edward the Fourth to the End of the Reign of Queen Elizabeth* (London: Mark Basket, 1770), pp. 247–50

[Henry VIII's *Act for the Dissolution of the Lesser Monasteries*, written by Thomas Cromwell (1485–1540), was designed to steal the wealth and property of the Catholic Church in Great Britain after Henry's break with the Pope during the English Reformation. The decree established ownership of Church lands and properties under the Crown and placed the king in the position to dispose of the wealth as he wished. Before the monks residing at these monasteries could sell off or protect the properties, commissioners and armed groups, sometimes local people, arrived to strip the lead from the roofs and windows, pack up the plate and religious artifacts, and lay claim to valuable artworks for the Crown. Even bells and doorknobs were stripped as the monasteries were turned into ruins.]

Stat. 27 H. VIII. c. 28. A. D. 1535.
All Monasteries given to the King, which have not Lands above two hundred Pounds by the Year [1]
Forasmuch as manifest, synne, vicious, carnal, and abominable Living is dayly used and committed commonly in such little and small Abbeys, Priories, and other Religious Houses of Monks, Canons, and Nuns, where the Congregation of such Religious Persons is under the Number of twelve Persons, whereby the Governors of such Religious Houses, and their Covent, spoyle, dystroye, consume, and utterly waste, as well their Churches, Monasteries, Priories, principal Houses, Farms, Granges, Lands, Tenements, and Hereditaments, as the Ornaments of their Churches, and their Goods and Chatells, to the high Displeasure of Almighty God, Slander of good religion, and to the great Infamy of the King's Highness and the Realm, if Redress should not be had thereof. And albeit that many continual Visitations hath been

---

1 The dissolution was made more palatable by apparently applying only to the smaller religious houses, but within a year the process of dissolution among even major institutions was complete.

heretofore had, by the Space of two hundred Years and more, for an honest and charitable Reformation of such unthrifty, carnal, and abominable Living, yet neverthelesse little or none Amendment is hitherto had, but their vicious Living shamelessly increaseth and augmenteth, and by a cursed Custom so rooted and infected, that a great Multitude of the Religious Persons in such small Houses do rather choose to rove abroad in Apostasy, than to conform themselves to the Observation of good Religion; so that without such small Houses be utterly suppressed, and the Religious Persons therein committed to great and honourable Monasteries of Religion in this Realm, where they may be compelled to live religiously, for Reformation of their Lives, the same else be no Redress nor Reformation in that Behalf. In Consideration whereof, the King's most Royal Majesty, being supreme Head on Earth, under God, of the Church of *England*, dayly studying and devising the Increase, Advancement, and Exaltacion of true Doctrine and Virtue in the said Church, to the only Glory and Honour of God, and the total extirping and Dystruction of Vice and Sin, having Knowledge that the Premises be true, as well by the Accompts of his late Visitations, as by sundry credible Informations, considering also that diverse and great solemn Monasteries of this Realm, wherein (Thanks be to God) Religion is right well kept and observed, be destitute of such full Number of Religious Persons, as they ought and may keep, hath thought good, that a plain Declaration should be made of the Premises, as well to the Lords Spiritual and Temporal, as to other his loving Subjects the Commons in this present Parliament assembled: Whereupon the said Lords and Commons, by a great Deliberation, finally be resolved, that it is and shall be much more to the Pleasure of Almighty God, and for the Honour of this his Realm, that the Possessions of such small Religious Houses, now being spent, spoiled, and wasted for Increase and Maintenance of Sin, should be used and committed to better uses, and the unthrifty Religious Persons, so spending the same, to be compelled to reform their lives: And thereupon most humbly desire the King's Highness that it may be enacted by Authority of his present Parliament, That His Majesty shall have and enjoy to him and his Heirs for ever, all and singular such Monasteries, Priories, and other Religious Houses of Monks, Canons, and Nuns, of what kinds of Diversities of Habits, Rules, or Order soever they be called or named, which have not in Lands, Tenements, Rents, Tithes, Portions, and other Hereditaments, above the clear yearly Value of two hundred Pounds. And in like manner shall have and enjoy all the Sites and Circuits of every such Religious Houses, and all the singular the

Manors, Granges, Meases,[1] Lands, Tenements, Rents, Reversions, Services, Tithes, Pensions, Portions, Churches, Chapels, Advowsons,[2] Patronages, Annuities, Rights, Entries, Conditions, and other Hereditaments appertaining or belonging to every such Monastery, Priory, or other Religious House, not having, as is aforesaid, above the said clear yearly Value of two hundred Pound, in as large and ample Manner as the Abbots, Priors, Abbesses, Prioresses, and other Governors of such Monasteries, Priories, and other Religious Houses now have, or ought to have the same in the Right of their Houses. And that also his Highness shall have to him and to his Heirs all and singular such Monasteries, Abbies, and Priories, which at any Time within one Year next before the making of this Act hath been given and granted to his Majesty by any Abbot, Prior, Abbess, or Prioress, under their Convent Seals, or that otherwise hath been suppressed or dissolved, and all and singular the Manors, Lands, Tenements, Rents, Services, Reversions, Tithes, Pensions, Portions, Churches, Chapels, Advowsons, Patronages, Rights, Entries, Conditions, and all other Interests and Hereditaments to the same Monastaries, Abbeys, and Priories, or to any of them appertaining or belonging; to have and to hold all and singular the Premises, with all their Rights, Profits, Jurisdictions, and Commodities, unto the King's Majesty, and his Heirs and Assigns for ever, to do and use therewith his and their own Wills, to the Pleasure of Almighty God, and to the Honour and Profit of this Realm.

II. And it is ordained and enacted by the Authority aforesaid, That all and every person and Persons, and Bodies Politick, which now have, or hereafter shall have, any Letters Patents of the King's Highness, of any of the Sites, Circuits, Manors, Lands, Tenements, Rents, Reversions, Services, Tithes, Pensions, Portions, Churches, Chapels, Advowsons, Patronages, Tithes, Entries, Conditions, Interests, or other Hereditaments, which appertained to any Monasteries, Abbies, or Priories, heretofore given or granted to the King's Highness, or otherwise suppressed or dissolved, or which appertaineth to any of the Monasteries, Abbies, Priories, or other Religious Houses, that shall be suppressed or dissolved by the Authority of this Act, shall have and enjoy the said sites, Circuits, Manors, Lands, Tenements, Rents, Reversions, Services, Tithes, Pensions, Portions, Churches, Chapels, Advowsons, Patronages, Tithes, Entries, Conditions, Interests, and all other Hereditaments, contained and specified in their Letters Patents

---

1 A messuage, or site for a dwelling house with outbuildings and land.
2 The right of presentation to a benefice or living.

now being thereof made, and to be contained and expressed in any Letters Patents hereafter to be made, according to the Tenor, Purport, and Effect of any such Letters Patents; and shall also have all such Actions, Suits, Entries, and Remedies, to all Intents and Purposes, for any Thing and Things contained in every such Letters Patents now made, or to be contained in any such letters hereafter to be made, in like Manner, Form, and Conditions, as the Abbots, Priors, Abbesses, Prioresses, and other chief Governors of any Religious Houses which had the same, might or ought to have had, if they had not been suppressed or dissolved.

III. Saving to every Person and Persons, and Bodies Politick their Heirs and Successors, (other than the Abbots, Priors, Abbesses, Prioresses, and other chief Governors of the said Religious Houses specified in this Act, and the Convents of the same, and their Successors, and such as pretend to be Founders, Patrons, or Donors of such Religious Houses, of any Lands, Tenements, or Hereditaments, belonging to the same, and their Heirs and Successors), all such Right, Title, Interest, Possessions, Leases for Years, Rents, Services, Annuities, Commodities, Fees, Offices, Liberties, and Livings, Pensions, Portions, Corrodies,[1] Synodies,[2] Proxies, and all other Profits as they or any of them hath, ought, or might have had in or to any of the said Monasteries, Abbies, Priories, or other Religious Houses, or in or to any manors, Lands, Tenements, Rents, Reversions, Tithes, Pensions, Portions, or other Hereditaments appertaining or belonging, or that appertained to any of the said Monasteries, Priories, or other Religious Houses, as if the same Monasteries, Priories, or other Religious Houses had not been suppressed by this Act, but had continued in their essential Bodies and States that they now be, or were in.

IV. Provided always, and be it enacted, That forasmuch as divers of the chief Governors of such Religious Houses, determining the utter Spoil and Destruction of their Houses, and dreading the Suppressing thereof, for the Maintenance of their detestable Lives, have lately fraudulently and craftily made Feoffments,[3] Estates, Gifts, Grants, and Leases, under the Covent Seals, or suffered Recoveries of their Manors, Lands, Tenements, and Hereditaments, in Fee-simple, Fee-tail,[4] for

---

1 A lifetime allotment of food, clothing, shelter, and care granted by religious establishments.
2 A synodal payment made by the inferior clergy to the bishop on the occasion of a synod (a formal assembly of clergy) or visitation.
3 A feoffment allowed property holders to transfer their land as well as the right to sell or bequeath it as an inheritance to others.
4 Fee-simple and fee-tail describe legal restrictions on land ownership. Fee-tail restricts who may inherit a piece of land and fee-simple indicates the permanent right to do whatever one wishes with a piece of land.

Term of Life or Lives, or for Years, or charged the same with Rents, or Corrodies, to the great Decay and Diminution of the Houses; that all such crafty and fraudulent Recoveries, Feoffments, Estates, Gifts, Grants, and Leases, and every of them, made by any of the said chief Governors of such Religious Houses, under their Covent Seals, within one Year next before the making of this Act, shall be utterly void and of none Effect: Provided always, That such Person and Persons as have Leases for Term of Life, or Years, whereupon is reserved the old Rents and Ferms[1] accustomed, and such as have any Offices, Fees, or Corrodies, that have been accustomed or used in such Religious Houses, and have bought any Livery or Living in any such Houses, shall have and enjoy their said Leases, Offices, Fees, Corrodies, Liberties, Liveries, and Livings, as if this Act had never been made.

V. And it is further enacted by Authority aforesaid, That the King's Highness shall have and enjoy to his own proper Use,[2] all such Ornaments, Jewels, Goods, Chattels, and Debts, which appertained or belonged to any of the chief Governors of the said Monasteries, or Religious Houses, in the right of their said Monasteries or Religious Houses, at the first Day of *March* in the Year of our Lord God 1535, or any Time sithen[3] whensoever, and to whose Possession soever they shall come, or be found, except only such Beasts, Grain, and Woods, and such other like Chattel and Revenues as have been sold before the said first Day of *March*, or sithen, for the necessary or reasonable Expences or charges of any of the said Monasteries or Houses.

Provided always, that such of the said chief Governors which have been elect, or made Abbots, Priors, Abbesses, or Prioresses, of any of the said Religious Houses sithen the first Day of *January*, which was in the year of our Lord God 1534, and by reason thereof be bounden to pay the First-Fruits[4] to the King's Highness at Dayes to come, limited by their Bonds made for the same, that in every such Case chief Governors, and their Sureties, or any of them, shall be clearly discharged by Authority of this Act, against the King's Highness, and all other Persons, for the Payment, of such Sums of Money as they stand bounden to pay for the said First-Fruits, or for any Part thereof: And forasmuch as the clear yearly Value of all the said Monasteries,

---

1 A variant of "farm"; some cultivated territory lent out for fixed payment.
2 Proper use here indicates that the king can take this as personal wealth and distribute it as he wishes, regardless of the nation's interests (as opposed to taking the wealth as a kind of tax revenue to be used for the nation).
3 Archaic for "since."
4 By ecclesiastical law, the first year's income paid by the holder of a benefice.

Priories, and other Religious Houses in this Realm, is certified into the King's Exchequer, amongst the Books of the yearly Valuation of all the Spiritual Possessions of this Realm, amongst which shall and may appear the Certainty and Number of such small and little Religious Houses as have not Lands, Tenements, Rents, Tythes, Portions, and other Hereditaments, above the said clear yearly Value of two hundred Pounds:

VI. Be it therefore enacted by Authority aforesaid, That the King's Highness shall have and enjoy according to this Act, the actual and real Possession of all and singular such Monasteries, Priories, and other Religious Houses, as shall appear by the said Certificate remaining in the King's Exchequer, not to have in Lands, Tenements, Rents, Tithes, Portions, and other Hereditements, above the said clear yearly value of two hundred Pounds, so that his Highness may lawfully give, grant, and dispose them, or any of them, at his Will and Pleasure, to the Honour of God, and the Wealth of this Realm, without farther Inquisition or Offices to be had or found for the same.

In Consideration of which premises to be had to his Highness, and to his Heirs, as is aforesaid, his Majesty is pleased and contented, of his most excellent Charity, to provide to every chief Head and Governor of every such Religious House, during their Lives, such yearly Pensions and Benefices as for their Degrees and Qualities shall be reasonable and convenient, wherein his Highness will have most tender Respect to such of the said chief Governors as well and truly preserve and keep the Goods and Ornaments of their Houses, to the Use of his Grace, without Spoil, Waste, or embezling the same; and also his Majesty will ordain and provide, that the Covents of every such Religious House shall have their Capacities, if they will, to live honestly and virtuously abroad, and some convenient Charity disposed to them towards their Living, or else shall be committed to such honourable great Monasteries of this Realm wherein good Religion is observed, as shall be limited by his Highness, there to live religiously during their Lives; and it is ordained by the Authority aforesaid, that the chief Governors and Covents of such honourable great Monasteries shall take and accept into their Houses, from Time to Time, such Number of the Persons of the said Covents as shall be assigned and appointed by the King's Highness, and keep them religiously, during their Lives, within their said Monasteries, in like Manner and Form as the Covents of such great Monasteries be ordered and kept.

Provided always, That all Archbishops, Bishops, and other Persons which be or shall be chargeable to and for the Collection of the Tenths granted, and going out of the Spiritual Possessions of this Realm, shall be discharged and acquitted of and for such Parts and Portions of the said Tenths wherewith the said Houses of Religion, suppressed and dissolved by this Act, were charged or chargeable to the King's Highness, except of such Sums of Money thereof, as they, or any of them have, or shall have received for the said Tenths, of the chief Governors of such Religious Houses.

Provided also, That where the Clergy of the Province of *Canterbury* stood, and be indebted to the King's Highness in great Sums of Money, remaining yet unpaid, of the rest of a hundred thousand Pounds granted and given to his Grace in their Convolution towards the Payment whereof the said Religious Houses should have been contributory if they had not been suppressed by this Act; and also some of the Governors of the said Religious Houses have been Collectors for levying of the said Debt, and received thereof great Sums of Money yet remaining in their Hands; the King's most Royal Majesty is pleased and contented to deduct, abate, release, defalk, to the said Clergy, of the said rest yet unpaid, as well such Sums of Money as any the chief Governors of such Religious Houses hath received, and not paid, as so much Money as every of the said Religious Houses, suppressed by this Act, were rated and taxed to pay in any one Year, to and for the Payment of the said hundred thousand Pounds; and also the King's Majesty is pleased and contented, that it be enacted by Authority aforesaid, that his Highness shall satisfy, content, and pay, all and singular such just and true Debts which be owing to any Person or Persons by the chief Governors of any the said Religious Houses, in as large and ample manner as the said chief Governors should or ought to have done if this Act had never been made.

Provided always, that the King's Highness, at any Time after the making of this Act, may at his Pleasure ordain and declare, by his Letters Patents under his Great Seal, that such of the said Religious Houses which his Highness shall not be disposed to have suppressed nor dissolved by Authority of this Act, shall still continue, remain, and be in the same Body corporate, and in the said essential Estate, Quality, and Condition, as well in Possessions as otherwise, as they were afore the making of this Act, without any Suppression or Dissolution thereof, or any Part of the same, by the Authority of this Act; and that every such Ordinance and Declaration, so to be made by the King's Highness, shall be good and effectual to the chief Governors of such Religious Houses which his Majesty will not have suppressed, and to their Successors, according to the Tenors and Purports of the Letters Patents thereof to be made, any Thing or Things contained in this Act to the contrary hereof notwithstanding.

Provided also, That where the Clergy of the Province of *York* stood, and be indebted to the King's Highness in great Sums of Money yet unpaid, of the rest of such Sums of Money which was granted by them to his Majesty in their Convocation, towards the Payment whereof the Religious Houses that shall be suppressed and dissolved by this Act, being within the same Province, should have been contributory if they had not been dissolved, and also some of the Governors of the said Religious Houses within the said Province, that shall be suppressed by this Act, have been Collectors for levying of Part of the said Sums of Money granted to the King's Highness, as is aforesaid, and have certain Sums thereof in their Hands yet unpaid, the King's Majesty is pleased and contented to deduct, abate, release, and defalk the said Clergy of the aid Province of *York*, of the rest of their said Debt yet unpaid, as well such of the said Sums of Money, as any chief Governors of any Religious Houses within the same Province, that shall be suppressed by this Act, hath been collected, and not paid, as so much Money as every of the said Religious Houses, suppressed by this Act, were rated and taxed to any one Year, towards the Payment of the said Sums of Money granted to the King's Highness.

VII. Provided always, That this act, or any Thing or Things therein contained, shall not extend, nor be prejudicial to any Abbots or Priors of any Monasteries or Priories being certified into the King's Exchequer to have in Possessions and Profits Spiritual and Temporal, above the clear yearly Value of two hundred Pounds, for or concerning such Cells of Religious Houses, appertaining or belonging to their Monasteries or Priories, in which Cells the Priors, or other chief Governors thereof, be under the Obedience of the Abbots or Priors to whom such Cells belong, as the Monks or Canons of the Covent of their Monasteries or Priories, and cannot sue, nor be sued, by the Laws of this Realm, in or by their own proper Names, for the Possession, or other Things appertaining to such Cells whereof they be Priors or Governors, but must sue and be sued in and by the Names of the Abbots or Priors to whom they be Obedi- encers, and to whom such Cells belong; and also be Priors or Gov- ernors dative, and removable from Time to Time, and Accountants of the Profits of such Cells, at the only Pleasure and Will of the Abbots or Priors to whom such Cells belong; but that every such Cell shall be and remain undissolved in the same Estate, Quality, and Condition, as if this Act had never been made; any Thing in this Act to the contrary hereof notwithstanding.

VIII. Saving always, and reserving unto every Person and Persons, being Founders, Patrons, or Donors of any Abbies, Prior- ies, or other Religious Houses, that shall be suppressed by this Act, their Heirs and Successors, all such Right, Title, Interest, Possession, Rents, Annuities, Fees, Offices, Leases, Commons, and all other Profits whatsoever, which any of them have, or should have had, without Fraud or Covin,[1] by any manner or Means, otherwise than by reason or occasion of the Dissolution of the said Abbies, Priories, or other Religious Houses, in, to, or upon the said Abbies, Priories, or other Religious Houses, whereof they be Founders, Patrons, or Donors, or in, to, or upon any the Lands, Tenements, or other Hereditaments, or appertaining or belonging to the same, in like Manner, Form, and Condition as other Persons and Bodies Politick be saved by this Act, as is afore rehearsed, and as is the said Abbies, Priories, or other Religious Houses, had not been suppressed and dissolved by this Act, but had continued still in their essential Bodies and Estates as they be now in, any Thing, in this Act to the contrary hereof notwithstanding.

IX. And be it further enacted, ordained and established by Authority aforesaid, That all and singular Persons, Bodies Politick and Corporate, to whom the King's Majesty, his Heirs and Successors, hereafter shall give, grant, let or demise any Site or Precinct, with the Houses thereupon builded, together with the Demeans of any Monasteries, Priories or other Religious Houses, that shall be dissolved or given to the King's Highness by this Act, and the Heirs, Successors, Executors and Assigns of every such Person, Body Politick and Corporate, shall be bound by Authority of this Act, under the Penalties hereafter ensuing, to keep, or cause to be kept, an honest continual House and Household in the same Site or Precinct, and to occupy yearly as much of the same Demeans in Ploughing and Tillage of Husbandry, that is to say, as much of the said Demeans which hath been commonly used to be kept in Tillage by the Governors, Abbots or Priors of the same Houses, Monasteries or Prioriess, or by their Farmer or Farmers occupying the same within the Time of twenty Years next before this Act.

X. And if any Person or Persons, Bodies Politick or Corporate, that shall be bounden by this Act, do not keep an honest Houshold of Husbandry and Tillage, in Manner and Form as is aforesaid, that then he or they so offending shall forfeit to the King's Highness for every Month so offending, six Pounds thirteen Shillings and Four-pence, to be recovered to his Use in any of his Courts of Record.

XI. And over that it is enacted by Authority aforesaid, That all Justice of Peace in every Shire where any such Offence shall be committed or done, contrary to the true Meaning and Intent of this

---

1 A financial agreement or collusion by two or more to cheat someone else, or, simply, a company.

present Act, shall, in every Quarter and General Sessions within the Limits of their Commission, inquire of the Premisses, and shall have full Power and Authority to hear and determine the same, (2) and to tax and assess no less Fine for every the said Offences, than is afore limited for the same Offences, (3) and the Estreats[1] thereof to be made and certified into the King's Exchequer, according and at such Time and Form, as other Estreats of Fines, Issues and Amerciaments been made by the same Justices.

2. From William Camden, *Britannia*, 1586 [Gough edition, 1789]

[Camden's book was the result of over two decades, beginning in 1577, spent walking, riding, and searching England for all of the sites of the religious houses that had vanished because of the dissolution. The first edition appeared in Latin in 1586, and five additional editions appeared before that of 1607, which was the first to include a full set of maps of England. The book was translated into English by Philemon Holland in 1610. Two more editions appeared in the eighteenth century, first in 1722, translated by William Gibson, and then in 1789, translated by Richard Gough. Each successive edition included additional material, further elucidating the history of the dissolution, as Camden (1551–1623) had hoped it would.]

From *Mr. Camden's PREFACE*

I am informed some are offended at my mention of religious houses and their foundations. I am sorry to hear this, but allow me to say, they would be as much offended, and perhaps would have forgotten that our ancestors were Christians, and that we continue so: since there never were more certain and more illustrious monuments to their Christian piety and devotion, nor any nurseries whence Christianity and learning were transmitted to us; however in a corrupt age they have been too much overgrown by weeds which it was necessary to root out.

From *DIVISIONS of BRITAIN*: Monasteries

Till the reign of Henry VIII. there were, if I may be allowed to say so, monuments of the piety of our ancestors, erected to the honour of God, the propagation of Christianity and learning, and support of the poor, religious houses, viz. monasteries or abbies, and priories, to the number of 645; 40 of which by favour of Pope Clement VII. were suppressed to oblige Cardinal Wolsey, who had begun two colleges, one at Oxford, the other at Ipswich. About the 36th year of Henry VIII. a

---

1 Exact copies of documents of fines or payments due.

storm burst upon the English church like a flood breaking down its banks, which, to the astonishment of the world and grief of the nation, bore down the greatest part of the religious with their fairest buildings. For what the Pope permitted the Cardinal to do, the king with consent of parliament took the liberty of doing. In 1536 all religious houses, with all their revenues, amounting to 200£. per. ann. or under, and in number 376, were granted to the king. The next year, under the specious pretense of destroying the remains of superstition, the rest, with all colleges, chantries, and hospitals, were surrendered to the king. At this time the remaining 605 religious houses were taxed or valued, 96 colleges, besides those in the universities, 110 hospitals, 2374 chantries and free chapels. These were almost all shortly after destroyed, their revenues squandered away, and the wealth which the Christian piety of the English had from the first conversion of England dedicated to God, in a moment dispersed, and, if I may be allowed the expression, profaned.[1]

3. From David Hume, *The History of England: Under the House of Tudor* (London: A. Millar, 1759)

[David Hume (1711–76) originally published his *History of England* in six volumes, between the years 1754 and 1762. Hume initially intended to write a history of only the Stuart monarchs, so the volumes were published out of sequence. Hume's history commanded a good deal of attention and was widely read, even though the author was disparaged by some as a free thinker and even as an atheist. Eventually, his would become the standard history in many school libraries. This excerpt, taken from the first edition of *The History of England under the House of Tudor*, was published in 1759, second to last in the order of publication, even though it occupies volumes 3 and 4 of the six-volume set.]

[In 1536] THE domestic peace of England seemed to be exposed to more hazard, by the violent innovations in religion; and it may be affirmed, that, in this dangerous conjuncture, nothing ensured public tranquillity so much as the decisive authority acquired by the King, and his great ascendant over all his subjects. Not only the devotion paid the crown, was profound during that age: The personal respect, inspired by Henry, was considerable; and even the terrors, with which he over-awed every one, were not attended with any considerable degree of hatred. His frankness, his sincerity, his magnificence, his generosity, were virtues which counterballanced his vio-

---

1 [Camden's note:] Henry VIII. by the first suppression got a yearly revenue of about 100,000*l.*

lence, cruelty, and impetuosity. And the important rank, which his vigour, more than address, acquired him in all foreign negotiations, flattered the vanity of Englishmen, and made them the more willingly endure those domestic hardships, to which they were exposed. The King, conscious of his advantages, was now proceeding to the most dangerous trial of his authority; and after paving the way for that measure by several expedients, he was at last determined to suppress the monasteries, and to put himself in possession of their ample revenues.

THE great encrease of monasteries, if matters be considered merely in a political light, will appear the radical inconvenience of the catholic religion; and every other disadvantage, attending that communion, seems to have an inseparable connection with these religious institutions. Papal usurpations, the tyranny of the inquisition, the multiplication of holidays; all these letters on liberty and industry, were ultimately derived from the authority and insinuation of monks, who being scattered every where, proved so many colonies of superstition and of folly. This order of men were extremely enraged against Henry; and regarded the abolition of the papal authority in England, as the removal of the sole protection which they enjoyed against the rapacity of the crown and of the courtiers. They were now subjected to the King's visitation; the supposed sacredness of their bulls[1] from Rome was rejected; the progress of the reformation abroad, which had every where been attended with the abolition of the monastic state, gave them reason to expect like consequences in England; and tho' the King still maintained the ancient doctrine of purgatory, to which most of the convents owed their origin and support, it was foreseen, that, in the progress of the contest, he would every day be led to depart wider from antient institutions, and be drawn nearer the tenets of the reformers, with whom his political interests naturally induced him to ally himself. Moved by these considerations, the friars made use of all their influence to enflame the people against the King's government; and Henry, finding their safety irreconcilable with his own, was determined to seize the present opportunity, and utterly destroy his declared enemies.

CROMWEL,[2] secretary of state, had been appointed vicar-general, or vicegerent, a new office, by which the King's

---

1 A papal bull: a formal legal statement of direction signed by the Pope by way of a seal called a bulla.

2 Thomas Cromwell (c. 1485–1540), a lawyer who served Henry VIII. Cromwell was a shrewd enabler who orchestrated Henry's separation from Anne Boleyn (c. 1501–36) and took charge of the dissolution of the monasteries, which gave Henry access to enormous wealth.

supremacy, or the absolute, uncontroulable power assumed over the church, was delegated to him. He employed Layton, London, Price, Gage, Petre, Bellasis, and others, as commissioners, who carried on, every where, a rigorous enquiry with regard to the conduct and deportment of all the friars. During times of faction, especially of the religious kind, no equity is to be expected from adversaries; and as it was known, that the King's intention in this visitation, was to find a pretence for abolishing monasteries, we may naturally conclude, that the reports of the commissioners are very little to be relied on. Friars were encouraged to bring in informations against their brethren; the slightest evidence was credited; and even the calumnies spread abroad by the friends to the reformation, were regarded as grounds of proof. Monstrous disorders are therefore said to have been found in many of the religious houses: Whole convents of women abandoned to lewdness: Signs of abortions procured, of infants murdered, of unnatural lusts between persons of the same sex. It is indeed probable, that the blind submission of the people, during those ages, would render the friars and nuns more unguarded, and more dissolute, than they are in any roman catholic country at present: But still, the reproaches, which it is safest to credit, are such as point at vices, naturally connected with the very institution of convents, and with the monastic life. The cruel and inveterate factions and quarrels therefore which the commissioners mentioned, are very credible, among men, who, being confined together within the same walls, never can forget their mutual animosities, and who, being cut off from all the most endearing connections of nature, are commonly cursed with hearts more selfish, and tempers more unrelenting, than fall to the share of other men. The pious frauds, practised to increase the devotion and liberality of the people, may be regarded as certain, in an order founded on illusions, lies, and superstition. The supine idleness, also, and its attendant, profound ignorance, with which the convents were reproached, admit of no question; and tho' monks were the true preservers, as well as inventors, of the dreaming and captious philosophy of the schools,[1] no manly or elegant knowledge could be expected among men, whose life, condemned to a tedious uniformity, and deprived of all emulation, afforded nothing to raise the mind, or cultivate the genius.

S OME few monasteries, terrified with this rigorous inquisition carried on by Cromwel and his commissioners, surrendered their revenues into the King's hands; and the monks received small

---

1 Scholastic religious philosophy, chiefly known through the works of Thomas Aquinas. Likely a reference to Thomas Aquinas (1225–74) and other theologians of the Middle Ages. After the Renaissance, scholasticism is often unfavorably contrasted to humanism.

pensions as the reward of their obsequiousness. Orders were given to dismiss such nuns and friars as were below four and twenty, and whose vows were, on that account, supposed not to be binding. The doors of the convents were opened, even to such as were above that age; and all those recovered their liberty who desired it. But as all these expedients did not fully answer the King's purpose, he had recourse to his usual instrument of power, the Parliament; and in order to prepare men for the innovations projected, the report of the visitors was published, and a general horror was endeavoured to be excited in the nation against institutions which, to their ancestors, had been the objects of the most profound veneration.

T HE King, tho' determined to abolish utterly the monastic order, resolved to proceed gradually in this great work; and he gave directions to the Parliament to go no further at present, than to suppress the lesser monasteries, who possessed revenues below two hundred pounds a year value.[1] These were found to be the most corrupted, as lying less under the restraint of shame, and being exposed to less scrutiny;[2] and it was esteemed safest to begin with them, and thereby prepare the way for the greater innovations projected. By this act three hundred and seventy six monasteries were suppressed, and their revenues, amounting to thirty two thousand pounds a year, were granted to the King; besides their goods, chattels, and plate, computed at a hundred thousand pounds more.[3] It appears not that any opposition was made to this important law: So absolute was Henry's authority! A court, called the court of augmentation of the King's revenue, was appointed for the management of these funds. The people naturally concluded, from the erection of this court, that Henry intended to proceed in spoiling the church of her patrimony.[4]

T HE act formerly passed, empowering the King to name thirty-two commissioners for framing a body of canon law, was renewed; but the project was never carried into execution. Henry thought, that the present confusion of that law encreased his authority, and kept the clergy in still greater dependance.

F ARTHER progress was made in compleating the union of Wales with England: The separate jurisdictions of several great

---

1 [Hume's note:] 27 Hen. VIII. c. 28.
2 [Hume's note:] Burnet, vol. 1. p. 193.
3 [Hume's note:] It is pretended, see Hollingshed [i.e., Raphael Holinshed (c. 1525–c. 1580)], p. 939, that ten thousand monks were turned out on the dissolution of the lesser monasteries. If so, most of them must have been Mendicants [itinerant friars vowed to poverty]: For the revenue could not have supported near that number. The Mendicants, no doubt, still continued their former profession.
4 [Hume's note:] 27 Hen. VIII. c. 27

lords or marchers, as they were called, which obstructed the course of justice in Wales, and encouraged robbery and pillaging, were abolished; and the authority of the King's courts was extended every where. Some jurisdictions of a like nature in England were also abolished[1] this session.

THE commons, sensible that they had gained nothing by opposing the King's will, when he formerly endeavoured to secure the profits of wardships and liveries, were now contented to frame a law,[2] such as he dictated to them. It was enacted, that the possession of land shall be adjudged to be in those who have the use of it, not in those to whom it is transferred in trust.

AFTER all these laws were passed, the King dissolved the Parliament; a Parliament memorable, not only for the great and important innovations which it introduced, but also for the long time it had sat, and the frequent prorogations which it had undergone. Henry had found it so obsequious to his will, that he did not chuse, during these religious ferments, to hazard a new election; and he continued the same Parliament above six years: A practice, at that time, quite unprecedented in England.

THE convocation, which sat during this session, were engaged in a very important work, the deliberating on the new translation which was projected of the scriptures. Tindal had formerly given a translation,[3] and it had been greedily read by the people; but as the clergy complained of it, as very inaccurate and unfaithful, it was now proposed that they should themselves publish a translation, which would not be liable to those objections. The friends of the reformation asserted, that nothing could be more absurd than to conceal, in an unknown tongue, the word itself of God, and thus to counteract the will of heaven, which, for the purpose of universal salvation, had published that salutary doctrine to all nations: That if this practice was not very absurd, the artifice at least was very barefaced, and proved a consciousness, that the glosses and traditions of the clergy stood in direct opposition to the original text, dictated by Supreme Intelligence: That it was now necessary for the people, so long abused by interested pretensions, to see with their own eyes, and to examine whether the claims of the ecclesiastics were founded on that charter, which was on all hands acknowledged to be derived from heaven: And that as a spirit of research and curiosity was happily revived, and men were now

---

1 [Hume's note:] 27 Hen. VIII. c. 4.

2 [Hume's note:] 27 Hen. VIII. c. 10.

3 William Tyndale (c. 1494–1536), English religious reformer and translator of the Bible into English. Condemned as a heretic, Tyndale was strangled and his body burnt.

obliged to make a choice among the pretensions of different sects, the proper materials for decision, and above all, the holy scriptures, should be set before them, and the revealed will of God, which the change of language had somewhat obscured, be again, by their means, revealed to mankind.

THE favourers of the ancient religion maintained, on the other hand, that the pretence of making the people see with their own eyes, was a mere cheat, and was itself a very barefaced artifice, by which the new preachers hoped to obtain the guidance of them, and seduce them from those pastors, whom the laws, whom ancient establishments, whom heaven itself had appointed for their spiritual direction: That the people were, by their ignorance, their stupidity, their necessary avocations, totally unqualified to choose their own principles, and it was a mocquery to set materials before them, of which they could not possibly make any proper use: That even in the affairs of common life, and in their temporal concerns, which lay more within the compass of human reason, the laws had, in a great measure, deprived them of the right of private judgment, and had, happily, for their own and the public interest, regulated their conduct and behaviour: That theological questions were placed much beyond the sphere of vulgar comprehension; and ecclesiastics themselves, tho' assisted by all the advantages of education, erudition, and an assiduous study of the science, could not be fully assured of a just decision; except by the promise made them in scripture, that God would be ever present with his church, and that the gates of hell should not prevail against her: That the gross errors adopted by the wisest heathens, proved how unfit men were to grope their own way, thro' this profound darkness; nor would the scriptures, if trusted to every man's judgment, be able to remedy; on the contrary, they would much augment, these fatal illusions: That sacred writ itself was involved in so much obscurity, was exposed to so many difficulties, contained so many appearing contradictions, that it was the most dangerous weapon which could be intrusted into the hands of the ignorant and giddy multitude: That the poetical spirit, in which a great part of it was composed, at the same time that it occasioned uncertainty in the sense, by its multiplied tropes and figures, was sufficient to kindle the zeal of fanaticism, and thereby throw civil society into the most furious combustion: That a thousand sects must arise, which would pretend, each of them, to derive its tenets from the scripture; and would be able, by specious arguments, or even without specious arguments, to seduce silly women, and ignorant mechanics, into a belief of the most monstrous principles: And that if ever this disorder, dangerous to the magistrate himself, received a remedy, it must be from the tacit acquiescence of the people in some new authority; and it was evidently better, without farther contest or enquiry, to adhere peaceably to ancient, and therefore the more secure establishments.

Appendix C: The Picturesque Abbey as Ruin or Great Mansion

1. George Keate, *The Ruins of Netley Abbey* (London: R. and J. Dodsley, 1764)

[George Keate (1729–97) was an English painter, poet, and traveler who became a friend of Voltaire (1694–1778) as well as of other eighteenth-century notables, including David Garrick (1717–79) and Samuel Johnson (1709–84). He published twelve volumes of verse; "Netley Abbey" was one of the best known and most frequently reprinted of his works. This is the complete text of the first edition of this popular poem. It was expanded and republished as *Netley Abbey: An Elegy* in 1769, along with "A Short Account of Netley Abbey."]

HENCE all the trivial Pleasures of the Crowd,
Folly's vain Revel, and that treach'rous Art
Which captivates the Gay, or sooths the Proud,
And steals each better Purpose from the Heart.

More welcome far the Shades of this wild Wood
Skirting the cheerful Green the seabeat Sands,
Where NETLEY, near the Margin of the Flood
In lone Magnificence a Ruin stands.

How chang'd, alas! from that rever'd Abode
Which spread in ancient Days so wide a Fame,
When votive Monks these sacred Pavements trod,
And swell'd each Echo with JEHOVAH's Name!

Now sunk, deserted, and with Weeds o'ergrown,
Yon aged Walls their better Years bewail;
Low on the Ground their loftiest Spires are thrown,
And ev'ry Stone points out a moral Tale.

Mark how the Ivy with Luxuriance bends
Its winding Foliage through the cloister'd Space,
O'er the green Window's mould'ring Height ascends,
And seems to clasp it with a fond Embrace.——

With musing Step I pace the silent Isle,
Each moss-grown Nook, each tangled Path explore,

While the Breeze whistles through the shatter'd Pile,[1]
Or wave light-dashing murmurs on the Shore.

No other Noise in this calm Scene is heard,
No other Sounds these tranquil Vaults molest,
Save the Complainings of some mournful Bird
That ever loves in Solitude to rest.

Haunts such as these delight, and o'er the Soul.
Awhile their grateful Melancholy cast,
Since through all Periods she can boundless roll,
Enjoy the Present, and recall the Past!——

Here, pious Hermits from the World retir'd
In Contemplation wing'd their Thoughts to Heav'n;
Here, with Religion's heart-felt Raptures fir'd,
Wept o'er their erring Days, and were forgiv'n.

Race after Race succeeding, in these Cells,
Learn'd how to value Life, learn'd how to die;
Lost are their Names, and no Memorial tells
In what lone Spot their mould'ring Ashes lie!

Mute is the matin[2] Bell which us'd to Call
The wakeful Fathers from their humble Beds;
No midnight Taper[3] glimmers on the Wall,
Or o'er the Floor its trembling Radiance sheds!

No sainted Shrine now pours its Blaze of Light
Bidding the zealous Bigot hither roam;
No holy Relick glads the Pilgrim's Sight,
Or lures his Foot-steps from a distant Home!——

Now fainter to the View each Object grows,
In the clear West the Day's last Gleams are seen,
On Night's dim Front the Star of Ev'ning glows,
And dusky Twilight aids the solemn Scene.

Again quick Fancy peoples all the Gloom,
Calls from the Dust the venerable Dead,

---

1 Large architectural object.
2 Morning. The first church service of the day is "Matins."
3 Candle.

Who Ages since lay shrouded in the Tomb,
And bids them these accustom'd Limits tread.

Swift as her Wish the shadowy Forms appear,
O'er each chang'd Path with doubtful Step they walk,
From their keen Eyes she sees Amazement stare,
And hears, or thinks she hears, the Spectres talk.

E'en now they pass, and fading like a Dream
Back to their hallow'd Graves again they go;
But first bequeathed one pitying Sigh, and seem
To mourn with me the Fate of all below!——

Disparted Roofs that threaten from above,
The tott'ring Battlement, the rifted Tow'r,
With many a scatter'd Fragment loudly prove,
All-conqu'ring TIME, the Triumphs of thy Pow'r.

These speaking Stones one sacred Truth maintain,
That Dust to Dust is Man's predestin'd Lot;
He plans, and labours,—Yet how much in vain!——
Himself, his Monuments, how soon forgot!——

Forgot on Earth,——but one there sits on high
Who bids our Virtues to his Throne ascend,
Pleas'd he beholds them with a Parent's Eye,
To give our Hope new Wings, and crown our End!——

And you, YE FAIR, of gayer Scenes the Grace,
If Chance should lead you from the jocund Train,
Curious to visit this sequester'd Place,
Amidst its Ruins wander not in vain.

Whence do they still our silent Wonder claim
E'en in this low, this desolated State?
'Tis from Remembrance of their former Fame:——
They once were beautiful, they once were great!

'Tis Goodness best adorns the female Heart;
Asks a Respect which must with Years increase,
Lives, when the Roses from the Cheek depart,
And all the Joys of Adulation cease!

Forgive the Muse, if with an anxious Love
She woos you to attend her friendly Lay;

Warns you, lest faithless to yourselves ye prove,
And in false Pleasures trifle Life away.

Know, in your Breasts is lodg'd a Spark divine
For ever prompting to each great Desire;——
Th' inconstant World must change, that still shall shine,
Nor Death's cold Hand e'er quench th'immortal Fire.

Ne'er may Dishonour's Blast an Entrance find,
O keep it sacred with a Vestal's Care,[1]
Feed it with all the Graces of the Mind,
Nor fail to pour the social Duties there.

So o'er your Forms when TIME his Veil shall cast,
And ev'ry Charm by Age shall be decay'd,
Your fair Renown shall triumph to the last,
And Virtue guard the Conquest Beauty made.

2. William Gilpin, "On Glastonbury and Ford Abbey," *Observations on the Western Parts of England* (London: T. Cadell, 1798)

[William Gilpin (1724–1804) was a schoolmaster, teacher, and amateur artist who took pleasure in exploring different regions of England and commenting on the natural and man-made beauties he discovered. He circulated manuscripts of his tour journals to friends, including Thomas Gray (1716–71); eventually he was persuaded to publish. Gilpin is credited with being one of the founders of the idea of "the picturesque." He is an outspoken opponent of modernization and new notions of beautification. Many travelers took his books with them on journeys, and he helped to make certain destinations popular, including the Lake District and Scotland. Here Gilpin reflects on the ruins of some great abbeys.]

SECT. XII.

THE ground on which the abbey of Glastonbury stands, is higher than the neighbouring district, which is a perfect flat; insomuch, that tradition says, it was formerly covered with the sea. If that was the case, the ground which the abbey occupies, if not an island, was at least a peninsula. To this day it bears the name of *the Isle of Avelon*; and the meadows around it seem plainly to have been washed and relinquished by the sea.

---

1 From Rome's vestal virgins, later referring to nuns.

The abbey of Glastonbury, therefore, does not enjoy that choice situation which the generality of religious houses possess. *Original foundations*, like this, were generally fixed by accidental causes. An escape from a shipwreck; a battle; a murder; the scene of some prince's death; with a variety of other circumstances, have commonly determined their site; so that if they enjoy a good situation, it seems to be accidental. Those religious houses whose situation we particularly admire, I should conjecture, have been chiefly colonies, or off-sets from the great religious houses. In *these* there might be a *choice of situation*.

The event which settled the situation of this abbey, is firmly attested, on the proof of Romish legends. When Joseph of Aremathea came to preach the Gospel in Britain, as it is asserted he did, he landed on the Isle of Avelon; and fixing his staff in the ground, (a dry thorn-saplin, which had been his companion through all the countries he had passed,) fell asleep. When he awoke, he found, to his great surprise, that his staff had taken root, and was covered with white blossoms. From this miracle, however, he drew a very natural conclusion, that as the use of his staff was thus taken from him, it was ordained that he should fix his abode in this place. Here, therefore, he built a chapel, which, by the piety of succeeding times, increased into this magnificent foundation.

Of this immense fabric nothing now remains, but a part of the *great church*, *St. Joseph's chapel*, an *old gate-way*, part of the *abbot's lodge*, and the *kitchen*.

Of the *great church*, the south side is nearly entire; some part of the east end remains; a little of the cross isle; and a remnant of the tower; all of the purest and most elegant Gothic. The north side was lately taken down, and the materials were applied to build a meeting-house. From this defalcation, however, the ruin, as a picturesque object, seems to have suffered little. In *correspondent* parts, if one only be taken away, or considerably fractured, it may possibly be an advantage. But we greatly regret the loss of the west end, which was taken down to build a town-hall. Still more we regret the loss of the tower; as the eye wants some elevated part to give an apex to the whole. Besides, in that part of the tower which remains, there is rather a formality. Two similar points, which have been the shoulders of a Gothic arch, arise in equal dimensions, and do not easily fall into a picturesque form.

St. Joseph's chapel, which stands near the west end of the great church, is almost entire. The roof indeed is gone; but the walls have suffered little dilapidation. This chapel was probably more ancient than the church, as it has evidently a mixture in it of Saxon architecture; but the style is very pure in its kind; and the whole is rich and beautiful. It is no little addition to its beauty, that ivy is spread about over the walls, in such just proportion, as to adorn without defacing them.

On the south-west of St. Joseph's chapel, stands the *Gate of strangers*, which seems to have been a heavy building, void of elegance and beauty. Not far from the Gate of strangers, and connected with it in design, are shewn the foundations of the Linguist's lodge: but no part of it, unless it be a postern, is now left. This was a very necessary part of an endowment, which was visited by strangers from all parts of the world.

The *Abbot's lodge* has been a large building. It ranges parallel with the south side of the church; and was nearly entire within the memory of man. It was a suite of seven apartments on a floor; but very little of it is now left. In the year 1714 it was taken down to answer some purpose of economy, though it seems never to have been a structure of any beauty.

Hard by the Abbot's lodge stands the *Kitchen*, which is to this day very entire, and is both a curious remnant of antiquity, and a noble monument of monkish hospitality. It is a square building, calculated to last for ages. Its walls are four feet thick, and yet strengthened with massy buttresses. They have, indeed, an immense roof to support, which is still in excellent repair. It is constructed of stone, and seems to be a work of very curious masonry, running up in the form of an octagonal pyramid, and finished at the top in a double cupola. The under part of this cupola received the smoke, in channels along the inside of the roof; and the upper part contained a bell, which first called the society to dinner, and afterwards the neighbouring poor to alms. The inside of the Kitchen is an octagon; four chimnies taking off the corners of the square. It has two doors, and measures twenty-two feet from one to the other, and a hundred and seventy from the bottom to the top. In this Kitchen, it is recorded, that twelve oxen were dressed generally every week, besides a proportional quantity of other victuals.

These are all the visible remains of this great house. Foundations are traced far and wide, where, it is conjectured, the cloisters ran; the monks' cells; the schools; the dormitories; halls; and other offices. The whole together has been an amazing combination of various buildings. It had the appearance indeed of a considerable town, containing perhaps the largest society under one government, and the most extensive foundation that ever appeared in England in any form. Its fraternity is said to have consisted of five hundred established monks, besides nearly as many retainers on the abbey. Above four hundred children were not only educated in it, but entirely maintained. Strangers from all parts of Europe were liberally received; classed according to their sex and nation; and might consider the hospitable roof, under which they lodged, as their own. Five hundred travellers, with their horses, (though they generally, I should suppose, travelled on foot,) have been lodged at once within its walls. While the poor from every side of the country waited the ringing of the alms-bell; when they flocked in crowds, young and old, to the gate of the monastery, where they received, every morning, a plentiful provision for themselves and their families: all this appears great and noble.

On the other hand, when we consider five hundred persons, bred up in indolence, and lost to the commonwealth; when we consider that these houses were the great nurseries of superstition, bigotry, and ignorance; the stews of sloth, stupidity, and perhaps intemperance; when we consider, that the education received in them had not the least tincture of useful learning, good manners, or true religion, but tended rather to vilify and disgrace the human mind; when we consider that the pilgrims and strangers who resorted thither, were idle vagabonds, who got nothing abroad that was equivalent to the occupations they left at home; and when we consider, lastly, that indiscriminate alms-giving is not real charity, but an avocation from labour and industry, checking every idea of exertion, and filling the mind with abject notions, we are led to acquiesce in the fate of these great foundations, and view their ruins, not only with a picturesque eye, but with moral and religious satisfaction.

This great house possessed the amplest revenues of any religious house in England. Its ancient domains are supposed *now* to yield not less than an annual income of two hundred thousand pounds. I have heard them calculated at much more.

Within a mile of the abbey stands the *Torr*,[1] which is by much the highest land in the island of Avelon, and had been our land-mark through an approach of many leagues. The summit of this hill is decorated with a ruin, which has its effect, though in itself it possesses no beauty. It is a structure of ambiguous intention. One tradition supposes it to have been a sea-mark, for which it is well adapted. Another makes it an oratory. To the abbot it certainly belonged.

Here the holy man, when Satan led him aside, might sometimes ascend, and looking round him, might see all the country his own; houses and villages filled with his vassals; meadows covered with innumerable flocks and herds to support the strength of his table; rivers and woods abounding with fish and game to furnish its delicacies; fields waving with corn to fill his granaries and his cellars; and, among other sources of luxury, no fewer than seven ample parks, well stocked with venison. Here was a glorious view indeed! His heart might dilate, as the vision expanded: and if he were not well upon his guard, he might easily have mistaken an earthly reverie for holy joy and religious gratitude.

---

1 Southwest England, from Celtic, commonly "Tor": abrupt rocky hill or free-standing heap of rock atop a hill.

Near the bottom of this hill are found great quantities of that species of putrefaction which resembles a coiled serpent; or, as it is often called, an *Ammon's horn*.[1]

The ruins of Glastonbury-abbey occupy a piece of ground, about a mile in circumference, which has no peculiar beauty, but might be improved into a very grand scene, if it were judiciously planted, and laid out with just so much art, as to discover the ruins to the best advantage. But such schemes of improvement are calculated only for posterity. A young plantation would ill accord with such antique accompaniments. The oak would require at least a century's growth, before its moss-grown limbs could be congenial with the ruins it adorned.

I should ill deserve the favours I met with from the learned anti-quarian, who has the care of these ruins, though he occupies only the humble craft of a shoemaker, if I did not attempt to do some justice to his zeal and piety. No picturesque eye could more admire these ven-erable remains for their beauty, than he did for their sanctity. Every stone was the object of his devotion. But above all the appendages of Glastonbury, he reverenced most the famous thorn which sprang from St. Joseph's staff, and blossoms at Christmas. On this occasion he gave us the following relation.

It was at that time, he said, when the King resolved to alter the common course of the year, that he first felt distress for the honour of the house of Glastonbury. If the time of Christmas were changed, who could tell how the credit of this miraculous plant might be affected? In short, with the fortitude of a Jewish seer, he ventured to expostulate with the King upon the subject; and informed his Majesty, in a letter, of the disgrace that might possibly ensue, if he persisted in his design of altering the natural course of the year. But though his conscience urged him upon this bold action, he could not but own the flesh trem-bled. He had not the least doubt, he said, but the King would imme-diately send down an order to have him hanged. He pointed to the spot where the last abbot of Glastonbury was executed for not sur-rendering his abbey; and he gave us to understand, there were men now alive who could suffer death, in a good cause, with equal forti-tude. His zeal, however, was not put to this severe trial. The King was more merciful than he expected; for though his Majesty did not follow his advice, it never appeared that he took the least offence at the freedom of his letter.

The death of the last abbot of Glastonbury is indeed a mournful tale, as it is represented by the writers of those times, and was calcu-lated to make a lasting impression on the country.

---

1 Old descriptive term for the fossil of a cephalopod.

This abbot is said to have been a pious and good man; careful of his charge, kind to the poor, and exemplary in his conduct. He is particularly mentioned as a man of great temperance; which, in a cloister, was not, perhaps, at that day, the reigning virtue. What was still as uncommon, he was a lover of learning; and not only took great care of the education of those young men, who were brought up in his house, but was at the expence of maintaining several of them at the universities. He was now very old, and very infirm; and having passed all his life in his monastery, knew little more of the world than he had seen within its walls.

It was the misfortune of this good abbot to live in the tyrannical days of Henry VIII., and at that period when the suppression of monasteries was his favourite object. Henry had applied to many of the abbots, and by threats and promises had engaged several of them to surrender their trusts. But the abbot of Glastonbury, attached to his house, and connected with his fraternity, refused to surrender. He was conscious of his own innocence; and thought guilt only had to fear from the inquisition that was abroad. But Henry, whose haughty and imperious spirit, unused to control, soared above the trifling distinctions between innocence and guilt, was highly incensed; and determined to make an example of the abbot of Glastonbury to terrify others. An order first came down for him to appear forthwith before the council. The difficulties of taking so long a journey, appeared great to an old man, who had seldom travelled beyond the limits of his monastery. But as there was no redress, he got into an easy horse-litter, and set out. In his mode of travelling, we see the state and dignity, which certainly required some correction, of the great ecclesiastics of that age. His retinue, it is said, consisted of not fewer than an hundred and fifty horsemen.

The King's sending for him, however, was a mere pretext. The real purpose was to prevent his secreting his effects; as it was never intended that he should return. Proper persons, therefore, were commissioned to search his apartments in his absence, and secure the wealth of the monastery. His steward, in the meantime, who was a gentleman of the degree of a Knight, was corrupted to make what discoveries he could. It was an easy matter in those days to procure evidence, where it was already determined to convict. In one of the abbot's cabinets some strictures upon the divorce were either found, or pretended to be found. Nothing else could be obtained against him.

During this interval, the abbot, who knew nothing of these proceedings, waited on the council. He was treated respectfully; and informed, that the King would not *force* any man to do what he wished him to *do freely*. However, as his Majesty intended to receive his final determination on the spot, he was at liberty to return.

Being thus dismissed, the abbot thought all was now over, and that he might be permitted to end his days peaceably in his beloved monastery.

He was now nearly at the end of his journey, having arrived at Wells, which is within five miles of Glastonbury, when he was informed, that a county-court (of what kind is not specified) was convened there on that day, to which he, as abbot of Glastonbury, was summoned. He went into the court room accordingly; and as his station required, was going to take his place at the upper end of it, among the principal gentry of the country; when the crier called him to the bar, where he was accused of high treason.

The old man, who had not the least conception of the affair, was utterly astonished; and turning to his steward, who stood near him, asked, if he knew what could be the meaning of all this? That traitor, whispering in his ear, wished him not to be cast down, for he knew the meaning of it was only to terrify him into a compliance. Though the court, therefore, on the evidence of the paper taken out of his cabinet, found him guilty of high treason, he had still no idea of what was intended. From the court he was conveyed to his litter, and conducted to Glastonbury; still in suspence how all this would end.

When he arrived under the walls of his abbey, the litter was ordered to stop; and an officer riding up to him, bad him prepare for instant death. A priest, at the same time, presented himself to take his confession.

The poor old abbot, utterly confounded at the suddenness of the thing, was quite unmanned. He begged with tears, and for God's sake, they would allow him some little time for recollection. But his tears were vain. Might he not then just enter his monastery; take leave of his friends; and recommend himself to their prayers? All was to no purpose. He was dragged out of his litter, and laid upon a hurdle, to which a horse being yoked, he was drawn along the ground to the Torr, and there, to make the triumph complete, was hung up, in his monk's habit, and in sight of his monastery. It was a triumph, however, that was attended with the tears and lamentations of the whole country, which had long considered this pious man, as a friend, benefactor, and father.

How far this shocking story, in all its circumstances of strange precipitancy, and wanton cruelty, may be depended on, considering the hands through which it is conveyed, may be matter of doubt: thus much, however, is certain, that if the picture here given of the royal savage of those days be not an exact portrait, it bears evidently a striking resemblance.

SECT. XXX.

FROM Axminster we left the great road to visit Ford-abbey. In a sequestered part of the country, where Devonshire and Dorsetshire unite, lies a circular valley, about a mile and half in diameter.

Its sides slope gently into its area in various directions; but are no where steep. Woody skreens, circling its precincts, conceal its bounds; and in many parts connecting with the trees, which descend into the bosom of the valley, form themselves into various tufted groves. Through the middle of this sweet retreat winds a stream, not foaming among broken rocks, nor sounding down cataracts; but mild like the scene it accompanies, and in cadence not exceeding a gentle murmur. From this retreat all foreign scenery is excluded. It wants no adventitious ornaments; sufficiently blessed with its own sweet groves and solitude.

> ——Such *landscape*
> Needs not the foreign aid of ornament;
> But is, when unadorned, adorned the most.[1]

This happy retirement was once sacred to religion. Verging towards one side of the valley stand the ruins of Ford-abbey. It has never been of large dimensions, but was a model of the most perfect Gothic, if we may credit its remains, particularly those of a cloister, which are equal to any thing we have in that style of architecture. This beautiful fragment consists of eight windows, with light buttresses between them, and joins a ruined chapel on one side, and on the other a hall or refectory, which still preserves its form sufficiently to give an idea of its just proportions. To this is connected by ruined walls a massy tower. What the ancient use of this fabric was, whether it belonged to the ecclesiastical or civil part of the monastery, is not now apparent; but at present it gives a picturesque form to the ruin, which appears to more advantage by the pre-eminence of some superior part.

At right angles with the chapel runs another cloister, a longer building, but of coarser workmanship, and almost covered with ivy. The river, which enters the valley at the distance of about half a mile from the ruin, takes a sweep towards it, and passing under this cloister, opens into what was once the great court, and makes its exit through an arch in the wall on the opposite side.

---

1 A paraphrase of lines 205–06 of James Thomson's "Autumn" from *The Seasons* (1726–30). The first line is Gilpin's addition.

This venerable pile,
—clad in the mossy vest of fleeting time,[1]
and decorated all over with variety of lychens, streaming weather-stains, and twisting shrubs, is shaded by ancient oaks, which, hanging over it, adorn its broken walls without encumbering them. In short, the valley, the river, the path, and the ruins are all highly pleasing; the *parts* are beautiful, and the *whole* is harmonious.

They who have lately seen Ford-abbey will stare at this description of it. And well may they stare; for this description antedates its present state by at least a century. If they had seen it in the year 1675, they might probably have seen it as it is here described. Now, alas! it wears another face. It has been in the hands of *improvement*. Its simplicity is gone; and miserable ravage has been made through every part. The ruin is patched up into an awkward dwelling; old parts and new are blended together, to the mutual disgrace of both. The elegant cloister is still left; but it is completely repaired, white-washed, and converted into a green-house. The hall too is modernized, and every other part. Sash-windows glare over pointed arches, and Gothic walls are adorned with Indian paper.

The grounds have undergone the same reformation. The natural groves and lawns are destroyed; vistas and regular slopes supply their room. The winding path, which contemplation naturally marked out, is gone; succeeded by straight walks, and terraces adorned with urns and statues; while the river and its fringed banks have given way to canals and stew-ponds. In a word, a scene abounding with so many natural beauties was never perhaps more wretchedly deformed.

When a man exercises his crude ideas on a few vulgar acres, it is of little consequence. The injury is easily repaired; and if not, the loss is trifling. But when he lets loose his depraved taste, his absurd invention, and his graceless hands on such a subject as this, where art and nature united cannot restore the havoc he makes, we consider such a deed under the same black character in matters of picturesque beauty, as we do sacrilege and blasphemy in matters of religion. The effects of superstition we abhor. Some little atonement, however, this implacable power might have made in taste, for its mischiefs in religion, if it had deterred our ancestors from connecting their mansions with ruins once dedicated to sacred uses. We might then have enjoyed in perfection many noble scenes, which are now either entirely effaced or miserably mangled.

---

1 A paraphrase of line 156 of Thomas Wharton's *The Triumph of Isis: A Poem* (1749). As above, Gilpin has written the first line and amended it to a line from another poet to incorporate their writing into his own.

Before we leave these scenes, I must relate a story of the monks of Ford, which does great credit to their piety. It happened (in what century tradition says not) that a gentleman of the name of Courtney, a benefactor to the abbey, was overtaken at sea by a violent storm; and the seamen having toiled many hours in vain, and being entirely spent, abandoned themselves to despair. "My good lads," (said Courtney, calling them together, and pulling out his watch, if watches were then in use,) "My good lads, you see it is now four o'clock. At five we shall certainly be relieved. At that hour the monks of Ford rise to their devotions, and in their prayers to St. Francis, will be sure to remember me among their benefactors; and you will have the benefit of being saved in my company. Persevere only one hour, and you may depend on what I say." This speech reanimated the whole crew. Some flew to the pump, others to the leak; all was life and spirit. By this vigorous effort, at five o'clock the ship was so near the shore, that she easily reached it; and St. Francis got all the credit of the escape.

3. From Sir Walter Scott, *Lay of the Last Minstrel* (London: Longman et al., 1805)

[Sir Walter Scott (1771–1832) was a prolific Scottish writer of historical fictions, plays, poems, and histories. His novels, including *Waverley* (1814), *Rob Roy* (1817), and *Ivanhoe* (1820), created a new standard for the historical novel and influenced continental writers, such as Victor Hugo (1802–85) and Leo Tolstoy (1828–1910), as well as every English-language novelist of the mid-nineteenth century. Developed from his interest in collecting folk songs from the Border regions, *Lay of the Last Minstrel* deals with the transition from one age of history to another, a favorite topic of Scott's. This most famous section of the poem describes the journey to Melrose Abbey in order to take the magic book from the tomb of the great wizard Michael Scott.]

Canto II

I.

IF thou would'st view fair Melrose aright,
Go visit it by the pale moon-light;
For the gay beams of lightsome day
Gild, but to flout, the ruins gray.
When the broken arches are black in night,
And each shafted oriel[1] glimmers white;

---

1 A kind of window.

When the cold light's uncertain shower
Streams on the ruined central tower;
When buttress and buttress,[1] alternately,
Seem framed of ebon and ivory;
When silver edges the imagery,
And the scrolls that teach thee to live and die;
When distant Tweed[2] is heard to rave,
And the owlet to hoot o'er the dead man's grave;
Then go—but go alone the while—
Then view St David's ruined pile;
And, home returning, soothly swear,
Was never scene so sad and fair!

II.

Short halt did Deloraine make there;
Little recked he of the scene so fair.
With dagger's hilt, on the wicket strong,
He struck full loud, and struck full long.
The porter hurried to the gate—
"Who knocks so loud, and knocks so late?"
"From Branksome I," the warrior cried;
And strait the wicket opened wide:
For Branksome's chiefs had in battle stood,
    To fence the rights of fair Melrose;
And lands and livings, many a rood,
    Had gifted the shrine for their souls repose.

III.

Bold Deloraine his errand said;
The porter bent his humble head;
With torch in hand, and foot unshod,
And noiseless step, the path he trod;
The arched cloisters, far and wide,
Rang to the warrior's clanking stride;
Till, stooping low his lofty crest,
He entered the cell of the ancient priest,
And lifted his barred aventayle,[3]
To hail the Monk of St Mary's aisle.

---

1   An architectural support.
2   The Tweed is a river in Scotland.
3   [Scott's note:] *Aventayle,* The visor of a helmet.

IV.

"The Ladye of Branksome greets thee by me;
　　Says, that the fated hour is come,
And that to-night I shall watch with thee,
　　To win the treasure of the tomb."
From sackcloth couch the Monk arose,
　　With toil his stiffened limbs he reared;
A hundred years had flung their snows
　　On his thin locks and floating beard.

V.

And strangely on the knight looked he,
　　And his blue eyes gleamed wild and wide;
　　"And, darest thou, warrior! seek to see
　　What heaven and hell alike would hide?
My breast, in belt of iron pent,
　　With shirt of hair and scourge of thorn;
For threescore years, in penance spent,
　　My knees those flinty stones have worn:
Yet all too little to atone
For knowing what should ne'er be known.
　　Would'st thou thy every future year
　　　　In ceaseless prayer and penance drie,
　　Yet wait thy latter end with fear—
　　　　Then, daring warrior, follow me!"

VI.

"Penance, father, will I none;
Prayer know I hardly one;
For mass or prayer can I rarely tarry,
Save to patter an Ave Mary,[1]
When I ride on a Border foray:
Other prayer can I none;
So speed me my errand, and let me begone."

1　Patter refers to muttering quickly and is related to "pater," a reference to the
　"Our Father." "Ave Mary" is a prayer, "Hail Mary."

VII.

Again on the Knight looked the Churchman old.
  And again he sighed heavily;
For he had himself been a warrior bold,
  And fought in Spain and Italy.
And he thought on the days that were long since by,
When his limbs were strong, and his courage was high:—
Now, slow and faint, he led the way,
Where, cloistered round, the garden lay;
The pillared arches were over their head,
And beneath their feet were the bones of the dead.

VIII.

Spreading herbs, and flowerets bright,
Glistened with the dew of night;
Nor herb nor floweret glistened there,
But was carved in the cloister-arches as fair.
  The Monk gazed long on the lovely moon,
    Then into the night he looked forth;
  And red and bright the streamers light
    Were dancing in the glowing north.
So had he seen, in fair Castile,[1]
    The youth in glittering squadrons start;
  Sudden the flying jennet[2] wheel,
    And hurl the unexpected dart.
He knew, by the streamers that shot so bright,
That spirits were riding the northern light.

IX.

By a steel-clenched postern door,[3]
  They entered now the chancel[4] tall;
The darkened roof rose high aloof
  On pillars lofty, and light, and small;
The key-stone, that locked each ribbed aisle,

---

1 A kingdom within what became modern Spain in the late fifteenth century.
2 Small Spanish horse, here turning a circle.
3 An entrance at the back of the church.
4 A space around the altar for the clergy and choir, usually blocked off from the
   nave by steps or a screen.

Was a fleur-de-lys, or a quatre-feuille;[1]
The corbells[2] were carved grotesque and grim;
And the pillars, with clustered shafts so trim,
With base and with capital flourished around,
Seemed bundles of lances which garlands had bound.

X.

Full many a scutcheon[3] and banner, riven,
Shook to the cold night-wind of heaven,
    Around the screened altar's pale;
And there the dying lamps did burn,
Before thy low and lonely urn,
O gallant chief of Otterhurne,
    And thine, dark knight of Liddesdale!
O fading honours of the dead!
O high ambition, lowly laid!

XI.

The moon on the east oriel shone,
Through slender shafts of shapely stone,
    By foliaged tracery combined;
Thou would'st have thought some fairy's hand,
'Twixt poplars straight, the osier[4] wand,
    In many a freakish knot, had twined;
Then framed a spell, when the work was done,
And changed the willow wreaths to stone.
    The silver light, so pale and faint,
    Shewed many a prophet and many a saint,
    Whose image on the glass was dyed;
Full in the midst, his Cross of Red
Triumphant Michael brandished.
    And trampled the apostate's pride.
The moon-beam kissed the holy pane,
And threw on the pavement a bloody stain.

---

1 Fleur-de-lys, the lily of France, an emblem of French kings; quatre-feuille, a
    four-leaved flower.
2 [Scott's note:] *Corbells*, the projections from which the arches spring, usually cut
    in a fantastic face, or mask.
3 An older form of "escutcheon," refers to a shield or emblem bearing a coat of
    arms.
4 Reed.

XII.

They sate them down on a marble stone,
 A Scottish monarch slept below;
Thus spoke the Monk, in solemn tone—
 "I was not always a man of woe;
For Paynim[1] countries I have trod,
And fought beneath the cross of God;
Now, strange to my eyes thine arms appear,
And their iron clang sounds strange to my ear.

XIII.

"In these far climes, it was my lot
To meet the wondrous Michael Scott;
 A wizard of such dreaded fame,
That when, in Salamanca's cave,
Him listed his magic wand to wave,
 The bells would ring in Notre Dame!
Some of his skill he taught to me;
And, warrior, I could say to thee
The words, that cleft Eildon[2] hills in three,
 And bridled the Tweed with a curb of stone:
But to speak them were a deadly sin;
And for having but thought them my heart within,
 A treble penance must be done.

XIV.

"When Michael lay on his dying bed,
His conscience was awakened;
He bethought him of his sinful deed,
And he gave me a sign to come with speed:
I was in Spain when the morning rose,
But I stood by his bed ere evening close.
The words may not again be said,
That he spoke to me, on death-bed laid;
They would rend this Abbaye's massy nave,
And pile it in heaps above his grave.

---

1 Any non-Christian, but especially a Muslim. From the French *paienime*, Latin
 paganismus.
2 A triple-peaked hill in the south of Scotland that overlooks the town of Eildon.

XV.

"I swore to bury his mighty Book,
That never mortal might therein look;
And never to tell where it was hid,
Save at his chief of Branksome's need;
And when that need was past and o'er,
Again the volume to restore.
I buried him on St Michael's night,[1]
When the bell tolled one, and the moon was bright;
And I dug his chamber among the dead,
Where the floor of the chancel was stained red,
That his patron's cross might over him wave,
And scare the fiends from the wizard's grave.

XVI.

"It was a night of woe and dread,
When Michael in the tomb I laid!
Strange sounds along the chancel past;
The banners waved without a blast"—
—Still spoke the Monk, when the bell tolled one!—
I tell you, that a braver man
Than William of Deloraine, good at need,
Against a foe ne'er spurred a steed;
Yet somewhat was he chilled with dread,
And his hair did bristle upon his head.

XVII.

"Lo, warrior! now the Cross of Red
Points to the grave of the mighty dead;
Within it burns a wonderous light,
To chase the spirits that love the night:
That lamp shall burn unquenchably,
Until the eternal doom shall be."
Slow moved the Monk to the broad flag-stone,
Which the bloody cross was traced upon:

---

1   The evening before Michaelmas (29 September in the Western liturgical calendar). Michaelmas is the feast in honor of St. Michael, the archangel who fought and defeated Satan (Revelation 12:7–13, also depicted in Book VI of Milton's *Paradise Lost*). English celebrations involved feasting, dancing, and games of various kinds.

He pointed to a secret nook;
An iron bar the warrior took;
And the Monk made a sign with his withered hand,
The grave's huge portal to expand.

XVIII.

With beating heart, to the task he went;
His sinewy frame o'er the grave-stone bent;
With bar of iron heaved amain,
Till the toil-drops fell from his brows like rain.
It was by dint of passing strength,
That he moved the massy stone at length.
I would you had been there to see
How the light broke forth so gloriously;
Streamed upward to the chancel roof,
And through the galleries far aloof!
No earthly flame blazed e'er so bright:
It shone like heaven's own blessed light;
And, issuing from the tomb,
Shewed the Monk's cowl, and visage pale;
Danced on the dark-brow'd Warrior's mail,
And kissed his waving plume.

XIX.

Before their eyes the wizard lay,
As if he had not been dead a day;
His hoary beard in silver rolled,
He seemed some seventy winters old;
A palmer's amice[1] wrapped him round,
With a wrought Spanish baldric[2] bound,
Like a pilgrim from beyond the sea:
His left hand held his Book of Might;
A silver cross was in his right;
The lamp was placed beside his knee:
High and majestic was his look,
At which the fellest fiends had shook;
And all unruffled was his face—
They trusted his soul had gotten grace.

---

1 A palmer is a pilgrim who has returned from the Holy Land; an amice is a religious garment that covered the head.
2 A finely wrought belt or girdle.

XX.

Often had William of Deloraine
Rode through the battle's bloody plain,
And trampled down the warriors slain,
     And neither known remorse or awe;
Yet now remorse and awe he own'd;
His breath came thick, his head swam round,
     When this strange scene of death he saw.
Bewildered and unnerved, he stood,
And the priest prayed fervently, and loud;
With eyes averted, prayed he,
He might not endure the sight to see,
Of the man he had loved so brotherly.

XXI.

And when the priest his death-prayer had prayed,
Thus unto Deloraine he said—
"Now speed thee what thou hast to do,
Or, warrior, we may dearly rue;
For those, thou mayest not look upon,
Are gathering fast round the yawning stone!"—
Then Deloraine, in terror, took
From the cold hand the Mighty Book,
With iron clasped, and with iron bound:
He thought, as he took it, the dead man frowned;
But the glare of the sepulchral light,
Perchance, had dazzled the warrior's sight.

XXII.

When the huge stone sunk o'er the tomb,
The night returned, in double gloom;
For the moon had gone down, and the stars were few;
And, as the Knight and Priest withdrew,
With wavering steps, and dizzy brain,
They hardly might the postern gain.
'Tis said, as through the aisles they passed,
They heard strange noises on the blast;
And through the cloister-galleries small,
Which at mid-height thread the chancel wall,
Loud sobs, and laughter louder, ran,
And voices unlike the voice of man;

As if the fiends kept holiday,
Because these spells were brought to day.
I cannot tell how the truth may be;
I say the tale as 'twas said to me.

Appendix D: Abbey Fictions

1. From Charlotte Smith, *Ethelinde* (London: T. Cadell, 1789)

[Charlotte Smith (1749–1806) was a poet and novelist. In *Ethelinde: Or, The Recluse of the Lake* (1789), Smith examines a marriage, having herself experienced a very bad marriage that left her in financial straits. The novel uses the Lake District as its central setting. The wife, whose money comes from the recent colonization of India, has no belief in the real or symbolic value of the possession of an abbey.]

CHAPTER I.

O N the borders of the small but beautiful lake called Grasmere Water, in the county of Cumberland, is Grasmere Abbey, an old seat belonging to the family of Newenden. The abbey, founded by Ranulph Earl of Chester, for forty Cistercian monks, was among those dissolved by Henry the Eighth; by whom it was given, with its extensive royalties, to the family of Brandon, from whence it descended by a female to Sir Edward Newenden, its present possessor.

His father, a man of boundless profusion, had at his death left every part of his property deeply mortgaged: but Sir Edward, on succeeding to it, had married the heiress of Mr. Maltravers, (a gentleman who had acquired an immense fortune in the East Indies,) and he had retrieved the fortune of his house, and disembarrassed his estates, by this opulent alliance.

Though much attached to Grasmere Abbey, which he venerated as the abode of his ancestors, and loved as the scene of his early pleasures, Sir Edward had not seen it for above four years. Lady Newenden had never been farther from the metropolis than to some of those places of public resort where all its conveniences and amusements are to be enjoyed; and her Ladyship had conceived a dread of a journey into Cumberland, which Sir Edward, to whom her slightest wish was a law, had never earnestly pressed her to conquer: but in the summer of 1784, as his presence there was absolutely necessary, he besought her as a favour to accompany him thither; and as a favour, granted with the most perfect consciousness of its value, she at length deigned to consent.

It was however almost the end of July before her Ladyship gave this reluctant acquiescence; and then, as she had persuaded herself that she was to be condemned for two months to a desart, she had accepted the offer of Miss Newenden, the sister of Sir Edward, to accompany her, and she had invited her cousin Ethelinde Chesterville, and Mr. Davenant, a young man not yet of age, who was distantly related to Sir Edward and was also his ward, to be of her party.

This gentleman, who was still at Oxford, arrived from thence at the house of Sir Edward, near Windsor, the evening preceding the day on which they were to set out from thence to London, on their way to the North. About twelve the next morning therefore he handed Lady Newenden to her coach, after she had taken leave of her three beautiful children. But Sir Edward lingered behind: he kissed repeatedly each of the lovely little creatures, earnestly recommended them to the care of their attendants; and when on the point of quitting them, again returned, renewed his caresses, and repeated his entreaties that they might have every attention shewn them during the absence of their mother. Then reluctantly tearing himself from them, he proceeded with his wife and Mr. Davenant to the house of Mr. Maltravers, her father, where they dined; and in the evening arrived at their house in Hanover Square, where they were to meet Miss Newenden and Ethelinde Chesterville.

They found Miss Newenden already there. As there had never been any great affection between her and Lady Newenden, they met without any warm expressions of pleasure. Their characters and manners were indeed wholly dissimilar. But though there was little friendship between them, there was less rivalry: the indolent apathy of Lady Newenden was not disturbed by the boisterous vivacity of her sister in law; who, occupied almost entirely by the stable or the kennel, considered her Ladyship as a pretty, insipid doll, whose mind was a mere blank, and whose person was fitted only to exhibit to advantage the feminine fineries which she herself despised—her own dress being usually such as was distinguished from that of a man only by the petticoat.

The first short compliments had no sooner passed, than Miss Newenden, addressing herself to her brother and Mr. Davenant, lamented that she had been prevented sending forward her horses the day before as she intended. "That devilish fellow, Jack Wildman's groom," said she, "put a confounded kicking horse into the stable with Meteor, the day before yesterday; and the dear soul in kicking at him in his turn, has got a strain in the back sinews. I am wretched about it; for I am sure he must be fired.[1] He'll be of no use to me all the

---

1 The horse needs to be treated with a red-hot iron implement applied locally to the site of an injury that is not healing. "Firing" a horse was (and is) a form of therapy used for cauterizing tissue. The new injury stimulates the flushing out of sources of original inflammation and speeds the healing process. Now called "pin firing," such thermocautery is used today—but with sedation and anesthetic for the animal not available in the eighteenth century.

summer, and I question if I shall get him sound by next season." Sir Edward heard her with more civility than interest; but Davenant, listening more attentively to her distress, they immediately began to consult on the probable advantages of a cold charge; and it was agreed that as soon as a celebrated farrier arrived, who was to be consulted, they would go together to the stable to inspect with him the condition of Meteor.

Their discourse was interrupted but not broken off, by the entrance of Colonel Chesterville and his daughter, neither of whom Mr. Davenant had ever seen before. Sir Edward introduced him to both. He bowed slightly to each; and then turning immediately to Miss Newenden, he continued with her a dissertation on the nature and consequences of a strain in the back sinews.

Colonel Chesterville, now near fifty, had been a remarkably handsome man. Military service in various countries, and sorrows suffered in his own, had had more share than time in marking the strong lines of his sensible and manly countenance with something of peculiar dejection. His manners, though perfectly those of a man of fashion, had yet a too visible coldness towards persons for whom he felt no particular esteem; but when he conversed with those for whom his heart owned an interest, especially when he spoke to or of his daughter, all that fire and energy which had been the leading feature of his character in the younger part of his life, seemed to return. His affections were almost entirely centered in his children: his son, who had entered early into the army, and was now with his regiment at Gibraltar, had by some youthful indiscretions taught the Colonel the anxieties of a father; but Ethelinde was in his opinion the most perfect of human beings; yet those who knew her best found but little of partiality or exaggeration in the exalted opinion he entertained of her.

Few girls of her age, for Ethelinde was not yet eighteen, can be said to have any decided character at all; but the circumstances of her life had taught her to think and to feel. In her twelfth year she had lost her mother by a lingering decline, and the deep melancholy into which her surviving parent had fallen in consequence of that event, the thoughtless conduct of her brother, and the encreasing anxiety which her father felt either from that or some other cause, had obscured her natural vivacity without diminishing her personal charms; and had given her a taste for solitude and reflection without lessening the natural sweetness of her temper. Her father's sorrows had redoubled her attachment toward him; her affection for her brother was encreased rather than diminished, since his imprudence had made him unhappy. To her he had disclosed his entangled circumstances even before he dared make them known to his father, and it was by her intercession that the Colonel had so easily pardoned him a second time, and had parted from him when he went to his regiment without any marks of displeasure.

Ethelinde however saw with great concern, that since that period her father had been more than usually unhappy, and that though he was less at home than was his general custom, he could with difficulty conceal, when they were together, the anguish that preyed on his heart.

Conscious of his own dejection, and fearing for the health and spirits of his daughter, which were evidently affected by it, he had, however unwilling to part with her, promoted her going to Grasmere Abbey with her cousin, Lady Newenden; and when she objected to it, because she was unwilling to leave him alone, he told her that she should take the opportunity of her absence to pay a visit of some months to his friend General Sandys, in the neighborhood of Bath. Ethelinde and her father were now to part; for a few months only; but even so short a separation, at the moment it was to take place, appeared so terrible to Colonel Chesterville, that he lost all his fortitude when it arrived. He had continued a very insipid conversation with Lady Newenden till a late hour, because he had not resolution enough to bid adieu to his daughter; but finding that the longer he delayed it more painful it became he at length arose, and approaching her, he kissed her and bade her hastily farewell. He trembled while he spoke; and Ethelinde, who felt and shared his emotion, found her eyes fill with tears, and her hand involuntarily clasped in his as if to detain him; while he, turning to Lady Newenden, said—"to you, Madam, and to Sir Edward, I confide almost the only good I have on earth." Lady Newenden curtseying, said something in a low voice; but Sir Edward advancing, cried with mingled politeness and tenderness— "We accept the trust, my dear Colonel, with the utmost pleasure; and we consider it as an high honor and happiness that we are thought worthy of a charge so precious."

Ethelinde held out her hand to her father; he pressed it to his heart, and then bowing to Miss Newenden and Mr. Davenant, (who gazed at him with an unmeaning stare) he hurried down the stairs and left the house.

Ethelinde finding it impossible to stifle her concern or stop her tears, hastily left the room. She was no sooner gone than Lady Newenden, who had thrown herself on a sopha, from which she had arisen on the Colonel's departure, cried, in her indolent way—"I wonder now what occasion Colonel Chesterville has to make such a fuss about parting from Ethy, as if she was never to come back again; it is really almost alarming to undertake to care of a person who is made of so much consequence."

"Surely, my love," said Sir Edward, mildly, "it is very natural to be attached to such a daughter, who is not only so extremely amiable and interesting, but is, as he told you, almost the only good he has on earth."

"Lord, brother," exclaimed Miss Newenden, "it is amazing to me that you can think her so handsome. I don't know whether it is quite civil to dispute the beauty of Lady Newenden's relation, but really now I have wondered an hundred times what you can possibly find in her; and I am surprised," added she, turning to Lady Newenden, "that your Ladyship allows Sir Edward to express these violent partialities."

"It is quite indifferent to me," answered she with a sort of languid haughtiness. "For my own part, Ethy seems to me to be just like other misses; I see nothing extraordinary in her either one way or the other, though her father has always made such a racket with her, that it is surprising she is not more pert and vain than girls generally are. If she had been entitled to a great fortune, he could not have lavished more expence upon her, or could there have been more rout about her beauty and her wit."

"Has she no fortune then?" said Davenant, who had been drumming on the arm of the sopha and whistling a few bars of an hunting song. This question, by turning half round towards Miss Newenden, seemed to be addressed to her.

"Upon my soul I don't know. Lady Newenden, what is Miss Chesterville's fortune? Here is Tom Davenant enquiring; perhaps he is smitten, and means to make proposals."

"Indeed," said Lady Newenden, "I cannot inform him; her mother was my father's sister, and I have heard that she and Chesterville ran away together when he was an Ensign, a great many years ago. She was dead before we came to England, and I never enquired much about them."

"Colonel Chesterville," said Sir Edward, who seemed very little pleased with the conversation, "is a younger brother of a noble house. While yet very young, he married one of the sisters of my wife's father, against the wishes of his own family and indeed of hers; for he had only an Ensigncy in a marching regiment; all his hopes of promotion depended on the interest of his father; and there was reason to fear that those prospects would be blasted by his marriage. His father, however, though he never was thoroughly reconciled, failed not to promote his interest in the army; and gave him at his death the same portion as he left to his other younger children; since which, some of his brothers are dead, and of their shares he participates; so that besides his regiment, he has an handsome income. Were however his circumstances such as you, Nelly, (turning to his sister,) seem fond of representing them, he might still claim the respect and veneration of the world for the goodness of his heart, as well as for his long military services."

"Dear Sir Edward," cried Miss Newenden, "I don't want I am sure to represent him as being in bad circumstances; only you know that he has had the character of playing monstrous deep."[1]

"I own I have heard that he plays; but I never saw any reason to believe, since I have known him, that he indulges that propensity to the prejudice of his fortune; and I know him to be so passionately fond of his children, particularly of Ethelinde, that I am persuaded he gratifies himself in nothing that is likely to be prejudicial to them."

Supper being now announced, Sir Edward sent a servant to summon Ethelinde, who instantly attended the table; her eyes were red and swollen, and frequent sighs stole from her bosom; but she struggled to conquer the pain she felt, and would have taken some share in the conversation, had not Miss Newenden and Mr. Davenant almost entirely engrossed it, and talked on subjects quite unknown to her—such as racing and hunting. Sometimes Davenant looked for a moment at her, as if trying to discover the beauty in whose praise Sir Edward had spoken but he otherwise noticed very little. Miss Newenden seemed not to know such a person was in the room; and Lady Newenden, who never spoke much, did not appear to consider herself obliged to make any unusual exertions for the entertainment of her own relation; and feeling less and less contented with her northern journey as it more nearly approached, she sat in an indolent yet somewhat sullen way, till the cloth was removed, and then retired to her own apartment.

The easy and affectionate attention which Ethelinde ever found in the behaviour of Sir Edward, made her more than amends for the indifference of the rest. He had now however some business to settle with his steward before he went into the North, which obliged him to leave the room immediately after supper; Ethelinde soon retired to her chamber, and Miss Newenden and Mr. Davenant went together to the stable, where they remained in conference with the grooms till it was time to separate for the night.

The next morning they began their journey: during the first two days of which, nothing remarkable passed. Lady Newenden, in proportion as she left London more distant, seemed to leave her good humour also; and she failed not to express her dislike of the roads, the country, and the inns, as if to remind her husband at every stage of the

---

1 The heroine's father, Colonel Chesterville, is betting very heavily on card games and other games of chance.

greatness of the sacrifice she was making—while he endeavoured, by the most attentive and tender manners, to oblige and entertain her; and with the most patient endurance of her pettish arrogance, and childish caprice, tried to convince her that he was sensible of her condescension in undertaking the journey. But he too often found that all his endeavours served only to encrease her discontent; and that the more earnestly he attempted to please her, the more difficult she became to please.

Her Ladyship, whose delicate frame and irritable nerves suffered extremely from the fatigue of travelling, usually retired to her bed as soon as they arrived at the inn where they rested for the night; Miss Newenden and Davenant then sat down to piquet; and Sir Edward and Ethelinde were left to entertain each other, with a book, or such conversation as the occurrences or remarks of the day afforded them.

CHAPTER II.

A FEW of these conversations convinced Sir Edward that the winning manners, and lovely person of Ethelinde, were her least perfections. The solidity of her understanding, the gentleness of her temper, and the softness of her heart, interested, while the vivacity of her conversation entertained him; and as she every day gained on his good opinion, he could not help reflecting with some pain on her situation. He had heard, in general conversation, that Colonel Chesterville had only a very small fortune; and from some circumstances which had occurred, he feared that his son's extravagance, if not his own propensity to gaming, had considerably diminished it; and Sir Edward could not without great pain represent to himself the probability there was that this young woman, so lovely in mind and person, might be left a necessitous dependent on the family of Maltravers; while all his tenderness for Lady Newenden, prevented him not from feeling that she had not that temper which was likely to soften or diminish the miseries of such dependence.

Mr. Maltravers, like most men who accumulate sudden and opulent fortunes, was wrapped up in the contemplation of his own consequence, and in the project he was ever forming to aggrandize his family by procuring an higher title for Sir Edward Newenden. Mrs. Maltravers had been a celebrated beauty; but of an obscure family, and destitute of fortune; she had therefore gone to the East Indies early in life, where those personal advantages had induced Mr. Maltravers to marry her, though he was many years older than she was. At the age of forty-two or three, she still retained much of her beauty; and though a grandmother was extremely unwilling to believe that she must relinquish all pretensions to admiration. This disposition did not greatly tend to enlarge her heart towards the young and beautiful: those indeed who have so great a partiality to their own perfections, being rarely found capable of doing justice to the perfection of others.

The other relations of Ethelinde, were an uncle, who inherited the small personal estate of his ancestors in the West of England, who retaining the rustic simplicity of an English yeoman, had brought up a numerous family to rural œconomy. Her only surviving aunt was the wife of a rich merchant at Bristol.

Of these relations, Mr. Maltravers, since his return from the East Indies, had taken little and reluctant notice; Ethelinde herself owing the preference which had been shewn her to her alliance with a noble family on the side of her father.

Colonel Chesterville's elder brother, now a peer, had married an extravagant woman of fashion. Embarrassed in his circumstances, and supporting his rank with difficulty, he had little power and less inclination to interest himself for the family of his brother; and his wife having several daughters whose establishment depended entirely on their personal attractions, could not help seeing how much Ethelinde excelled them, and therefore he gave little encouragement to her to be often with them. Thus in the midst of numerous relations on both sides, Ethelinde, amiable as she was, had few friends; and though she complained not of the little affection she found from them, Sir Edward saw that she felt and lamented it.

The gentle sensibility of her heart, thus forbidden to extend itself towards her relations, centered more warmly in her father and brother. Next to them, she had learned to love Sir Edward Newenden, from whom she always received attention, tenderness, and respect. She considered him as an elder brother; and was always happy in his company, and delighted with his praises; while in cultivating so fine an understanding, Sir Edward found a new source of pleasure and gratification. During the journey, they read together in Italian and Spanish; in the first of which, Ethelinde was tolerably proficient, and in the latter he had been her instructor. Lady Newenden, on whose education great sums had been lavished, had learned every thing, but could do nothing; nor had she the least ambition to be any thing but a very pretty woman. As long therefore as Ethelinde disputed not with her the palm of beauty, she was content to leave her all the praise that should be due to knowledge; and her Ladyship beheld with great apparent indifference, the preference which Sir Edward sometimes too evidently gave to the society of Ethelinde.

Davenant, had a mind, which resembling the imaginary qualities of the camelion, received its predominant colour from the object which was most immediately near it. Deficient in that strength of intellect which gives determinate character, he was

"Every thing by turns, and nothing long."[1]

At Oxford, he drank, without loving wine; and kept hunters,[2] without loving violent exercise. In town, he sauntered about all the morning, without pleasure or pursuit; and went to a gaming table at night, though he always lost his money—an operation to which he had a very great aversion.

He was the mere creature of the day: his dress, his expences, his pleasures, his sentiments, being regulated by the opinion of others, rather than by his own inclinations.

From that facility of temper, which at an early period had been remarked in him, Sir Edward had been taught to hope that he might be rendered a useful if not a brilliant member of society. But his guardian soon found, that the same easiness of disposition which would, if he had fallen into good company only, have rendered him respectable, now laid him open to the influence of numberless debauched and dissipated young men, who without having more sense, had more vivacity than himself. Of these he became the copyist; and committed folly with no other hope and to no other end than to obtain the suffrage of fools.

His fortune however was not yet hurt; and Sir Edward, who had seen but little of him since the preceding year, (because he had passed the last vacation in another part of England) still hoped, that by detaching him from the society which had misled him, and opening to him new pursuits of domestic comfort and literary amusements, he might give new energy to his mind, and great rectitude to his morals. Davenant however had not been three days with Sir Edward, before he saw the fallacy of this hope, and of that which had for a moment led him to suppose that his ward might become worthy of the honor of being the lover and the husband of Ethelinde Chesterville.

Occupied entirely by Miss Newenden, Davenant noticed her very little. Yet neither the person or manners of Miss Newenden were calculated to attract esteem or admiration: her person, without being tall, was hard and masculine; her features, though not large, were sharp and harsh; and from being constantly exposed to the air, her complexion had contracted an unpleasant redness, particularly about her nose and forehead, that gave it a certain coarseness, which, without adding to the general spirit of her face, certainly encreased the fire or rather the fierceness of her quick, grey eyes.

---

1 A misquoted line from John Dryden's "Absalom and Achitophel" (1681), line 548: "Was everything by starts, and nothing long."

2 Horses used for fox hunting.

She had lost her mother when she was not more than ten years old; and from that period had been left entirely to the care of a governess, who found it more to her own interest to gratify than to contradict her. Her father, himself a keen sportsman, was pleased with the courage and agility she shewed on horseback, and had been accustomed to indulge her in following the hounds, while yet a child. Animated by the praises that were then bestowed upon her, she had imbibed a notion that to possess a good horse was the first point requisite to human happiness; and to be able to ride well, the first of human perfections. Her father dying when she was about sixteen, she became entitled to the whole of what was at his death to descend to younger children; as she was an only daughter, and had no brother but Sir Edward. This sum amounted to about sixteen thousand pounds; a fortune which would probably have procured her a respectable establishment; but Miss Newenden, far from having any views of that sort, immediately furnished her stables with valuable hunters, doubled her number of grooms, and took a small hunting seat in Dorsetshire; where, though she sometimes prevailed on a maiden aunt to reside with her, she oftener passed whole winters alone. Sir Edward, who would have loved her extremely if he had met with any affection in return, often pressed her to take up her abode part of the year with him; but she seldom accepted his invitations, unless for a few weeks at a time, either during an hard frost, or some capital sale at Tattersall's.[1] As she advanced in life, (and she was not near eight and twenty) her passion for field sports, for the stable, and the kennel, encreased rather than diminished. Many who knew that her fortune would be convenient to them, had, during the first years of her being mistress of her actions, addressed her with offers of marriage; but she had without hesitation dismissed them all; and though she still suffered some of them to attend on her in her favourite amusement, and shewed frequent preference to those who best understood the merits of an horse, or who displayed the most judgement in the hunt, she never thought of marrying, and soon ceased to be considered as an object of pursuit. Nothing indeed but her fortune had ever made her appear so; and the gentlemen who had with that view addressed her, were easily repulsed, and desisted without any great pain from addressing a young woman who had little other merit, and no other language and manners, than those of a stable boy.

The vapid and vacant mind of Davenant, ever open to momentary impressions, was amused with her singularity, and he fancied himself instructed by her skill in horse flesh. To keep up a conversation with

1 The most famous market in London for high-quality horses.

Sir Edward, demanded more knowledge than he had acquired, and more attention than he was willing to exert. From him therefore he generally tried to escape. Yet in despite of that imbecility of mind, which ever required that he should be told what he was to like or dislike, he was often attracted by the animated beauty of Ethelinde; and as she conversed with Sir Edward by the table where he was at cards with Miss Newenden, he insensibly neglected his game while he gazed at her. But from these short fits of absence he was generally recalled by Miss Newenden, with "Come, Tom, what the devil are you thinking of? if you cannot attend I'll play no more." Startled by this reproof, Davenant again attended to his cards, and seemed to have forgotten the object that had thus momentarily drawn his attention from them.

As they travelled very slowly, lest Lady Newenden should be too much fatigued, it was not till the afternoon of the sixth day after quitting London that they arrived within a few miles of Grasmere Abbey. As soon as the tall blue heads of the fells were very distinctly seen, Sir Edward, who was then in the coach with Lady Newenden, his sister, and Ethelinde, expressed forcibly the pleasure he felt in seeing them. "They are," said he, delighted at the sight, "as the sight of old friends, and bring back to my mind the pleasant days I used to pass when, at the holidays, I went down to Grasmere Abbey with my father. On that towering hill to the left, which at this distance seems an immense pile of purple rocks, the first grouse fell by my gun. I was not more than ten years old; and the delight with which I saw Humphrey, my old servant, put it in the net, the triumph with which I shewed it, on my return to my father, I shall never forget. Look, my love," continued he, "at the wild grandeur of that varied and bold outline; observe the effect of the sun's rays on the summits of the crags, while the large and swelling clouds that pass over seem almost to touch them and give them numberless shades in their progress."

"I see but little beauty in those dreary mountains," answered Lady Newenden, with a cold and disdainful smile. "Perhaps you had better apply to Ethelinde. You may teach *her* as she is a young lady of *sublime taste* you know, to admire what I, who am a creature without any, really want faculties to enjoy."

There was something in this speech more disobliging than usual; but Sir Edward, turning to Ethelinde, said with assumed gaiety, "Well then, my fair cousin, I must have *you* for a pupil, and you must learn to admire my country, for admired it must positively be. And you, Ellen," addressing himself to his sister, "have you acquired by absence and refinement a dislike to the scenes where you passed your early life? and do you prefer the flat, uninteresting country round London?"

"No," answered she, "not exactly the country round London; but I like many countries better than I do this, to be sure. Great part of Dorsetshire for example, and Hampshire; where one may gallop upon turf for ten or twelve miles on end, without check or leap. This is well enough for the eye, but I own for myself I cannot think it very desirable otherwise."

Sir Edward, smiling at an objection so strongly in character, then dropped the conversation, and soon after got on horseback. Miss Newenden, however, who sometimes rode with him, now remained in the coach; where, as they advanced among the fells, a deeper gloom fell on the countenance of Lady Newenden; Miss Newenden took out of the coach pocket, the sporting calendar, where she was endeavouring to trace the pedigree of an horse, about which she held an argument with Davenant the evening before; and as neither of them spoke to Ethelinde, she contemplated without interruption the novelty and grandeur of the scenery around her.

She had been much accustomed to travel with her father; who, having himself an elegant and enlightened understanding, had improved that turn for observation which genius had given to the mind of his daughter; and she had learned to see the face of nature with the taste of a painter, and the enthusiasm of a poet; while to Lady Newenden all was a blank, which offered nothing to gratify either her personal vanity, or the consequence she assumed from her splendid fortune.

Their road become now more slow by the necessity of winding among the hills; and every mile presented some new beauty, affording to Ethelinde the purest and most exquisite delight. At length they came within view of Grasmere Water, and passing between two enormous fells, one of which descended cloathed with wood, almost perpendicularly to the lake, while the other hung over it, in bold masses of staring rock, they turned round a sharp point formed by the root of the latter, and entering a lawn, the abbey, embosomed among the hills, and half concealed by old elms, which seemed coeval with the building, appeared with its gothic windows, and long pointed roof of a pale grey stone, bearing every where the marks of great antiquity. The great projecting buttrasses were covered with old fruit trees, which from their knotted trunks seemed to have been planted by the first inhabitants of the mansion. In some of the windows the heavy stone work still remained, and they were totally darkened at the top by stained glass; in others, sashes had been substituted; and the windows had been contracted by brick work to make them appear square within; but, even in these, the stained glass had been replaced, which generally represented the arms of Newenden surcharged with those of Brandon.

When the coach stopped, Sir Edward appeared at the door of it; and taking the hand of Lady Newenden, he led her into an hall, saluted her tenderly, and bade her welcome to Grasmere Abbey.

Instead, however, of attempting to gratify him by expressing any pleasure at that which evidently gave him so much, she turned abruptly away, and exclaimed—"Don't keep me, Sir Edward, in this great, cold place; it strikes as damp as a family vault. I hope you have ordered fires. I assure you that my departure will be a much fitter subject of congratulation than my arrival."

Sir Edward, a good deal hurt, led her without speaking into a long and old fashioned, but well furnished parlour, where he left her, and returned towards Ethelinde and his sister. He met Ethelinde in the hall; but Miss Newenden was gone with Davenant to the stables to chuse which she would have for her own horses.

A settee of rich cut velvet, with massy gilt feet, was in the room; which seemed to have in its time supported many of the venerable figures, and fair but faded forms, which were represented in the great portraits that covered the wainscot. On this settee or sopha, Lady Newenden sat down; and wrapping her cloak round her, complained of the excessive coldness of the house. By this time an old house-keeper, who had lived many years in the family, appeared, and in the broad dialect of the northern country, enquired—"Wat my lady wad please to have aufter her journey?"

"Have!" exclaimed her Ladyship, with evident marks of disgust; "why I would have a little warmth, good woman, if it is possible in these rooms; do make a fire instantly, and if my own people are come, send Powell to me."

"Your servants," said Sir Edward, "are yet at some distance; one of the post horses of the chaise lost a shoe about two miles from hence, which has detained them. Dickenson however will execute any orders you may have to give her."

"She can do nothing for *me*," sullenly replied his wife. "I should be glad indeed to have my own bed made up, but I must wait I see till Powell comes."

Mrs. Dickenson, who had long served the mother of Sir Edward, one of the best tempered and mildest women, began to find herself extremely hurt at the haughtiness of her new lady; and spreading out her clean white cloth apron, she with a sort of half curtsey approached nearer, saying—"Indeed, my Lady, I shud ha been glad to ha known as your Ladyshep weshed for to have fires, and then sure they shud ha ben leetted all aboot the hoose; bot my leet lady she niver hud fires tull aboot the eend of Siptimber ur begennen of Ooctoober, an I cud na knaw your Ladyshep wud leek of um, for my leet lady she——"

"Tell me not of thy late lady, Mrs. Nicholson," said Lady Newenden, (wilfully mistaking the name); "but since I am condemned to remain in this comfortless and dreary place, do prithee bestir thyself, to save me if possible from dying of an ague."

"Go, Dickenson," said Sir Edward, "and send in the housemaid to make a fire here; while you yourself see that others are made immediately in Lady Newenden's dressing and bed rooms."

The housekeeper immediately obeyed. Sir Edward, more vexed with his wife than he desired to appear, walked about the room in silence; and Ethelinde, depressed by the ill humour of her cousin, and concerned at the effect it had on Sir Edward, seated herself in the window, and looking at the surrounding hills, recollected how very far she now was from her father; and in that recollection felt deserted and forlorn.

By this time Miss Newenden joined them, and being better satisfied with the stable than her sister was with the house, she came gaily into the room with Davenant, who enquired of Lady Newenden how she found herself?

"More than half dead, I assure you, Davenant," said she, with her usual languor; "and all that amazes me is, how any creature can take such a journey as this for pleasure."

"I am very sorry, Lady Newenden," said Sir Edward, unable any longer to conceal his chagrin, "that *you* have undertaken it at all."

"Indeed, Sir Edward, so am I," answered she.

"I can't imagine why," cried Miss Newenden with quickness; "for I am sure you are no worse for it."

"Not the worse, Ma'am? why I am shaken to death, dissociated in all my joints, and after having been martyred the whole way in jolting in extreme heat, I come into this cold, damp, desolate place, which really is fit only for the nuns and friars that you told me, I think, used to inhabit it."

"Its inhabitants since that, Madam," said her sister in law, with encreased tartness, "were persons, of whom I may venture to say, that few of our present nobility are so *well*, certainly none *better* born. They were of a family with which at least *mere modern opulence* may be proud to boast it's alliance."

"Dear Miss Newenden," answered her Ladyship contemptuously, "nobody disputes it; I only wish that the last and present possessors of the place had been contented to remain as quiet here as the owners did who lived at it two or three hundred years ago; then I suppose they would not have spent so much money as has obliged them to have recourse to *modern opulence* to prevent these dreary rooms from being made into barns or granaries, or tumbling quite down."

"My dear cousin!" exclaimed Ethelinde, unable to repress her astonishment at this speech.

Sir Edward, finding that all his tenderness for Lady Newenden could not check the anger which this proud and contemptuous spirit provoked, now hastily left the room. Davenant, always an indifferent spectator of scenes where no kind of dissipation bore a part, strolled into the garden; but Miss Newenden, whose family pride (the only pride she had) was now roused, returned to the charge.

"Most women, let me assure your Ladyship, whatever may be their fortune, would think themselves too happy to share it with such a man as *my* brother."

"Not *too* happy surely," with a malicious smile, answered Lady Newenden, "if part of their lives was to wear away in banishment in the nunnery of Grasmere."

"But let me inform you, Lady Newenden——"

"Not to night, dear Ma'am—do not inform me to-night; for I am really fatigued to death, and cannot keep myself awake to hear any more about your ancestors. Doubtless they were all Knights and Esquires of high degree; only I wish their old fashioned nunnery had fallen into the lake before I had been dragged a thousand miles to catch my death in it."

At this moment her woman, Mrs. Powell, and her Indian servant, entered the room.

"Ah! Powell," exclaimed she, "it is comfortable to see you. Get my drops and my chocolate. I shall go instantly to bed. Why, what a while you have been coming?"

"Good heaven! my dear Lady," drawled out her attendant, "I thof that to have got here at all was a thing impossible. Gracious me! I thof of all things we should have been killed by one of them there great large *ills*; and then squish squash through such a deal of water! I am sure your Ladyship must be quite tired out of your life."

"Tired indeed! I hope every thing is ready for me?"

"Oh! yes I got every thing ready as soon as I came in for your Ladyship."

"Help me then," cried she, with redoubled languor, "help me to my bed. Good night, Ethy. Your humble servant, Miss Newenden. I congratulate you both on being so very robust, that even the fatigue of *such* a journey does not disable *you* from taking a pleasant rural walk, or an evening ride perhaps, over those sweet hills to see prospects. You cannot fail of entertainment; so I shall make no apology for leaving you."

She then, leaning on her two attendants, left the room.

2. From Regina Maria Roche, *The Children of the Abbey* (London: Minerva Press, 1796)

[Regina Maria Roche, née Dalton (1764–1845), was born in Waterford, Ireland, and moved to Dublin as a child. After her marriage to Ambrose Roche in 1794, she moved to England. *Children of the Abbey* is deeply interested in the relationship between England and Ireland. Very critical of English attitudes toward the Irish and Ireland, the novel uses various settings within the British Isles to elicit views of conflict and cultural disparity. *Children of the Abbey* rivalled the popularity of Anne Radcliffe's *Mysteries of Udolpho* (1794). Although officially the Roches must have been considered Anglicans, the first names of Regina and her husband indicate a Catholic background, and Roche uses Catholic characters in her novel.]

CHAPTER XI

> From the loud camp retired and noisy court,
> In honorable ease and rural sport;
> The remnant of his days he safely passed,
> Nor found they lagged too slow nor flew, too fast.
> He made his wish with his estate comply,
> Joyful to live, yet not afraid to die:
> One child he had—a daughter chaste and fair,
> His age's comfort, and his fortune's heir. —PRIOR.[1]

OSCAR'S regiment, on his first joining it in Ireland, was quartered in Enniskellen, the corps was agreeable, and the inhabitants of the town hospitable and polite. He felt all the delight of a young and enterprising mind, at entering, what appeared to him, the road to glory and pleasure; many of his idle mornings were spent in rambling about the country, sometimes accompanied by a party of officers, and sometimes alone.

In one of his solitary excursions along the beautiful banks of Lough Erne, with a light fusee[2] on his shoulder, as the woods, that almost descended to the very edge of the water, abounded in game; after proceeding a few miles he felt quite exhausted by the heat, which, as it was now the middle of summer, was intense; at a little distance he perceived an orchard, whose glowing apples promised a delightful repast; knowing that the fruit in many of the neighboring

---

1 Lines 51–58 of Matthew Prior's "Henry and Emma" (1709).
2 Flintlock musket, or firearm.

places was kept for sale, he resolved on trying if any was to be purchased here, and accordingly opened a small gate, and ascending through a grass-grown path in the orchard to a very plain white cottage, which stood upon a gentle sloping lawn, surrounded by a rude paling, he knocked against the door with his fusee, and immediately a little rosy girl appeared; 'tell me, my pretty lass,' cried he, 'whether I can purchase any of the fine apples I see here.' 'Anan!' exclaimed the girl with a foolish stare. Oscar glancing at the moment into the passage, saw, from a half opened door, nearly opposite to the one at which he stood, a beautiful fair face peeping out; he involuntarily started, and pushing aside the girl, made a step into the passage; the room door directly opened, and an elderly woman, of a genteel figure and pleasing countenance, appeared. 'Good Heaven!' cried Oscar, taking off his hat, and retreating, 'I fear I have been guilty of the highest impertinence; the only apology I can offer for it is by saying it was not intentional. I am quite a stranger here, and having been informed most of the orchards hereabouts contained fruits for sale, I intruded under that idea.' 'Your mistake, sir,' she replied with a benevolent smile, 'is too trifling to require an apology; nor shall it be attended with any disappointment to you.'

She then politely showed him into the parlor, where, with equal pleasure and admiration, he contemplated the fair being of whom before he had but a transient glance; she appeared to be scarcely seventeen, and was, both as to face and figure, what a painter would have chosen to copy for the portrait of a little playful Hebe;[1] though below even the middle size, she was formed with the nicest symmetry; her skin was of a dazzling fairness, and so transparent, that the veins were clearly discernible; the softest blush of nature shaded her beautifully rounded cheeks; her mouth was small and pouting, and whenever she smiled a thousand graces sported round it; her eyes were full and of a heavenly blue, soft, yet animated, giving, like the expression of her whole countenance, at once an idea of innocence, spirit, and sensibility; her hair, of the palest and most glossy brown, hung carelessly about her, and, though dressed in a loose morning-gown of muslin, she possessed an air of fashion and even consequence; the easy manner in which she bore the looks of Oscar, proclaimed her at once not unaccustomed to admiration, nor displeased with that she now received; for that Oscar admired her could not but be visible, and he sometimes fancied he saw an arch smile playing over her features, at the involuntary glances he directed towards her.

---

1 Hebe, Zeus's daughter and goddess of health, was the female cupbearer to the Greek gods.

A fine basket of apples, and some delicious cider, was brought to Oscar, and he found his entertainer as hospitable in disposition as she was pleasing in conversation.

The beautiful interior of the cottage by no means corresponded with the plainness of the exterior; the furniture was elegantly neat, and the room ornamented with a variety of fine prints and landscapes; a large folding glass door opened from it into a pleasure garden.

Adela, so was the charming young stranger called, chattered in the most lively and familiar terms, and at last running over to the basket, tossed the apples all about the table, and picking out the finest presented them to Oscar. It is scarcely necessary to say he received them with emotion; but how transient is all sublunary bliss! A cuckoo-clock, over Oscar's head, by striking three, reminded him that he had passed near two hours in the cottage.

'Oh, Heavens!' cried he, starting, 'I have made a most unconscionable intrusion; you see, my dear ladies,' bowing respectfully to both, 'the consequence of being too polite and too fascinating.' He repeated his thanks in the most animated manner, and snatching up his hat, departed, yet not without casting

One longing, lingering look behind.[1]

The sound of footsteps after him in the lawn made him turn, and he perceived the ladies had followed him thither. He stopped again to speak to them, and extolled the lovely prospect they had from that eminence of the lake and its scattered islands. 'I presume,' said Adela, handling the fusee on which he leaned, 'you were trying your success to-day in fowling?' 'Yes; but as you may perceive, I have been unsuccessful.' 'Then, I assure you,' said she, with an arch smile, 'there is choice game to be found in our woods.' 'Delicious game, indeed!' cried he, interpreting the archness of her look, and animated by it to touch her hand, 'but only tantalizing to a keen sportsman, who sees it elevated above his reach.' 'Come, come,' exclaimed the old lady, with a sudden gravity, 'we are detaining the gentleman.' She took her fair companion by the arm, and hastily turned to the cottage. Oscar gazed after them a moment, then, with a half-smothered sigh, descended to the road. He could not help thinking this incident of the morning very like the novel adventures he had sometimes read to his sister Amanda as she sat at work; and, to complete the resemblance, thought he, I must fall in love with the little heroine. Ah! Oscar, beware of such imprudence! guard your heart with all your care against tender impressions, till fortune has been more propitious to you! Thus would my father speak, mused Oscar,

---

1 Thomas Gray, "Elegy Written in a Country Churchyard" (1751), line 88.

and set his own misfortunes in terrible array before me, were he now present: well, I must endeavor to act as if he were here to exhort me. Heigh ho! proceeded he, shouldering his fusee, glory for some time to come must be my mistress!

The next morning the fusee was again taken down, and he sallied out, carefully avoiding the officers, lest any of them should offer to accompany him; for he felt a strange reluctance to their participating in either the smiles of Adela or the apples of the old lady. Upon his arrival at the orchard, finding the gate open, he advanced a few steps up the path, and had a glimpse of the cottage, but no object was visible. Oscar was too modest to attempt entering it uninvited; he therefore turned back, yet often cast a look behind him; no one, however, was to be seen. He now began to feel the heat oppressive, and himself fatigued with his walk, and sat down upon a moss-covered stone, on the margin of the lake, at a little distance from the cottage, beneath the spreading branches of a hawthorn; his hat and fusee were laid at his feet, and a cool breeze from the water refreshed him; upon its smooth surface a number of boats and small sail-vessels were now gliding about in various directions, and enlivened the enchanting prospect which was spread upon the bosom of the lake; from contemplating it he was suddenly roused by the warble of a female voice; he started, turned, and beheld Adela just by him. 'Bless me!' cried she, 'who would have thought of seeing you here; why, you look quite fatigued, and, I believe, want apples today as much as you did yesterday?' Then, sitting down on the seat he had resigned, she tossed off her bonnet, declaring it was insupportably warm, and began rummaging a small work-bag she held on her arm. Oscar snatching the bonnet from the ground, Adela flung apples into it, observing it would make an excellent basket. He sat down at her feet, and never, perhaps, felt such a variety of emotions as at the present moment; his cheeks glowed with a brighter color, and his eyes were raised to hers with the most ardent admiration; yet not to them alone could he confine the expression of his feelings; they broke in half-formed sentences from his lips, which Adela heard with the most perfect composure, desiring him either to eat or pocket his apples quickly, as she wanted her bonnet, being in a great hurry to return to the cottage, from which she had made a kind of stolen march. The apples were instantly committed to his pocket, and he was permitted to tie on the bonnet. A depraved man might have mis-interpreted the gaiety of Adela, or at least endeavored to take advan-tage of it; but the sacred impression of virtue, which nature and edu-cation had stamped upon the heart of Oscar, was indelibly fixed, and he neither suspected, nor, for worlds, would have attempted injuring, the innocence of Adela; he beheld her (in what indeed was a true light) as a little playful nymph, whose actions were the offspring of innocence.

'I assure you,' exclaimed she, rising, 'I am very loth to quit this pleasant seat; but, if I make a much longer delay, I shall find the lady of the cottage in anxious expectation.' 'May I advance?' said Oscar, as he pushed open the gate for her. 'If you do,' replied she, 'the least that will be said from seeing us together, is, that we were in search of each other the whole of the morning.' 'Well,' cried Oscar, laughing at this careless speech, 'and if they do say so, it would not be doing me injustice.' 'Adieu, adieu,' said she, waving her hand, 'not another word for a kingdom.'

What a compound of beauty and giddiness it is! thought Oscar, watching her till she entered the cottage. As he returned from the sweet spot he met some laborers, from whom he inquired concerning its owner, and learned she was a respectable widow lady of the name of Marlowe.

On Oscar's return from Enniskellen, he heard from the officers that General Honeywood, an old veteran, who had a fine estate about fourteen miles from the town, was that morning to pay his compliments to them, and that cards had been left for a grand *fête* and ball, which he annually gave on the 1st of July, to commemorate one of the glorious victories of King William.[1] Every person of any fashion in and about the neighborhood was on such occasions sure of an invitation; and the officers were pleased with theirs, as they had for some time wished for

---

1 This celebratory picnic in the ruins of an old abbey marks the Battle of the Boyne (1 July 1690). In 1688, the Dutch William of Orange (1650–1702), son-in-law of the Catholic King James II of England (r. 1685–88), was invited by certain English Protestant aristocrats to invade England and oust King James. On 1 July, William's invasion of Ireland crossed the Boyne and began the attack upon the Irish and French defenders. Led by the new Dutch king, the English troops were completely successful; James was defeated along with his English, Irish, and French troops. In this late battle of the "Glorious Revolution" (so called by Protestants), most of the army went over to William. King James was allowed to escape to France. The color orange forever after signified the Protestant cause and English victory over Ireland.

Roche's novel makes evident the historical conflict within an apparently pleasant summer event. The color orange that the servants are made to wear proclaims the Protestant cause and emphasizes English and Protestant victory over the Irish and Catholicism. The picnic flaunts the presence of "field pieces"—moveable cannons, fit for a field of battle. The Irish will know who is in charge. The first day of July was long commemorated as the anniversary of a glorious Protestant victory, although in later years the Orange Order has celebrated its cause on 12 July.

an opportunity of seeing the general's daughter, who was very much admired.

The general, like a true veteran, retained an enthusiastic attachment for the profession of arms, to which not only the morning, but the meridian of his life had been devoted, and which he had not quitted till compelled by a debilitated constitution. Seated in his paternal mansion he began to experience the want of a faithful companion, who would heighten the enjoyments of the tranquil hour, and soothe the infirmities of age: this want was soon supplied by his union with a young lady in the neighborhood, whose only dowry was innocence and beauty. From the great disparity of their ages it was concluded she had married for convenience; but the tenor of her conduct changed this opinion, by proving the general possessed her tenderest affections; a happier couple were not known; but this happiness was terminated as suddenly as fatally by her death, which happened two years after the birth of her daughter; all the general's love was then centered in her child. Many of the ladies in the neighborhood, induced by the well-known felicity his lady had enjoyed, or by the largeness of his fortune, made attempts to engage him in matrimonial toils; but he fought shy of them all, solemnly declaring, he would never bring a stepmother over his dear girl. In her infancy, she was his plaything, and as she grew up his comfort; caressed, flattered, adored from her childhood, she scarcely knew the meaning of harshness and contradiction; a naturally sweet disposition, and the superintending care of an excellent woman, prevented any pernicious effect from such excessive indulgence as she received; to disguise or duplicity she was a perfect stranger; her own feelings were never concealed, and others she supposed equally sincere in revealing theirs; true, the open avowal of her regard or contempt often incurred the imputation of imprudence; but had she even heard it she would have only laughed at it—for the general declared whatever she said was right, and her own heart assured her of the innocence of her intentions. As she grew up the house again became the seat of gaiety; the general, though very infirm, felt his convivial spirit revive; he delighted in the society of his friends, and could still

Shoulder his crutch, and show how fields were won![1]

Oscar, actuated by an impulse, which if he could he at least, did not strive to account for, continued daily to parade before the orchard, but without again seeing Adela.

At length the day for General Honeywood's entertainment arrived, and the officers, accompanied by a large party, set off early for Woodlawn, the name of the general's seat. It was situated on the borders of

---

1 Oliver Goldsmith, "The Deserted Village" (1770), line 158.

the lake, where they found barges waiting to convey them to a small island, which was the scene of the morning's amusement; the breakfast was laid out amid the ruins of an ancient building, which, from the venerable remains of its Gothic elegance, was most probably, in the days of religious enthusiasm, the seat of sacred piety; the old trees in groups formed a thick canopy overhead, and the ivy that crept along the walls filled up many of the niches where the windows had formerly been; those that still remained open, by descending to the ground, afforded a most enchanting prospect of the lake; the long succession of arches, which composed the body of the chapel, were in many places covered with creeping moss, and scattered over with wallflowers blue hair-bells, and other spontaneous productions of nature; while between them were placed seats and breakfast-tables, ornamented in a fanciful manner.

The officers experienced a most agreeable surprise on entering; but how inferior were their feelings to the sensations which Oscar felt, when, introduced with the party by the general to his daughter, he beheld in Miss Honeywood the lovely Adela! She seemed to enjoy his surprise, and Mrs. Marlowe, from the opposite side of the table, beckoned him to her with an arch look; he flew round, and she made room for him by herself: 'Well, my friend,' cried she, 'do you think you shall find the general's fruit as tempting as mine?' 'Ah!' exclaimed Oscar, half sighing, half smiling, 'Hesperian fruit,[1] I fear, which I can never hope to obtain.' Adela's attention, during breakfast, was too much engrossed by the company to allow her to notice Oscar more than by a few hasty words and smiles. There being no dancing till the evening, the company, after breakfast, dispersed according to their various inclinations.

The island was diversified with little acclivities, and scattered over with wild shrubs, which embalmed the air; temporary arbours of laurel, intermingled with lilies, were erected and laid out with fruits, ices, and other refreshments; upon the edge of the water a marquee was pitched for the regimental band, which Colonel Belgrave had politely complimented the general with: a flag was hoisted on it, and upon a low eminence a few small field-pieces[2] were mounted; attendants were everywhere dispersed, dressed in white streamers, ornamented with a profusion of orange-colored ribbons; the boatmen were dressed in the same livery; and the barges, in which several of the party were to visit the other islands, made a picturesque appearance with

---

1 The mythical golden apples guarded by nymphs became associated with oranges.

2 Moveable cannons.

their gay streamers fluttering in the breeze; the music, now softly dying away upon the water, now gradually swelling on the breeze, and echoed back by the neighboring hills, added to the pleasures of the scene.

Oscar followed the footsteps of Adela; but at the very moment in which he saw her disengaged from a large party, the general, hallooed to him from a shady bank on which he sat; Oscar could not refuse the summons; and, as he approached, the general, extending his hand, gave him a cordial squeeze, and welcomed him as the son of a brave man he had once intimately known. 'I recollected the name of Fitzalan,' said he, 'the moment I heard it mentioned; and had the happiness of learning from Colonel Belgrave I was not mistaken in believing you to be the son of my old friend.' He now made several inquiries concerning Fitzalan, and the affectionate manner in which he mentioned him was truly pleasing to Oscar. 'He had once,' he said, 'saved his life at the imminent danger of his own, and it was an obligation, while that life remained, he could not forget.'

Like Don Guzman in Gil Blas,[1] the general delighted in fighting over his battles, and now proceeded to enumerate many incidents which happened during the American war,[2] when he and Fitzalan served in the same regiment. Oscar could well have dispensed with such an enumeration; but the general, who had no idea that he was not as much delighted in listening as he was in speaking, still went on. Adela had been watching them some time; her patience at length, like Oscar's, being exhausted, she ran forward and told her father 'he must not detain him another minute, for they were going upon the lake; and you know, papa,' cried she, 'against we come back, you can have all your battles arranged in proper form, though, by the bye, I don't think it is the business of an old soldier to intimidate a young one with such dreadful tales of iron wars.' The general called her saucy baggage, kissed her with rapture, and saw her trip off with his young friend, who seized the favorable opportunity to engage her for the first set in the evening. About four the company assembled in the Abbey to dinner; the band played during the repast; the toasts were proclaimed by sound of trumpet, and answered by an immediate discharge from the Mount. At six the

---

1 A nobleman in Alain-René Lesage's (1668–1747) novel *Gil Blas de Santillane* or *The Adventures of Gil Blas* (1715–35), which adopts the Spanish-style "picaresque" story of the wanderings of a young man who must live on his wits.

2 The American Revolutionary War (1775–83).

ladies returned to Woodlawn to change their dresses for the ball, and now

Awful beauty put on all its charms.[1]

Tea and coffee were served in the respective rooms, and by eleven the ballroom was completely crowded with company, at once brilliant and lively, particularly the gentlemen, who were not a little elevated by the general's potent libations to the glorious memory of him whose victory they were celebrating.

Adela, adorned in a style superior to what Oscar had yet seen, appeared more lovely than he had even at first thought her; her dress, which was of thin muslin, spangled, was so contrived as to give a kind of aerial lightness to her figure. Oscar reminded her of the promise of the morning, at the very moment the colonel approached for the purpose of engaging her. She instantly informed him of her engagement to Mr. Fitzalan. 'Mr. Fitzalan!' repeated the colonel, with the haughty air of a man who thought he had reason to be offended; 'he has been rather precipitate, indeed; but, though we may envy, who shall wonder at his anxiety to engage Miss Honeywood?'

Dancing now commenced, and the elegant figure of Adela never appeared to greater advantage; the transported general watched every movement, and, 'Incomparable, by Jove!—what a sweet angel she is!' were expressions of admiration which involuntarily broke from him in the pride and fondness of his heart. Oscar, too, whose figure was remarkably fine, shared his admiration, and he declared to Colonel Belgrave, he did not think the world could produce such another couple. This assertion was by no means pleasing to the colonel; he possessed as much vanity, perhaps, as ever fell to the share of a young belle conscious of perfections, and detested the idea of having any competitor (at least such a powerful one as Oscar) in the good graces of the ladies. Adela, having concluded the dance, complained of fatigue, and retired to an alcove, whither Oscar followed her. The window commanded a view of the lake, the little island, and the ruined Abbey; the moon in full splendor cast her silvery light over all those objects, giving a softness to the landscape, even more pleasing than the glowing charms it had derived from the radiancy of day. Adela in dancing had dropped the bandeau from her hair; Oscar took it up, and still retained it. Adela now stretched forth her hand to take it: 'Allow me,' cried he, gently taking her hand, 'to keep it; tomorrow you would cast it away as a trifle, but I would

---

1 A misquotation of lines 139–40, Canto I, of Alexander Pope's *Rape of the Lock* (1712): "Now awful Beauty puts on all its Arms; / The Fair each moment rises in her Charms."

treasure it as a relic of inestimable value; let me have some memento of the charming hours I have passed to-day.' 'Oh, a truce,' said Adela, 'with such expressions!' (who did not, however, oppose his putting her bandeau in his bosom); 'they are quite commonplace, and have already been repeated to hundreds, and will again, I make no doubt.' 'This is your opinion?' 'Yes, really.' 'Oh, would to Heaven,' exclaimed Oscar, 'I durst convince you how mistaken a one it is.' Adela, laughing, assured him that would be a difficult matter. Oscar grew pensive. 'I think,' cried he, 'if oppressed by misfortune, I should of all places on earth like a seclusion in the old Abbey.' 'Why, really,' said Adela, 'it is tolerably calculated for a hermitage; and if you take a solitary whim, I beg I may be apprised of it in time, as I should receive peculiar pleasure in preparing your mossy couch and frugal fare.' 'The reason for my liking it,' replied he, 'would be the prospect I should have from it of Woodlawn.' 'And does Woodlawn,' asked Adela, 'contain such particular charms, as to render a view of it so very delightful?'

At this moment they were summoned to call a new dance—a summons, perhaps, not agreeable to either, as it interrupted an interesting *tête-à-tête*. The Colonel engaged Adela for the next set; and though Oscar had no longer an inclination to dance, to avoid particularity he stood up, and with a young lady who was esteemed extremely handsome. Adela, as if fatigued, no longer moved with animation, and suddenly interrupted the colonel in a gallant speech he was making to her, to inquire, if he thought Miss O'Neal (Oscar's partner) pretty—so very pretty as she was generally thought? The colonel was too keen not to discover at once the motive which suggested this inquiry. 'Why, faith,' cried he after examining Miss O'Neal some minutes through an opera glass, 'the girl has charms, but so totally eclipsed,' looking languishingly at Adela, 'in my eyes, that I cannot do them the justice they may perhaps merit: Fitzalan, however, by the homage he pays her, seems as if he would make up for the deficiency of every other person.' Adela turned pale, and took the first opportunity of demanding her bandeau from Oscar; he, smilingly, refused it, declaring it was a trophy of the happiness he had enjoyed that day, and that the general should have informed her a soldier never relinquished such a glorious memento. 'Resign mine,' replied Adela, 'and procure one from Miss O'Neal.'—'No!' cried he, 'I would not pay her charms and my own sincerity so bad a compliment, as to ask what I should not in the least degree value.' Adela's spirits revived, and she repeated her request no more. The dancing continued after supper, with little intermission, till seven, when the company repaired to the saloon to breakfast, after which they dispersed.

3. From Jane Austen, *Northanger Abbey* (London: John Murray, 1817)

[The historical commentary of Jane Austen (1775–1817) in her novel *Northanger Abbey* has been little understood and greatly oversimplified. Those who focus on the delightful naiveté of the heroine overlook the deeper and darker flaws of the Tilneys. Their ownership of an abbey is a sign of their imperfection. In this section, Austen depicts the inexperienced heroine as almost overwhelmed by the attentiveness of the owner of the abbey, General Tilney.]

Volume II, Chapter V.

Mr. and Mrs. Allen were sorry to lose their young friend, whose good-humour and cheerfulness had made her a valuable companion, and in the promotion of whose enjoyment their own had been gently increased. Her happiness in going with Miss Tilney, however, prevented their wishing it otherwise; and, as they were to remain only one more week in Bath themselves, her quitting them now would not long be felt. Mr. Allen attended her to Milsom-street, where she was to breakfast, and saw her seated with the kindest welcome among her new friends; but so great was her agitation in finding herself as one of the family, and so fearful was she of not doing exactly what was right, and of not being able to preserve their good opinion, that, in the embarrassment of the first five minutes, she could almost have wished to return with him to Pulteney-street.

Miss Tilney's manners and Henry's smile soon did away some of her unpleasant feelings; but still she was far from being at ease; nor could the incessant attentions of the General himself entirely reassure her. Nay, perverse as it seemed, she doubted whether she might not have felt less, had she been less attended to. His anxiety for her comfort—his continual solicitations that she would eat, and his often-expressed fears of her seeing nothing to her taste—though never in her life before had she beheld half such variety on a breakfast-table—made it impossible for her to forget for a moment that she was a visitor. She felt utterly unworthy of such respect, and knew not how to reply to it. Her tranquillity was not improved by the General's impatience for the appearance of his eldest son, nor by the displeasure he expressed at his laziness when Captain Tilney at last came down. She was quite pained by the severity of his father's reproof, which seemed disproportionate to the offence; and much was her concern increased, when she found herself the principal cause of the lecture, and that his tardiness was chiefly resented from being disrespectful to her. This was placing her in a very uncomfortable situation, and she felt great compassion for Captain Tilney, without being able to hope for his good-will.

He listened to his father in silence, and attempted not any defence, which confirmed her in fearing that the inquietude of his mind, on Isabella's account, might, by keeping him long sleepless, have been the real cause of his rising late.—It was the first time of her being decidedly in his company, and she had hoped to be now able to form her opinion of him; but she scarcely heard his voice while his father remained in the room; and even afterwards, so much were his spirits affected, she could distinguish nothing but these words, in a whisper to Eleanor, "How glad I shall be when you are all off."

The bustle of going was not pleasant.—The clock struck ten while the trunks were carrying down, and the General had fixed to be out of Milsom Street by that hour. His great coat, instead of being brought for him to put on directly, was spread out in the curricle in which he was to accompany his son. The middle seat of the chaise was not drawn out, though there were three people to go in it, and his daughter's maid had so crowded it with parcels, that Miss Morland would not have room to sit; and, so much was he influenced by this apprehension when he handed her in, that she had some difficulty in saving her own new writing-desk from being thrown out into the street.—At last, however, the door was closed upon the three females, and they set off at the sober pace in which the handsome, highly-fed four horses of a gentleman usually perform a journey of thirty miles: such was the distance of Northanger from Bath, to be now divided into two equal stages. Catherine's spirits revived as they drove from the door; for with Miss Tilney she felt no restraint; and, with the interest of a road entirely new to her, of an abbey before, and a curricle behind, she caught the last view of Bath without any regret, and met with every milestone before she expected it. The tediousness of a two hours' wait at Petty-France, in which there was nothing to be done but to eat without being hungry, and loiter about without anything to see, next followed—and her admiration of the style in which they travelled, of the fashionable chaise and four—postilions handsomely liveried, rising so regularly in their stirrups, and numerous outriders properly mounted, sunk a little under this consequent inconvenience. Had their party been perfectly agreeable, the delay would have been nothing; but General Tilney, though so charming a man, seemed always a check upon his children's spirits, and scarcely anything was said but by himself; the observation of which, with his discontent at whatever the inn afforded, and his angry impatience at the waiters, made Catherine grow every moment more in awe of him, and appeared to lengthen the two hours into four.—At last, however, the order of release was given; and much was Catherine then surprised by the General's proposal of her taking his place in his son's curricle for the rest of the journey:—"the day was fine, and he was anxious for her seeing as much of the country as possible."

The remembrance of Mr. Allen's opinion, respecting young men's open carriages, made her blush at the mention of such a plan, and her first thought was to decline it; but her second was of greater deference for General Tilney's judgment; he could not propose anything improper for her; and, in the course of a few minutes, she found herself with Henry in the curricle, as happy a being as ever existed. A very short trial convinced her that a curricle was the prettiest equipage in the world; the chaise and four wheeled off with some grandeur, to be sure, but it was a heavy and troublesome business, and she could not easily forget its having stopped two hours at Petty-France. Half the time would have been enough for the curricle, and so nimbly were the light horses disposed to move, that, had not the General chosen to have his own carriage lead the way, they could have passed it with ease in half a minute. But the merit of the curricle did not all belong to the horses;—Henry drove so well,—so quietly—without making any disturbance, without parading to her, or swearing at them; so different from the only gentleman-coachman whom it was in her power to compare him with!—And then his hat sat so well, and the innumerable capes of his great coat looked so becomingly important!—To be driven by him, next to being dancing with him, was certainly the greatest happiness in the world. In addition to every other delight, she had now that of listening to her own praise; of being thanked at least, on his sister's account, for her kindness in thus becoming her visitor; of hearing it ranked as real friendship, and described as creating real gratitude. His sister, he said, was uncomfortably circumstanced—she had no female companion—and, in the frequent absence of her father, was sometimes without any companion at all.

"But how can that be?" said Catherine, "are not you with her?"

"Northanger is not more than half my home; I have an establishment at my own house in Woodston, which is nearly twenty miles from my father's, and some of my time is necessarily spent there."

"How sorry you must be for that!"

"I am always sorry to leave Eleanor."

"Yes; but besides your affection for her, you must be so fond of the abbey!—After being used to such a home as the abbey, an ordinary parsonage-house must be very disagreeable."

He smiled, and said, "You have formed a very favourable idea of the abbey."

"To be sure, I have. Is not it a fine old place, just like what one reads about?"

"And are you prepared to encounter all the horrors that a building such as 'what one reads about' may produce?—Have you a stout heart?—Nerves fit for sliding panels and tapestry?"

"Oh! yes—I do not think I should be easily frightened, because there would be so many people in the house—and besides, it has never been uninhabited and left deserted for years, and then the family come back to it unawares, without giving any notice, as generally happens."

"No, certainly.—We shall not have to explore our way into a hall dimly lighted by the expiring embers of a wood fire—nor be obliged to spread our beds on the floor of a room without windows, doors, or furniture. But you must be aware that when a young lady is (by whatever means) introduced into a dwelling of this kind, she is always lodged apart from the rest of the family. While they snugly repair to their own end of the house, she is formally conducted by Dorothy, the ancient housekeeper, up a different staircase, and along many gloomy passages, into an apartment never used since some cousin or kin died in it about twenty years before. Can you stand such a ceremony as this? Will not your mind misgive you when you find yourself in this gloomy chamber—too lofty and extensive for you, with only the feeble rays of a single lamp to take in its size—its walls hung with tapestry exhibiting figures as large as life, and the bed, of dark green stuff or purple velvet, presenting even a funereal appearance? Will not your heart sink within you?"

"Oh! but this will not happen to me, I am sure."

"How fearfully will you examine the furniture of your apartment!—And what will you discern?—Not tables, toilettes, wardrobes, or drawers, but on one side perhaps the remains of a broken lute, on the other a ponderous chest which no efforts can open, and over the fireplace the portrait of some handsome warrior, whose features will so incomprehensibly strike you, that you will not be able to withdraw your eyes from it. Dorothy meanwhile, no less struck by your appearance, gazes on you in great agitation, and drops a few unintelligible hints. To raise your spirits, moreover, she gives you reason to suppose that the part of the abbey you inhabit is undoubtedly haunted, and informs you that you will not have a single domestic within call. With this parting cordial she curtsies off—you listen to the sound of her receding footsteps as long as the last echo can reach you—and when, with fainting spirits, you attempt to fasten your door, you discover, with increased alarm, that it has no lock."

"Oh! Mr. Tilney, how frightful!—This is just like a book!—But it cannot really happen to me. I am sure your housekeeper is not really Dorothy.—Well, what then?"

"Nothing further to alarm perhaps may occur the first night. After surmounting your *unconquerable* horror of the bed, you will retire to rest, and get a few hours' unquiet slumber. But on the second, or at farthest the *third* night after your arrival, you will probably have a violent storm. Peals of thunder so loud as to seem to shake the edifice to its foundation will roll round the neighbouring mountains—and during the frightful gusts of wind which accompany it, you will probably think you discern (for your lamp is not extinguished) one part of the hanging more violently agitated than the rest. Unable of course to repress your curiosity in so favourable a moment for indulging it, you will instantly arise, and throwing your dressing-gown around you, proceed to examine this mystery. After a very short search, you will discover a division in the tapestry so artfully constructed as to defy the minutest inspection, and on opening it, a door will immediately appear—which door being only secured by massy bars and a padlock, you will, after a few efforts, succeed in opening,—and, with your lamp in your hand, will pass through it into a small vaulted room."

"No, indeed; I should be too much frightened to do any such thing."

"What! not when Dorothy has given you to understand that there is a secret subterraneous communication between your apartment and the chapel of St. Anthony, scarcely two miles off—Could you shrink from so simple an adventure? No, no, you will proceed into this small vaulted room, and through this into several others, without perceiving anything very remarkable in either. In one perhaps there may be a dagger, in another a few drops of blood, and in a third the remains of some instrument of torture; but there being nothing in all this out of the common way, and your lamp being nearly exhausted, you will return towards your own apartment. In repassing through the small vaulted room, however, your eyes will be attracted towards a large, old-fashioned cabinet of ebony and gold, which, though narrowly examining the furniture before, you had passed unnoticed. Impelled by an irresistible presentiment, you will eagerly advance to it, unlock its folding doors, and search into every drawer;—but for some time without discovering anything of importance—perhaps nothing but a considerable hoard of diamonds. At last, however, by touching a secret spring, an inner compartment will open—a roll of paper appears:—you seize it—it contains many sheets of manuscript—you hasten with the precious treasure into your own chamber, but scarcely have you been able to decipher 'Oh! thou—whomsoever thou mayst be, into whose hands these memoirs of the wretched

Matilda may fall'—when your lamp suddenly expires in the socket, and leaves you in total darkness."

"Oh! no, no—do not say so. Well, go on."

But Henry was too much amused by the interest he had raised to be able to carry it farther; he could no longer command solemnity either of subject or voice, and was obliged to entreat her to use her own fancy in the perusal of Matilda's woes. Catherine, recollecting herself, grew ashamed of her eagerness, and began earnestly to assure him that her attention had been fixed without the smallest apprehension of really meeting with what he related. "Miss Tilney, she was sure, would never put her into such a chamber as he had described!—She was not at all afraid."

As they drew near the end of their journey, her impatience for a sight of the abbey—for some time suspended by his conversation on subjects very different—returned in full force, and every bend in the road was expected with solemn awe to afford a glimpse of its massy walls of grey stone, rising amidst a grove of ancient oaks, with the last beams of the sun playing in beautiful splendour on its high Gothic windows. But so low did the building stand, that she found herself passing through the great gates of the lodge into the very grounds of Northanger, without having discerned even an antique chimney.

She knew not that she had any right to be surprised, but there was a something in this mode of approach which she certainly had not expected. To pass between lodges of a modern appearance, to find herself with such ease in the very precincts of the abbey, and driven so rapidly along a smooth, level road of fine gravel, without obstacle, alarm, or solemnity of any kind, struck her as odd and inconsistent. She was not long at leisure however for such considerations. A sudden scud of rain, driving full in her face, made it impossible for her to observe anything further, and fixed all her thoughts on the welfare of her new straw bonnet:—and she was actually under the Abbey walls, was springing, with Henry's assistance, from the carriage, was beneath the shelter of the old porch, and had even passed on to the hall, where her friend and the general were waiting to welcome her, without feeling one awful foreboding of future misery to herself, or one moment's suspicion of any past scenes of horror being acted within the solemn edifice. The breeze had not seemed to waft the sighs of the murdered to her; it had wafted nothing worse than a thick mizzling rain; and having given a good shake to her habit, she was ready to be shewn into the common drawing-room, and capable of considering where she was.

An abbey!—yes, it was delightful to be really in an abbey!—but she doubted, as she looked round the room, whether anything within her observation, would have given her the consciousness. The furniture was in all the profusion and elegance of modern taste. The fireplace, where she had expected the ample width and ponderous carving of former times, was contracted to a Rumford,[1] with slabs of plain though handsome marble, and ornaments over it of the prettiest English china. The windows, to which she looked with peculiar dependence, from having heard the general talk of his preserving them in their Gothic form with reverential care, were yet less what her fancy had portrayed. To be sure, the pointed arch was preserved—the form of them was Gothic—they might be even casements—but every pane was so large, so clear, so light! To an imagination which had hoped for the smallest divisions, and the heaviest stone-work, for painted glass, dirt, and cobwebs, the difference was very distressing.

The General, perceiving how her eye was employed, began to talk of the smallness of the room and simplicity of the furniture, where everything, being for daily use, pretended only to comfort, &c.; flattering himself, however, that there were some apartments in the Abbey not unworthy her notice—and was proceeding to mention the costly gilding of one in particular, when, taking out his watch, he stopped short to pronounce it with surprise within twenty minutes of five! This seemed the word of separation, and Catherine found herself hurried away by Miss Tilney in such a manner as convinced her that the strictest punctuality to the family hours would be expected at Northanger.

Returning through the large and lofty hall, they ascended a broad staircase of shining oak, which, after many flights and many landing-places, brought them upon a long wide gallery. On one side it had a range of doors, and it was lighted on the other by windows which Catherine had only time to discover looked into a quadrangle, before Miss Tilney led the way into a chamber, and scarcely staying to hope she would find it comfortable, left her with an anxious entreaty that she would make as little alteration as possible in her dress.

4. From George Gordon, Lord Byron, *Don Juan* (1819; London: John Hunt, 1823)

[George Gordon, Lord Byron (1788–1824) produced many popular and political works of poetry, including *English Bards and Scotch Reviewers* (1809), *Childe Harold's Pilgrimage* (1818), *The Vision of Judgment* (1821), and his masterpiece, the unfinished *Don Juan* (1819–24). In this section of *Don Juan*, the mock-hero Juan visits an

---

1 A modernized fireplace designed by Count Rumford.

aristocratic couple in their comically titled "Norman Abbey." Juan, a Spanish Catholic, recognizes the Catholic nature of the images he is viewing. This tension between the Catholic past and the aristocratic Protestant present runs throughout the last sections of the poem (Cantos XIII–XVIII). Byron satirizes the nature of the politician's entertainments and the qualities of the guests.]

From Canto the Thirteenth.

LV.

To Norman Abbey whirled the noble pair,—
  An old, old monastery once, and now
Still older mansion, of a rich and rare
  Mixed Gothic, such as Artists all allow
Few specimens yet left us can compare
  Withal: it lies perhaps a little low,
Because the monks preferred a hill behind,
To shelter their devotion from the wind.

LVI.

It stood embosom'd in a happy valley,
  Crown'd by high woodlands, where the Druid oak
Stood like Caractacus[1] in act to rally
  His host, with broad arms 'gainst the thunder-stroke;
And from beneath his boughs were seen to sally
  The dappled foresters—as day awoke,
The branching stag swept down with all his herd,
To quaff a brook which murmur'd like a bird.

LVII.

Before the mansion lay a lucid lake,
  Broad as transparent, deep, and freshly fed
By a river, which its soften'd way did take
  In currents through the calmer water spread
Around: the wild fowl nestled in the brake

---

1 Caractacus, who was a first-century king of the Britons, resisted the Roman Empire under the leadership of the emperor Claudius for nearly a decade. The captured hero allegedly made a successful speech in his own and his people's defense, an occasion frequently referred to by historians and artists.

And sedges, brooding in their liquid bed:
The woods sloped downwards to its brink, and stood
With their green faces fix'd upon the flood.

LVIII.

Its outlet dash'd into a deep cascade,
  Sparkling with foam, until again subsiding
Its shriller echoes—like an infant made
  Quiet—sank into softer ripples, gliding
Into a rivulet; and thus allay'd,
  Pursued its course, now gleaming, and now hiding
Its windings through the woods; now clear, now blue,
According as the skies their shadows threw.

LIX.

A glorious remnant of the Gothic pile,
  (While yet the church was Rome's) stood half apart
In a grand Arch, which once screened many an aisle.
  These last had disappear'd—a loss to Art:
The first yet frown'd superbly o'er the soil,
  And kindled feelings in the roughest heart,
Which mourn'd the power of time's or tempest's march,
In gazing on that venerable Arch.

LX.

Within a niche, nigh to its pinnacle,
  Twelve saints had once stood sanctified in stone;
But these had fallen, not when the friars fell,
  But in the war which struck Charles from his throne,[1]
When each house was a fortalice—as tell
  The annals of full many a line undone,—
The gallant Cavaliers,[2] who fought in vain
For those who knew not to resign or reign.

---

1 The English Civil War (1642–51) included the beheading of King Charles I in
  1649.
2 The principal combatants in the English Civil War were the Roundheads, who
  supported Parliament, and the Cavaliers, who supported King Charles.

LXI.

But in a higher niche, alone, but crowned,
  The Virgin Mother of the God-born child,
With her son in her blessed arms, look'd round,
  Spared by some chance when all beside was spoil'd;
She made the earth below seem holy ground.
  This may be superstition, weak or wild,
But even the faintest relics of a shrine
Of any worship, wake some thoughts divine.

LXII.

A mighty window, hollow in the centre,
  Shorn of its glass of thousand colourings,
Through which the deepen'd glories once could enter,
  Streaming from off the sun like seraph's wings,
Now yawns all desolate: now loud, now fainter,
  The gale sweeps through its fretwork, and oft sings
The owl his anthem, where the silenced quire
Lie with their hallelujahs quench'd like fire.

LXIII.

But in the noontide of the Moon, and when
  The wind is winged from one point of heaven,
There moans a strange unearthly sound, which then
  Is musical—a dying accent driven
Through the huge arch, which soars and sinks again.
  Some deem it but the distant echo given
Back to the night wind by the waterfall,
And harmonized by the old choral wall:

LXIV.

Others, that some original shape, or form
  Shaped by decay perchance, hath given the power
(Though less than that of Memnon's statue,[1] warm

---

1 Memnon is named in Homer's *Iliad* as an Ethiopian nobleman or king who died
   in the Trojan War. When the Greeks admired two giant sculptures in Egypt, they
   named them after Memnon. The statue taken to be that of Memnon himself
   emitted a low note or whistle as the first rays of sun hit it. According to the geog-
   rapher Strabo, this was effected by a crack resulting from an earthquake. Modern
   archaeology identifies the statues (still visible) as guardians of the burial place of
   the pharaoh Amenhotep III (r. 14th c. BCE).

In Egypt's rays, to harp at a fixed hour)
To this grey ruin, with a voice to charm.
  Sad, but serene, it sweeps o'er tree or tower;
The cause I know not, nor can solve; but such
The fact:—I've heard it,—once perhaps too much.

LXV.

Amidst the court a Gothic fountain play'd,
  Symmetrical, but deck'd with carvings quaint—
Strange faces, like to men in masquerade,
  And here perhaps a monster, there a Saint:
The spring gush'd through grim mouths, of granite made,
  And sparkled into basins, where it spent
Its little torrent in a thousand bubbles,
Like man's vain glory, and his vainer troubles.

LXVI.

The mansion's self was vast and venerable,
  With more of the monastic than has been
Elsewhere preserved: the cloisters still were stable,
  The cells too and refectory, I ween:
An exquisite small chapel had been able,
  Still unimpair'd, to decorate the scene;
The rest had been reformed, replaced, or sunk,
And spoke more of the baron than the monk.

LXVII.

Huge halls, long galleries, spacious chambers, join'd
  By no quite lawful marriage of the arts,
Might shock a Connoisseur; but when combined,
  Form'd a whole which, irregular in parts,
Yet left a grand impression on the mind,
  At least of those whose eyes are in their hearts.
We gaze upon a Giant for his stature,
Nor judge at first if all be true to Nature.

LXVIII.

Steel Barons,[1] molten the next generation
To silken rows of gay and garter'd Earls,
Glanced from the walls in goodly preservation;
And Lady Marys blooming into girls,
With fair long locks, had also kept their station;
And Countesses mature in robes and pearls:
Also some beauties of Sir Peter Lely,[2]
Whose drapery hints we may admire them freely.

LXIX.

Judges in very formidable ermine
Were there, with brows that did not much invite
The accused to think their Lordships would determine
His cause by leaning much from might to right:
Bishops, who had not left a single sermon:
Attornies-General, awful to the sight,
As hinting more (unless our judgments warp us)
Of the "Star Chamber" than of "Habeas Corpus."[3]

LXX.

Generals, some all in armour, of the old
And iron time, ere Lead[4] had ta'en the lead;
Others in wigs of Marlborough's martial fold,[5]

---

1   Portraits of past male aristocrats wearing armor.
2   Sir Peter Lely (1618–80), a prominent portraitist of the seventeenth-century
    English court. Lely painted high-born women with bare bosoms in an erotic
    collection that won him a knighthood and a stipend.
3   The Star Chamber was a court of the King's Privy Councillors held from the
    late fifteenth to the middle of the seventeenth centuries, the name of which
    became synonymous with abuses and injustice. As a legal concept, *habeas
    corpus*, literally "that you have the body," requires that prisoners be produced at
    court to be accused. Since *Magna Carta* (1215), *habeas* has been considered a
    foundational right of law, requiring that one be given a fair trial.
4   Lead was used to make shot. Here Byron puns on the transition from the iron
    age to the age of lead, which could pierce iron or steel armor.
5   General John Churchill, 1st Duke of Marlborough (1650–1722) was a long-
    serving officer in the English army. His storied and infamous career included
    service to five monarchs, victory in Monmouth's Rebellion, the successful
    installation of William of Orange on the English throne, and leading the allied
    forces during the War of Spanish Succession.

Huger than twelve of our degenerate breed:
Lordlings, with staves of white or keys of gold:[1]
 Nimrods, whose canvass scarce contain'd the steed;
And here and there some stern high Patriot stood,
Who could not get the place for which he sued.

LXXI.

But ever and anon, to soothe your vision,
 Fatigued with these hereditary glories,
There rose a Carlo Dolce[2] or a Titian,[3]
 Or wilder group of savage Salvatore's:[4]
Here danced Albano's[5] boys, and here the sea shone
In Vernet's[6] ocean lights; and there the stories
Of martyrs awed, as Spagnoletto[7] tainted
His brush with all the blood of all the sainted.

LXXII.

Here sweetly spread a landscape of Loraine;[8]
There Rembrandt[9] made his darkness equal light,
Or gloomy Caravaggio's[10] gloomier stain
 Bronzed o'er some lean and stoic Anchorite:—
But, lo! a Teniers[11] woos, and not in vain,
 Your eyes to revel in a livelier sight:
His bell-mouthed goblet makes me feel quite Danish
Or Dutch with thirst—What, ho! a flask of Rhenish.[12]

---

1 Staves is plural of staff. A white staff indicates the office of Lord Chamberlain.
  The Groom of the Stole, who historically presided when the king was in the
  privy, wears a golden key that opens that chamber.
2 Florentine Baroque painter (1616–86).
3 Tiziano Vecelli (c. 1490–1576), painter of the Venetian school.
4 Salvator Rosa, Italian Baroque painter, poet, and printmaker (1615–73).
5 Francesco Albani, Italian Baroque painter (1578–1660).
6 Claude Joseph Vernet, French painter (1714–89).
7 Lo Spagnoletto ("the little Spaniard"), Jusepe de Ribera, Spanish Tenebrist
  painter (c. 1591–1652).
8 Claude Lorrain (c. 1600–82), French Baroque painter.
9 Rembrandt Harmenszoon van Rijn, Dutch painter, printmaker, and art collec-
  tor (1606–69).
10 Michelangelo Merisi da Caravaggio, Italian Baroque painter (1571–1610).
11 David Teniers the Younger, Flemish painter (1610–90).
12 Fine wine originating from the regions surrounding the river Rhine.

LXXIII.

O reader! if that thou canst read,—and know,
  'Tis not enough to spell, or even to read,
To constitute a reader; there must go
  Virtues of which both you and I have need.
Firstly, begin with the beginning—(though
  That clause is hard;) and secondly, proceed;
Thirdly, commence not with the end—or, sinning
In this sort, end at least with the beginning.

LXXIV.

But, reader, thou hast patient been of late,
  While I, without remorse of rhyme, or fear,
Have built and laid out ground at such a rate,
  Dan Phœbus[1] takes me for an auctioneer.
That Poets were so from their earliest date,
  By Homer's "Catalogue of ships" is clear;[2]
But a mere modern must be moderate—
I spare you then the furniture and plate.

LXXV.

The mellow Autumn came, and with it came
  The promised party, to enjoy its sweets.
The corn is cut, the manor full of game;
  The pointer ranges, and the sportsman beats
In russet jacket:—lynx-like is his aim,
  Full grows his bag, and wonder*ful* his feats.
Ah, nut-brown Partridges! Ah, brilliant Pheasants!
And ah, ye Poachers!—'Tis no sport for peasants.

LXXVI.

An English autumn, though it hath no vines,
  Blushing with Bacchant coronals[3] along

---

1 Phœbus, the Roman name of the Greek sun-god Apollo. "Dan" (from *dominus*) was a Latin honorific like "Sir," meaning "Lord" or "Master."

2 Long section of Homer's *Iliad* (c. 762 BCE, 2.494–759) listing the states that supplied ships and men for the war on Troy, in lines more historical than poetic.

3 Grape vines and leaves as Bacchic crowns. Bacchus is the Roman name for Dionysus, the Greek god of agriculture and wine.

The paths, o'er which the far festoon entwines
 The red grape in the sunny lands of song,
Hath yet a purchased choice of choicest wines;
 The Claret light, and the Madeira strong.
If Britain mourn her bleakness, we can tell her,
The very best of vineyards is the cellar.

LXXVII.

Then, if she hath not that serene decline
 Which makes the Southern Autumn's day appear
As if 'twould to a second spring resign
 The season, rather than to winter drear,—
Of in-door comforts still she hath a mine,—
 The sea-coal fires the earliest of the year;[1]
Without doors too she may compete in mellow,
As what is lost in green is gained in yellow.

LXXVIII.

And for the effeminate *villegiatura*[2]—
 Rife with more horns than hounds—she hath the chase,
So animated that it might allure a
 Saint from his beads to join the jocund race;
Even Nimrod's self might leave the plains of Dura,[3]
 And wear the Melton[4] jacket for a space:—
If she hath no wild boars, she hath a tame
Preserve of Bores, who ought to be made game.

---

1 Coal that came by ship from the northeast to London.
2 Retreat to residence in the country, and (Byron indicates) a group enjoying
   such a summer holiday.
3 In some accounts, Nimrod ordered the Tower of Babel built in his kingdom
   (Babylon), which included the plains of Dura. Dura is also the location of the
   golden idol to himself constructed by King Nebuchadnezzar (Daniel 3:1).
4 Developed in the Leicestershire town of Melton Mowbray, Melton was cloth of
   woven wool and was used to make the durable weatherproof jackets worn for
   fox hunting.

Appendix E: The Reception of Barford Abbey and Other Works by Gunning

1. Review of *Barford Abbey*, *Critical Review*, vol. 24 (1767): 422–30

Barford Abbey. *A Novel. In a Series of Letters. Two Volumes*, 12.*mo.*
Pr. *6s.* Cadell.

THE title of this novel is taken from the place where its principal scenes are laid. Miss Warley, the heroine of the piece, a nonpareil of beauty, virtue, and *all that*, has just lost her generous protectress by the death of Mrs. Whitmore. She meets, however, with another, in the person of lady Mary Sutton, who is at the German Spa, and presses Miss Warley to come over to live with her; in the mean time she remits her three hundred pounds: she likewise engages one Mr. Smith and his wife, who are coming over at the same time, to take care of Miss Warley on her journey and in her passage.

Miss Warley retires to the house of Mr. Jenkings, a worthy old man, steward to Sir James Powis, the lord of Barford Abbey, which is situated in the neighbourhood. Jenkings has his reason for being particularly fond of, and respectful to Miss Warley; and he being treated by Sir James and his lady, a most amiable woman, rather as a companion than servant, Miss Warley is invited to their house, where she is no sooner seen, than she wins the love and esteem of all. Lord Darcy,[1] a young nobleman, of about two thousand pounds a year fortune, and a ward of Sir James, becomes enamoured of our heroine. The great foible of Sir James is a love of money; and his son having fallen in love with a lady possessed of little or none, had lived for many years upon a government abroad, to the great concern of lady Powis. It appears by the letters which pass between Miss Warley and Lady Mary, that Mr. Powis is a most accomplished gentleman, and corresponds with his mother. Lord Darcy's father had, upon his death-bed, in the most pathetic, affectionate manner, bequeathed the care of his son to Sir James; so that he is master of the young lord's state, especially in the affair of marriage. Darcy, who is by no means indifferent to Miss Warley, hints his passion to his guardian, who absolutely discourages the notion, because she is supposed to have no fortune. Darcy entertains such a regard for the commands of his dying father, that he dares

---

1 The reviewer has "Darcy" for Gunning's "Darcey" throughout.

not think of disobliging Sir James; and his behaviour is such as puzzles Miss Warley through the first volume.

The second volume opens with the following letter, which we lay before the reader as a specimen of the author's manner, as well as to acquaint him with the situation of the amour at that period.

[Here the reviewer reprints *Barford Abbey*, Letter XXIII.]

In the meantime the plot thickens. The two lovers become passionately fond of each other, and Jenkings and his wife begin to talk of doubts and mysteries which are to be cleared up by a certain day. This throws the young couple into terrible quandaries, *puzzleations*, and suspicions; but Lord Darcy not being explicit enough in his courtship, Miss Warley endeavours to get rid of her passion, and disposes every thing in good earnest to go over with Mr. and Mrs. Smith to lady Mary, and actually sets out with the former in a post-chaise for Dover.

Lord Darcy, soon after her leaving Barford Abbey, prevails with his guardian to consent that he shall marry Miss Warley, who proves to be the daughter of Mr. Powis; and he, with his lady, returns to England. Darcy flies after his mistress to Dover, where he and his friend Mr. Molesworth receive a certain account that the packet which carried Miss Warley had gone to the bottom of the sea, and that every soul on board had perished. Lord Darcy is distracted, and falls so ill, that his life is despaired of. Captain Risby, another friend of Darcy's, communicates the melancholy news to the family at Barford Abbey, where Mr. and Mrs. Powis had been most affectionately received by their parents. This produces a most interesting and affecting scene, in which we think the author has done great justice to the subject, particularly in describing the sensations of Mr. Morgan, an honest fox-hunter, but a great humourist, and possessed of a handsome fortune, which he had some thoughts of leaving to Miss Warley, who had entirely captivated his esteem, but without the mixture of any other passion. The detail, however, is too long to be inserted here, and the particulars are too interesting for any of them to be omitted. Captain Risby remains still at Barford Abbey, where his chief companion is Edmund, son to Mr. Jenkings, and excellent young man. Molesworth having informed Risby that Miss Warley's body is thrown ashore, that gentleman sends him the following letter, which we think is well composed and finely imagined.

[Here the reviewer reprints *Barford Abbey*, Letter XXXII]

In the next letter Miss Warley comes to life, and is found at the house of Mr. Delves, a banker, where she had just lain in—of the small-pox; and from which she had recovered without any blemish to her beauty. Here we are entertained with a harlequinade, which is the most exceptionable part of the work. Mr. Smith, in carrying our heroine to Dover, where his wife was to receive them, makes love to her on the road; and concealing himself in her room at the inn where they lay, attempts to ravish her, but she screams out, and is rescued by Mr. Delves, who was banker to lady Mary Sutton, and who carries her to his house. On the road, she throws her eyes on a child newly recovered from the small-pox, and catches that distemper. The packet certainly went to the bottom; but the body thrown on shore was that of one Miss Frances Walsh, whose linen was marked with the initial letters of Miss Warley's name. The revealing such floods of good news to Darcy and the afflicted family at the Abbey, proves a matter of almost as much difficulty and delicacy, as the disclosing the former melancholy tidings. The reader may easily imagine that Darcy recovers, though slowly, and that his hand is joined in marriage with his admirable Miss Powis. Lady Mary Sutton returns to England; and towards the close of the novel, we are introduced to a lord and lady Hampstead, their son lord Hallum, and their two daughters; one of whom captivates Mr. Molesworth; and lord Hallum falls in love with Miss Delves, a sprightly black-eyed girl, daughter to the banker. Here the curtain drops,—to be drawn up, perhaps, in a third volume.

We cannot help making an exception of this novel from the common run of such publications. Few or none of the incidents are, indeed, new; but they are well wrought up. There is a great delicacy in all the characters, except that of Smith; which we wish had not been introduced, because the part he acts might have been supplied with more propriety and probability.

2. Review of Minifie's *Coombe Wood, British Magazine and Review*, vol. 2 (1783): 127–28

Art. IV. *Coombe Wood. A Novel in a Series of Letters. By the Author of Barford Abbey, and the Cottage.* 2 vols. 12mo. 5s. Baldwin.

THIS performance, in point of language and sentiment, is infinitely superior to the generality of novels; and the characters it contains are drawn with much delicacy of colouring.

The author has discovered no mean abilities in the pathetic.

'What a change does death make even in the appearance of the outside of a house! Not a blink of light to be seen from either the

windows—*no* chearful sounds within—no lamps burning in the hall—
no hospitable doors thrown open—no rooms lighted up—no comfortable circle surrounding a chearful fire—darkness, silence, and sorrow,
now succeeded to this *once* happy spot.

'I was on top of the steps more than a minute before I could find
in my heart to touch the door; at last a gentle effort, and it creaked on
its hinges: I drew back my hand, sighed from the bottom of my soul,
and was about to enter, when I heard, by a slow step, somebody was
approaching.

'It was the old butler coming from an inner room with lights; I
asked him for his lady, but his reply was only, "Oh, Sir!" and shaking
his head, his eyes streaming with tears, pointed toward the staircase,
respectfully walking on for me to follow him.

'There was such a solemn stillness presided through the house, that
I declare the sound of my own voice, though I spoke in a low accent,
reverberated on my ear; and my voice, on every step as I ascended,
appeared to echo and re-echo round the wall.

'At the dressing-room door my conductor turned towards me, and
sobbing out something I did not understand, I whispered him to
announce me; but instead of doing as I desired him, he touched me on
the arm with one of his poor trembling hands, and beckoning me to a
little distance from the door, whispered, in an agitated voice, that his
lady was going to leave them.

'"Going!" returned I, with surprize. "Good God! where is she
going?"—"Oh!" said the good soul, "that we can't tell, Sir; it is a great
secret, *but* she is *going* to-morrow morning, and we are all breaking our
hearts." And then, with his eyes and hands lifted up to heaven, he burst
into such a shower of tears, and sobbed so loud, that I begged him to go
down, and ventured myself to tap gently at the door.'

The author has been no less successful in painting the fastidious
extravagancies of a thorough-bred woman of fashion.

'I thought I should have left my bones with them the fortnight I
once spent in their old *frightful* castle. Country visits—horrid! Family
circles—*worse!* Reading and working parties—*insupportable!* But the
old hen, *trailing* her chickens after her from the *lawn* to the *garden*,
from the garden to the *poultry*-yard, from the poultry-yard to the
dairy-house, is more stupid, vulgar, and savage, than I am able to
express.

'I am dying with the vapours; for my sake—for your *own* sake—and
for the sake of every thing that is pleasant—let us find refuge in town.
Don't think a moment about your *shape:* if you lace tight it will do very
well. I do not wonder that you hate the *man:* but one must marry, you
know; and few fashionable people think any thing about the *creature*
they are obliged to take for the incumbrance.

'What is a woman of five-and-twenty, without her *town-house*—her equipage—her *jewels*—her *own* parties—and the consequence which all married women have with the pretty young men. They keep themselves at an *aweful* distance till *fashion* constitutes an intimacy: they are safe with *married* women; a girl they are afraid of; nobody would choose to be questioned by *fathers*—by *brothers*—by uncles—and by *grandfathers*: a man can't visit *now* six months in a family but he is called upon for an explanation.

'I *must* marry; and, if next winter does not prove propitious, that awkward, unfashioned, conceited *thing*, swaddled in callicoe and lace, *must* be the man: a fortune of *two* hundred thousand pounds sounds *well*, and what are the *nabobs*[1] to me? I have a title to *tag* on to their *mean* extraction; no body will ask, if I have money, *who* I married; the appellation will be, "Lady Lucy's *husband*."

'I suppose his fortune will last me ten years: an age to be doing such a dirty affair. I shall try to shorten the time, or I shall be much behind *all* my acquaintance: *few* of us live till we are forty, so I shall have time for every thing; and what is to become of us in the *other* world is an enquiry no *fashionable* women has any occasion to make.'

We are not disgusted, in this work, with the profusion of sentiment that weighs down the present goodly race of morality novels; in which the authors seem generally to think, that just observations, and refined opinions, are able to compensate a total defect of character and incident.

There are few admirers of this species of writing, who are unacquainted with Miss Minifie's former productions; and to such it will be sufficient to say, that Coombe Wood is not less worthy their attention than Barford Abbey and the Cottage.

3. From a Review of Gunning's Poem *Virginius and Virginia*, *Critical Review*, vol. 5 (1792)

[The story of Verginia and her father Verginius is recorded in Livy's first-century BCE history of Rome. Verginius murders his daughter in the Forum rather than hand her over as commanded to the lustful Appius Claudius. In various tellings, the incident raises questions of individual honor, class power, and (in the eyes of some) the right of a woman to her own body. Whig interpretations saw in it the contest between the virtuous higher middle classes and a controlling aristocratic elite. The story of Verginius and his daughter had been adapted by earlier authors in English, from Chaucer onward. Gotthold

---

1   A slightly derisive term especially applicable to the new rich who acquired their wealth in India.

Ephraim Lessing's drama *Emilia Galotti* (1772) is the most notable eighteenth-century variant version of this theme; in the play, Lessing takes the same line as Gunning's poem, celebrating the young woman's self-sacrifice. In Goethe's *The Sorrows of Young Werther* (1774), Werther has been reading Lessing's play just before he shoots himself. Gunning's poem thus participates in investigating a struggle of current interest: the conflicting values of the bourgeoisie and the aristocracy.]

We would advise Mrs. Gunning to rest her literary fame on the basis of that credit, whatever it be, which she has acquired as a novellist. Her poetical abilities, if we may judge by this production, will never entitle her to any exalted seat among the favourites of the Muses. The story of Virginius and Virginia has been represented on our stage, and is well known to every classical reader. It is a subject capable of the highest poetical ornaments, and calculated to excite the tenderest pity, or severest indignation. The following scene, in the hand of a master, would have produced that effect. Appius commands Claudius, his agent, who claimed Virginia as his slave, to lead her off. The lover and father are of course extremely enraged upon the occasion: but the simile particularly had the sex of the beast been changed, would have been more appropriate to the latter than the former.

> As, looks the lioness, before her den,
> Growling, to guard her whelps, from *dangers ken*!
> So, look'd Icilius; so, his eye-balls glare,
> So, fierce he flow'd, so upright stood his hair;
> Virginius, saw his sad, distracted mind,
> And, in his looks, rage, vengeance, death *defin'd*!

The words noted in Italics seem to shew that Mrs. Gunning occasionally found some difficulty in completing her rhymes. But to proceed: Virginius opposes the attempt, and appeals to the people.

[Excerpt from the poem follows, with commentary.]

The *costume* is but little attended to in this extract. The Romans were not apt to die of grief at the loss of a mistress, or the dread of being bound in chains, as Icilius, contrary to historic testimony, is here represented to have done. Nor was it natural for Virginius, or any one, to feel 'a stern delight' at the loss of a friend, particularly at the time he stood in need of his assistance; nor to *pray* in so very humble a manner that Appius *would 'hear his confession.'* This expression of an old roman in the times of the commonwealth, though we do not suppose it was meant as allusive to a penitent of the roman church, has an odd effect on the mind, and impresses it with modern ideas: and Virginia's being compared to 'an angel,' and her thoughts to those of 'a pilgrim at this shrine,' are Christian images, and totally ungenial to the characters of the story. Virginius, likewise, soon after says, that it would be no pleasure to meet his daughter gain [sic], *'on this side heav'n.'*—Why Nutamora is substituted for Numitorius, the uncle of Virginia, we know not. Some grammatical defects, and they are too frequent in the poem, occur in the lines preceding and subsequent to that wherein Claudius is called a brute, who *'monster'd* human shape.'—It is, on the whole, a tame and tiresome performance. The dedication to Fashion, however, possesses some original humour and fair satire, but no poetry.

Appendix F: Writing and Scandal: The Life of Susannah Minifie Gunning

Susannah Minifie (Gunning) (1739/40–1800) was born in Somerset, the daughter of a clergyman. Her father, the Reverend Doctor James Minifie, matriculated at Wadham College, Oxford and described himself as a "gentleman." He was posted to a small parish in Staplegrove, Somerset where Susannah was born. She and her sister Margaret wrote two novels together: *The Histories of Lady Frances S——, and Lady Caroline S——* (1763) and *The Picture* (1766). Margaret may have written two novels on her own, though these were traditionally thought the product of the two sisters.

Susannah's *Barford Abbey* appeared shortly before she married John Gunning in August 1768. She wrote no more fiction for nearly two decades. John Gunning was the son of John Gunning of County Mayo, Ireland, and Bridget, daughter of Viscount Bourke. John, a military man, was to fight on the British side at Bunker Hill. Much more famous were his two older sisters, Maria (1733–60) and Elizabeth (1733–90). In 1748, Viscountess Petersham gave a ball at Dublin Castle. The teenaged girls (then 15 and 14) had no clothes to wear. Thomas Sheridan (1719–88) of the Smock Alley Theatre was sympathetic and gave them a couple of theatre costumes (Lady Macbeth and Juliet). Thus attired, the beautiful girls appeared at the ball where they were presented by the Earl of Harrington. Shortly after this debut, Bridget Gunning took her daughters back to England—a venture that seems to have been supported (for some reason or other) by a pension for Bridget from the Earl of Harrington. Eventually, the girls were taken to London and presented at Court. They made a great sensation. According to Horace Walpole (1717–97), Elizabeth Montagu referred to "those goddesses the Gunnings"; people crowded to see them; every artist wanted to paint their picture. Elizabeth married first—in a clandestine midnight wedding in Mayfair Chapel, reputedly using a ring from a bed curtain. She became the Duchess of Hamilton. The following year (1752), Maria married the 6th Earl of Coventry and became Countess of Coventry.

Maria did not live long. According to accounts, she died of blood poisoning brought on by lead-based cosmetics. Elizabeth survived her first husband and married John Campbell, Marquess of Lorne (1723–1806), who succeeded to the title of Duke of Argyll. The beautiful Gunning sisters and their astounding marital success struck the popular imagination. They were stellar celebrities. In contrast, their younger brother's military career, forwarded by a spot of patronage from his in-laws, won him no fame. It might have been hard for Susannah to compete with the reputations of two such dashing and celebrated sisters-in-law.

Before marrying John, Susannah Minifie had published *Barford Abbey*. After her marriage, Susannah did not publish for some time. The marriage does not seem to have been happy, but she and John had one child, the beautiful Elizabeth (1769–1823). Why should there not be a new beautiful Gunning at the center of the social scene? According to all reports (including James Gillray's caricatures, Appendix G), young Elizabeth Gunning was handsome, and by many counts she was herself well-born. Not only had Elizabeth's great-grandmother been a Viscountess, but she was the niece both of the Countess of Coventry and of the Duchess of Argyll. A splendid marriage for her daughter would compensate Susannah for her trials, placing her lovely girl in a stellar position in the world.

Then things went terribly wrong. In 1791 a scandal broke. Elizabeth was accused of writing feigned letters and spreading false rumors that she was going to marry George Spencer-Churchill (1766–1840), the Marquess of Blandford, heir to the Duke of Marlborough. A denial from the Duke of Marlborough set publicity spinning and put an end to any prospect of a marriage with the duke's son. Some speculated that these letters had actually been forged to make Elizabeth seem like a desirable prospect and encourage the attention of George Campbell, the Marquess of Lorne. Susannah wrote a pamphlet defending her daughter, claiming that Elizabeth's father, Susannah's husband John, had spread the forged letters in order to disgrace Elizabeth and prevent her marriage, simply so that he would not be liable to pay for a dowry. It has not escaped commentators that the turmoil was created by letters, epistles that seemed in some sense or other to be fictional, strongly connected with a novelist expert in the epistolary mode. The connection has been explored by Thomas O. Beebee in an article entitled "Publicity, Privacy, and the Power of Fiction in the Gunning Letters." Beebee does not, however, spend time on the letters in Gunning's own novels.

The Duke of Marlborough (George Spencer, 1739–1817) was the descendant of a great military ancestor, John Churchill (1650–1722), who was rewarded for his military prowess with his title and given Blenheim Palace (near Oxford) as the gift of a grateful nation. It was a tremendous misfortune for the Gunnings to be at odds with the great and powerful Churchill family. But the head of Clan Campbell was important too. The scandal was tasty because it was a scandal of *high* life. Susannah's self-published contribution to the furor, *A Letter from Mrs. Gunning Addressed to his Grace the Duke of Argyll*, attracted immense public interest. It went through at least four editions. In this letter, Susannah tried to vindicate Elizabeth's virtue and innocence, endeavoring—fruitlessly—to save the situation.

Susannah Gunning's story of innocence wronged turns into a kind of mystery story, with Susannah seizing on clues and counteracting the conspirators against herself and Elizabeth. This piece of journalism would have benefited from an editor—adjectives proliferate (unlike *Barford Abbey*). There is an undeniable excess of italics. But a variety of other factors make for considerable narrative interest. Susannah tries to create layers of impressions of her husband and his hangers-on, especially the led captain,[1] Essex Bowen. Susannah has on her side only her sister Margaret—an old maid, loyal but poor. A party of helpless women—a mother and an aunt and a defenseless girl—holds out against a crew of villains.

Susannah as a lone champion works as a detective, examining alleged letters:

> I told them *some tricks* had certainly been played with the
> letter, and pointed out their observation, that the coronet
> was reversed in sealing it, and that instead of St. James's, it
> was written the direction St. James Place. (*Letter* 26)

Susannah vividly conveys her own sense of an ordeal borne with outward calm. When Mrs. Bowen tells her of the incriminating letters allegedly penned by Elizabeth, Susannah says she listened patiently:

> And all *this* without a *tear* of *disappointment,* or a *sigh* of
> *anguish*; I am not at all conscious that I did not go through
> the whole task with exactly the same *indifference,* as I should
> have *written* a ballad or *read* a paragraph in the news papers
> *concerning* the national debt. It answered the ends I *hoped* it
> would; she thought me *securely* fixed in her Trap. (63)

The narrative builds up to a climax on the terrible day, 9 February 1791. On that day, Elizabeth, in low spirits and temporarily unwell, is told that her father commands her to leave his house:

> I was sitting by the bedside of my dear injured innocent,
> and holding one of her hands between mine, when her aunt
> came up into the room with a face paler than ashes, and agi-
> tated beyond all description, though she *evidently endeav-*
> *oured* to conceal it—what's the matter with you *Auntee Peg* (a

---

1 A sycophant or hanger-on (*OED*).

name which from infancy she has always called her by) what makes you put on such a long face? asked the angel. I said nothing, but my heart was not the less alarmed—my love, replyed her aunt, I have had a very extraordinary conversation with your father and then ... she broke to us the false accusations, and the cruel *most* cruel messages that accompanied them.... (101)

Some of the biographical dictionaries still say that John Gunning threw out both his wife and daughter, but Susannah sarcastically scotches that rumor:

It is *most* certain that I was not *commanded* to leave his house on that day, the General is *too* good a *manager* of his *fortune*, and has *earned* that *fortune* by too many *sacrifices*, to have given *me* a claim, by the *laws* of my country, to *any* part of it. No, to do him *justice*, the act of leaving his house was *entirely* my *own*. (105)

If Susannah's husband actually *ordered* her to leave the matrimonial home, the wife would be entitled to legal redress; the likely result would be a formal separation, with a court-ordered regular allowance paid to the wife by the husband. John would not risk that. Through accretion of suggestive detail Susannah paints a dodgy John, with his extreme unwillingness—or inability—to part with money. That is ultimately the *solution* to her mystery story. John Gunning created these falsehoods to prevent any engagement of his daughter to either of the young men concerned—as he was deeply unwilling (or even unable) to give the girl a dowry. True, his sisters had married men so infatuated with their looks that they would waive a dowry, but lighting seldom strikes twice—and definitely not thrice.

Susannah complains that "the combined plotters" among their "ridiculous insertions" in the newspapers have "accused me of Novel writing":

Particularly of a book called Waltham-Abbey; which is made up they say of tricks, of stratagem, and of forged letters. I must assure them their mistake is a very palpable one, for though to have been the author of that book might possibly have done honour to my genius, yet, as I never have seen such a book, or ever before heard there was such a book written, I cannot without great injustice lay any claim to the credit of being its writer. (89)

Waltham-Abbey is a believable title—based on *Barford Abbey*. (A fresh joke enters in "Waltham," a place associated with poachers, disguise, and rebellion.) *Barford Abbey*, though not playing with forgery, is certainly epistolary, and engages issues of epistolarity. Susannah is a published and acknowledged writer, and her defense in the letter to Argyll is essentially concerned with reading and writing. Her pamphlet is full of documents, of affidavits or formal statements witnessed or certified, of letters false and true. Susannah narrates her heroism in journeying an arduous 140 some miles by coach while fasting—evidently to give the packet of materials to the Duke. (She doesn't mention Blenheim directly but inserts the mileage to help the reader to figure out where she went.)

The pamphlet attracted attention. Ironically, Susannah's work as a novelist counts against her with the public. The better her story, the more willing readers are to believe it is a fiction. There was a pamphlet war. Her *Letter to Argyll* was followed by a quick riposte from Essex Bowen: *A Statement of Facts, in Answer to Mrs. Gunning's Letter addressed to his Grace the Duke of Argyll*. The reason he won't sue, he loftily declares, is that punishment and damages would be too small. So he and his wife will get their own back in their *Statement*. The contention of Essex Bowen and his wife is that Elizabeth was deceiving her mother, as well as other people. The girl allegedly explained to Mrs. Bowen,

> if her mother was undeceived in respect of her attachment
> to Lord Lorne, to use her own words, "'twould produce
> such a rumpus in the family" that it would be the means of
> separating her father and mother. (20)

There was a "rumpus in the family," certainly. Essex Bowen is obviously serving Major-General John Gunning. John's implied case is bolstered not only by denigration of both Susannah and Elizabeth but also by exhibition of the two women at odds. John Gunning tries to keep out of the direct line of fire, partly because he has his own troubles. He is being accused of adultery with a Mrs. Duberly. Charged by the aggrieved husband (as was customary in a case of "criminal conversation"), John had to defend himself and his money in the trial of 22 February 1792. When the wronged husband was awarded damages of £5,000, John Gunning fulfilled all negative expectations. He eloped to Napoli with Mrs. Duberly, his married inamorata, to avoid having to pay the £5,000 he legally owed to the lady's husband. Thus he offered (a year too late) some confirmation of Susannah's contention that what he most cared about was money. There was implicit vindication of the wife and daughter during the adultery trial. The cele-brated barrister Thomas Erskine (1750–1823), counsel for Mr. Duberly, sarcastically attacks John Gunning for his treatment of his daughter: "This is the man whose principles are so honourable; this is the man who ejects his daughter for some supposed incorrectness of conduct."[1]

What purported to be John Gunning's *Apology for the Life* ap-peared in 1792; this autobiography seems patently ghostwritten (at least in part) and may be designed for readers in search of the comic and bawdy. The author (or authors) of the *Apology* manage with some subtlety to adapt the theme to the topic of epistles. The lubri-cious John claims to have been inspired by his reading of modern books:

> My library chiefly consisted of such books as tend to vitiate the mind, and debauch the understanding. L[or]d

---

1 *The Trial between James Duberly, Esq. Plaintiff. And Major-General Gunning, Defendant, for Criminal Conversation with the Wife of the Plaintiff* (London: J. Ridgway, 1792), 10. Erskine later returns to the charge that John Gun-ning took what he calls a "romantic" course in sending off his wife and daughter:

> I said that General Gunning did what was most romantic, conquering
> every affection, forgetting every tie that nature has implant [*sic*] in our
> breasts, by shutting his door against his wife and his child.—Yet this,
> this is the man who now runs into the extreme of vice and debauchery.
> (*Trial* 38)

In his speech in the law court Erskine continuously draws attention to the age of the adulterer (who was nearly 60 when he first met the Duberlys in 1788). This hoary sinner is represented as infirm and ugly: "General Gunning's frame is infirm and disjointed—his hands are crippled—his feet lame" (5).

Thomas Erskine was a highly effective speaker, and already the best paid barrister in Britain by the 1780s. He had signed a statement for Essex Bowen but apparently had doubts about John Gunning, whose capacity for plotting and underhand dealing is displayed in narratives of the circumstances involved in the adultery case. Erskine was also a man of liberal views, a defender of justice and freedom. A couple of years after the Duberly case he would defend some of the leading advocates of civil liberty in the "Treason trials"; he successfully defended Horne Tooke and John Thelwall. Erskine's political and social views are thus on the opposite side from those of James Gillray (see Appendix G). Erskine seems to think that Gunning's wife and daughter were oppressed and treated unjustly. The case against John Gunning and the conduct of the adultery trial—as well as its verdict—may be considered as a social payback for the wrongs endured by Elizabeth and Susannah Gunning.

C[hesterfiel]d's Letters and C[lariss]a H[arlowe][1] were generally my morning's amusement. From the former I learnt
all the ARCANA and inexpressible refinements of a man of
intrigue, and from the latter all the principles and practice of
an accomplished v[illai]n The spirit of L——ss ["Loveless,"
i.e., "Lovelace"] took possession of my bosom; a congenial-
ity of sentiment and coincidence of desires made me in love
with his character ... which bore so strong a resemblance to
myself.

John's fashioning himself into a comic character does not help Susannah but drags her further into a comic pornotopia. By this time,
however, she has already suffered enough damage from James Gillray's
caricatures (see Appendix G).

In writing and publishing her *Letter to Argyll*, Susannah Minifie had
used the familial society to go out of the realm of the family and to
appeal to a wider public. She really is successful *as a writer* if one
judges by the sales of her pamphlet. But she can succeed only by
gaining publicity—and publicity makes her funny and ever weaker.
There is a harsh central paradox. A father defending his daughter's
virtue is heroic and moving. His story is essentially a tragic story—as
in *Virginius and Virginia* (see Appendix E3) or *Emilia Galotti* (or *Rigo-
letto*).[2] The father often kills the daughter in order to save her. A *woman*
defending her daughter's virtue is merely funny. Yet such a person is

---

1   *The Letters of Lord Chesterfield* (1774), worldly-wise epistles to his son by Philip
     Dormer Stanhope, Earl of Chesterfield (d. 1773), evoked Samuel Johnson's
     comment to James Boswell that "they teach the morals of a whore, and the
     manners of a dancing master" (*Life of Samuel Johnson*, ed. R.W. Chapman,
     Oxford World's Classics, 1970, p. 188). In Samuel Richardson's novel *Clarissa*
     (1747–48), the aristocratic rake Robert Lovelace, failing in ingenious attempts
     to seduce the heroine, resorts to rape.
2   Gunning's poem shares in the investigation of issues of current interest. Samuel
     Crisp's *Virginia: A Tragedy* was produced in London in 1754. The heroine of
     Gotthold Ephraim Lessing's drama *Emilia Galotti* (1772) begs her father to kill
     her to save her from her own attraction to the aristocratic rake. Goethe's
     Werther in *The Sorrows of Young Werther* (1774) has been reading Lessing's play
     just before he shoots himself. The Verginius story in its variations turns on the
     sacrifice of (particularly female) personal desire to patriarchal propriety. Verdi's
     opera *Rigoletto* (1851), based on a banned play by Victor Hugo, is a variant on
     the same motif—with the twist that the father kills the desirous daughter by
     fatal error. A father trying to protect and control his daughter is a tragic figure;
     a woman (like Susannah Gunning) endeavoring to defend a daughter or her
     reputation is merely comical.

perhaps a trifle threatening to social order, after all. The more public she gets, the more she becomes an antagonist, an outsider to good society. And so the more scarecrow and absurd her little posse must be made to seem. Three female persons—or four if we include the aged Duchess of Bedford—are up against the world. That is not the role for a woman. A woman's virtue is too shaky a matter for someone as ignorant as another woman to endorse and defend. Entrance into a public arena renders the speaker grotesque. Public speech, public intervention—these are bound to be self-defeating. Susannah, when trying to write Elizabeth out of social obloquy, had embarked upon a hopeless cause.

Perhaps both mother and daughter had been enchanted by the first generation of the "Gunning Goddesses"—their celestial rise, their glow of glamour. What once had seemed easy now was not. The appeal of the beautiful and glamorous was pressed down by the urgency of the possibility of war and social revolt. Perhaps England wanted some kind of payback for the adulation lavished on the "Gunning Goddesses" over 40 years earlier. In his own vindication John Gunning blames his sisters' elevation for his own problems:

> The beauty of my sisters was for years the theme of admiration, and it is no wonder it raised them from a state of dependence to grace the first dignities in the kingdom. Their beauty and situation were unequalled, and under the flattering auspices of their protection I was first introduced into the world. A scene of prosperity and pleasure now seemed to open on me ... while I was thus employed in imbibing these intoxicating pleasures, I had neither time nor inclination to examine the situation of my affairs. My expences (*sic*) far exceeded the income of my estate.... It is true, the affluence and affection of my sisters left me no reason to complain of pecuniary embarrassments: but their generosity was exceeded by my extravagance.[1]

The whole story becomes a story about class. James Gillray reads the gender issues ultimately as class conflict. This is a society of women, trying to stick together, but it become a ridiculous society, in the end

---

1 *An Apology for the Life of Major General G—, Containing A full Explanation of the G-NN-G MYSTERY, and of the Author's Connexion with Mr. D--BER-YS FAMILY of SOHO-SQUARE* (London: J. Ridgway, 1792), 4–5. That the same publisher printed the trial and the "Apology" indicates that somebody saw an easy continuity between the two works; presumably John Gunning needed money too much to mind putting himself in a bad light.

a comically evil little club, a sort of criminal coven of gypsies. Susannah's trust in indignant virtue and sworn statements is mocked as well as her supposed ambition or the alleged participation in her daughter's forgeries. The Gunning women's hope to seize any control, to have a *say* in a social and legal—and sexual—situation is in itself a kind of forgery. After all, Mrs. Duberly had no say in the trial over her adultery.

As Horace Walpole explained in a letter to Agnes Berry, "The Gunninghiad is compleated—not by a marriage, like other Novels of the Minifies."[1] In February 1792, John Gunning's trial for "criminal conversation" with another man's wife went against him. For the crime of stealing another man's wife, he was assessed for damages, in accordance with the law of the time, which saw a wife as another man's property that had been stolen. John Gunning bore out negative opinions of him in the upshot, when he eloped to Napoli with the married woman of his affections in order to prevent having to pay the legal damages of £5,000 he owed to the lady's husband after he lost the suit.

After a short time abroad, Susannah returned to England and to the literary scene as a novelist. She enjoyed some success with works like *Anecdotes of the Delborough Family* (1792), *Memoirs of Mary* (1793), and other novels. She drew on her experience of the Gunninghiad scandal for material, for instance, her long poem *Virginius and Virginia*. Her later writing for the Minerva Press is more confident than some of the earlier work and takes a wider social view. She is interested in family relations, money, and class differences. This period, the mid- to late 1790s, also marks Gunning's most experimental period, including the long tragic poem and an interesting work called *Delves, a Welch Tale*, which attempts to translate the style and tropes of writing for the theatre into novel form.

Gunning's writing received mostly lukewarm notice in the eighteenth century. According to its publisher, William Lane, *Anecdotes of the Delborough Family* received enormous attention in the lead-up to its publication, and it quickly sold into a second edition. Most literary historians agree that this attention derived from Gunning's notoriety thanks to the scandal. Some of the earlier novels, both those written with Margaret and Susannah's single-authored works, ran to multiple editions and received some mild praise, but critics rarely describe them with any real enthusiasm.

---

1 Horace Walpole, *Correspondence*, Vol. 11, edited by W.S. Lewis, Yale, 1944, p. 196.

Appendix G: James Gillray's Caricatures of the Gunninghiad

Before Susannah and her daughter Elizabeth left England to wait out the storm of scandal and ridicule, she and her sister Margaret published sworn affidavits in the *Public Advertiser* (3 May 1791) attesting that they had "never written, or caused to be written, any letter or letters, note or notes," nor were they "in any shape ... instrumental in framing a correspondence, in the name of his Grace the Duke of Marlborough, or the Marquis of Blandford, or any other person or persons." The depth of public opprobrium and the extent of the ridicule these women faced during the Gunninghiad scandal (see Appendix F) can be measured by the appearance of three caricatures by political cartoonist James Gillray (1756–1815) in March 1791. The first, "The Seige of Blenheim—or—the new System of GUNNING discoverd" (5 March 1791) obscenely rejoices in the overthrow of the younger woman's erotic and social ambitions (Figure 1).

Figure 1. James Gillray, "The Seige of BLENHEIM—or—the new system of GUNNING, discoverd" (1791)

A handsome if blowsy Elizabeth, with much leg showing, sits astride a gun. She declares, "O Mother, Mother! My mask'd Battery is discovered, & we shall be blown up!" Beside her, Susannah, an aging woman, covers her head with the Duchess of Bedford's skirts. She holds the feather pen with which she has touched off the gun that bombards a building named BLENHEIM. She exclaims, "Good heavens! Who could have thought that the Seige of a Coronet would have ended in smoke and stink?" The duke, buttocks bared at the window of his "Blenheim," blasts the women with a stream of excrement, while General John Gunning sneaks away. "I find our Stratagem won't take effect," John says as he creeps out of the scene, "& therefore I'll be off." Gillray's satire is at its strongest when touched by pornography, or the pornographic and scatological mixed, as in this instance.

The aging Duchess of Bedford was the maternal grandmother of the Marquess of Blandford. Surprisingly, she had come to the defense of Susannah and Elizabeth. In her letter to the Duke of Argyll, Susannah pays her very grateful compliments, emphasizing their long-term friendship. This valued friend is Elizabeth's benefactor in a crisis. The caricatured figure here sheltering Susannah with her huge skirt is a wispy patroness indeed—and obviously aged. She somewhat resembles the thin Margaret Minifie—who appears in both of the other caricatures—save that the duchess has good stockings and handsome shoes. The Duchess of Bedford becomes one of the comically ineffective crew of women in the wrong. They are all uselessly setting themselves up against male power. Central cultural metaphors are made explicit in this picture, which combines traditional elements of satire (sex, violence, and shit) with competing effects. The sexy beauty of Elizabeth only adds to the ridicule of her aggressive ambition and overreach. Taking on the male role in the sex game brings her to ignominious defeat.

The second illustration of this scandal (Figure 2), which Horace Walpole would later dub the "Gunninghiad," recalls the case of a missing teenage girl. On 1 January 1753, Elizabeth ("Betty") Canning disappeared. On 29 January she reappeared, claiming that she had been abducted to a house in Enfield where she was stripped of her clothes and the woman of the house tried to make her turn whore. Betty's story aroused great sympathy. Henry Fielding (1707–54), magistrate and novelist, was one of Betty's strongest defenders. The women were tried, and the "gypsy" woman, Mary Squires, who had taken Betty's stays, was sentenced to hang. Sir Crisp Gascoyne (1700–61), Lord Mayor of London, was not happy with the accuracy of the charge or with the justice of the verdict. The Mayor worked to have the verdict overturned, for which he was furi-

Figure 2. James Gillray, "BETTY CANNING revived:—or—A peep at the Conjuration of Mary Squires, & the Gypsy Family" (1791)

ously attacked. For a while, Betty was a popular heroine. She herself was tried, however, and found to have been lying about her alleged abduction and imprisonment by the poor women. Sentenced to transportation, Betty was taken to Connecticut in an ordinary ship—and not, as was customary, with a band of prisoners. In Connecticut she was put in charge of a minister in whose house she lived, and whom she later married. So her penal excursion to America turned out quite well for her.

Despite the reversal of events, a populist Betty Canning was still the virtuous victim, imprisoned by a gang of low-class non-English rogues. To others, she was a brazen liar, willing to swear to anything. In his second caricature of the Gunninghiad, Gillray takes the conservative view of Betty Canning as an outstanding liar—thus a good parallel with Elizabeth Gunning. Even the names rhyme. Notice in the picture the "Affidavit of Eliz. Canning" beside the poster of the pillory—just above Elizabeth—hinting the penalty she should be headed for. While holding a pack of cards instead of a Bible, Elizabeth vows: "I swear, that I never wish'd or tried, directly or indirectly, to get a Coronet: that I never saw or went to Lord B——[Blandford]—or Lord L——[Lorne] in all my Life:—that Men are my aversion—& that I never had anything to do with the Groom, in all my born days: will that do, Dad?" She extends her left hand to the Devil under the table,

Figure 3. James Gillray, "Margaret's Ghost" (1791)

his arm reaching into her skirts, who insists that she "Swear!" This Betty is in league with the gypsies, not complaining against them. Margaret (in rags) is cooking, and Susannah is encouraging the fire with a bellows (her *Letter to Argyll*). This caricature makes fun of Susannah's reliance on statements, affidavits, and the swearing of solemn oaths. Susannah is not the prime agent of evil here but is herself taken in, as she is so besotted with her daughter. Betty is willing to touch the devil—her Dad—as an antidote to her (false) oath. "Mary Squires" the gypsy knows better about the full range of Betty's schemes and lies.

The third of Gillray's caricatures of the Gunning women, "Margaret's Ghost" (25 March 1791), shows Elizabeth abed, being nursed in illness by a bloated Susannah, as an emaciated "Auntee Peg" appears before them (Figure 3). This is a fairly straightforward illustration of the scene described in Susannah's pamphlet, which even includes quotations from that letter in its captions (*Letter to Argyll*, 101). The connection is made very clear in "Auntee Peg"—the affectionate name itself a vulgarism, reeking of lower-class custom. In this all-female bedroom scene there are only the three vulgar middle-class women, all physically weakened and at a loss. "Peg," with her bad news, must announce the Gunning women's exclusion from any male sphere, their loss of status with the coverage of marriage. The absence of the strength of the male sphere is reflected in Susannah's narrative language, her gushing, over-the-top praise of her daughter. The more the positive words are heaped on Elizabeth, the less credible any of them seem. Blinded by stupid affection, the caricatured Susannah cannot see through the illusions conjured by the two-faced scheming Elizabeth. This is a reading better supported by the Bowen narrative. All the power that Susannah has left is her cornucopia of words. And these are mistaken.

All three of these caricatures of 1791 cast the Minifie women as lower-class, even vagabonds, ridiculous agents of mayhem. They are all ludicrous—fat Susannah with her attempts at fashion, in contrast with the badly dressed scrawny Peg, with her torn stockings and no proper shoes. The women do not understand the system that they are trying to blow up. By 1791 the feelings over the French Revolution had grown cooler. Although in its early stages the Revolution had many warm supporters in England, there were conservatives who saw it as a threat from the start. James Gillray attacked both Tories and Whigs, or radicals like Charles James Fox (1749–1806), but after the outbreak of the French Revolution the caricaturist's feelings ran much more strongly against the radical or revolutionary side. His antipathy to Susannah Gunning is justified in a way, since her novels deal with changes of class and relations between classes. These caricatures tell us that Gillray saw Susannah Gunning (née Minifie) and her daughter as upstarts who were trying to push their way into inappropriately high social status. His animus apparently derives from a view of both women as intruders. They are like—or they *are*—revolutionaries, invading a social level in an attempt to dislodge true aristocrats. Their attempt must be shown to be futile. Gillray is antipathetic to the lower sort of people, including the working poor, females, and slaves. He is opposed to their gaining much say over their own lives. He remained a staunch opponent of *any* emancipation.

Susannah and Elizabeth had to run away to the Continent for a while to escape the full blaze of ridicule. Their lives were seriously affected. Susannah's marriage was over—as were Elizabeth's marital prospects. The mother and daughter offered an impressive example of women brought down for their ambition. These unrealistic females are entertainingly punished for adopting the foolish idea that they could wield for themselves the levers of power regarding marriage, class, and money. The central group—two sisters and a daughter—forms an absurd and unnatural feminine social unit. Their interrelationship is part of the fun for Gillray's view of the helpless officiousness of women. These images are energized by political resentment. To Gillray, the Gunning women are "low" people, determined to change class without permission. Instead of knowing their place, they are *gunning* for power. This group wants to attack, to take from the rightful rulers. Marlborough is Gillray's big symbol of rightful rule and potency, not the Scottish Argyll. Susannah and Elizabeth become one with the rabble who brought down the Bastille and the women who forced the king from Versailles back to Paris. A female society is in itself sufficient to alarm—the mockery is the shit-artillery that can embarrass and silence them.

Works Cited and Select Bibliography

Works by Susannah Gunning

Anecdotes of the Delborough Family. W. Lane, 1792.
Barford Abbey. T. Cadell, 1768.
Coombe Wood. R. Baldwin, 1783.
The Cottage. T. Durham, 1769.
Delves, a Welch Tale. Lackington, Allen, and Co., 1796.
Family Pictures, A Novel. Containing Curious and Interesting Memoirs of Several Persons of Fashion in W——re. W. Nicoll and T. Durham, 1764.
Fashionable Involvements. T. Gillet, 1800.
The Heir Apparent, Revised and Augmented by Miss Gunning. James Ridgway, 1802.
Love at First Sight. H. Lowndes, 1797.
Memoirs of Mary, A Novel. J. Bell, 1793.
Virginius and Virginia; A Poem in Six Parts. W. Lane, 1792.

With Margaret Minifie

The Hermit. H. Gardner, 1769.
The Histories of Lady Frances S——, and Lady Caroline S——. R. and J. Dodsley, 1763.
The Picture. J. Johnson and Co., 1766.

Secondary Sources

Epistolarity and Women Writers

Batchelor, Jennie. "Influence, Intertextuality and Agency: Eighteenth-Century Women Writers and the Politics of Remembering." *Women's Writing*, vol. 20, no. 1, 2013, pp. 1–12.

Beebee, Thomas O. *Epistolary Fiction in Europe, 1500–1800.* Cambridge UP, 1999.

———. "Minifie, Margaret and Susannah." *The Encyclopedia of British Literature, 1660–1789*, vol. 1, edited by Gary Day and Jack Lynch, Wiley, 2015, pp. 797–98.

———. "Publicity, Privacy, and the Power of Fiction in the Gunning Letters." *Eighteenth Century Fiction*, vol. 20, no. 1, 2007, pp. 61–88.

Gevirtz, Karen Bloom. "Ladies Reading and Writing: Eighteenth-Century Women Writers and the Gendering of Critical Discourse." *Modern Language Studies*, vol. 33, no. 1/2, 2003, pp. 60–72.

Johnston, Elizabeth. "'Deadly Snares': Female Rivalry, Gender Ideology, and Eighteenth-Century Women Writers." *Studies in the Literary Imagination*, vol. 47, no. 2, 2014, pp. 1–21.

Mitford, Jessica. *Hons and Rebels*. New York Review Books, 2004.

Precup, Amelia. "Please for Respectability: Eighteenth-Century Women Writers Theorizing the Novel." *American, British and Canadian Studies Journal*, vol. 30, no. 1, 2018, pp. 9–26.

Schellenberg, Betty A. *The Professionalization of Women Writers in Eighteenth-Century Britain*. Cambridge UP, 2005.

Thomason, Laura E. *The Matrimonial Trap: Eighteenth-Century Women Writers Redefine Marriage*. Bucknell UP, 2014.

Todd, Janet. "Marketing the Self: Mary Carleton, Miss F and Susannah Gunning." *Studies on Voltaire and the Eighteenth Century*, vol. 217, 1983, pp. 95–106.

———. *The Sign of Angellica: Women, Writing and Fiction, 1660–1880*. London, 1989.

Turner, Cherly. *Living by the Pen: Women Writers in the Eighteenth Century*. Routledge, 1992.

Reformation in England and the Dissolution of the Abbeys

Ashton, Margaret. *Broken Idols of the English Reformation*. Cambridge UP, 2016.

Doody, Margaret Anne. *Jane Austen's Names: Riddles, Persons, Places*. U of Chicago P, 2015. [See Chapters 2 and 3.]

Duffy, Eamon. *The Stripping of the Altars: Traditional Religion in England, 1400–1580*. Yale UP, 1992, 2005.

Moore, Roger Emerson. *Jane Austen and the Reformation: Remembering the Sacred Landscape*. Routledge, 2016.

Moorhouse, Geoffrey. *The Last Divine Office: Henry VIII and the Dissolution of the Monasteries*. BlueBridge, 2012. [Reprint of *The Last Office*, Weidenfeld & Nicolson, 2008.]

From the Publisher

A name never says it all, but the word "Broadview" expresses a good deal of the philosophy behind our company. We are open to a broad range of academic approaches and political viewpoints. We pay attention to the broad impact book publishing and book printing has in the wider world; for some years now we have used 100% recycled paper for most titles. Our publishing program is internationally oriented and broad-ranging. Our individual titles often appeal to a broad readership too; many are of interest as much to general readers as to academics and students.

Founded in 1985, Broadview remains a fully independent company owned by its shareholders—not an imprint or subsidiary of a larger multinational.

For the most accurate information on our books (including information on pricing, editions, and formats) please visit our website at www.broadviewpress.com. Our print books and ebooks are also available for sale on our site.

broadview press
www.broadviewpress.com